"As chilly as the icy sea, as haunting as the prospects of ghosts, *The Salvage* is a novel to keep you up all night. Anbara Salam is a master of suspense. Be careful when you start this book, because you won't want to stop."

—RENE DENFELD,
bestselling author of *The Child Finder*

"A rich, gothic mystery, *The Salvage* has a moody, salt-drenched atmosphere and layers of intrigue that span centuries. I couldn't put it down."

—FLYNN BERRY,
bestselling author of *Northern Spy*

THE SALVAGE

ALSO BY ANBARA SALAM

Hazardous Spirits

Belladonna

Things Bright and Beautiful

THE SALVAGE

a novel

AMBARA SALAM

TinHouse

A zando IMPRINT

NEW YORK

Tin House

The characters and events in this book are fictitious. Any similarity to real persons, living or dead, is coincidental and not intended by the author.

Copyright © 2025 by Anbara Salam

Zando supports the right to free expression and the value of copyright. The purpose of copyright is to encourage writers and artists to produce the creative works that enrich our culture. Thank you for buying an authorized edition of this book and for comply- ing with copyright laws by not reproducing, scanning, uploading, or distributing this book or any part of it without permission. If you would like permission to use material from the book (other than for brief quotations embodied in reviews), please contact connect@zandoprojects.com.

Tin House is an imprint of Zando.
zandoprojects.com

First US Edition 2025
Manufacturing by Lake Book Manufacturing
Cover and text design by Beth Steidle

The publisher does not have control over and is not responsible for author or other third-party websites (or their content).

Library of Congress Cataloging-in-Publication Data is available.

978-1-963108-47-7 (paperback)
978-1-963108-54-5 (ebook)

10 9 8 7 6 5 4 3 2 1

Manufactured in the United States of America

For Struan

THE SALVAGE

AUTHOR'S NOTE:

On Christmas Eve 1962, an intense cold front plunged Scotland, England, and Wales into the "Big Freeze": the coldest winter on record since 1740. Blizzards and Arctic conditions gripped Great Britain over the following months, and the next frost-free day didn't arrive until March 6, 1963.

SATURDAY, OCTOBER 20, 1962

WHEN I ARRIVE AT PORT MARY HARBOUR, THERE ARE ALREADY men in the fishing boats. Their oilskin aprons creak as they winch in ropes and haul rusted cages, seawater rolling down their arms. Nudging one another, they fall silent as I walk along the pier. I raise my head, keeping my eyes on Colin's boat. He's sitting on the stern, drinking from the cup of a plastic thermos, the radio tuned to a drama. As I approach, he leans into the wheelhouse and clicks the dial to the BBC World Service for the news.

"Is that you ready, then?" he says, looking me over.

I'm wearing a dirty fleece and holding a margarine tub containing two jam sandwiches, likely not what he imagined of a professional diver. "Yes, I'm all ready."

"Thought there'd be more"—he gestures—"bits."

"All my *bits* are already here." I point to the wheelhouse, where my equipment was locked overnight. My tone is sharp, and I try to offset it with a smile.

"Aye, fair enough." He tips his head. "Come on, then."

Colin starts the motor, and as we pull through the harbour, the fishermen stop working to watch us—lines go slack, ropes slop into the water. I check that the batteries are in the camera, the pressure gauge is set, the seals around the mouthpiece are intact, my torch is working. When I turn to look over my shoulder, the eyes of the men are still on us. A young man in a green pullover lifts his cigarette butt overhead, like a javelin, and tosses it in our direction. Behind us, Port Mary's coastal street stretches into view—a row of pastel pebbledash houses, two splintered benches, the boarded-up windows of the old pleasure pavilion. The roof of the Grand Hotel looks shabbier from this distance; the whole island seems improbably exposed, a scribble on slate. Colin's boat knocks through the waves, and as Cairnroch Island grows smaller, my heart starts jittering. It's my first dive down to survey the shipwreck, and I have to get it right. This is my chance to do something right.

After nearly an hour Colin must feel me looking at him, and he slows the engine, checks the map, the compass. "Here."

I'm looking down at my own map and compass. He's farther away than I'd like, but I nod. Colin looks deliberately away while I shrug off my fleece. I check the camera again, the pressure gauge, the fit of my regulator, the torch. Heaving on my air tank, I'm gripped by sudden paranoia. Alex mixed my tank up for me before I left Edinburgh. I check the taste now through my regulator—he wouldn't—no, it just tastes normal, like rubber. Surely even Alex doesn't hate me that much. Sitting on the gunwale, I squeeze into the flippers, attach my belt. Oily water from the motor splatters over my knees as Colin lobs the anchor overboard.

"Do you feel confident with the signals we discussed yesterday?" I ask.

"Aye," he says.

I wait a moment, but he doesn't offer more detail. Realistically, Colin's not going to be able to do anything if I have a problem while I'm down there, anyway. It's forty miles and an unreliable ferry between me and anyone qualified to help me if my equipment fails. Diving alone is against every code of honour in the trade, but clearly my safety isn't Alex's priority right now.

"I'll see you in about half an hour," I say, giving Colin a thumbs-up, which, even while I'm doing it, makes me feel foolish. He nods at me.

I strap on my mask, click my neck, breathe out, and push myself back, over, and down, into the water.

§

IT'S EVEN COLDER than I'd expected, a blow that knits my muscles together. Pushing all my strength into kick kick kick I swim down down, concentrating only on moving. My heart is racing from the slap of cold. As I reach ten feet, I paddle in place, circling my arms, waiting for my heart and breathing to settle. I unfold the waterproof map, check the compass again. I was right, Colin was off—stupid of me to waste time and air. The pain of the cold pulls back, replaced by a fizzing in my limbs. My breath is loud and regular in the mask, and I have a strange urge to do a somersault. I'd forgotten how much I missed this. Kelp towers above me, collared with fluffy crimson algae. I weave through the boughs, the wet lick of the fronds against my legs, slim fish flashing tin in the bubbles. Kicking through a patch of seaweed disturbs a cloud of trembling jellyfish the size of buttons, and they shimmer alongside me as I swim northeast, following the dip of the seafloor.

The seabed drops abruptly to a plateau. I'm down on the shelf now; it's darker here, sheltered by the kelp forests to either side. I descend four more feet, into the shadowy water near the seabed. A flickering, gloaming light filters through the kelp, and orange tentacles of seaweed furl and unfurl around my legs. I switch on my torch. And there she is.

HMS *Deliverance*.

None of the scoping material did her justice. The Arctic waters where the ship was found have preserved it like it was stoppered in a bottle. The greenheart wood planks are intact; the name plaque on the stern is barely tarnished. My skin is tingling. I knot the end of the guideline to the clip of the inflatable buoy, then put my mouthpiece to the balloon, tie it, and let it float to the surface. Hopefully, Colin is watching and will bring the boat around. I try not to imagine what will happen if I surface and he has just sailed away.

The camera is weightless in my hands, and I steady it to take the first photograph. The flash lights up the name plaque, the fresh lichen the ship has collected since being towed to Scottish waters. Swimming towards the aft deck, I take more photos—the dents in what I can see of the retractable rudder, the ice scarring on the greenheart, the clamps along the gunwale from the towing gear. The main hatch is already open, a small mercy for my purposes, and my torchlight shines back on a wooden ladder, paint worn in the centre of each rung where the crew's footsteps buffed it away. I pull myself down through the hatch and into the ship.

The first dive into a ship is an otherworldly experience. It's travelling into a moment that has been paused in time. When Jenine and I were young, we used to play a game where we peeked through other people's windows and made up stories about their lives. It was a winter game, best played after the brooding Glasgow sunset, when strangers' front rooms would be lit up by the fire, teakettles whistling from back kitchens. The boards of HMS *Deliverance* are lacy with algae, and I trace my fingers over knots in the wood. It gives me the same kind of thrill I felt back then, as the unseen observer of someone else's world. Like I have become both invisible and all-powerful. Being the first diver to visit the ship after her relocation means that I'm exploring a place almost nobody has been in over a hundred years, since she sank. I have her all to myself.

Inside the passage, the lips of water beyond my torchlight are coal black, stippled with freckles of sediment. Slowly, I ease myself along the narrow corridor that leads to the crew quarters. The cabins along the right-hand side are frozen in Victorian grandeur. They look exactly as they must have in 1849, when the boat last left Port Mary Harbour: wooden panelling, narrow bunks built into the walls. I expected there would be breakage from when the ship was towed back here, but she was made for movement: furniture nailed to the walls, drafting pens fixed to writing desks. I take photographs of the crew quarters, the flash glinting on shaving mirrors shrouded in webs of algae. I've never seen a site like this before—it seems almost staged in its completeness, like a doll's house. Through the silt I spot an ivory-handled clothes brush and a tin spectacle case tucked into the rail of the first officer's bunk. Lord and Lady Purdie will have their pick of trophies for their museum. After taking pictures in the next three rooms, I kick gently down to the far end of the starboard side. A silver-coloured pollock has slipped in from the kelp on the seabed and darts in startled zigzags as I approach the reason for my trip to Cairnroch Island: Captain Purdie's bunk.

The door is sticking to the floorboards, and I deliberate for a moment before sliding my knife through the algae and dragging open the door, a fog of silt seeping into the water. I float against the ceiling of the passage until it's settled enough for me to see my own hands again, and pull myself through into the room. The skeletal remains of Captain James Purdie appear in the frame of torchlight. Curled on the bottom bunk, his knees are drawn to his chest, wisps of hair drifting softly around his skull. His skeleton is well preserved, his bones dappled with gooey-looking sediment. Nestled under the remains of Purdie's hands is a chunky golden ring—unusual for a Calvinist of this era, but perhaps it was a guild gift. I have to focus at close range to take a photograph, illuminating the faint outline of a barque engraved on the bezel. The Purdies will lose their minds over the ring—there couldn't be a more perfect museum showpiece. Through the speckles of silt I peer through the doors of a glass-fronted cabinet, which contains a pair of bone snow goggles, a horn comb, and a toothbrush, the bristles still intact. There is no porthole, but dents in the wall mark where nails must once have held up maps or schedules, maybe photographs from home, and slotted into a niche in the wall is a small gilt mirror. On the table next to Captain Purdie's bunk is what looks like a copper coin, a fringe of glutinous seaweed smothering it to the surface of the wood. The discovery report recorded that the top drawer of the desk contains the provisioner's ledger and the captain's expedition journal, but the Danish team who found the ship were pessimistic about the likelihood of the books surviving the tow. The drawer has become gummed with seaweed, and I carefully drag my penknife through the fronds, praying I haven't accidentally cut the material. When I prise open the drawer, the two leatherbound books inside seem to have held up much better than anticipated. Gingerly, I open the books and take photos at random to send back to Sophie, the textual expert at the museum in Edinburgh, for review. The captain's diary contains pre-lined boxes for recording the latitude and longitude, as well as wind speeds and temperature. But I can't make out the writing—visibility is too poor, and deciphering handwriting isn't my strong suit in any case.

Swimming away from Captain Purdie's remains, I squeeze through the passageway into the galley kitchen, where two metal spoons still hang from pegs on the wall. There is a horn cup engraved with Captain Purdie's initials attached by a snap hook above the grate. It must have been his personal drinking vessel. I haven't seen this type of fixture before; it's a clever little grooved latch to stop items from falling during bad weather, and I take a couple of extra photographs. The pantry is stacked with corroding tins and stoneware jugs nailed into position with wooden dowels. It's odd the crew would have left this many tins here before abandoning the ship, but I suppose they must have taken the dried pemmican with them. Maybe one day their remains will also be discovered. I wonder if Lord and Lady Purdie will pay for their repatriation, too, or if their generosity only stretches to their ancestors.

My regulator glitches; it hiccups with a start, and I brace myself in the corner of the room. *Don't panic*, I say to myself, *release the valve*, and it cocks back again. For a moment, I give myself permission to miss Alex, knowing that we could always rely on each other during a dive, if not above water. On the other side of the kitchen is the saloon, the only space on the ship large enough for group meals or socialising. The walls of the saloon curve inwards, and it feels smaller than I'd expected, silt gently coasting in the water like snowfall. It must have been claustrophobic for the crewmates to spend the dark Arctic winter cooped up in here while they planned their escape across the ice. The table riveted to the floor has gouges cut into it, someone marking down time, measuring wins or losses. As I take a picture of the grooves, a cupboard door on the far side under the porthole smacks open. I jump, and the circle of torchlight swings to the ceiling. The bubble of my laughter echoes in my mouthpiece. I right the torch. The storage cupboard is only knee-high and set at an angle with a latch to prevent it from knocking open on rolling seas. In my surprise, I've unsettled the sediment, and it is rippling in creamy ribbons that fill the room, like ash. It's hard to take photos in such poor conditions, so I lever myself against the table to swim back the other way. As I begin to pull myself from the saloon, a flicker of movement behind me catches my eye. The cupboard door is closing again. Slowly, this time. I must have created an eddy of pressure. Or it's a fish, knocking against the wood. I blink back into the room through the ripples of silt, raising my camera.

And there, underneath the window, a man is crouching.

2

SUNDAY, OCTOBER 14, TO
MONDAY, OCTOBER 15, 1962

TO CATCH THE FERRY TO CAIRNROCH ISLAND, I'D DRIVEN from Edinburgh up to Inverness and spent the night in a cheap bed-and-breakfast near the rail lines, headlamps from freight trains chattering in the gap between the curtains. I was the first customer in the co-op in the morning when I went in to pick up supplies for the island, eliciting an arched eyebrow from the girl at the till, who must have supposed I was preparing for an eccentric breakfast of batteries and sanitary napkins. As I set off along the coast, a belt of fog rolled over the road and I drove slowly, hearing rather than seeing the waves against the rocks. Every so often, a box of late-season apples left by the side of the road appeared out of the mist, and I stopped near Greenacre and stood over the hot hood of the car, the apples limp and leathery between my teeth.

Signs for the Cairnroch ferry appeared after Galen, and the turning revealed a black-and-gold teahouse shaped like a pagoda, sitting improbably in a loading station clogged with oil drums and lobster crates, slick, gritty puddles of cigarette stubs and sluiced water from dripping mackerel. Mr. Tibalt, the manager of the Cairnroch Grand

Hotel, had told me over the phone that it was hard to come by gas on the island, so I'd decided against bringing my Ford Prefect for the sake of only a few weeks. There were no other patrons in the tea shop, and through the window I watched people calling to one another from amidst the jumble of fishing wire and felt self-aware that I was the sole ferry passenger sheltering indoors. My skirt, which had seemed positively modest in Edinburgh, now felt far too short. An old woman wearing a maid's mob cap delivered the tea in a teacup made of such thin china I could have read the Bible through it.

Half an hour before the ferry was due to leave, I asked for the bill, and when the woman came back she lingered, hovering over me so that I felt compelled to add an extra shilling to my plate.

"You're it, are you?"

I looked up, bemused.

"The diver."

"Yes, that's me. I'm me."

"Thought they'd send someone at the top for something as important as this?"

I gave her an insincere smile. "Well, I volunteered for this assignment. Don't worry, my boss is still in charge."

She nodded but didn't move. I wasn't sure what she wanted from me, so I said, "Are you from Cairnroch yourself?"

"Oh, no. We used to go on holidays as a child, but not since . . ." She gestured at the faded pictures of Rathdunon Castle framed on the walls. The castle was destroyed by a German strike during the war, now apparently not much more than a pile of rubble. Cairnroch never recovered its place as an affordable summer holiday spot. Even now, the paintings of the Purdies' ancestral home have the same nostalgic dolour of a cardboard memorial photo of an airman gunned down by the Luftwaffe. Lewis had a well-thumbed souvenir postcard of the castle on the cage of his electric meter in his flat. A relic from the last trip home before his dad died, the last summer he was happy, he said. Never passed up an opportunity for a bit of melodrama.

"And is it true that he's down there?" She leaned forward.

I licked my lips. "Captain Purdie?"

She tutted, as if I'd said something stupid. "Yes, Auld James. He's really come home?"

As a corpse, I thought. Out loud I said, "In a sense."

She looked around the tea shop. "Imagine. Sailing back home again in his own ship. And now he's getting to his rightful resting place." She reached out and gripped my hand. "God bless the Purdies. Everything round here will be changed. Like the good old days."

It occurred to me she might have been working in the tea shop since before the war. Twenty years of boiling the same kettle, wiping away other people's lipstick smudges. The thought depressed me. "You might get a better uniform," I said, aiming for a joke.

Her expression tightened then. "Better get going. They're punctual around here."

I looked out the window. If they were punctual, it would be the first island I'd ever visited in my life that didn't have a magnanimously long-era sense of time. A man wearing a waxed cap appeared at the door and gave me a hard stare before leaving again.

I hurried after him. "Are you looking for me?"

He chuckled. "No, hen. Get one of the men on the dock to help you with your bags."

I cleared my throat. "I don't need help with my bags. I'm the diver. Mr. Tibalt mentioned I should check in with someone."

He jerked his head back. "Oh. That's you, is it? I heard the Purdies were sending someone. I thought . . ."

I could guess what he thought—that he was looking for a man. "No, yes, no," I said.

Running his tongue over his teeth, he said, "I wouldn't have expected a nice girl like you to be in this line of work."

"Well, that's me." Then I added, "Sorry." Although I wasn't sure what I was apologising for. Not being a nice girl, perhaps. A squirm of self-hatred passed through me.

"Right, well, I'm supposed to load the . . ." He looked around me.

"My equipment."

He tipped his cap at me, winking. "Right you are, then. No one says no to a Purdie."

§

OVERCOMPENSATING FOR BEING the only indoor patron at the loading dock, I sat outside on the deck of the ferry for the journey, which I should've known would be an error from how the locals huddled inside. The fog doused me in frigid droplets, the waves below the colour of pencil lead, and the other ferry goers watched me curiously through the window. I braced myself against the drizzly veil and tried not to think of Alex, back at the museum. How by now, he'd be drinking coffee at his desk. How by now, he would no doubt feel relieved that I was gone.

It was three hours before Cairnroch came into sight. A sudden gleam of sun on the red-and-white ice cream swirl of the Captain James Purdie Lighthouse, a hint of a rainbow in the sea spray. A row of pastel-coloured houses stretching along the waterfront puffed coal smoke from narrow chimneys. As we entered the deep bowl of Port Mary Harbour, the ferry slid through oily slicks in the sheltered water, drawing up into a waiting crowd.

Clearly the arrival of the ferry was something of an occasion—little boys in school shorts were crouching on the jagged stone walls, and behind them were perhaps twenty women with overcoats blowing aside to flash glimpses of sherbet-coloured pinafores. People muttered to one another and gestured to me with raised eyebrows. Mr. Tibalt, a thin man in his sixties with a carefully trimmed moustache, was waiting to meet me off the ferry. He was wearing his hotel uniform of a double-breasted navy jacket and braided cap, standing to attention next to an old-fashioned chrome luggage trolley onto which he insisted on loading my equipment. As Mr. Tibalt wheeled the trolley along the path to the hotel, I was forced to walk behind, feeling somehow like the sole mourner at a funeral. Between the gulls and chatter of the ferry passengers, I struggled to understand his accent—the Cairnroch manner of speaking, as if one is holding a sweetie in the mouth that is in danger of leaping out unless kept in place with the tongue.

"Course the war . . ." I heard. Then, as we began passing the row of pastel-coloured houses: "Used to be a fish-and-chip shop . . . now it's gone." Later, as we approached a shuttered stand overlooking the harbour: ". . . ice cream . . ." and then a long sigh.

The breeze blew salty and sour with gull droppings, and as Mr. Tibalt sighed and pointed, I scrutinised the seafront. Lewis was the only person I've ever known from Cairnroch. After a few drinks he would get misty-eyed about donkey rides and the pleasure pavilion and the dark thrill of trips to the outdoor privy in winter. Now, the pleasure pavilion was boarded up and the beach littered with abandoned bathing huts bleeding rusted crab cages. But maybe not for long, if the Purdies' plan works.

Mr. Tibalt stopped in a shallow heather garden at the front of the Grand Hotel to give me a hotel history lesson which I wasn't much listening to. The building was fashioned out of the island's grey stone, and it looked much more severe than the luxurious spot for local honeymooners that Lewis had described. But then as a child I'd thought that sugar sandwiches were luxurious.

As Mr. Tibalt opened the hotel doors, the purpose of my trip to Cairnroch was reflected back at me. The mahogany-panelled lobby was in the process of being renovated from a loose hunting theme to a nautical one. Oil paintings of stags in majestic, steaming splendour were propped carefully on the floor, ousted to make way for paintings of majestic, steaming ships being tossed on roiling seas. On my left-hand side, a man in overalls was at the top of a ladder, nailing an anchor over the counter of an art deco–style cocktail bar.

Mr. Tibalt led me towards an imposing staircase and, next to that, a desk with a single amber-bulbed lamp. I gave him my old address at first, out of habit, and as I was double-checking the bedsit phone number, I looked up to see a maid in a white apron watching me over the banister, before quickly withdrawing.

"Purdie hunting tartan," Mr. Tibalt said, pointing to the sash around his desk. I had been idly running my fingers around the seam and pretended now to admire it.

"Oh, so do the Purdie family also own the hotel?" I asked. He gave me such an astonished look that I gathered the answer to this question had formed most of his earlier lecture about the building. He blinked into the small coal fireplace before recovering. "Forgive us . . . no television."

I felt my face drop. "That's fine," I said. "I'll have time to read." But there was already a sense of panic creeping over me. The ferry to the mainland only runs every five weeks. Stuck here for over a month with no television, and no fresh newspapers. Feeling Lewis everywhere. "Can I send telegrams?"

"Post office, main street, most Thursday afternoons. Telephones . . . lobby. Lady Purdie can reach the American air base for anything urgent."

I nodded, pretending to be reassured. No one would need to contact me urgently; even my parents and I hadn't spoken since my birthday in February.

"Your luggage already . . . room. Flora . . . upstairs," Mr. Tibalt said, gesturing to the maid in the white apron.

I gave him a polite goodbye and followed the maid along a strip of worn teal carpet to the doors of a lift that she cranked open with some effort.

"There's no need," I said. "I can take the stairs."

"Mr. Tibalt insists," she said, primly. As the doors closed with a juddering series of screeches, her voice became more conspiratorial. "We only use it for guests," she said. "It gets stuck." The gears wound and she crossed herself.

"Do you get a lot of guests here this time of year?" I said.

She laughed. "Oh no. We have longer-term residents, but you're the only tourist."

"I'm here for work."

"Yes." She looked me up and down. "The diver. I didn't think you'd be a girl."

I shrugged.

Flora withdrew a strand of hair from her bun and pulled it across her lips. "They'll have to bring more people on at the hotel, won't they? Once people start coming back here to visit like they used to."

"Perhaps?"

She nodded, as if I'd said something wise. "I've been telling my sister she doesn't need to leave to find work. That there'll be more jobs coming here soon, but she won't listen to me. Maybe you can tell her, she might believe it coming from an outsider."

"I don't know," I stuttered, but the lift doors finally creaked open on the second floor. Flora pointed out the bathroom at the end of the hallway, and I spotted a green-veined marble floor and a chipped claw bathtub.

"Here you go, number 7."

The floorboards outside the room squeaked underfoot and the door opened onto a large L-shaped room, tucked into the corner of the building. The window on the far wall overlooked the still cup of the harbour, and in the corner was a ceramic-tiled coal fireplace nursing red embers. A modest walnut bed underneath the second window offered an easterly view over the ballroom roof, the cracked lights of the old pleasure pavilion just beyond. My luggage had already been delivered to the room and I hurried to pull my diving tank away from the fireplace. Above the writing desk was a painting of HMS *Deliverance* set fast in Arctic ice, a pearly, endless sunshine glinting off the rime. It was clearly newly installed for my arrival since a border of unfaded green wallpaper surrounded the frame. The blotter held a few thin sheets of writing paper that looked suspiciously as if they had been crumpled up and then ironed. I sat on the edge of the bed. It wouldn't be worth writing to Alex, since I'd probably arrive back in Edinburgh in advance of the post. It wasn't as if I could say anything to make things better between us, anyway.

Back down on the ground floor of the hotel I made my way to the cocktail bar. The man with the ladder was now twisting a braid of marine rope over the fireplace on the far side of the room. A blonde woman was stocking bottles in a cupboard behind the counter, and when she turned, I saw she was roughly my age, a little shorter than me. Pretty, in a full-fat milk sort of way, with heavy cheeks and thick brown lashes.

"Oh, it's you!" she said.

I looked behind me in confusion.

She laughed. "I'm sorry, I just was expecting the new guest today. You're Marta?"

I came forward and sat at the counter. "Nice to meet you."

"Elsie," she said. Her handshake was strong, and up close, the fullness in her face and figure afforded her a kind of sulky languor.

"The diver," she said, leaning her elbows on the counter. "I thought . . ."

"You thought I'd be a man?"

She frowned. "I thought you'd be taller." She motioned to the wall behind her. "A wee dram as a welcome?"

Gratefully, I received the whisky, trying not to gulp down the whole glass at once.

"So, will you need to get rubbed all over with oil?"

I laughed, coughing on the whisky. "I'm sorry, what?"

She kicked the bottom of the counter, and my glass wobbled. "Goose fat or oil. For the cold."

"Oh." I grappled with the spectre of a joke, something about massaging the fat on me, or me being slippery; something coy and flirtatious. "Sometimes I put a little Vaseline on my face. Suits only come in men's sizes so it doesn't fit me very well at the best of times, without adding oil to the equation," I said instead.

Elsie nodded. "When do you have to go down there?"

"I'll need to find a fisherman to take me out to the site. Perhaps a week or so? Then the captain's bones will go straight for burial."

She edged down the bar towards the open cabinet and recommenced filling the shelves. The way she moved was deliberate and weighted, as if she were swimming against a strong current. "Funeral."

"Sorry?"

"The Purdies will prefer if you say 'funeral.'"

"Ah, good point."

"And he's Auld James around here, not 'the captain.' Only outsiders call him Captain Purdie."

"I don't feel like I know him well enough for a nickname," I said.

Elsie raised her eyebrows. "Digging up his skeleton ought to get you two acquainted."

I waited until I was sure she was joking before laughing.

She turned to me, a bottle of lemonade in hand. "I don't know how you could do that for a job. Going down into that dark water. It would scare the hell out of me."

"Everything that's down there is already dead," I said, and she winced. Through the glass of the cabinet door, I saw her figure flicker as she made the sign of the cross.

LATITUDE 60°, 0' N, LONGITUDE 9°, 18' W

Men already yearning to return to Port Mairi. Rather foul breeze and heavy pitching ... insubordination ... The men would not look upon me in the face but grumbled.

SATURDAY, OCTOBER 20, 1962

GULLS ARE CIRCLING COLIN'S BOAT AS I HEAVE MYSELF OUT of the water. His hands are in the pockets of his trousers and he's watching me almost suspiciously as I drag my limbs over the gunwale. Sliding off the air tank, I pull one of the hotel towels over my head, throwing another somewhere in the direction of my chest. My stomach clenches from the cold, and I grip the side of the boat, squeezing my nails into the softened wood.

"Finished?" Colin says, rocking on his heels.

"Yes, for now," I say. I aim for a smile, but my jaw is so tight I feel a crooked grimace cross my face. He stops rocking on his heels. "Excuse me." I motion to the wetsuit and Colin turns away, although if he wanted, he could watch me undress in the reflection in the window of the wheelhouse. I check the reflection, to see if he wants. He doesn't want. Clumsy shaking fingers on clumsy shaking skin, my ill-fitting wetsuit peels off easily, revealing green veins, gooseflesh. I climb into my wool sweater and trousers and try and rub the circulation back into my face.

"Didn't bring anything back up, did you?" Colin says.

"Do you see anything?" I snap. I take a breath and try again. "No, I was only taking photographs."

He sucks his teeth, his hand resting on the motor pull. If I wait, he won't be able to hear me over the wind.

"Did you see any seals come by? Dolphins?"

"A dolphin?" he repeats, as if it's the most absurd proposition anyone has ever made.

"One of the doors in the ship opened." I hold his eyes. "It helps my work if I know what kind of animals might be feeding in or around the vessel."

He scoffs. "Dolphins, this time of year." Under his breath, he says, "Mainlander," as we motor back towards the island.

An itch spreads over my belly and thighs as I start to warm up. It feels like my skin is crawling, as if I've brushed against something noxious. I peer down into the glaucous water rolling underneath us and try not to picture the figure, down in the ship. Watching me.

§

BACK AT THE HOTEL, the gas heater in the bathroom clicks with a thunderous flicker before the rumble of the hot water heater, and as the tub fills, I inspect the bowl of seashells left by the window that is obliged, by law, in every hotel in the United Kingdom. From here, the water in the harbour is turquoise, a ripple of white sand in a cove farther down the coast that makes false tropical promises. I get into the tub and reach for a bar of hotel soap. It's wrapped in thick cream paper, like an old-fashioned wedding dress. Pummelling the bar into a frail jacket of suds, I watch the silt that crept inside my wetsuit rub off and collect in grey welts at the bottom of the bath. I picture the swirls of the stuff in the saloon, the ripples, the something, crouching. I start to shake. My limbs tremble in the tub, the bathwater quivering. I wrap my arms around my knees and squeeze them to my chest as hard as possible. *I can't do this. I can't be here.* My heart is fluttering in half beats; the air in the room is too thin. I take the deepest breath I can manage and submerge myself in the water, blowing the air out in a slow stream of bubbles until I feel more in control. I have to get a grip on myself. This is the least I can do for Lewis, even if it's not enough.

When I'm dressed, I let myself out of the hotel by the side door next to the old ballroom and make my way through narrow back lanes to the high street. Port Mary's main thoroughfare is a narrow, cobbled road that runs from east to west behind the harbour. There's a general store selling methylated spirits, paraffin, loose tea, stale biscuits; all at an eye-watering price. The pharmacy next door has a shelf of ancient cod-liver oil bottles in the window. Elsie advised me to avoid the pharmacy unless in case of emergency, since the Irene who works there, Big Irene, is apparently zealous in her role as island directory of everybody's dandruff and haemorrhoids. Two small redheaded boys are kicking a football across the cobbles. They are both wearing school shorts even though it's a Saturday. A woman with a bonnet over her rollers is pouring something into the drain outside her kitchen, and she stands at her doorway, crossing her arms as I pass. Agnes? Irene? I smile at her, but she turns back into her house.

Taking a left at the shuttered post office, I pass the shuttered fish-and-chip shop and join the road where it meets the coast. Elsie's bike is leaning against the phone booth, where I left it yesterday—oops—unlocked. It is one of the old hotel bikes, so it would be too obvious to steal. Probably. Seagulls wail from posts along the water's edge; the breeze is light, spiderweb clouds overhead. By the lamppost at Roiner's Point the water dimples, and a seal's head bobs above the froth, eyes glossy, bulbous. Then it retreats into the water. That's all it was, down in the ship. A seal, or a crab, come in from the kelp. It's easy to be spooked by nothing when you're diving—your brain tricks you into seeing faces everywhere, in old shopping bags, divots in the rock. I cycle along the winding road that leads up the hill, and the castle looms above me in the distance. Young, rusty-coloured pine trees kneel in shallow hollows along the hillside, and as I climb higher, the stretch of copse that runs parallel to the castle comes into view. The trees have been fighting against the wind, and they trail down the slope in stretched lines, as if they've been given one good hard tug through with a comb.

And then I'm at the path up to Purdie Castle. It's what they call Scottish baronial style, more like a mansion than a true castle, two turrets flanking the southeasterly facade. It is built from the island's grey stone and set across a Z pattern, with a walled garden at the back, and alcoves where bees used to be kept. The picture-book medieval glamour of Rathdunon Castle may have drawn in the tourists, but Purdie Castle has long been the real residence of the Purdie family. Auld James himself spent his childhood here, although the castle was renovated in the 1840s, and his old nursery was apparently converted into a guest bedroom. I leave Elsie's bike on the far side of the hedge, think about locking it, promise myself I'll lock it tomorrow. Mr. Scruff barks as I enter the kitchen, and I let him lick my palm, waiting for Janet, the housekeeper, to come through.

"Don't feed him," Janet says, bustling in from the passage to the larder.

"I haven't," I say, stroking his silky ears.

"I just gave him his food ten minutes ago," Janet says. "He just had his food."

She isn't really talking to me, she's talking to the dog, so I readjust my bag and take the steps two at a time. If I linger, I'll get caught in a description of Mr. Scruff's morning timetable. How he chased a sheep, or a mouse, or his tail. "He wanted breakfast early today, he did," Janet is saying.

"Oh dear." My hand turns the doorknob faster than is polite; the door opens with a creak. The narrow back corridor is dark after the lightness of the kitchen. It runs along the length of the building and would have been of use only for servants in the olden days. The doorways along the right-hand side that each open into a different room are muffled with red velvet curtains, as if each one framed a puppet show. I walk as quietly as I can along the corridor; if I make even a small whisper, I'll have to—

"Janet?" Lady Purdie shouts, in the voice of someone accustomed to shouting for people.

I take a breath. I was hoping to have more time to sit with my reports before talking to Lady Purdie, but I can appreciate why the Purdies are impatient. "Good morning, Lady Purdie." I put my head around the doorframe into the morning room. It is decorated in dusky rose–coloured wallpaper patterned with intertwining green thistles.

"Marta." Lady Purdie looks up from her desk by the window, her elbows resting on a partially finished letter. She takes off her glasses. "You've been down there already?"

"Yes, Lady Purdie."

"How is it? How is he?"

I edge into the room and contemplate sitting down, but people from a certain social class like to have their workers standing to attention. "The ship is in astonishing condition, completely furnished. There's been a small amount of damage from the tow, but there are some objects that will be a real highlight for the museum. The captain has an unusual gold ring, and there's an interesting coin in his cabin."

She lifts her pen and taps the lid across her teeth. The pen is silver-plated; it catches a flare of light from the window. "And from above, the ship would be appealing for swimmers?"

"Absolutely. Exceptional for snorkelling trips. In the summer, that is."

She sits back in her chair with an exhalation of breath. I feel sorry for her, then. The weight of expectation, the sheer audacity of their plan to coax people out to the island. The planning, the expense, the imagination.

"The quality of the water?"

I picture the figure in the mist. "Good," I say, after a moment.

"And the captain?"

"He looks just as if he were sleeping, Lady Purdie. I think it's likely he passed that way, in his sleep." Of course there is no way to know that, but as her expression relaxes, I know that I delivered the lie in the right way.

"Isn't that how we'd all like to go?" she says.

I feel the horror of the sea rolling over him, the salt choke in his throat. Behind my back I squeeze my hands together.

She is watching me. "Tiring, is it? You look a bit pale. Well, pale for you."

The terror pulls back. Funny how something as simple as annoyance can do that; it's like stabbing yourself with a pin to distract from the pain of the dentist's drill.

"So what happens next?" Lady Purdie says, all business now.

"I'm waiting for some—" I hesitate; she won't like the word "hoist." "Some specialist equipment to be delivered, before we can lay the captain to rest."

She nods. "I've spoken to the groundsman at the kirk. That crypt is in terrible shape, there's a leak down there that's rotten right through one of the walls. That field always caused me trouble. Why you'd put a sheep drain so close to a graveyard is beyond me, all the silage pours down there. Stinks in the summer."

Maybe she wouldn't have minded the word "hoist" after all. There's a certain type of aristocratic countrywoman of that age, who saw things during the war, who takes a brutal sense of achievement from snapping the necks of rabbits, who prides herself on never being cold. Women who fetishise work, the paraphernalia of work, the suffering of work.

"I should get to work," I say.

She turns back to her letter. "Off you trot, then," she says, with a dismissive flash of the silver pen, and for a second, I hate her.

§

BACK ALONG THE CORRIDOR, I pass the drawing room and then am emptied out into the former entranceway flanked by heavy oak doors that are never used. They call this hall the Elephant Gallery, on account of the one taxidermied elephant head over the fireplace, as if the two dozen antlers don't count. On the other side of the entranceway are the formal sitting room, the huge, octagonal "Ceylonese Room," and the castle museum. As of now, the museum really isn't much more complicated than a room with a couple of cabinets. There are a few coins belonging to other ancestral Purdies, along with a selection of colonial curios dispatched here by way of the family estates in Ceylon and, before that, Jamaica. In the corner, next to a rack of sun-bleached postcards, Lester, the curator of the castle museum, is humming as he tries to fit keys into a locked cabinet.

"Good morning, Marta," he says, nudging his spectacles back up to the bridge of his nose. Then he snaps to attention. "You went down this morning, didn't you?"

I nod.

"Well? Don't torture a poor old man." He grips the keys so tightly that his fingertips blanch.

"Everything is looking promising. The temperature and the low oxygenation have kept everything in an ideal condition. I'm going to develop my photos now, then we can maybe look at them together."

Lester clasps his hands, staring at his knees, and when he looks back at me, his eyes are wet. I feel embarrassed, as if I've been witness to a private emotion. "Thank you," he says. He has a reason to be grateful. Captain Purdie's treasures are the discovery of a lifetime, not just for the island, but for him personally.

"It's my pleasure," I say. I turn the words over as I let myself out behind the museum into the long, narrow room where the Purdie collections live. Drawers of Ceylonese moths, Jamaican wood carvings. It's not pleasure, exactly, but I do have a guilty sense of satisfaction at finally being useful. Being able to prove to Alex how much the museum needs me, to prove to myself I can do something right.

My darkroom is set up at the very back of the wing, in the old stillroom, and I unclip the photos hanging up there of shallow kelp, some of the interior of the hotel, a couple of pictures of Elsie behind the hotel bar. I pull the old war blackout curtains over the windows, stuff a towel under the door. The camera roll I unwind into the reel, pour in the developing fluid, rinse, then add the fixer. I set my stopwatch to five minutes.

I hate these five minutes. It's an in-between time, when you can't do anything except sit in the dark. All the uneasy confidence of moments ago flushes away, and my mouth fills with a bitter taste. Alex's face that day at the kitchen table. I need these photos to be good. I can't afford to give Alex any excuse to fire me—my reports have to be beyond reproach. *It's all going to be OK*, I say to myself. *Don't panic, just keep going.*

My hands are shaking as I tip out the fixer and give the roll one final rinse. As I hang the negatives up to dry, they look promising. Sharp, clear focus. There's good definition in the shots of Captain Purdie's remains. A few photos I don't remember taking but I'm glad I did—the outside of his door where I cut through the lichen, the labels on the tin cans in the galley. I run through the roll, wondering if the movement from the seal or the spider crab might have compromised the last few pictures. But I don't have to worry, because the final picture isn't blurred at all. It captures the saloon of the ship perfectly. The clouds of silt, but also the cupboard door on the far side of the room. And next to that, the figure, crouching.

4

SUNDAY, OCTOBER 21, 1962

I'VE ONLY JUST DROPPED INTO SLEEP WHEN CHURCH BELLS wake me the next day. From my bedroom window I watch the slow procession of people making their way up the slope towards the kirk. Too late, I realise I probably should have gone as well—goodness knows how scandalised the locals would be if they found out I'm technically a Catholic.

Instead, I dress and let myself out by the hotel's front doors. A surprised brown mouse bounds out of the heather and scurries across the road. The harbour is full of fishing boats—even the fishermen must observe the Sabbath around here. I walk to the easterly side of the harbour until I meet the marshy turf that stretches out towards the island's second lighthouse. This one is a modest whitewashed affair, nestled into the cliffs. Everyone calls it "the other lighthouse." Storm petrels circle the roof, and a puffin, proud and silly as a boarding school boy in his first-day uniform, struts out from a cleft in the rock and then retreats. I feel almost sorry for this humble lighthouse. It can't compare with the postcard-worthy structure that sits near the harbour, supposedly built by Captain Purdie himself.

I walk back on myself and follow the wide, well-paved road out to the site of what used to be Rathdunon Castle, the home of the ancestral Purdies. Officially, this road was renamed James Purdie Road in the early 1900s, although nobody refers to it like that. On the sparse maps of the island, Auld James has lent his name to a well near Gluckathy, a strip of rocky beach, and of course the James Coal Mine. And now he's due to return and revive the fortunes of the whole island. It's a lot of pressure on one man. And on me.

Along the road, faded signs for the castle now point to a bombed-out hole in the ground, surrounded by startled-looking piles of grey rubble. I wander among the stones, running my fingers over their fuzzy brooches of lichen. We never took summer holidays as children; Mama always was anxious at the idea of travelling, swallowing nervous hiccups if we had so much as a bus ride to Edinburgh. It's odd to think of Lewis standing on this very spot. His parents helping him navigate the stone steps of the castle. Now they're all dust. A seagull coasts overhead, landing on a jagged lip of rock and watching me with hopeful, canny eyes for any sign of scraps. I flash back to the darkness inside the cabin, the shape in the photograph. I can feel it now, the stare fixed on me. Leaning on one of the sloping rocks, I rest my head in my hands. The feeling of being watched grows so strong that I can't help but look around me. A whistling hum is creeping over the broken stones, stirred by the wind. Behind me, a shadow skulks in the grass, and I find myself standing up, my heartbeat thrumming. But there's nothing there. A rabbit, maybe. As I walk back to the hotel, I turn my collar up to protect the back of my neck. I can still feel the stare.

I linger in the hotel hallway, absently passing between the paintings of barques in full tilt. A fretful restlessness has crept up on me, and the idea of being alone in my bedroom is unbearable. I bring my satchel down from my room and sit in a bucket seat near the telephone, smoking one cigarette after another. When Elsie crosses the hallway, I sit up and she laughs, surprised.

"Does the bar have set hours?" I try not to sound too desperate.

She thinks about it. "We don't usually open on a Sunday, but I won't mention it to Mr. Tibalt if you don't?"

She pours me a whisky and fixes herself a gin and lemonade, leaning her elbows on the bar to sip from her glass. She's talking about the medieval leper hospital attached to the church, and the restless gloom fills me again at the idea of those poor people shut away there, their bodies mouldering away beneath them.

"Is it tiring, the diving?" Elsie says, eventually.

This is a polite way of excusing me for not listening to her.

"I'm sorry. I don't mean to be distracted."

"Sure you're not coming down with something? You're a funny colour."

I light another cigarette. "That's what Lady Purdie said."

Elsie blushes. "I didn't mean it like that."

"I know, I'm sorry." God, what's wrong with me? I can't accept a mild solicitous gesture without being prickly.

She tucks a lock of hair behind her ear, then crosses to sit on the barstool next to me. "How was it yesterday?"

I hesitate, and her eyes travel over my face. There is a single, tear-shaped freckle underneath her left eye. I can't remember the last time someone willingly offered me their full, focused attention like this. I have a sudden impulse to kiss her, startling myself. Not that I haven't kissed a girl before, but that was long before Alex and I got married. I take another sip of whisky. "It was fine. Murdo was driving up near the air base, so he took up the photographs. They'll go out on a drop tomorrow."

"The dive, though. How did it go?"

I stretch my shoulders, shift my weight on the stool, swallow. "Could I show you something?"

"Of course." Her face brightens, and I think I might have been able to get away with kissing her.

We go next door into the reading room where the light is better. As usual, there's nobody in there, although a smoky fire is gurgling in the grate. Elsie coughs, tutting as she opens the flue on the side of the fireplace. "Flora always forgets," she grumbles. The table by the window is sticky, and I unfold a week-old copy of the *Scottish Herald* before putting my satchel on the table. As I slide out the envelope, I realise that I'd been waiting to show the photographs to her, otherwise I wouldn't have brought my bag down in the first instance. "This is the ship."

Her shoulder is warm against mine. "Oh, it's big!"

I flip to the next picture. After a moment, she turns to me. "I don't know what I'm looking at."

"That's the rudder."

"I see." She studies it for longer than I expected.

"You can keep going," I say. "I don't know why I'm turning them for you."

"What if I get them dirty?"

"It doesn't matter, they're just copies," I say. "Go ahead."

Carefully, she looks through the photographs. I point out the broken masts, the bowsprit, the hatch, the passageway.

At the first photo of Captain Purdie, she pauses. "Oh."

"I should have warned you, sorry." I make to go past it, but she bats me away, her fingers glancing against my wrist.

"How do you think it happened? Did he really volunteer to go down with the ship?"

I shrug. "Honestly, I think he likely died before the ship went down, otherwise his position wouldn't be like that. It could have been illness, starvation, anything."

"A lot of those sailors had scurvy, didn't they?"

"Yes, although see all the tins here?" I skip ahead to the pictures of the galley. "People knew about scurvy by then, they had antiscorbutics with them. Tinned fruit, lime juice."

She smiles at me.

I can't help but smile back. "What is it?"

"Could anyone learn to dive?"

I tip my head back. I think, *No*, but I say, "Yes."

"Is it dangerous?"

"No," I lie. "Not really. Sometimes. You have to keep cool, that's all."

"I never heard of a woman archaeology diver before. How many are there?"

"Not many. Yet."

She looks at me appraisingly, and I have a wild compulsion to urge on the glint of whatever is in her eyes. "Some other archaeologists taught us—me—in Turkey, there's an incredible site there. It's practically a whole new science, excavating underwater. You could come back with me next year, I could show you."

Her expression shifts to a blend of sadness and pity, as if I'm patronising her. Maybe I am. I want to take it back, but she covers for it quickly. "Do you have to do any experiments on the bones?"

"No. Straight to burial. I'll only need to go down again a couple more times after that to collect some of the items for the Purdies' museum. Colin doesn't seem too happy about taking me, though."

Elsie wrinkles her nose. "Oh, don't mind him, he's just superstitious about that shipwreck."

My mouth is dry. "Superstitious of what?"

"Fishermen have their own ways. Maybe it's just that nobody's really that fond of the Purdies, but we can't exactly go around saying so after all the money they've spent on the shipwreck, among other things."

"How wealthy are they?"

Elsie shrugs. "Nobody's really sure, but it's not endless, is it? I don't know how they've been keeping this hotel going all these years. And then bringing the whole boat back here."

I start to talk about the towing operation, about how the Danish engineers refloated the ballast tank, but somewhere around describing the kind of sheaves they used on the gunwales, I realise Elsie is watching me with a bemused expression.

She puts a hand on my wrist. "Marta, I'm sorry to tell you this, but good grief, that's boring."

I laugh, feeling the blood in my cheeks. "OK. Well, after I collect the objects, Lester will get the museum going. Snorkelling trips to the site could start next summer. Then I suppose they can start getting their money back. You all can."

"We'll have to have a party, here at the hotel," Elsie says, looping a strand of her blonde hair around her finger. "See you off."

I feel irrationally offended that she's not more upset to think of me leaving, so I don't respond. A few minutes pass as she shuffles through the pictures. I stop her hand as it comes to the final image.

"There," I say. My voice is hoarse.

"What? It looks like dust."

"Nothing else?" I point to the figure.

She shrugs. "Patterns in the dust."

I steady myself against the sticky surface of the table.

"What was I supposed to see?" she says, watching me.

The man I killed, I think. Instead, I say, "Nothing."

LATITUDE 56°, 13'N, LONGITUDE 46°, 17'W

Ince sighted mollimauk flying overhead, herald of near ice. High sea, swells like rolling glass bottles . . . no whales to be seen, the men refute every order. Drever tied to crow's nest for disobedience.

5

ALEX AND I HADN'T BEEN MARRIED FOR LONG BEFORE WE started arguing. Misunderstandings at first. Him leaving the dance hall without me, because he couldn't find me and assumed that I'd left without him. When I took a trip up to the Albert Institute in Dundee, I took his set of keys with me as well as my own and he was locked out of the flat over the weekend. The misunderstandings proliferated. Alex had asked me to tidy up my papers from the kitchen table, and I returned to find they'd been thrown away, he claimed by accident. We'd come home after nights at the dance hall and stay up late bickering about subtleties of blame, disagreements that dissolved into sharp words and stormy silences. I began to associate Saturday morning headaches with the shameful squalor of a post-argument kitchen: shattered glasses, cigarettes stubbed out in saucers of hardened butter. It seemed that the qualities Alex had loved about me before marriage became too much too quickly, as if my volume dial had been turned up after the ceremony. I was careless instead of carefree. I was possessive instead of passionate. And the worst part was, he was right. I would watch myself overreacting and feel powerless to stop myself.

It wasn't all bad. He was promoted quickly at the museum and I was proud of him, proud to be married to him. And when we weren't at work, we were fun. We went camping on the weekends, laughing in the same itchy sleeping bag. We swam naked in the sea on cold evenings, spilled too much wine into meals. Alex had a curatorial fondness for eccentrics. Drunk men raving at bus stops, little old ladies brimming with irrational grievances. He had a talent for goading out odd phrases and then turning to me, smiling with complicit mischief. I knew that he was performing for me, the only audience that mattered. But his temperament was mercurial, and never being able to anticipate his mood left me anxious, hunting for clues that his humour was about to turn. I'd watch him watching other women and store it all up somewhere prickly, only to produce examples with a flourish when he was at his most reticent and grumpy. Desperate for privacy, he'd snap at me, "Christ, Marta, leave me alone."

He never understood that he was all I had.

After his thirty-fourth birthday in November something changed, and I realised, with a bitter kind of regret, how tame his previous withdrawals had been, by comparison. He began spending weekends in Stirling with his brother, or so he said. He'd come back home with his shirts ironed, and I know it wasn't his brother doing his laundry. He started taking long walks after leaving the museum, "to clear his head," sometimes not coming home until the wee hours of the morning. I bought a Turkish cookbook and tried to re-create the food from our diving trips. I smiled as he sparkled with charm and affability in the office, and yet slunk home, despondent and taciturn. I could feel that he was pulling away from me.

In May, I started sleeping with his friend Lewis. Alex and Lewis had gone to high school together in Edinburgh, and we didn't see him often, but when we did, he'd always make a point to linger a little longer near me, deliver strange pinches to my stomach that I at first thought were aggressive, then I realised were hungry.

One evening, Lewis called the flat when Alex was out. When I told him Alex was with his brother, he laughed into the phone. "How about I take you out instead?"

A roaring flush passed over my body. I wanted to punish Alex. I wanted to hurt him, before he hurt me. A preemptive strike to prove something to myself. I don't know what. I dressed in new stockings before I went out to meet Lewis that night; I could hear in his voice what he wanted from me. And three drinks later, in the corner of the pub near the station where no one either of us knew would be, Lewis put his hand on my stomach and kissed me. It was a soft kiss, with a question in it. I hadn't been kissed like that in a long time. That night, I went home alone, and when Alex climbed into bed around three, I put my arm around his chest and held him to me.

A week later as I was leaving the museum, I spotted Lewis at the bus stop across the street. We walked until my feet hurt, not saying anything, intoxicated by the knowledge that when we stopped walking, something would happen. I both wanted it and didn't want it. I wanted to be wanted. I followed him back to his flat and he undressed me on his bed. Afterwards, he ran his hands over my body, his expression territorial and predatory. "He doesn't know what he's got," he said.

It sounds ridiculous, but I never considered what would happen. It was like the sensation of exalted, alert terror that comes when driving through a blizzard, and all you can think of is maintaining balance on the road for a few moments at a time.

The first weekend in July, Alex announced he was going camping with his brother, and I gathered, from how late on Friday he announced it, that I wasn't invited. I watched him leaving on Saturday without the car keys, the tent, the camping stove, the torch, any food or matches. After the door shut behind him, I called up Lewis at his flat. We drove down to Crag's Head that afternoon; Lewis had a fondness for blustery seaside spots, a holdover from growing up on Cairnroch. He insisted on driving, whistling an off-key rendition of "Tom Dooley" and drumming his fingers on the steering wheel. His jauntiness jangled my nerves, and when we stopped for gas at Gadsby I almost asked him to turn back. I've thought about that moment a great deal since then.

The bed-and-breakfast was damp and smelled of wallpaper paste. We ate fish and chips on the shingle from paper cones, drinking bottles of beer that we buried in the sand to keep cool. When we had sex that night his hip bones dug into mine, and over his shoulder I traced alien shapes in the pebbledash ceiling. On Sunday around eight a.m., he squeezed my foot at the end of the bed. I caught something about a swim but didn't pay much attention.

When I woke again, it was past nine and the sun had turned grey. From the grimy window in the shared bathroom the water was white, all soft, frothy peaks. By ten, Lewis still hadn't returned, and I begged the man at the desk to give us an extra hour, which he did, begrudgingly. Irritated with Lewis, I set out to find him. No doubt he had found some dodgy pub willing to prop its back door open on a Sunday morning and was two drinks down, sharing his cigarettes with rheumy-eyed widowers drowning their lack of a home-cooked dinner. I roamed the seafront, cursing him under my breath. Then I spotted his clothes and a hotel towel, down by the water. A surge dragged the bundle into the foam; farther down along the shore his shoes were being tossed in spirals. I stumbled down the beach towards them. Bells clanked on the rocking buoys. "Lewis?" I croaked. He was nowhere in sight. Again, his shoes skittered over in the tide. I turned behind me to the shuttered shops, dismayed beachgoers huddling along the seawall in sweaters and blankets. I knew I should call for help. But there would be a lifeboat, a search, a telephone call to Alex. It felt like I was watching myself, through the sticky frame of a Polaroid. I watched myself return to the hotel room, collect my bag, and leave.

6

MONDAY, OCTOBER 22, 1962

MR. TIBALT KNOCKS ON MY BEDROOM DOOR AT FIVE A.M. ON Monday. Someone from the mine left a message with the night porter: The hoist is on its way. The room is lurching around me, and I tug on the window sash until cold air blows over my temples. Too much whisky last night, but I couldn't bear to risk dreaming about Lewis. The chicken pox scar between his eyebrows, his tuneless whistling, the roughness of his fingertips. His cries for help that I didn't hear. I rest my forehead against the windowsill. I knew it would be like this, being on Cairnroch. That I would feel him everywhere. But doing something positive for the place he loved so much, it seems like the least I can do for him.

When I get to the harbour an hour later, people are already lined up along the wall: women in plastic rain bonnets, babies in knitted bonnets. This isn't the mainland ferry; it brings the miners down from the north of the island every few weeks, and there's a celebratory restlessness to the waiting crowd. As the puffer docks, off-duty miners stream down the gangway, deposit kisses under bonnets, pass over wage packets. Then some of them are rounding the corner towards the Black Hare, the only pub on the island, but most linger on the waterfront, conspicuously pointing me out to one another and then pretending not to be watching when I turn towards them. Curtains are twitching in front rooms; more little boys in school shorts are playing football precariously near to the puffer. It's not just the boat docking that has got people excited; today is the day to collect Auld James.

The skipper is leaning against the prow of the puffer, chatting to a man holding a brace of mackerel. After the mackerel exchange hands, I step forward. "I'm expecting a hoist," I say. "It would have been loaded on by James Mine 2?"

"C2?" The skipper sucks his teeth. "No, nothing come on board there."

I wait, in case he's joking. There is a particular flavour of island humour that involves outright lying to your face.

"Ah, it's here, right enough," he says, elbowing me. The mackerel smacks against my coat. "No one says no to a Purdie."

I give him a weak smile.

"Don, there's someone here about your winch," he shouts, into the boat.

A man comes down from the upper deck; he's in his early fifties with a pale, lined face. "You're the diver?" he says, incredulously.

"Yes. Marta Khoury." I put out my hand, but he doesn't shake it or introduce himself.

"Some equipment," he says, looking me over with an incredulous expression.

"Yes," I say.

"And this is for the—" He points out to sea.

"The corpse, yes," I say, unable to resist the urge to shock him.

He clears his throat, then performs a strange gesture, a readjusting of his collar. It's as if he used to cross himself and hasn't broken himself of the habit. "Today's the only day I have for it," he says.

"It's the only day I need," I say, trying to match his tone. But as I turn back to the hotel, I feel the eyes of all the men from the puffer watching me. The schoolboys throwing rocks, the old ladies gossiping at their garden gates. In the bottom of my coat pocket there's a hole in the lining, and I push my index finger through, ripping it larger.

§

FOR THIS DIVE, I have an audience. The puffer has been emptied of coke, which has left a grainy coating of black powder that rubs onto the backs of the men's jackets. No one has told me who the men are, but it's not difficult to distinguish them. The fishermen are windburned, quietly sceptical. The miners are wiry, talkative, giddy on their first day of leave, passing bottles between them, horsing around and pretending to throw one another overboard. Someone's mother is here, wearing a set of plastic pearls and flesh-coloured stockings. Lady Purdie and Lord Purdie are standing at the prow of the boat in matching oilskin jackets, a polite but firm border of space between them and the other passengers. Lady Purdie has a pink silk scarf tied around her hair that makes her face look angular and stubborn, like a whippet. I change into my too-large wetsuit in the wheelhouse and kneel on the floor, taking deep breaths. Clouds of white silt, his hand, reaching for me. I press my fingertips against my eyeballs. *Concentrate*, I tell myself. *This is no time to panic, focus on the real danger.* I think back to the rockslide I survived in the quarry near Aberdeen, the ice dive in Norway where my air cut out and Alex and I had to share a regulator, passing it between our chattering teeth. Except this time, I only have myself to rely on.

The men rest their elbows on the railing as I position myself on the side near the buoy I left last time. I hope they can't see how much my hands are trembling as I clip on my torch, my belt, my mask. I check that the man from the mine is positioned next to the hoist; then, crossing my arms, I breathe out and throw myself backwards into the water.

The cold this time is a jolt through my bones. I'm electrified back into existence, as if I'd been sleepwalking for the last two hours. As I kick down, following the guideline, I scream into the regulator, a gargling sound that somehow makes me feel better. Threading the guideline through my fingers, I swim until the ship appears before me, then tug on it twice. I kick in place, keeping my eyes fixed on the hatch. *There's nothing to be afraid of*, I tell myself. I picture all the people above me on the boat, waiting for me, watching me. I shine the torch around me. Seaweed drifts, soft, baby soft. A fish nibbles at my flipper. I kick until it darts away. Overhead, the cage is being lowered down into the water, and I tug the guideline again when it's level with the ship. Slowly, it grinds to a halt. I attach the torch to my shoulder strap, slide the wire tray out of the cage, and swim it over to the deck. At the hatch, I take hold of the torch again for one last look around me. Then I count three breaths and force myself down, into the ship.

The saloon first. I need to know. Dropping the tray on the floor of the passage, I float outside the door, trying not to disturb the silt. My skin is tingling as I pull myself through into the room. My eyes flick straight to the space under the porthole. It's empty. I want to cry with relief. Of course it's empty. Nobody under the table, nobody in the corners. Behind me, the galley is as it was. There is nobody in the pantry, nobody hiding by the rack of delftware plates. One of the pegs over the grate is empty, where I'm almost certain Purdie's horn cup was hanging. There's a splinter in the wooden snap hook—must have been knocked off by a fish. Even ghosts don't need utensils.

The seaweed furring the saloon billows, rippled by unseen currents. I hesitate for a few seconds before paddling towards the porthole. The cupboard door is latched from the outside with the same mechanism from the galley. I unclick the latch, and the door pops ajar. Shining my torch in the crack, I pull it open and brace myself. Something brushes against my elbow—I scream. The torch swings around on nothing, nothing, nothing. A minnow the size of my little finger scuttles through the porthole. I hear myself croak a laugh into the regulator. The cupboard is bare. Along the back is some feathering in the wood where fish or crabs have been nibbling. But there's nobody here, there never was. Of course not.

As I float through to Captain Purdie's bunk, I berate myself. Letting my guilt and imagination get in the way of doing something right for once. Conjuring up ghosts. I need to stop drinking so much whisky.

I take the final measurements and photographs of the captain's body. Pulling the tray over to the bunk, I pass it over the bedside table. Only then do I notice that on the surface of the table, there is a perfect circle of algae in the wood. The coin is missing. I look closer. There's a slash in the wood where a blade or a screwdriver has dug in to prise off the coin. I stare at it, hardly able to believe what I am seeing. Someone has been down here, in the room, and taken the coin.

I look away and back again. I pull myself closer to Purdie's remains, my heart jittering. The captain's gold ring is gone. How had I not noticed? How is it even possible? And then I remember—the buoy! Anyone would have known where to come for the wreckage. It's not even that deep; if you were accustomed to the cold, it would be manageable in short trips. I punch my own leg. My heart is thudding in my eardrums, but the anger has cleared something out—all the cobwebby horror of before. I've been worrying about a dead man and forgot about all the unscrupulous bastards who are still alive. Looking around the captain's room, it's obvious now, the places where things are missing. His gilt mirror, and the pair of ivory snow goggles in his cabinet at least. I take photographs of the captain's bunk and then swim back through the ship and photograph the other rooms in turn. A silver knife and fork are missing from the galley, and the horn cup is gone. Stolen in less than a week. I click through the whole roll of film, and my air tank is approaching seventy bars—only around forty minutes left—so I force myself to make my way back to Captain Purdie's bunk and finish the exhumation.

I'm unfocused as I slide the tray under his remains, nudge it too hard, and a slick film oozes into the water, seeping into my wetsuit. One of his ribs crumbles as it rolls back and forth. When his whole skeleton is collected on the tray, I snap the sides and slowly guide it out of the room, down the passage, and through the hatch before connecting it back to the hoist cage. I tug on the guideline, and after a moment, the hoist grinds up. Captain Purdie is released, up to the living.

I pause on the guideline on the way back up. It's not deep enough that I need to decompress, but I'm not ready to face the people on the puffer. Lord and Lady Purdie. Lester, back at the museum, his cabinets waiting for items that are already missing. The site that I botched in only a few days. My breathing quickens in the regulator. This was meant to be my redemption, and I've managed to fuck it up. All Alex needed from me was one more mistake, and I've given it to him. Of course I have.

Eventually, when I climb onto the boat, everyone is silent. Lord and Lady Purdie are looking stoically into the waves. The men are moving in tight little gestures, lighting cigarettes, adjusting caps, shaking change in their pockets. The sight of the captain's body has spooked everybody. The blackness clinging to the bones, the spidery fragments of hair. None of them were ready for his teeth, the teeth.

7

MONDAY, OCTOBER 22, 1962

THE REMAINS OF CAPTAIN JAMES PURDIE ARE WHISKED UP TO the castle in the back of Murdo's Land Rover, accompanied by Lord and Lady Purdie. And as soon as the car has turned the corner by the kirk, the crowd relaxes, shoulders drop, top buttons are released, pipes are lit. Island festivities can now begin in earnest. A piper strides along the waterfront, seals tumbling from their rocks in confusion. A flurry of tables appear on the high street, heaving with piles of shortbread and fairy cakes daubed with the lightest lacquer of jam, tablecloths flapping furiously in the breeze. The lobby of the hotel is packed with celebrants, rosy-cheeked Jocks mopping their foreheads, bony Irenes sipping shandies. A middle-aged man, who I presume to be an officiant of some kind as he is wearing a tartan sash, climbs onto the table in the window booth of the cocktail bar, and the crowd falls silent. He toasts:

Here's tae us.
Wha's like us?
Gey few,
And they're a'deid.
Mair's the pity!

He climbs down and withdraws a sgian dubh from his sock. With a slash of the ceremonial knife, he opens the wax seal on a battered whisky cask. Everyone cheers. Glasses are raised in my direction, and there is no way to withdraw without calling attention to myself. Instead, I sit on a wobbly stool near the dartboard and sip Captain Purdie's whisky. Grown from his own fields up north, the story goes, the whisky was intended to celebrate his return to the island, and when he never came back from his trip to the Arctic, three barrels were set aside in his honour. The whisky is strong and oddly sweet, but it's flowing freely, and my body feels heavy. Conversation falls to only one topic, the island darling himself.

"And Auld James gave the boy his own shoes . . ."

"The crow never returned . . ."

"He blessed the fields and ploughed them single-handedly . . ."

"The snake withdrew . . ."

As the evening goes on, the stories become more improbable. Auld James once saw a ghost at the kirk crossroads who warned him never to sleep with his head facing north, and that's why the bedrooms at Purdie Castle all face east (not true). Auld James learned the whole Bible by heart in "the Inuit language" so he could preach to the whaling villages in their own tongue (unlikely). Auld James was born under a meteorite that travelled across the sky, then retreated back up into heaven (no).

The coal fire in the grate and the press of the crowd and the whisky are smothering the room with a humid, dank heat, and sweat is trickling under my arms. Three different men loudly toast ancestors among the crew of the *Deliverance*, brave souls who followed Auld James to the edge of the world and gallantly met their fate. Pushing through the celebrants towards the window, I press my forehead to the cold glass. I'm going to lose my job. I'm going to lose everything I worked so hard for. I came here thinking I would be doing something positive for once, that helping this island would be my way of commemorating Lewis. I failed him on that beach and now I've failed him again. I take a gulp of whisky. I should have collected more items when I retrieved the remains—what if someone goes back there and loots it all? But the Purdies are up at the top of the hill waiting for the captain's gold ring; is saving his toothbrush going to make much difference? The cool, iodine smell of the sea rolls through a crack at the bottom of the window. The whole island is waiting for this wreck to bring it back to life. The very room that I am standing in has been converted into a shipwreck-themed hotel. Everyone's livelihoods are resting on me. What am I going to do?

A pale man sidesteps towards me from between two Irenes. I don't recognise him as the miner who brought the hoist until he's close enough to touch his elbow to mine. "Well, you brought him home, all right."

I don't answer, just tip my glass towards him.

"Some job you have there."

"Dark, cold, lonely," I say. "We could start a union."

He chases a laugh with his drink. Then he leans his weight farther towards me, his elbow tracing lightly across my forearm. I look up at him. There is a suggestion in his eyes, and just for a second, I consider it. No one would notice two people leaving this crush, plenty of empty rooms to slip away to. A moment of escape. Feeling nothing, just hunger. But the hollowness afterwards, the futility. I turn pointedly away from him and back towards the window. My blouse is damp under my arms. It's too hot in this room, there's not enough air. I tug on the window. The sky outside is lightening, a tinge the colour of peach pudding dappling the clouds. For a heartbeat I think that the evening has become so late that we've drunk our way to dawn, but it's only just before eight p.m. That's when the church bells start to ring, and people pause mid-drink, looking at one another in confusion, before the first shouts of "Fire!" can be heard.

§

WE SPILL OUT onto the street, stumbling in the sudden darkness after the brightness of the hotel chandeliers. Men throw their jackets onto the side of the road, running in shirts and suspenders towards the harbour. The fire is coming from the captain's lighthouse. It stands on a craggy islet to the south, and the blaze picks out men rowing unsteadily towards the fire. The rest of the island crowd stands in silence along the edge of the water. A little girl is crying and being scolded by a grandmother who is bending to wipe her nose. Black smoke is pouring into the night, and even on the waterfront people are coughing, holding handkerchiefs over their faces. A retriever is nosing happily through people's legs, holding in its mouth a scorched seagull with blackened wings scabbed with patches of blistered red flesh. It twitches horribly in the dog's mouth, evidently still alive. The beam of the lighthouse is somehow still throbbing, flickering now in odd angles. I break into a run, but someone grabs me from behind.

"What are you doing?" It's Elsie.

I turn, shaking her off before I realise what I'm doing. "Helping."

She squeezes my arm. "Leave them to it, Marta, there's no saving it now," Elsie says.

Orange spears race up the lighthouse; hot billows of air scream across the harbour. The heat is tremendous. With a thick, crackling groan, the top of the building crumbles into itself, bricks tumbling into the waves with heavy swallows. Feathery cinders float across the harbour, men on watch at the boats to throw buckets of water at any blazing debris.

The mood has quickly become reverent. "It's a sign. The pillar of fire," an elderly man mutters from the crowd. "The Lord is with us."

Heads around us nod gravely. I look at Elsie for a translation from Calvinism.

"God guided the Israelites through the wilderness at night by a pillar of fire," she says, after a moment.

"Auld James has come home all right," the old man says. "His own lighthouse is the vessel for the Lord's word." Unsteadily, he lifts a glass of whisky to the sky. "To Auld James!"

The still water of the harbour is a bowl of reflected flame as the church bells ring out into the night. I don't know how they can see God's blessing in all this destruction. All I can think of is Lewis, that this is his way of showing that he's here. That he's watching me.

LATITUDE 64°, 05' N, LONGITUDE 56°, 32' W. DAVIS'S STRAITS.

Rude and unpolished Huskys approached in a small canoe, uninterested in labour but willing enough to trade fresh seal meat which Grimball did prepare . . . Do the Scots not also need sealers, or must the heathen Danes alone line their pockets with oil? Told Gilchrist I would cast him out to perich on the ice and he ceased whistling. Charts wrong.

8

MONDAY, OCTOBER 22, TO
TUESDAY, OCTOBER 23, 1962

THE LIGHTHOUSE IS STILL SMOULDERING AS I MAKE MY WAY back inside the hotel, glips of oily water reflecting light from the fishermen's torches.

As I approach the bottom of the staircase, Elsie calls to me. "Going to bed?"

"Yes?" I say, looking at my watch. It's almost midnight. I feel heavy with the dive and my failure and the smoke. I just want to go to sleep, or as close to it as I can manage.

"They're going to announce something on the radio. I thought you might want to hear it. A speech."

"What do you mean? A speech about the lighthouse?" I rub my face with the back of my hand, and it comes away coated in black soot.

"I'm not sure. President Kennedy is talking about something. Berlin, I think. We're listening in the reading room." Elsie's expression is earnest. It's as if she wants something from me, but she doesn't know what.

"Let me wash up." I gesture to my face.

Her expression relaxes. "I'll save you a spot."

The staff and full-time residents of the hotel are crowded around the radio in the reading room. On the left is Alice, Elsie's grandmother, who also works in the hotel. She must be in her early seventies at least, although I've seen her carrying a bucket of coal up the stairs while still having enough breath to hum "The Road to Dundee." Sitting next to Alice is Mrs. Eleanor, a sixty-something widow who grew up on the island and returned after her husband died. She's been living in the hotel for weeks in anticipation of Auld James's exhumation, carrying a Bible around as if it were a purse. Everyone's clothes are dusted in soot, and the atmosphere is as tense as a hospital waiting room. I take a seat next to Francis, a student from the University of Aberdeen, who is tweaking the edges of a week-old newspaper.

My first night at the hotel, Alice was serving at the bar, and Francis and I were the only guests. As my whisky and waters became less watery after nine, my heart started to feel heavy; a battered, rotten plum in my chest. And Francis was there, crossing and recrossing his legs. Young, perhaps twenty, the self-conscious posture of a virgin; likely bad, but willing, and I'd contemplated seducing him. Then, after talking to him for only ten minutes (he came to the island for dissertation research—worms), I regretted wasting any seductive energy in his general latitude. Looking at him now in the glow of the smoky coal fire, I feel a vertiginous sense of having escaped a disaster. It's not the way he looks as much as the spindly way he moves his fingers, the flickering grey eyes. He has the scuttling disposition of a silverfish.

"The lighthouse was a sign that Auld James is with us," Mrs. Eleanor is saying. She touches the cross around her neck. "He knew this was coming."

No one replies. Mr. Tibalt stands and turns the handle on the chimney flue. Flora, the maid, lights a cigarette and passes the pack around the room.

The radio beeps for midnight and we all stop fidgeting. As President Kennedy talks about Cuba and the nuclear missiles trained on America, everyone fixes their eyes on the carpet. After the broadcast, Alice turns off the radio, and the room is silent.

"The base," the hotel's cook says, at last. "If the missiles can reach Hudson Bay, then they could reach here." He is a powerfully built bald man in his sixties who has never yet looked me in the eye. I still don't know his name; I've only heard him called Cook.

"Oh, surely not." Mrs. Eleanor twists her necklace.

Francis clears his throat. "Regardless of if those exact missiles could reach here, the US base makes Cairnroch a legitimate target for all Soviet allies."

"Communists wouldn't be interested in us, would they?" Flora whispers.

"The Axis had less reason than that during the war, and they still got us," Cook says.

"We can't go taking the word of that papist." Mrs. Eleanor scowls accusingly at the radio. I shift in my seat. "We only need to trust in the Lord's hands. He's showing us that through Auld James, we are the chosen people. Protected."

"How is burning his lighthouse down supposed to protect Cairnroch?" Francis says.

"You too, young Francis." Mrs. Eleanor points a bony finger at him. "You're a child of this island as much as I am."

"Just because I was born here doesn't mean Auld James is shielding me from rockets."

Mrs. Eleanor raises her voice to speak over him, twittering, "The Lord went before them by day in a pillar of cloud, to lead the way, and by night as a pillar of fire, to give them light, so they could travel by day and night."

Cook stands. "It's the coward's way, missiles," he says, before striding out of the room.

Alice pats Elsie back down into her armchair. "I'll go see to him. You know how Jock gets about the war." So Cook does have a name—I should have guessed.

Francis acquires a sharp, badgerish look and turns the radio back on, switching the dials to catch any incoming news. Elsie takes her grandmother's pile of knitting from her vacated chair and straightens the stitches along the needle.

"Do you think we'll be safe here?" Elsie says.

"Of course," I lie. "The politicians would never let it get that bad."

§

WHEN THE MORNING COMES, radios all over the hotel are competing with one another, slightly out of sync, so the BBC stammers through the building. I dress in a pair of corduroy trousers and my green wool sweater, lock up my bedroom, and come down to find the breakfast room empty, eggs cold in their cozies, the porridge hardened to cement. Most of the noise is coming from the lobby, so I pour myself a lukewarm cup of tea and follow the commotion. Half the island seems to be mingling between the telephones and the cocktail lounge. Elsie spots me from behind the bar counter and beckons me over.

"We all need this today," she says, raising a bottle of Auld James's whisky. She pours a generous slug into my teacup.

"What's everyone doing here?" I say, but we are joined at the counter by a man in his fifties with wild white eyebrows. He lifts his teacup and shouts. "To Auld James, guiding the elect until the last."

There is a cheer through the lobby. He leans his elbows on the counter. "You're the one who went down for him," he says.

Elsie shoots me an apologetic glance. "That's me," I say.

"Strange profession for a wee girl," he says.

"Maybe I'm a strange wee girl," I say, as sweetly as possible.

Elsie motions for me to follow her behind the bar, and so I abandon my teacup and duck under the counter, following her into the deep pantry along the side of the bar where the glassware is kept.

"I think you should get away," she says, quietly. Her breath smells of whisky. "Colin's off on a fishing trip, but I spoke to his brother, Ollie. He'd take you to the mainland." A faint blush is creeping over her face.

"Colin's gone, is he?" The pieces are snapping into place. I should never have trusted him. No doubt he led people back to the site within hours of our visit. "And how long has Colin gone for?"

"I'm not sure."

THE SALVAGE | 51

Elsie must read my irritation at Colin's trip as an internal grappling with a crisis of conscience, because she leans back against a shelf. "You're an outsider."

I surprise myself by feeling stung. As I stutter a response, she interrupts me. "I mean, you're not from here. There's no reason for you to put yourself in danger by staying here on the island if it's an obvious Soviet target."

I take a deep breath. "Listen, yesterday, when I went back down to the ship, some things were missing."

"What do you mean?"

"Items taken from the wreckage. A ring, a coin, a mirror, perhaps more. Someone else must have gone down to the ship in the two days between my first and second dives."

She shakes her head. "How could anyone possibly get down there without your"—she gestures vaguely around my head—"equipment?"

"It's not that deep. If you were used to swimming out here, you could do it in a series of quick trips."

"But—"

"Sometimes people steal things from shipwrecks to sell. Colin's long fishing trip sounds like suspicious timing to me."

She flinches. "Steal?"

"Well, what would you call it?"

"I don't know." She looks down at the floor. I've lost her; she's offended. "It's not stealing, is it, if the ship's already gone down? More like recovery."

I bite the inside of my cheek. "Well, the Purdies are paying me to *recover* those items for the museum. Wrecks like this are protected by the law—technically it'll be Lester who'll have to account for it all; he's an agent of the receiver of the wreck."

"What does that mean?"

"It means Lester is the person designated to file government reports on the ship. He's sitting up in the castle polishing the inside of his cabinets, waiting for me to bring him objects that have already been stolen. And my boss is back in Edinburgh waiting for me to file a report on a site that got looted on my watch. I'm supposed to be here to fix things." My voice comes out strangled.

After a moment, Elsie says, "Look on the bright side, maybe we'll all get nuked by the Soviets."

I laugh, despite myself. "Why don't you and your granny take Colin's brother up on his offer?"

She shakes her head. "No, Granny won't go anywhere. I already tried to convince her. She said the only way she's leaving here is in a box."

"Cheery. Anyway, listen." I put my hands either side of her shoulders and give her a squeeze. Her arms are surprisingly muscular, probably from lifting all those casks of beer. "I promise that we're not going to get blown apart by the Soviets."

"You're really not worried?"

I can't help the urge to reassure her, despite the acid in my stomach. "No."

Someone out at the bar is ringing the bell at the counter. It's the man with the wild eyebrows. He is shaking his empty teacup meaningfully.

"I should go," Elsie says. "I expect it will be a busy day here, with the funeral."

"Oh no, did someone die in the fire?"

She stares at me, astounded. "Auld James's funeral."

§

ELSIE'S BICYCLE IS lying out by the telephone booth, unlocked. I check my watch again. I'm already late up to the castle, Captain Purdie is already dead. Somehow, the anonymity of this bleak little phone booth makes it feel like an easier place to talk to Alex than back at the hotel. My shilling chimes in the slot, and I twist the cord around my wrist while the phone rings. Emily at the front desk picks up. "Curatorial?"

"Alex Dimiroulis, please," I say, in a deep voice. I don't want Emily to realise it's me, in case she's tempted to listen in on the conversation. Lord knows she's overheard enough about our marriage.

"Who's speaking, please?"

Damn. "It's Marta."

She hesitates. "Oh. Marta. You sounded different."

In my normal tone I say, "The line must be odd. It's quite remote out here, rather poor connection."

"I'm sure," she says, primly. "I'll check if Alex is in."

This is a lie, a form of torture. From where Emily sits, she can already see if Alex is at his desk. The only reason she would need to "check" is in case he doesn't want to talk to me.

"Hi." It's Alex. The sound of his voice from so far away tugs at something deep inside me.

"Hi. I'm calling from Cairnroch."

"Yes, I gathered," he says.

There is a horrible silence.

"Did you need something?" His tone is cool, as if I'm a stranger, not his wife.

"Have the photographs from the ship arrived yet?"

"Not yet."

"The air base took them on a run last week," I say.

"OK. Anything interesting?"

I can't tell him. I can't do it. Why did I call him? Why did I think this would be a good idea?

"Hello?" he says.

"Yes. Yes, documents. I took pictures of the journal and logbooks, for Sophie to look at. I couldn't make out the handwriting." That will be safe. No one ever steals paper from a wreck.

"OK," he says.

"Have you heard about the missiles?" As I say it, I realise I'm even more scared than I thought.

"Yes, I heard."

"You don't think there's anything to worry about, do you?"

There is silence. "Listen," he says. His voice is quieter, closer to the phone. Somehow, I know that he's taken the earpiece around the corner from the phone, into the space we call the cubby. I can picture it now, the ten-year-old poster from an Etruscan pottery exhibition, the out-of-date telephone book, the abandoned tube of lipstick, Cherries in Snow. I know that he's where the others can't see him. "I've been meaning to say something."

My pulse is shooting along my body. He misses me. He's missed me. He's changed his mind about the divorce.

"Since you mentioned Sophie, I thought you should know. She and I are together."

The blood rushes from my head so fast I have to bend down in the booth. The phone doesn't even reach my mouth down here; I hold it with one hand on my forehead. Alex is still talking.

"We had a wee party last weekend, invited people from the office, so I thought you should know as well, since everyone else here does," he is saying.

I try to control my breathing.

"Marta?" he says, at first confused, then annoyed. "Marta?"

"I'm here," I say. My voice catches.

"So now you know," he says.

I nod into the phone even though he can't hear me. I manage to squeak, "OK."

"Call the office back in a week, after the next set of photographs," he says. "If the world still exists."

I wait, swallowing, trying to control my voice so I can say something, anything. I should respond in the way a normal person would. Wish him happiness, promise discretion. A dial tone echoes from the phone. He has already hung up.

§

ON THE CYCLE UP to the castle, all I can think of is Sophie. Sophie, her posh Edinburgh accent, her short black curls, those rings she wears, the rings, I see them now on her fingers, green and sharp, sparkling as they touch him as they open the door to his flat to our flat as they uncork a bottle of wine for a party our party my table. Sophie with the curls the long legs the bite marks on the end of her glasses her glasses on my bedside table her ringed fingers on my husband. It's only fair after what I did I'm being punished I deserve to be punished it's my fault—

§

I GET off the bicycle and stand pointlessly for a moment, reeling. Then back on the bike.

§

MY HUSBAND in the sea the Turkish sea the sun the green water his hand on her his hand on her—

§

THERE IS A HORSE and carriage outside the castle and I stop, panting for breath. Near the formal front doors with the cannon in front of them, a bagpiper is smoking a cigarette. Mr. Scruff is barking from somewhere inside the building. Maybe I can throw the bike somewhere and slip into the museum; there's enough commotion that no one will notice that I'm late.

"Marta." Lady Purdie appears from around the back of the building. She is wearing a long tweed overcoat over a knee-length black dress, and muddy Wellington boots. She looks me up and down. "You know, it's traditional to wear black to a funeral."

There are wet patches on the knees of my corduroy trousers, and I can smell the urine from the phone booth. The president's address isn't going to get me out of this; people with enough money consider themselves impervious to the apocalypse. "Late night with the lighthouse," I say, weakly.

She sighs. "What a pity. Not that the whisky would have been drinkable, anyway."

I blink at her. "Whisky?"

"The first barrel from the captain's fields, put there in the 1850s I believe, when he didn't return from his voyage. Symbolic, I suppose. Foolish place to keep it in the first place, but history makes fools of us all."

"So you don't think it was a sign?"

She peers at me. "A sign of what, exactly?"

My voice dries in my throat. Lady Purdie marches over to the horse and carriage and puts one hand on the horse's flank. "Right. Go and clean yourself up. Ask Janet to look you out my black wool dress with the Peter Pan collar, it should fit you. And hurry up, for goodness' sakes."

When I enter the kitchen, Mr. Scruff is running around in a circle.

"Don't mind him, he's all in a tizzy because of the hubbub," Janet says.

I let him nose into my pockets. "Lady Purdie said I should borrow her dress with the Peter Pan collar."

"Oh, aye, the maternity one."

Lady Purdie, you bitch, I think.

"Am I to get it, am I?" Janet says.

I'm not sure if she's teasing me. "I can go?"

"Oh, don't bother yourself, no, no, don't bother yourself, I'll do it."

"Thank you, Janet," I say, trying and failing to smile.

"Go wash in Lady Purdie's bathroom."

I expect her private bathroom to be luxurious; bottles of unguents and lotions and tablets of buttery soap made from heather honey. But of course, I'm forgetting what old money looks like. The window is speckled with mildew and jammed open a few inches, so chilly October air is blowing in. On the edge of the tub is one ancient towel with its nap worn down to bobbles, and inside the tub is a half-empty bottle of what is apparently horse shampoo. In the mirror I'm yellow toned, dry lipped. It's no wonder Alex chose Sophie. Could they have been flirting all the time we were married? Maybe even involved with each other? I try to think of any times when I saw them together. But he used to complain about her. About the rustle of her cough drops, about how careful she was on the reports, how she would spend hours moving commas around, retyping a whole page on the typewriter if she made even one error. And yet he chose her. How could I ever go back there and sit and watch them? I sit on the edge of the bath and put my head in my hands. This is how he guarantees that I'll never come back to the museum. Between Sophie and the missing objects, my career will never go anywhere. Maybe this is what I deserve.

Janet knocks on the door. "Here you are, hen." She hands over a prewar dress with stained sweat pads under the armpits.

"And some stockings too."

I look down at the thick woollen stockings. I'm not going to fit into Lady Purdie's stockings. She is half my size. I put the dress and the stockings on. They pinch into the fat above my knees and the dress rustles when I walk and the collar is too tight. What am I going to tell the Purdies? Lester and his empty museum. And it's a victory for Alex. Firing me with solid, justifiable cause. Oh, how he'll relish moving his new girlfriend over to my desk. And once he's let me go, he'll lift the phone to his old boys' network. What will they say about me? A divorced woman? A Syrian divorced woman? A cheating, Syrian divorced woman? I'll never work again. I turn on the tap and run the cold water over my wrists until my pulse settles.

§

DOWNSTAIRS, THE SERVANTS are lined up along the hallway to the Ceylonese Room. I join the back of the queue in front of Janet. As we inch forward, I can smell the cedarwood panelling. I've never been in the room before; it's one of the public areas that are open to touring in the summer, not that they've had many visitors recently. Finally, the footman in front of me crosses himself and turns away from the spectacle in the centre of the room. Captain Purdie's skeleton has been laid into a narrow birch casket, and somehow it looks even more macabre resting on a velvet cushion than it had done down in the ship. The bones have a wet jelly look, puddle grey and seeping. His teeth are set into a leering grimace. On the remains of Captain Purdie's rib cage is balanced a white porcelain saucer with what looks like a pile of salt.

I turn behind me to Janet. "What's that?" I whisper.

"It's for the dead. Keeps it from swelling," she says.

"But—"

Janet tuts. "It's tradition. Don't you have traditions, back where you're from?"

"I'm from Glasgow," I say, but she is looking behind her into the hallway. I feel rather than hear the sweep of servants standing deferentially aside, as Lord and Lady Purdie travel down the antlered stairway and through the corridor and pause at the entrance of the room.

Lord Purdie is a tall man in his early seventies, with a grey crown of hair and large, powerful hands. He peers down at me. "And who might you be?"

I've been introduced to him on at least three separate occasions, but nevertheless, I put out my hand.

"This is Marta Kerry," Lady Purdie says.

"Khoury," I say.

She looks right past me and into the room.

"Ah." Lord Purdie looks into the middle distance. "Remind me, my dear, didn't there used to be a Kerry out near Tomconney?"

"Yes, you are quite correct," Lady Purdie says. "There was a Kerry out there. Magnus. That would have been 1937 or '38."

"Yes, that's the one," Lord Purdie says. "1938 I would have believed. And he had a lovely Labrador. Poor chap. Shot himself in the head."

"Yes," Lady Purdie says. "Lovely Labrador."

"Perhaps this is a good moment to explain briefly about the site," I say, knowing full well that this is a terrible moment.

"The site?" Lady Purdie squints at me.

"HMS *Deliverance*."

"Well, what about it?" She reaches past me to shake the hand of a man I don't recognize.

"You see, when I was retrieving the captain's remains today, I measured some changes in conditions that might cause the more valuable objects to become fragile on land. Of course, we want to be cautious, so I recommend that all artifacts stay longer in situ while I investigate the," I hesitate, "water acidity, and the microorganisms and also the electrical conductivity and—"

"Yes, yes," Lady Purdie says. "Investigate whatever you need to."

"It means I won't be able to collect any objects for a couple more weeks at least."

Outside, the piper has started up, and Lord Purdie gives me a brief, dismissive tap on the forearm. "Very good, Mary, we'll leave it in your hands."

§

AS THE PIPER PLAYS "Going Home," footmen bring the now-closed coffin out through the formal front doors and place it inside the carriage. The horse walks slowly down the hill, led by the piper, and Lord and Lady Purdie follow behind the carriage. Lester walks behind the Purdies, then the rest of the household staff, then, finally, me. It's a bright day, filaments of light sparkling on the water. From above, I can see the spires of boats filling the harbour before the blackened husk of the lighthouse comes into view. I realise the lighthouse could very well belong to the Purdies too. They might end up having to pay for it to be rebuilt. At the very least a lightship will need to take its place. Even more expenses that the wreck will need to cover.

The only church in Port Mary is a medieval grey-stone affair on the western edge of the island, on a slope overlooking the village on one side and, on the other, bordering a steep drop into black coastline. As we approach the church, men in the waiting crowd remove their caps and stand reverently aside. Each face we pass is pale and puffy. Apparently it was a long night for everyone.

Inside the church, I put my shoulder to the grey stones and tiptoe to the back pew, leaving a trail of snagged black threads, like a hirsute slug. A tall, plump woman with frizzy iron-grey hair looks up as I approach the final bench. She is wearing an unusual cloak with zigzag patterns picked out in light green thread. Pinned to the front of her cloak is a Celtic knot brooch that holds a sprig of dried white flowers.

"You're the diver."

"Yes," I whisper, lowering my weight onto the bench.

"Violet McCloud," she says, offering me her hand, which is cold, her skin papery. As I take her hand in mine, she grips my fingers, tugging me towards her. "You shouldn't have touched him," she says. "He won't like that at all."

"Touched who?" I try to wrestle back control of my fingers.

"Auld James." She releases my hand. "Oh no, he won't like that at all."

I stare at her, lost for words.

"We'll have something in common, then," she says, with a crooked smile, and I realise she might be a bit unhinged. "Something else in common."

I give her the half-humouring nod you afford to a lunatic that has cornered you at a bus stop.

"I'm a curator too." She leans forward. Her breath is sour, and I have to turn aside. "The Neolithic museum up north. You should come."

"Maybe," I say.

"I can hardly see anything from here." Shaking her head, she clutches a baggy grey knitted purse and moves to the row in front.

Her off-kilter intensity has rattled me, and I begin tugging at the loose seams of Lady Purdie's dress. The church fills with more people than I have seen in one place on the island, even at the lighthouse fire. All of Port Mary must be here. Fishermen with chapped hands, gawping schoolchildren in oversized Sunday outfits being given swift, corrective smacks on the side of the head to drive them to their pews. Ancient and wobbly white-haired women are guided the closest available seats; young men from the farms self-consciously wipe the mud off their boots at the doors. Eventually I recognise a couple of the teenage bellboys from the hotel, then Flora, then Mr. Tibalt and Mrs. Eleanor, Francis, and finally Elsie with Alice on her arm. As Elsie settles her grandmother into a row near to the front, I half stand from the bench and wave at her.

She's wearing a long navy-blue dress and her hair has been combed. I've never seen her without her usual flicks of eyeliner, and she looks sweet and scrubbed as a fresh new potato. "You look really nice," I say, as she approaches.

"You look terrible," she laughs, standing back to get a fuller view of Lady Purdie's dress. "I think I prefer you in the trousers with the hole in the knee."

For some absurd reason, the fact that my trousers do indeed have a hole at the knee, and that Elsie has noticed my disrepair, tips me over from numbness. My eyes sting. She gives me a pitying look and motions for me to nudge along the pew, taking a seat next to me. "Don't worry if no one will sit here. It's church, isn't it?"

THE SALVAGE | 61

I hadn't even noticed that I was being snubbed. It was my own self-pity that I was thinking of. Alex and Sophie. My career. How much work it has been to claw my way up to get to this point. Failing myself. Failing in my one pathetic attempt to do something in honour of Lewis's memory.

Elsie pats my shoulder and the padding rustles. "Listen, you can be a hero come to bring him home and still be an outsider. There's a boy I went to school with who came here to live with his granny when he was four, and people still call him New Jim."

I try to smile. "I won't take it personally."

"None of this would have happened without you," she says.

I nod, but it doesn't make me feel better. This funeral has gathered together everyone on this island who I have also let down. The collar of Lady Purdie's dress is digging into my throat. I look at the leper squints in the walls of the church, which once allowed the patients held here to watch services without mingling with the congregation. Heaven only knows what they would have done around here with a resident Catholic. I stand up. "Maybe I should go. This is an island occasion."

She pulls me down to the bench by my sleeve. "No, don't leave, for heaven's sake. That would be worse—you're supposed to stay, where they can judge you for being an apostate mainlander."

I wonder if she knows exactly how apostate I am. Will there be a good opportunity to reveal myself to her as papish?

"But listen." She wrinkles her nose. "Don't come to the wake back at the castle."

"Wouldn't they enjoy judging me there?"

"Oh yes, but you can't win that one. Either you won't eat enough so you'll be being rude, or you'll eat too much, which is also rude. And you won't drink enough so you're being stuck up, or you're drinking too much and being disrespectful. Stay for the service and then get out, go back to the hotel."

"Thanks," I say.

The minister takes to the lectern. He's in his early seventies with grey hair that has something of the intention of a curl about it. He begins without any of the usual throat clearing or welcoming preamble.

"Proverbs 16:33 tells us that the Lord has ordained every roll of a dice, every toss of a coin, and so, He has seen it come to pass that Captain James Purdie, child of this island, has come to rest his earthly remains at his earthly home."

I think, now, of Lewis's grave, back in Edinburgh. I've never been to visit it. They never found anything to bury. With a jolt, I realise that Lewis must have been inside this very church. He would have spent each Sunday of the summer holidays staring at these walls. I should have talked to him more about his time here; I should have talked to him more about everything. The minister is reading a statement about Captain Purdie's life. The youngest son of the Cairnroch Purdies, after several years in whaling he found himself the beneficiary of what the minister calls "generous familial compensation." I have to swallow my scoff—what the minister means by this amply cushioned euphemism is further profit from enslavement in Jamaica. The restoration of Purdie Castle absorbed some of this money, and the captain used the rest to refit his whaling ship, *Scrimshaw*, in Dundee. There, it became HMS *Deliverance*, ready for her new mission to spread the gospel to the Arctic. According to the minister, on the first of such trips, the icebound crew of the *Deliverance* attempted to reach safety across the floes, never to be heard from again. Purdie, meanwhile, bravely went down with the ship, allowing his men time to escape.

I shift on the bench and it squeaks. Unlikely, I think. Nobody lies peacefully in bed as a ship gets crushed by the ice. I've seen plenty of wrecks—if it had been sunk through ice pressure, the girders would have bent; the entire vessel would have been crumpled like a matchbox.

"Total depravity," the minister announces, pressing his finger into the lectern as if he's boring a hole in the wood. "Every man, woman, and child on this earth was born into a state of total depravity." I feel as if he is looking directly at me, and drop my gaze to my lap.

"We are all, even the babes, servants of sin. John 8:44 tells us that we have the same nature as Satan. Yet the Lord, in his infinite mercy, has chosen some among us to be his elect and have our hearts open to regeneration."

I unhook the pearl button at the collar of Lady Purdie's dress. So this is what the good people of the island believe. God decides who is worth saving and who is doomed. And there's nothing anyone can do to change their fate. If you really believed that, why would you even bother to get out of bed in the morning? What would be the point in doing anything?

"Captain Purdie's example among the heathen of the Arctic should serve as a reminder to all of us of the Lord's directive in Matthew 28, verses 19 and 20: 'Go, therefore, and teach all nations, baptising them in the name of the Father, and of the Son, and of the Holy Ghost. Teach them to observe all things that I have commanded you.'"

I become aware of a slow scratching sound, like someone drawing a rusty nail over a shard of slate. At first I think it is coming from underneath my bench, a mouse perhaps, but one by one, the other churchgoers turn their heads until they are looking in my direction. My face burns, and I stare at my feet. The clatter picks up again, a deliberate scrape against the back wall of the church. Schoolchildren playing a trick with snaps of wood? But everyone in Port Mary, maybe even everyone in the south of the island, is inside this church.

The minister falls silent.

The scratching trails around the back to the side of the church. It clicks into the divots in the masonry, drawing against the leper squints in the wall. The heads of the people in the church follow the sound of the scratch. Somewhere towards the middle of the church, a little girl starts up laughing, a hysterical giggle that makes the clawing noise seem even worse. After a few mumbles of consultation, an older man near the front of the church crosses to the heavy oak doors and pulls them open. He steps outside, and people peer over one another's heads. Everyone seems to hold their breath. After half a minute, the man steps back into the church with a shrug. "Must've been a deer."

The congregation falls silent as this piece of information is digested. People look at one another, lips pursed, eyebrows raised.

"Rutting season," someone whispers.

"Must be."

"Saw Red Angus this morning, I did. Probably him."

The minister raps his knuckles on the lectern until the attention is settled back on him. "'Go, therefore, and teach all nations, baptising them in the name of the Father, and of the Son, and of the Holy Ghost,'" he repeats. "For the Lord has selected to open the hearts only of the elect, but only he knows which amongst us can be saved, and which are reprobates, left to dwell forever in their sins. Overnight, the world again faces the attacks of Satan and his godless Soviet minions. But we must look to Captain James Purdie as an example of a man sealed by his election. The Lord says, 'I will not turn away from them, to do them good; but I will put my fear in their hearts, that they shall not depart from me.' Just as the Lord has provided for this child of the island to return, he will not forsake us now."

§

AT THE END of the service, the crowd shuffles out of the church, respectfully bowing and taking their hats off to Lord and Lady Purdie, who are standing to solemn attention by the exit. Outside, the propped-open doors of the church have shallow, spindly gouges running through them, at roughly shoulder height. There are four clear lines; in some places, five. Deliberate enough to splinter the wood of the doors, to etch staves into the stonework. It is deer season. Perhaps it was a deer, ambling towards the noise and vibration of the church in full service, running its antlers against the stone in its quest for a mate. Perhaps.

As Lester passes through the church doors, he catches my eye and gives me a demure wave before coming to stand next to me.

"I thought I'd see you up at the castle this morning. How are you getting on?" he whispers.

When I look down into his face, I see my own pale reflection shivering in his half-moon spectacles. "I—when—I—"

He scrutinises me for a moment before squeezing me gently on the shoulder. "Try not to worry, there's a nice strong bunker down in the village, saw us through the war."

I force my attention down to the weeds growing through the gaps in the flagging.

"Would you look at that," he mutters. "Old habits die hard." He nods towards the church doors, where a switch of dried leaves and white flowers is hanging. It looks like the same plant that I noticed attached to Violet's brooch.

"What is it? Some kind of mistletoe?" Not that it seems likely that Cairnroch Islanders would be bestowing festive kisses on one another for yuletide conviviality. It's probably a spiteful cousin of mistletoe; instead of a kiss you receive a slap with a hymnbook.

"No," Lester says, with a chuckle. "That's pearlwort. Stops a dead man from returning."

A prickle crawls over my skin. "Sorry?"

"Tradition after a funeral. The minister doesn't approve, but people will respect the old ways regardless. Supposed to keep the dead in their place, after they've been laid to rest. Protects the threshold."

Even though I've undone the button, the collar of Lady Purdie's dress is still digging into my throat. I find myself edging away from Lester and closer to the doorway, where I reach out and select a sprig of the dried pearlwort. It nestles into the pocket of my coat with a spidery rustle. From here, the scratches don't look like marks from a deer. They look like someone has crept around the building, clawing their fingernails into the stone.

I give Lady Purdie's dress a sharp tug away from my neck and hear thread rip somewhere along the seam. Suddenly, I can feel Lewis everywhere. Swinging his legs on one of the hard benches in this church. Kicking a football along this road. Here, now, watching me. Turning my back on the congregation, I run as fast as I can manage away from the kirk, down the hill, and towards the hotel.

I enter through the side doors near the kitchen, catching my breath by Mr. Tibalt's desk. Mounted onto the wall behind the desk is a glass-fronted cabinet containing all the room keys. Colin could easily have sold objects from the wreck to someone in the hotel, and I'll never get another chance like this to search. I yank open the cabinet and grab the master key from the bottom hook.

Cook's room first. He doesn't seem to like me, and Elsie said that he sells on the hotel's milk. His room on the first floor is immaculately neat, and the bed has been made with a naval man's attention to detail. There is a cross nailed to the wall, a pair of worn leather slippers by the bed. I check the drawer of his bedside cabinet—a two-year-old fishing magazine, a pocket watch with a faded inscription I can't read, a bottle of multicoloured antacid pills. A clothbound Bible has a tasselled bookmark in Timothy 1. There's a faded photo of a woman in a headscarf standing at a gate; I find it tucked into a cigar box at the bottom of the wardrobe. That's it.

Francis's room next. He has a large, L-shaped room on the opposite side of the building. He's messier than Cook, but nothing on me. Next to his bed are a half-eaten packet of digestive biscuits and a Superman comic: the belongings of a child. I remember again, with horror, the night I considered seducing him. The desk in his adjoining room smells like chemicals, and on glass plates in an index card box are the worms, preserved in their own helicoid cuneiform. Also on the desk is a softbound notebook of indecipherable handwriting that I flick through. Sophie would be able to read it. Sophie. A lurch of bile shoots into my throat. The flash of her rings on my husband, her hands on—

I steady myself against Francis's desk. He's exactly the sort to want to take a keepsake from a wreck, sitting in his room, hoarding his collections. He's the type who had marbles and seashells and birds' eggs and fossils. His childhood bedroom had a lock on it that his father gave him the key for, with a sharp little talk about responsibility. I want to shatter all of Francis's little glass plates, step his worms into the carpet. I think of the plastic tubs Jenine and I shared in our bedroom back in Glasgow. The slugs creeping spittly trails across the carpet, the mouldy curtains, the newspapers, the foil lids from milk bottles glinting in crates like Christmas ornaments. I pull open more of Francis's drawers now, his boxes of coloured pencils, his bottles of preserving solutions and jars of cotton balls. If he has anything, he's hidden it away very carefully. I check the pockets of a pair of trousers thrown across one of the velvet chairs: snotty tissues, bubble gum. A child, an actual child.

There is a noise from outside the hotel, a seal barking. I put Francis's trousers back on the chair. My hands are shaking. I let myself out of Francis's room and start opening all the doors on the first floor. I needn't have bothered with the master key, none of them are locked. In Mr. Tibalt's room: a cross above the bed, a pair of tweed slippers, a Bible on the nightstand. George the bellboy's room: the slippers by the side of the bed, the cross leaned against the window, the Bible on the pillow. I stand at the bottom of the servants' staircase, pressing the master key into the palm of my hand. Mrs. Eleanor would never touch stolen goods, nor would Alice. And then I remember the safe. The safe!

The safe is in a narrow cupboard between two bedrooms on the first floor, almost directly underneath my own room. I step in and shut the door behind me. Hotel blankets are stored in a cabinet on the left, and then on the far wall is a series of shelves containing a warden's helmet from the war, a torch, and the safe. I often see Flora ironing in here, with the door propped open. I grope for the metal light chain, and the single bulb turns on. The master key doesn't even fit in the lock of the safe. I curse myself. Of course it doesn't—there must be another key somewhere. I turn to exit the cupboard, but when I push on the door, nothing happens. The handle turns, slick, in my hands. I twist it back and try again, but it slips round and round. I heave myself against the door. Nothing.

All my hectic energy drains, and I slide down to the bottom of the door. There's a narrow grate which looks out onto the hallway, whisking through a light breeze from a window open somewhere in the hotel. I put my face to the mesh and call into the hallway. But of course, there's no one there. I'll be stuck here until after the funeral. The sweat trickling down my back is cooling to a chill. Pulling one of the blankets down from the cabinet, I tuck it around my knees. Sophie's hands on my sheets, her fingers folding down the blanket. *Don't think about it*, I tell myself.

It's then that I hear footsteps on the main staircase.

"Hello?" I shout. No reply. Surely everybody will be at the wake for hours; who would pass up the chance to celebrate Auld James on the Purdies' penny? The tread on the stair creaks again, a mouse, maybe. No, it's larger than a mouse. "Anyone there?" I call, but there is nobody out there. I fold the blanket into a pillow and prop it under my head. The breeze from inside the building carries the scent of old carpet and bicarbonate of soda. Old buildings like this are always creaky, only usually the sound is covered up by people coming and going. Sophie's lips on my husband, breakfast at our table, Alex in his place, her in mine. My clothes are still hanging in the bedroom wardrobe. I picture her fingers gliding over my woollens, her nose wrinkling at the visible darns. I shake my head, trying to dislodge the image. My mind goes back to the minister's sermon. The chosen and the reprobates. And all those people sitting on their hard benches in the hard church, believing themselves to be saved and watching their neighbours for evidence of damnation. How can Elsie bear to live here among all the silently judging eyes? And then I imagine myself slinking back to work at my desk in the museum, and a sort of sick recognition bubbles in my stomach. I know how Elsie can bear it: because there is no alternative.

This time I distinctly hear footsteps climbing the main staircase. Through the grate, the hallway looks empty, but the sounds are travelling up towards the second floor. The only way someone could climb the stairs without being visible from here is if they were crawling on their hands and knees.

At the top of the landing on the second floor outside my room there are three squeaky floorboards. Elsie said there was a storm a couple of years ago and a leak dripped all into the wood. They warped then, and even though Mr. Tibalt put down new carpet, the boards don't fit together quite right, and there's not much to be done about it. I hold my breath, listening for those floorboards.

Nothing.

And then I sit up, the hairs on the back of my neck tingling. Footsteps, above me. There is someone in my bedroom. The horror creeps over my skin; I can't move. I am holding my room key in my right hand, and the master key in my left hand. Nobody could possibly get into my bedroom. The hinge didn't grate, and in any case I know

THE SALVAGE | 69

that I locked my door this morning. I think about where I am in the hotel. It's unmistakable. Above me is my bedroom, and somebody is in there.

Lewis.

He's followed me here, come out from the water. He came searching at the kirk, and he's up there, right now, looking for me.

9

WEDNESDAY, OCTOBER 24, TO
SATURDAY, OCTOBER 27, 1962

APPARENTLY THE ISLAND'S OLD AIR RAID SIREN IS BROKEN, because after an initial test on Wednesday it keeps going off in starts; a stuttering wail that echoes between the hill and the water before winding into an abrupt, stunned silence. It's funny how you never forget the horror of that sound. As a child, I found it almost exciting at first, the chaos of being bundled out of bed in the middle of the night; the forced cheeriness of the adults in the shelter. Jenine and I always went a little feral in the surreal moments we emptied out onto empty streets, pigeons scattering as we cartwheeled between exhausted, wild-eyed adults. The bleats of the Cairnroch siren are only a few seconds long, but from the window of my bedroom I watch a middle-aged woman hanging laundry behind her house pause, sheet in hand, until the siren trails off.

I'm supposed to be up at the castle, but I still don't know how I'm going to explain the theft to the Purdies and Lester. Colin hasn't returned from his fishing trip. If I tell Alex, I can say goodbye to my job. I can hardly bring myself to look at Alice after she discovered me dishevelled and jittery, locked in the linen cupboard. And my bedroom. It doesn't look any different. But I know I heard someone in here. I know it.

I avoid the hotel as much as possible, walking anonymous spots around Cairnroch that Lewis never spoke about. I march through boggy grass that whirs with puffs of dozy little flies near the second lighthouse. I wander among the worn headstones in the kirkyard, the boom of waves echoing against the bottom of the cliff. I climb the hill near the castle and walk among marmalade-coloured mushrooms while milky columns of sunlight shine on the heart-shaped tracks of deer printed into the mud. The light on the island is constantly shifting, dancing through clouds, opening in sudden blasts of exuberant revelation on mossy boulders. But something about the restless sunlight adds to the sense of being watched, followed. As if there is something knowing, almost capricious, lingering among the island's dark stones. It's full autumn now; winds plunge upon me from conflicting directions so that every now and again while walking, I'm forced to my hands and knees in the foggage among oblivious sheep. The siren keeps shrieking. The plane from the US air base roars overhead, then back again, and women stop to watch from their back gardens, headscarves fluttering.

On Friday morning when I let myself out of the front of the hotel, there are several staff members already outside, whitewashing the frames of the windows. George, one of the bellboys, is balancing precariously at the top of a ladder to reach the windows on the second floor. Cook has one noncommittal elbow on a lower rung to hold it steady while he packs his pipe. It's not just the hotel; farther along the street there are Irenes dressed in pinafores in almost every front garden with their own buckets of whitewash.

I find Elsie painting one of the old ballroom windows, her hair tied in a scarf that looks like it was once a tea towel. "Is this some kind of island tradition?" I say.

Elsie drops her paintbrush in a bucket and gives me a suspicious look, as if I might be making fun of her. There is a smudge of white paint on her neck. "Government advice," she says. "For an atomic attack. It's supposed to help with the nuclear flash."

I shift my weight. "Oh." We stand in silence for a few seconds. I want to ask if white paint will stand much of a chance against a nuclear warhead, but saying it out loud will only make me sound cruel. Instead, I say, "Does Colin stay here in the village?"

"Why?"

"Just wondering." My face must betray me. I was thinking it over in the wee hours of last night. I'm going to break into his place and search it for the missing objects.

"You're not going to try and go to his place to search for your objects?"

"Of course not."

Elsie shakes her head. "Colin's trustworthy."

"Nobody's trustworthy," I spit.

"Well, he's married and lives with his bedridden old mum as well, so you'd never get in there unnoticed."

"Oh." I grip my room key, feeling the bite of it into my palm to stave off the panic.

"I know you've got a bad impression of us because of the ship, but you probably don't need to be locking your room," Elsie says, gently. "I promise there's not much crime around here."

I put my key in my pocket. At night I leave the key in my bedroom lock and get up three, four times to check that it hasn't turned. It's not just theft that I'm worried about. Without thinking about what I'm doing, I reach forward and rub the smear of paint from Elsie's neck. Her throat is hot, her pulse throbs under my finger. She gives me a startled smile, and I pull back, amazed at myself. We study each other for a moment.

"Going out for another walk?" she says, eventually.

I nod.

"Want some company?"

"Shouldn't you—" I gesture to the paint.

Elsie puts her hands on her hips and surveys the window frame. "Somehow, I don't get the sense a lick of paint is going to do much against an atomic bomb. Come on."

She leads me behind the high street to a mossy knoll and down into a little patch of grass next to a brook that feeds into the river.

The grass is the colour of toast just before it burns. I take a seat on a slab of gneiss. Near us, a mouselike thing, a water vole maybe, leaps through the exposed roots of a clump of rushes and into a hole in the earth. I pick a blade of sedge from the edge of the brook and strip it into threads.

"People have been buying things from the shop," Elsie says. It's such an odd thing for her to say that I turn to look at her.

"Excuse me?"

She twirls a fallen leaf in her fingers. "People usually don't buy much from the shop," she says. "Too expensive. But all this talk about the rockets—everyone's on edge."

I put my hands deep into the wet grass. The squelchy, damp earth feels sobering under my fingers. I take a deep breath of the cold smirr drifting from the flowing brook. "Yes," I say.

"Are you doing all right?"

I nod. "I suppose it's not just the end of the world that's got me on edge."

She stares at me. "Nuclear war not enough for you? Oceans poisoned? The land covered in ash, nothing growing? How about everyone on the whole planet being blasted into shadows?"

I fall silent, chastened. She's right. I haven't been thinking about the fate of all the innocent people across the world, about birds choking on white dust. I've been thinking about me. I haven't even called my parents to check on them. I picture Mama's face at the slit of our letterbox, worried about imaginary cameras spying on her from next door. God knows how frightened she must be about imminent global war. I should call them. Maybe Jenine has called them. Yes, Jenine's probably called them.

"It's not selfish to think about the island," I say, churlishly. "If the Purdies' plan doesn't work, it will affect you too. Your granny."

"True, but right now I just want to live to see thirty."

I twist a ribbon of sedge around the tip of my finger until it blanches.

Elsie nudges me with her shoulder. "There's other things left in the boat, surely? And the ship is still there, people will still come to look at it, assuming we're all still here and not living in a bunker. I suppose I don't understand why you'd be so worried about one coin."

"The most valuable items are missing—Auld James's things—and I let it happen. I already told Lady Purdie about the ring, and the coin, and now they're gone! I don't even have an excuse. This is my mistake, it's all my fault. I was supposed to fix things."

She looks at me strangely.

I glance down into the wet grass again. After a moment, I say, "So how does anyone survive if they don't use the shop?"

"Oh, everybody has their sources, there's an unofficial trade. A black market, I suppose. The shop is only for emergencies."

"Black market?"

She nods.

"What kind of things would someone be able to get hold of?"

"Cigarettes, coal." She runs a finger over her knees, dropping her voice to a whisper. "I get my stockings that way. Don't tell anyone."

"Who is it that does the selling?"

Elsie looks away, as if she regrets leading me to this kind of conversation. "Mostly fishermen."

I can tell she doesn't want to be disloyal by naming anyone. I picture all the Irenes secretly queuing up by the shop under the cover of night, furtively buying soap flakes and stale biscuits.

"I suppose if the island is meant to be protected by Auld James, nobody wants to admit that they're scared of the end of the world," I say. "If you're elect, then death is nothing to be afraid of."

Elsie scrapes a drop of white paint from the back of her hand with a fingernail. "People round here wouldn't admit to being afraid of a falling sword."

I turn to her. "There's something I don't understand. If you are elect, and you've been chosen by God for salvation, what happens if you do something bad?" My heart picks up as I search for an example. "Say, rob a bank, for example. Are you still guaranteed to go to heaven?"

She purses her lips. "You can't."

"You can't go to heaven?"

"I mean, you can't rob a bank. If you're elect, you live a life of moral virtue. You just *do*, because you're irresistibly saved," she says. "You're not going to go around robbing banks."

"But isn't forgiveness the whole point of God?" I say. "What is he even doing all the time if he's decided some people are already saved and the bad people are damned forever?" I know that I'm pushing a little too far. I can hear a pleading, panicked tone in my voice. But I want her to have an answer. Any answer.

"'They shall never perish, nor will any man pluck them out of my hand.'"

I stare at her, startled. I get a horrible queasy feeling in my stomach. I'd been goading her, and she believes in all of it. Here I've been thinking myself to have a rapport with her. But she's saved, and I'm forsaken. "Wow," I say, covering for my discomfort with a strangled laugh. "Impressive."

Elsie's cheeks are pink. "The minister doesn't change his tune much of a Sunday. It's bound to sink in eventually."

I say nothing.

"Even if a member of the elect sins, they will always be brought back to God," Elsie says, softly. "People that fall into sin can't be elect, or else they would have been brought back."

"So the good are good and the bad are bad? It's really that simple?"

She shrugs. "That's the idea."

§

BACK AT THE HOTEL, the end of the world has improved Cook's professional skills. There is real butter in the mashed potato. Lamb for dinner, with baby leeks and salted radishes. Sponge pudding with the very last of the season's raspberries, trembling in fresh custard. Only while I'm eating a third helping of raspberries and custard on Friday evening does it occur to me that Cook might be using up what isn't going to keep in a bunker.

§

BY SATURDAY MORNING all the tablets of soap in the hotel's bathroom have vanished. From up on the hill by the kirk I spot fresh divots in Port Mary back gardens where people's vegetables have been surreptitiously dug up. The stony fields around the farmland have been harvested but not replanted. Apparently even the elect are quietly preparing themselves for the worst. For lunch I eat venison pie and creamed spinach, drink Auld James's whisky. The apocalypse has its comforts, it seems.

§

IT'S AROUND FIVE in the afternoon when the BBC announces that a US plane has been shot down. It's around half an hour later when the radio in my room turns to static. I turn the dial all the way through. The island has lost signal.

§

THIS TIME, when the siren sounds, it doesn't turn off. Someone downstairs in the hotel is blowing a whistle, and I open the door of my room to a scene of chaos. Flora is helping a tearful Mrs. Eleanor down the stairs with a suitcase. Francis is bolting up and down the hallway, seemingly without reason, slamming doors. It's Mr. Tibalt with the whistle. He's standing in the middle of the lobby, dressed in an overcoat and gumboots, wearing the warden's helmet from the war that I spent all those hours staring at while locked in the cupboard. George the bellboy is pushing a wheelbarrow piled with tinned milk and candles through the hallway. I can't see Elsie or Alice. I can't even think over the sound of the siren.

"Time . . . shelter," Mr. Tibalt barks over the din.

My skin zips with electric tingles. I stare at him, my mouth opening and closing. Oh my God, it's actually happening. We're actually all going to die. All my breath leaves my body. I grip the banister.

He points with his whistle, indicating that I should follow George. "Shelter," he says, louder.

I turn around hopelessly on the staircase—what do I need from my room? There's nothing I need—my parents—I should have called my parents. The feeling travels back into my limbs and I run down the stairs two at a time.

Cook and George and Flora and Mrs. Eleanor are trailing along the corridor to the side exit, and as we spill into the narrow lane, the passageway is clogged with Irenes and Jocks and dogs barking at one another. Everyone is stealing glances up into the sky. Francis is holding an old copy of the *Scotsman* over his head, as if he's trying to stave off drizzle instead of rockets. Up on the high street, people are neatly queued up to enter the pharmacy, politely refusing to panic, even for Armageddon. My pulse is bouncing between my heart and my brain. I force myself to use my dive breathing. I will not disgrace myself by falling apart in front of all these stoic old ladies in their anoraks and stout shoes. The line for the bunker winds behind two houses within touching distance of each other, where two concrete doors stand propped open with buckets filled with wet sand. I've passed these doors tens of times in the last week without realising they were the old village war shelter. I can't hear Mr. Tibalt's whistle anymore and turn back through the crowd to look for him. Then I remember he has an elderly mother; maybe he's gone back for her. The minister is standing at the bunker doors, waving people into the space. Inside the shelter, grey-faced Irenes sit quietly on benches along the wall, hunched in the thin-lipped, braced position. Something about their silence strikes me as odd, sterile, almost. Then I realise it's the lack of prayer. No muttered entreaties to Our Lady, no one singing "Ya Oum Allah," no clicking of the rosary. Aren't you supposed to pray, at the end of the world?

"In you go," the minister says to me. "To the back on the left."

As I shuffle through the doors, an Irene in a black-and-blue-flowered headscarf stands up and raises her hand. "No."

I stop shuffling.

"No." She's shaking her head. "We can't have her in here."

At the back of the shelter, Elsie's face appears in the band of light between the doors. The minister looks at me properly for the first time. "Where are your belongings?" he says. I can't get a handle on what's happening. I try to explain that I didn't bring anything, but the woman in the flowered headscarf is pointing at me.

"If she comes in, I'm going out," she's saying.

"And who the hell are you?" I snap.

There is a chorus of tuts and indrawn breaths throughout the bunker. It was the wrong thing to say, I know, but I'm stretched tight as a rubber band.

"She's an outsider," the flowered headscarf says.

My eyes are burning; a surge of desperation is rolling through me, running acid into my veins. Francis's face peers out from among the gathered islanders. He's perched on a wooden apple crate, holding a brown leather briefcase in his hands. I point into the shelter. "What about him? He's not one of yous either."

"His grandfather was Tall Jock from Gluckathy," someone in the bunker says. "He belongs here, with the saints."

A horrible, wet laugh escapes from my throat.

"Auld James gave us the sign, the pillar of light," the woman in the headscarf is saying. "Only the elect are protected."

A reedy voice pipes up from somewhere in the corner. "We can't pollute ourselves with reprobates."

The minister's eyes on me are blank. "Aren't you going to say anything?" I say, with a croak. I want to grab him by the lapels, but my hands hang uselessly by my sides.

"You have spent your years on earth satisfying your desire. You have fattened yourself for the day of slaughter," a middle-aged woman behind me whispers.

The minister's breath is warm on my face. Still, he says nothing.

Slowly, I turn away from the doors and walk back against the crowd. The panic has dribbled away from me now, and I feel strangely numb. I should have called my parents. The image of my mother praying for the forgiveness of her attacker comes back to me, the twin divots in the carpet by the window where she knelt so frequently that her posture rubbed away the weave. This is really it. This is what Lewis was marking me for. This is what I deserve. Maybe it's not so bad. A flash of lightning, a shadow in the grass. What have I got left to fight for, anyway?

Elsie wriggles through to the doors of the shelter, nudging past the minister, calling over the shoulder of the woman in the headscarf, "Marta."

I turn as she approaches and woodenly squeeze her hand. "Say thank you to your granny for me."

She steps around a man in a cap who is trying to file into the bunker. "Come on, let's go."

"What? No."

But she's gripped my hand in hers and pulls me down between the stone buildings. "Come on, don't make it worse." She starts running, yanking me behind her, and I follow, our footsteps swallowed by the siren. Elsie is fast; I have to let go of her hand. Every few steps she looks behind to check I'm still with her, then up, at the sky.

§

AT THE HOTEL, she slams the side door by the ballroom, then motions me down through a door into a cupboard by the kitchen, kneeling and wrenching open a wooden hatch in the floor. Her face is pink and dripping with sweat.

"Quick," she says, "go, go."

The ladder at the hatch disappears into a dark cellar and I climb down first, finding myself on an unfinished dirt floor. Elsie descends after me, pulling down the hatch and bolting it. After a few seconds, a torch clicks on, her hands sweaty against mine as she hands it to me. I hold the beam on her as she fumbles with a matchbox, lighting a paraffin lamp hanging from the ceiling. I turn off the torch. The room is cool and dank, a row of beer casks against the wall. At the back is a rack of dusty bottles of wine. A trickle of a breeze is blowing from a chink in the bricks, and there's a thin, yeasty smell in the air.

"What did you do?" I say. I can't tell if the siren is still blaring or if it has somehow been inscribed on my hearing. We are both still trying to catch our breath; there's a pain underneath my ribs. "You have to go back. Just leave me here."

Elsie shakes her head, her chest heaving.

"You're insane," I say. "Why would you do that for me?"

She shrugs, with a short, coughing laugh.

Without thinking of what I'm doing, I cross to her, put my hands either side of her face, and kiss her on the mouth. She kisses me back, hungrily, her tongue against mine, her hand in my hair. I lean her against the bricks, we stumble on the uneven floor, and she laughs. Slipping my hand inside her sweater, her skin is damp with sweat. I kiss her neck, rub my thumb over her nipple, and she takes a sharp inhale of breath. Her body is hot against mine, her hand on the small of my back under my shirt. I nudge my knee between her legs; chalky dust rains from the walls as her head grazes the bricks. Then she tugs me down to the unfinished dirt floor.

10

SUNDAY, OCTOBER 28, 1962

SO THE WORLD DIDN'T END.

At the sound of footsteps overhead, I follow Elsie out of the cellar. Initially, we'd thought someone had made a mad dash back to the hotel to collect something, or perhaps even to steal something. But as the steps became heavier and steadier, we knew the danger was over. It's just after six in the morning as we emerge, blinking, into the hotel. Someone is playing "Wild Mountain Thyme" on the old piano in the lobby, and I'm almost certain I can hear Mrs. Eleanor singing along. Through the glass in the storeroom door, I can see people already lined up at the bar, Alice on the other side, pouring generous measures of Auld James's whisky into waiting teacups. Elsie brushes off her knees and turns to me. We both look as bedraggled as each other. Her hair is matted on the side; there is a greasy grey dust coating her skin. My sweater I had to retrieve from a puddle of fetid liquid behind a keg, and I can feel it sticking to my stomach.

I open my mouth to say something to her, but as I take a breath, I have no idea what I'm supposed to say.

Elsie probes her thatch of hair with tentative fingers. "Uh—"

"I might—" I point up to the direction of my room.

"Of course," she says. "Yes, of course. I'd like to—" She gestures towards her grandmother.

"Oh, yes," I say.

"Well," she begins, but I'm talking over her and I stop. "I'll be seeing you, I suppose," Elsie says. Her cheeks are pink. She moves towards me and I lean forward, thinking she might be aiming for an embrace, but she was only putting her hand out for the door. I leap back as if I've been scalded.

"Sorry," I say. "Bye."

I turn and rush through the door, then as soon as I'm around the corner, I pause to let the swell of embarrassment roll over me. What was I thinking? What was she thinking? Oh, there's a special humiliation in being someone else's moment of madness. I hobble slowly up the stairs. My neck is cramped, my hand is cramped, my hip is stiff from the hard flagstone floor of the cellar. From the other room, I hear the cheers of celebration, the toasts to the island's saviour and his role in averting disaster.

Upstairs in my room, I kick off my shoes and peel off the wet, beer-soaked sweater. There are fresh bruises on my arms from last night, and another surge of embarrassment engulfs me at remembering the confusion when we parted. Elsie thought it was the end of the world, and now it will be awful between us. That should never have happened. For a start, I'm married. I rub my face, a sprinkle of dust falling from my hair. I never anticipated that doomsday would be so mortifying. With a sudden give of energy, I slump down to the floor and lean against the bed, burying my face in the blanket.

When I look up, I see it for the first time.

On the window is a perfect, wet handprint.

I pull myself up from my kneeling position and climb onto the bed. It's a large print, much larger than my own. A man's hand. I edge closer to the window, my knees shaking.

The handprint is on the outside of the glass.

SUNDAY, OCTOBER 28, 1962

"IT'S SEAWEED," FLORA SAYS, TAPPING THE GLASS.

I'm standing by the door to my room, clutching my elbows. "Not possible."

She tuts. "Aye, it is." Flora points at the mark. "That slapjack splits into five leaves. We call it 'old man's handshake'—you never heard that?"

I shake my head.

"The wind were high last night and it got tossed about." She nods down towards the street. "See for yourself, there's plenty down there in the gutters."

I don't want to get too close to the print.

"Go on, down there."

I edge towards the window, still holding on to my elbows. Where she's pointing, I can vaguely see brown leaves collected in the guttering of the old pleasure pavilion. But there's nothing that looks like a hand down there. The mark on the window has started to melt, drips of condensation steaming on the glass. "Can someone bring a ladder, clean it off?"

She raises an eyebrow. "You're asking me for someone to clean it off."

"Yes."

"Today?"

"Yes."

"On a Sunday?"

A headache is creeping over my skull. Last night, Elsie and I opened a few of the wine bottles by putting them in her shoe and slamming it against the bricks. "Tomorrow then."

Flora sucks her teeth. She must think that I've lost my mind to care about a dirty window after all that happened last night, but I'm beyond caring. I try to remember if she was already in the shelter by the time I was turned away yesterday, but all I can see is the pinched expression of the woman in the headscarf. Flora would have heard about what happened, though, by now. I picture the whole village huddled inside the bunker overnight, praying through the darkness, congratulating themselves on being the chosen ones, protected by their private saint, Captain James Purdie.

§

I TAKE A LONG, hot bath, watching the seagulls wheel over the harbour from the window on the opposite side of the room. All the soap is still missing, but I keep draining and refilling the water whenever it cools, swishing my hair until it's free of dust. The church bells begin to ring, and from the tub, I laugh until I'm hiccuping.

After I've dressed, I stand at the edge of the door to the breakfast room, where Francis and Mrs. Eleanor are sitting in their usual places. From his seat at the table, Francis looks up at me loitering in the doorway. I remember the betrayed expression on his face as I tried to throw him to the wolves in the bunker. He drops his gaze back to his black pudding. He didn't speak up for me either; perhaps that makes us even.

Mrs. Eleanor is saying, "I thought I might walk to Speeland Point today after church. I want to visit the well where Auld James was baptised. Pay my respects for protecting the island yesterday."

Francis says nothing. Maybe he's come around on Auld James as the island saviour, after last night.

Despite how hungry I am, I let myself out of the side doors and walk out into the daylight. The world is all still here. Grass slick with dew, spiderwebs catching orbs of moisture, blackbirds swooping through the hedgerows. In the distance, the ocean tumbles white foam. I want to lift handfuls of the briny grey soil to my mouth and kiss it. Gusts of wind gallop in strange chutes down the hill, ruffling my right ear but not my left. I take huge lungfuls of the cool air, breathing in the smell of rotting leaves and seaweed and gorse. When I turn back to look down the hill, a line of people are making their way up to the church.

A bitter twist cinches inside me. This island. Righteous until it matters. They just shut the doors on me and left me to be bombed into pieces. Drinking whisky and watching one another for signs of damnation. Why should I worry about helping this place? I can feel Lewis here. The things I liked about him seem hard to remember. I force myself to picture the hole in his knitted vest he used to push his finger through absent-mindedly when he was nervous. His habit of throwing things in the air and catching them while you were talking to him. Not that we did much talking. All I remember of him are flashes. Replaced now by the footsteps, the fingernails at the church door, the handprint. A judgement. Wind roars down the hillside and I close my eyes and let it thrust against my eyelids, lift my hair like a whip. If I can't get this to work, I will have nothing to return to. And what will happen to Elsie and her grandmother if the Purdies' plan fails? All Cairnroch wants is to celebrate Auld James; once I give that to them, I can get off the island knowing that I've done my duty. The next ferry is on November 19. I have three weeks to mend this, then I can try and rescue the rest of my life.

I'm still here. I'm still alive. I have another chance to make things right.

LATITUDE 78°, 04' N, LONGITUDE 72°, 01' W

At Huski village winter turf huts being set up. Noone of intelligence, only filthy tents and a woman giving suck to a child that I wished instead to be drinking from. Danish Governor has not been here in months and yet none would agree to my terms of recruitment even under threat of pistol. Scots deserve the Huski seals and their oil . . . Grimball prepared most delicious tarmigan eggs . . . in channel the charts proved wrong again, wasted day turning around. Ice berg passed us by on Westerly side.

12

WEDNESDAY, OCTOBER 31, 1962

I'M SITTING IN THE LOBBY, HOLDING A DOG-EARED COPY OF *Time* magazine from February 1957 without actually looking at it. On Sunday I developed the two sets of prints to compare, and I've been over the photographs more times than I can count. The key items that are missing all seem to be the personal belongings of Auld James. What I can see so far is a set of cutlery engraved with his initials, his horn cup, his mirror, the pair of Inuit snow goggles from inside his cabinet, the coin, and, most worryingly of all, his gold ring. It's a start to know the items weren't taken at random, but everyone on this island wants a piece of Auld James, so my discovery doesn't really narrow things down.

Elsie's face appears over the top of my magazine. She leans on the back of one of the other armchairs. She's wearing a white apron streaked with orange grime, and her hair is tied back in a ponytail.

"Excited about the Purdies' Halloween party later?" she says.

I put the magazine down with a rustle. I've been conspicuously avoiding her since we escaped the apocalypse. But here she is, smiling, relaxed.

"I'm not sure that I'm invited," I say.

"Of course you're invited! The whole island is invited!"

Lifting a glass of whisky in a room full of people who ushered me out into nuclear annihilation. "I don't think so."

"You're not going to stay behind here all alone, are you?"

I picture creeping the hallways of the dark, empty hotel over the evening of Halloween. Sitting in my room under the blankets as I have been for the last three nights, alert to every squeak in the building, knowing nobody else is there. "Could we go together?" I say.

"Of course." She smiles. "Come on, we're making tumshies out of turnips. Come along."

I follow her as she crosses the hallway and opens the door to the hotel kitchen. I've never been in here before. It's a long room with a polished chrome table along the right-hand side, and on the far wall, a preparation area with two sinks large enough to bathe pigs in. Above the sinks are high rectangular windows, no bigger than envelopes, that must vent out onto the narrow lane behind the side door.

Sitting on stools along the chrome table are Cook, the bellboys George and John, Flora, and two other maids whose names I keep getting confused: Ellen and Helen, I think. On the table in front of them, like some gruesome vegetal postmortem, is a row of turnips in varying stages of Halloween surgery.

"Marta's going to carve a tumshie with us. Move up," Elsie says, motioning to George to move stools.

One of the maids, the curly-haired one, looks down at the turnip in front of her. I remember her then, her face at the back of the bunker.

"There you go, Marta," Elsie says, slapping the still-warm stool vacated by George. I sit down, and she takes the seat next to me.

Cook passes me a neep without looking at me.

"They're a bit soft, sorry," Elsie says.

As I take a knife and begin to carve, I think, *They're soft because they were pulled early to go into the bunker. The bunker I was excluded from.* But I say nothing, cutting a hole into the turnip. After a few minutes, George and John begin trying to play their neeps like flutes, laughing in the spluttery way only adolescent boys can. Helen and Ellen chatter to each other about their favourite

Halloween costumes. Even Cook is humming under his breath. I suppose everyone is in a good mood, now that we're not mounds of radioactive dust.

§

HALF AN HOUR LATER, Alice calls, "Guisers are coming," from the lobby, and we all brush down the table for the tumshie peelings, which Cook collects in a pot. I stand aside and let the others go first, and as I bring up the rear, Elsie slips her arm through my elbow. It's the first time we've touched since the other night, and the shock of it travels through my body.

Alice has set up chairs in a semicircle facing the front doors, and we all take seats. The fire is roaring, and maybe because of the generous pours of Auld James's whisky or the exceptionally still night, the room feels overwarm; everyone's cheeks are rosy.

Flora clambers on the leather booth by the window. "Oh, here they are!" she squeals.

The flickering lights of tumshies appear along the front path, and soon after there is chapping on the front door.

Mr. Tibalt pulls it open to a crowd of miniatures. A small boy wearing a knitted orange sweater, cheeks and nose rouged to look like a clown. A ghost, with holes cut into a pillowcase for eyes. A girl with another pillowcase with a red cross drawn onto it, a tiny, stern nurse.

The clown steps forward, clearly the leader of the gang. He clears his throat and recites, into the back of the room: "The tattie-bogle wags his airms—"

At this, the other children join in, shouting, "Caw! Caw! Caw!"

Slightly out of sync with one another, stumbling over the words, they recite the rest of the poem together:

> *He hasna onie banes or thairms:*
> *Caw! Caw! Caw!*
>
> *We corbies wha hae taken tent,*
> *And wamphl'd round, and glower'd asklent,*

Noo gang hame lauchin owre the bent:
Caw! Caw! Caw!

When they finish, everyone applauds, and the children look expectantly at Mr. Tibalt. He carries a dish covered by a silver cloche from a tea tray by the kitchen doors and kneels in front of them, lifting the cloche with a flourish to reveal a plate of brazil nuts, which the children take as solemnly as if it were part of a ritual to swear a sacred oath.

Over the next half hour, more swinging tumshies appear in the window as we are visited by more tiny ghosts, diminutive clowns, one knight in a tinfoil hat. The radio signal is still down, but Alice sits at the piano and we all sing along to "The Bonnie Banks o' Loch Lomond." Jenine and I were never allowed to go guising as children. When we complained that the other children in our tenement were going, Mama insisted they were a "rough crowd." We would turn off the lights on Halloween and huddle in the kitchen, pretending not to be in, ignoring the raps on the door, the faces of confused frogs and fairies pressed against the hallway window. We heard a lot about it later at school—it was strange, unfriendly, hostile even, not to welcome visitors on Halloween. Since we were already considered strange and unfriendly, I leaned into the whispers. I told Jean Mackenzie that we went to a special church service on Halloween evening, and then the whispers became rumours that we were heathenish. It didn't matter. We could never bring people back to our warren of rubbish anyway, even if anybody had wanted to be friends with us. As I grew up, Halloween became almost invisible to me; I carried only a vague awareness of giggles on the street, the occasional chewed apple discarded in the gutters. Last year, Alex and I had people over the Saturday before Halloween. It ended in a row when Alex, already tipsy, knocked over a bottle of red wine and it smashed onto the kitchen linoleum. I made a joke about it, a cheap, plasticky joke to slick it over, and then he turned on me: "You think you're so perfect, do you?" Senga made panicked eyes across the room at Marion, and when I saw the alertness to danger in that exchange, something in me shrivelled in shame, like one of Francis's worms.

My stomach turns now, as I remember that night. The broken glass that I wrapped in newspaper and then hid even from Alex at the bottom of the bin, worried that seeing the bundle would humiliate him again and we'd get into another fight. He didn't drink that much, but when he did it filled him with air, made him pompous, prone to grand statements that I interpreted as judgement at me, for not being posh enough, clever enough, nice enough. Maybe being among people who shut me out to get bombed isn't the worst way to spend Halloween. At least the Cairnroch Islanders made their decision and condemned me quickly.

§

AT SIX, EVERYONE DISPERSES to change their clothes for the party. I didn't bring any nice clothes with me, so I put on the black turtleneck and the skirt I was wearing on the ferry over. My face looks tired in the mirror. There is a sharp crack behind me and I jump, peering into the room. But it's only the window frame settling. Suddenly, I want nothing more than to be up at Purdie Castle.

When I come down, Flora and the two other maids are already in the lobby, wearing cocktail dresses in sober colours that are at least five years out of style. I feel conscious of the strip of leg between my skirt and my boots.

"You look nice," Elsie says, standing up from the booth by the window. Like the others, she's wearing a dated sleeveless cocktail dress that's cinched at the waist.

"I'm underdressed," I whisper, pulling my coat on.

She shrugs. "Nobody will be looking at you once the bonfire gets going," she says, and I choose to believe her.

All along the road, homemade tumshies flicker and bob as the island travels up to Purdie Castle. There is little wind tonight; the murmur from partygoers carries down across the dark fields, and I lower my voice to lean into Elsie.

"Does anyone have a grudge against the Purdies around here?"

"What do you mean?"

"I'm just trying to think of anyone else who might have been in with Colin. Is there anyone who might want to ruin their plans, or to get back at them somehow?"

Elsie thinks about this. Her tumshie has smoked out and she stops to relight it, the gobliny face grinning a yellow crescent onto her dress. "I don't know," she says eventually. "Does anyone really *like* their landlord? People respect them, though. And everyone is proud of Auld James. No one would want to get in the way of him being honoured. And for what it's worth, Colin has run their odd jobs for years. I really don't think he'd betray them."

"Well who do you think it is then, if it's not him?"

Elsie squeezes my arm. "Sorry, Marta. Their money is filling in gaps all over the island. And this plan with the museum and the shipwreck, bringing Auld James home. I just can't see anybody wanting to get in their way."

§

LORD AND LADY PURDIE are waiting in a reception line inside the formal oak doors at the front entrance to the castle. Lady Purdie is wearing a prewar navy evening gown, and as I shake their hands, she has to introduce me to Lord Purdie, again.

The floor in the entrance hall has been polished to a slippery sheen, the fire bouncing spears of light off the antlers above. On the left, the Ceylonese Room has been opened for the occasion, benches pushed back against the walls where glasses of whisky and lemonade and platters of black bun are set out. A fiddler in the corner is tuning his violin. "There'll be a ceilidh dance later," Elsie says.

"Cei-lonese," I say, and Elsie snorts. I don't deserve the laugh, but as our eyes meet I get an urge to kiss her here, in front of everyone.

Elsie hands me a tumbler filled with Auld James's whisky, and we clink our glasses together. "To surviving the end of the world," she says.

"Thanks to you."

Elsie looks down at the floor, embarrassed. I feel awkward now, as if I've said the wrong thing. Maybe I shouldn't have reminded her. Maybe she regrets everything we did that night.

"I'm going to look for Lester," I say, and turn away before I have a chance to see any relief on her face.

"Don't feed him," Janet calls, as I let myself into the kitchen. Mr. Scruff is scampering around in a circle and leaps to greet me. I feel the light scratch of his paws on my belly.

"I won't." I nuzzle his head, his warm flank. He might like me most of anyone on the island at the moment. He's overexcited, vaulting around the room, barking occasionally in the direction of the hallway, his ears alert.

"Poor wee man," Janet says. "He wants to go to the party too."

Janet has been released from her uniform tonight; she's wearing a frilled concoction of a dress that looks a little like a tea cozy. "Have you seen Lester?" I ask her.

"He's about somewhere." Her eyes narrow and she takes a step closer to me, licking her thumb and rubbing it against my cheek. Her fingers are rough under my chin, her grip strong. "There you go. Had a bit of soot on you."

The gesture reminds me of my own mother, and an unexpected surge of emotion bubbles up in me. "So how was the end of the world around here?" I say.

Janet flaps her hand dismissively. "Oh, that haver."

"Where did you go? Is there a bunker in the castle?"

She shakes her head. "Dungeon."

I laugh, spitting out my whisky. "There are dungeons?"

"Just the one." She frowns, as if I'm making fun of her. "Had a prisoner down there in the 1700s. Blue Bobby."

I'm almost afraid to ask. "Why was he blue?"

"On account of the cold, I suppose. Water comes in down there through the storm tunnels in the winter, fills up the basement."

"Bloody hell," I say, then apologise when I catch her expression. Lord and Lady Purdie must have hated being shuffled into the dungeon along with all the maids. The pinched, polite conversations the poor staff must have had to endure listening to as they considered it might be the last evening of their lives.

"It's dry enough down there right now, anyway," Janet says.

"And Mr. Scruff?"

She stares at me, horrified. "Of course Mr. Scruff. Why would you say such a thing? We weren't going to leave him out to be bombed!"

Mr. Scruff had better chances than me. I imagine myself wandering alone on the island, pressing my cold, radioactive hand against the windowpanes.

Lester crosses towards the passageway and I run towards him, giving Janet a farewell wave. He's dressed in a shirt and kilt, his hair freshly trimmed. "Hello, my dear." He smiles at me, his eyes warm. Another rush of sentiment wells up in my chest. Maybe I did the right thing in coming up to this party. At least there are some people on the island who are pleased to see me.

"May I talk to you, privately?" I point towards the narrow hallway that leads to the other side of the castle.

He gives me a polite bob of the head. "Certainly."

I follow him down the hallway and into the morning room. One of Lady Purdie's statuettes looks at us with blank marble eyes from a Queen Anne dresser. "What can I help you with, my dear?"

"Lester," I begin, then stop. The fiddler has started to play in the Ceylonese Room, and I run my finger around the rim of my glass. I can't ruin his celebration, see the disappointment in his face. "Do you stay here, in the castle?" I ask.

"Yes, I'm lucky enough to have rooms in the east wing."

I think of the clipped formality between Lord and Lady Purdie. I wouldn't want to live here. The winds that shrill through the cracks in the walls, the angles of the antlered gallery by firelight. "You wouldn't rather be in the hotel?"

"Oh no, there's always been plenty of accommodation for the staff here."

I hadn't really thought of him as staff, and it surprises me that he would be so willing to consider himself on the same level as Janet. "Doesn't it get lonely?"

He chuckles. "I've been a confirmed bachelor all my life. No, the peace and quiet suits me."

"That's nice." I look down into my glass.

"Now, Marta, what's troubling you? Out with it, come along! Do you need some more whisky?"

"No, it's just, I could use your advice. I'm having trouble with my . . . my personal belongings."

His eyes widen, which I take as permission to continue.

"It seems as if some of my belongings at the hotel have been . . ." I drop my voice to a whisper. "Taken."

Lester winces. "Taken? From your room?"

"My room, yes. And the odd thing is, these are antique objects. I wouldn't expect anyone to know what they were worth." I'm hoping that he's not going to ask what they are. Quickly, I decide on miscellaneous Syrian antiques.

He puts a hand on my shoulder, shaking his head. "I'm so sorry, Marta. And in the hotel, too. Have you mentioned it to Alice?"

"No, I wouldn't like her to think I'm accusing anyone."

"Of course."

"I thought perhaps you might know if there's a market on the island for antiques like that."

He blows air out of his lips, adjusting his bow tie. "Oh, Marta, I can't think anyone would be so calculated. I'm sure your things will turn up in time."

But I can tell from the quick movements of his hands, the fingertips over buttons, the tug on his collar, that he's holding something back. "Has anything like this happened before?"

He looks at me for a long moment before shaking his head. "I really couldn't say."

"It will be confidential between us, one professional to another," I say, knowing that will appeal to his sense of vanity.

He glances into the corridor. "Did you know we had a flood down in the tunnels?"

I shake my head.

"Oh, it was a good few years ago, now. Back when my hair wasn't so grey."

He's waiting for me to smile, so I do.

"Now, you'd think, because of the hill, that we're too far up for the water to reach us. But there are storm drains all over the island."

"Yes, Janet mentioned."

"One of them empties down in the cellars. And back in the winter of '45 there was a terrible storm. The water surged right up and into the front basement. Oh, we had a time of it."

I nod, suffocating the urge to hurry him along.

"Well, we ended up having to dig down to put in a new drain after that, and we uncovered all kinds of things. An axe, a Pictish engraving, right in the original drainage system. Of course, you've seen them in the museum."

"Oh, of course." The eerie, swirling Pictish gravestone is propped somewhat unceremoniously behind the door to the museum. I don't recall seeing the axe.

"Well, what we haven't widely disclosed is that those are not the originals. We were forced to have re-creations made. The originals..." He shakes his head. "Well, unfortunately, they went missing."

I hold my breath.

He leans against the wall, his posture slumped, as if he has suddenly been weighed down. "We never could prove anything, but there was a younger woman working here at the time. An apprentice curator, so to speak. She was the only person who had access to the items. It was a terrible time. I didn't want to ruin the lady's career, but anyone with eyes could see they were there one minute and gone the next."

"I understand. What happened to her?"

"Well, she had to leave the employ of the castle museum, of course. Eventually she took up residence farther north."

"She's still on the island, then?"

"Oh yes. The lady in question went on to ply her skills at another museum, but alas, her career never recovered."

I remember now the shock of iron-coloured hair in the church. "Violet McCloud."

"I'd prefer not to confirm that," he says. "A sad affair, really. It was a good job we at least had the photographs to work from, for the sake of posterity. And as I said, we could never prove anything about the culprit. I'm sure you can imagine how people around here talk."

"Yes, I can imagine." I straighten up, repressing the urge to hug him. He's so petite and merry and round, like a Toby jug. "I won't say anything."

"This may not have anything to do with your missing antiques," Lester says.

I'd almost forgotten the story I just sold him. "Of course."

"But still, people become desperate, and then there's no reckoning with them," he says, squeezing my shoulder. "Now why don't you go forget your troubles for a bit. Goodness knows we could all use it after this week."

I thank him again and travel back down the passage, across the hallway, and into the Ceylonese Room. The windows are now running with condensation, and the room is heavy with the distinct smell of sweat into flannel petticoats. Violet was at Purdie's burial service, so it's possible she's here tonight. If she lives up north, maybe she's even checked into the hotel this evening. But strange as she seemed, would she be so brazen as to return to a place she'd been dismissed from? Surely Lord and Lady Purdie wouldn't invite a woman they thought had stolen from them. Perhaps I could convince Murdo to give me a lift up to the Neolithic museum. I let myself out of one of the glass doors on the far side of the Ceylonese Room and light a cigarette on the wraparound balcony that faces out over the peaty hills. A sheep calls out from somewhere in the darkness.

Another glass door opens and Elsie climbs out. "I thought it was you, skulking out here."

Her tone is jovial, but I prickle. "I'm not skulking," I say. I am, however, leaned over the unlit balcony, by myself, looking out into the black October night. It's exactly the sort of thing someone who is skulking would do. I stand up straight. "You haven't seen Violet McCloud at this party, have you?"

"Violet?" Elsie shakes her head. Her expression is almost offended. "Why are you looking for her?"

I stab out my cigarette and toss it over the rail of the balcony and into the earth. "I just want to ask her something."

"May I have one?" Elsie says, pointing to my pack, and I offer her a cigarette.

"What do you want with Violet?" she says. Her cheeks are in high colour from the dancing, a loop of blonde hair sweaty against her forehead.

"Did you know she used to work here?"

Elsie shakes her head.

"Lester seems to think that she has sold on antiques in the past. I thought she might know something about the items missing from the ship."

Blandly, she nods, before turning to me. "Wait, you mean she might have had something to do with it?"

The incredulity in her voice irks me. Even if it turns out to be a dead end, at least this is a start. "Perhaps. Will you tell me if you see her?"

"Why?" Elsie's face is light, as if she's expecting me to make a joke.

I stare at her. "What do you mean, why? I've got less than three weeks to try and find anything I can before the next ferry, and I can get out of here with a career to go back to."

She drops her cigarette onto the boards and grinds it under her heel. "Didn't realise you were so keen to get away."

We look at each other. I think about the awkwardness of the moment when we parted after our night in the cellar. Another rejection is more than I can withstand. I say, "It was only ever a temporary job."

"Right," she says, turning away. "Right."

Elsie marches off through the thrum of people dancing in the room, closing the door behind her with a smack. Immediately, I'm full of regret. Why can't I be nicer, kinder? But she didn't speak to me for days after the bunker; I don't need to waste more time being someone else's mistake. Back in the Ceylonese Room, kilts are waving and hands are being held. I push through the crowd, turning my face away from the rows of Irenes and Jocks sitting out the dances to tap their feet along with the music. In the entranceway I take a seat on an uncomfortable plush velvet chair which is not, nor was it ever, intended to function for sitting. At least from here, I'll be able to see if Violet appears.

It's an hour and three glasses of Auld James's whisky later when the ornamental gong in the Ceylonese Room sounds, and people begin to file through into the hallway, bringing with them a fug of damp cheer.

Lord and Lady Purdie take a few steps up the staircase, the antlers mounted above them throwing notched shadows over the walls.

"Thank you so much for joining our Samhain celebration," Lord Purdie says. "We will be lighting the fire in the garden shortly, if you'd like to use the door to the left."

§

OUT IN THE GARDEN, a slinky mist is pooling over the grass. At first, I can't see much beyond the heads and shoulders of people relieved for the fresh air over their warm limbs. And then I realise that at the back of the garden is a bonfire and, in the centre, a wooden effigy of a young woman holding a bunch of flowers in her hand.

My blood thickens. I stop walking, the crowd of people spilling around me. A groundsman puts a lit torch to the base of the effigy, and a small lick of flame gathers around her skirts. The wood pops and the crowd in the cold garden is silent as it burns. From the copse beyond the fields, an owl hoots. Heat from the burning figure bastes the faces of the crowd, and I turn away, picking my way back to the house. Near the back door, I recognise Alice sitting on a stool and cross to stand by her side.

"Alice," I whisper, until she turns to me. "What is this about?" My voice is shaky.

The light dances over her face. "It's Brìghde," she says, with surprise.

"Who is that?"

"Brìghde, the goddess of spring," Alice says. "It's time for us now." She laughs. "The crones."

I shake my head at her.

"The Cailleach, Marta." She sits back on the stool and tuts. "They don't teach you anything in school these days."

"I don't understand," I say.

She sighs. "On Samhain, Brìghde, the goddess of spring, passes control to the Cailleach, the old woman. She rules the world of winter. We'll be due the first of her cold winds any day from now."

"Oh." I look back at the smouldering effigy. It's absurd, it's paranoid, it's self-centred, but I wrangle with a faint apprehension that the burning young woman had something to do with me. I give silent thanks that no one seems to have figured out that I'm technically a Catholic.

"The bonfire is Samhain tradition," Alice says. "We do the same in March for the Cailleach, and her husband."

"She's married?"

Alice folds her hands on her lap. "Oh yes. She has a husband, the Bodach. He's like a ghost that creeps around spreading frost during the icy months."

"I'm going to get a drink," I croak. Back inside the house, I can smell the bitter smoke on my clothes. The Ceylonese Room is empty, sticky patches on the floor from spilt lemonade, and I pour myself another glass of whisky. Someone has propped open one of the doors that lead out onto the balcony, and the glass shimmers with an orange haze.

In the reflection, a small, white face appears underneath the table behind me.

I scream, spinning, to see a wide-eyed young clown, caught in the act of sipping whisky from an abandoned glass. We stare at each other, my heart racing. Mumbling something incomprehensible even to me, I leave the room. My good mood has plummeted, and now even being trapped in my hotel room, waiting for a ghost, is preferable to being corralled into this house with all these people who wished me bombed to splinters. I collect my coat from my chair in the entranceway, and just before leaving, I turn back to use the bathroom. When I open the door to the toilet, I bump it straight into the hip of a woman standing at the sink.

Violet.

"Oh, come on in," she says. "I'm just finishing up."

I hesitate before entering and pulling the door closed behind us. It's not much larger than a cupboard, and the dark blue wallpaper gives the space an underwater melancholy.

"Do you have any lipstick?" she says, inspecting herself in the mirror. "I'm so pale I could be the Cailleach herself, tonight." She laughs with a whoop and a wheeze.

"No, sorry."

"Never mind." She pinches her cheeks. "I suppose it doesn't matter what I look like, does it?" She puts her hand out for the door handle.

"Someone mentioned you used to work here." My voice is louder than I'd intended.

She turns back to me. "Yes, that's right. Many moons ago. Or suns. Or stars."

"Lester mentioned it, in fact. He told me what happened."

A suspicious narrowing tightens her face. At least I have her attention now.

"Listen." I take a breath. "You live here, you know what Auld James means to people. The Purdies need it all back. They only want to encourage more visitors to come here, which may end up being good for your museum too."

"Have it all back," she echoes. "Gosh, doesn't that sound nice?"

"At least the ring," I say. "That, at the least. Please."

She cocks her head to the side as if she doesn't understand me. An urge to shake her comes over me and I clench my hands into fists. "Auld James's ring. Do you still have it?"

"Ah, the captain," she says dreamily, standing next to me so that I have to look at her reflection in the mirror. "I don't think he'd like you very much."

"That might be the case," I say, hearing a stout, dour schoolmistress in my tone. "But please, do you still have the things?"

"You know what he did, don't you?" Violet says, to my reflection.

"I don't know, something about a miracle with a snake? And preaching?" Someone knocks on the door. "Just a minute," I shout.

"A snake, oh, that I'm sure of."

I shift aside so that she has to look at me directly, not in the mirror. "Violet, I'll meet you wherever you like. No one needs to know about this. I haven't said a word, and I don't intend to. Not to Lester, not to anybody."

Violet gives me a smile as she reaches for the door handle. "Yes, preaching. It's funny, isn't it? That the devil himself would take to preaching."

THURSDAY, NOVEMBER 1, 1962

THE NEXT MORNING I'M UP AND OUT AT THE HARBOUR LOOK-ing for Colin before the sun rises. The fishermen down at the pier barely acknowledge me when I call across to them; they didn't like me even before I went down to the ship. At this rate, no one on the island is going to look me in the eye again. It's not long after seven when the church bells toll and a stream of Irenes pour out of the kirk to scurry back to their hearths. Church at sunrise on a Thursday morning. I suppose there's not much else to do here. And the women who don't farm or fish otherwise seem to spend a lot of their day hanging over their fences and watching one another. Then I spot Elsie's blonde hair. She's walking arm in arm with Alice back towards the hotel, and when she looks up at me, I take a deep, steadying breath and point towards a bench up on a knoll overlooking the sea. She glances down at the path, hesitating, before patting Alice on the elbow and releasing her arm.

"Hello," she says, as she approaches. The tip of her nose is pink.

"Church on a Thursday morning?" I say.

"It's Hallowmas," she says, as if that explains anything. We sit side by side on the bench in uncomfortable silence while churchgoers stream past us.

"I wanted to apologise about last night," I blurt out.

She looks at me out of the corner of her eye but doesn't reply, so I continue.

"I didn't mean to offend you."

"I wasn't offended," she says, diffidently.

"I'm sorry. I wasn't thinking how it would sound when I said I was trying to escape from here." Her eyeliner is smudged; I wonder if she's hungover at all after last night. If last night at the party she met anyone, kissed anyone.

"It's OK," she says, with a sigh. "I suppose I thought you were avoiding me, after Saturday."

"You were avoiding *me*!"

She stares at me. "Marta, you're impossible. Hiding yourself in your room all the time, off on your odd wee walks. What am I supposed to do, dress in Purdie hunting tartan and go tracking you down in the hills?"

I take a breath. "My boss, back in Edinburgh, he's not pleased with me."

"Oh?" She's confused by the diversion in topic.

"I made some mistakes," I say, looking down at my knees. "Personal and professional. If my boss finds out the site has been looted on my watch, he'll use it as the final excuse to let me go. It's why I've been so on edge."

"But that's not fair," Elsie says. Her outrage almost amuses me.

I shrug. "He's been waiting for a slip-up from me, and I provided it." I fiddle with the piping on my gloves.

"Couldn't you just get a new job?"

"It's not like that. There are about five places in the world that would pay me for what I do. The kind of training to get to this point. The kind of convincing, the number of people who said no—I can't watch it all go to waste, everything I've worked for." I swallow. "And I'm helping my parents, financially. And I don't have—"

"OK, I understand," she says. She has no reason to be so generous. I hate myself for eliciting her sympathy. "Why don't you stay here a bit longer then? The ferry runs every five weeks, so there'll be another one on Boxing Day."

"Stay here for longer? On the island?" I try to hide my dismay.

"It's only an extra few weeks, it'd give you more time to find everything. Wouldn't it be worth it, to have as much time as you need to make things right?"

Down in the water a halo of bubbles forms around the snout of a seal. Alex isn't going to care how long I'm on the island; he'd probably be pleased to have me out of his way for another two months, and I can't do anything until I've spoken to Colin. But then there's Lewis. Here. Everywhere.

I put my face in my palms. "I don't know that I could bear it."

Elsie laughs, bitterly. "Now I'm really trying not to be offended."

I look through my interlaced fingers at her. "No, I don't—"

"I'm not stupid," Elsie says, looking out at the pale streamers of sun spiking through the clouds over the horizon. "I didn't think it meant anything, the other night."

I start to interrupt her, but she puts up her hand to stop me.

"I just don't want to feel disposable," she says.

A barb of guilt tugs at my gut. "Of course you're not disposable. You might be the nicest person I've ever met. Helping me to go down into the cellar that night—it was the kindest thing anybody has ever done for me." As I say it, I realise how true it is, and my eyes start to burn from self-pity.

She squeezes my hand, misreading my expression as thankfulness. "If you stayed a bit longer . . ." She leaves the rest of the sentence unfinished.

Unexpectedly, I feel a rush of blood to my cheeks. She is smiling at me. There is a twinkling of something inside me, hopefulness, maybe. I haven't felt that in a long time. It's been a long time since someone looked at me like I'm redeemable.

"I'm sorry for hurting your feelings. I didn't mean to be cold towards you."

"Forgiven," she says.

"You're too good for me," I say, and I mean it.

"So." She slaps her knees, as if a decision has been made. "You're staying for longer, then?"

I bite the inside of my cheek. She's right. It's the only way to have a real chance to mend everything. "I don't know. I'd have to try to convince the Purdies to pay for me to be here for longer. As it is, they think I need longer to review the site conditions before bringing up the captain's belongings, so that has bought me some time. I might be able to think of another reason to stretch out my stay. But everybody here hates me."

"They don't hate you," Elsie says.

I fix her with an incredulous look. "They locked me out to be flattened by missiles."

"Yes, but that wasn't hate. That was because you're damned."

Despite myself, I laugh. "Either way, I really need you to help me. Please? Maybe I'd even be able to come back next summer. If I manage to find Auld James's things, then the Purdies might be open to further excavation on the site."

"The whole summer?" she says.

I nod, even though I know the Purdies want to have tourists on day trips out there next summer. The last thing they would be interested in is paying for me to come back and take more measurements. It's not really a lie, more like a sugaring of the truth. "But first I need you to help convince people to talk to me. Colin, when he reappears. And Violet. I got nothing out of her last night. I won't be able to do anything without you."

Elsie smiles. "I'll see what I can do."

A rush of gratitude courses through me. I look around, then lean in and kiss her on the cheek. She turns her chin and catches my lips, and as I kiss her back a tangle of emotions tumble inside me, like a carnival trick. Thankfulness and panic and preemptive, vertiginous regret. What if people see us? What am I even doing? But it's over in a flash and she's there and she's smiling at me, and I can still feel the cold imprint of the tip of her nose on my cheek.

"Are you busy tonight?" she says.

"Oh yes, I'm going to the pictures. Then the opera, and then an Indian restaurant."

She rolls her eyes. "I have a silly tradition on Hallowmas. If you promise not to judge, would you like to come with me?"

I nod.

She stands up. "Let's go back, it'll be time for breakfast."

I take her arm and we walk back through the frail, lemonade-coloured grass towards the hotel. Another month here could be bearable, if I have Elsie on my side.

As we walk through the front doors, the smell of toasting tattie scones and black pudding drifts through from the kitchen.

"Hello," a man's voice booms from behind us.

Elsie and I jump.

"Oh dear. Sorry to startle you, Elisabeth, Margaret."

Lord Purdie is standing in the door to the reading room, wearing a blue velvet dressing gown and a pair of North African leather slippers. Elsie and I shoot each other an uncomfortable look.

"Good morning, sir," Elsie says. "Is Lady Purdie also with you this morning?"

"No, just me. I ran poor Jock down last night and decided to make an evening of it," Lord Purdie says.

"Tea, sir?"

"Oh yes, please, dear. I'll take it in my usual seat." He gestures back towards the reading room.

Elsie hustles me along the corridor, dropping her voice to a whisper. "I'd better check Mr. Tibalt knows he's here. Go on, talk to him now, while he's on his own."

I edge into the reading room.

Lord Purdie is still standing to attention inside the door, his hands clasped behind his back, as if he's surveying his kingdom. I suppose he is.

"As it happens, it's fortunate that I'm able to speak to you. I've been hoping to tell you how remarkable the findings from the ship have been," I say, summoning my plummiest tones.

Lord Purdie takes several steps towards me, and I'm forced to back up into the corner of the room. "Is that so?" he says.

"Yes, my colleagues in the museum have been astounded," I say, trying to put an armchair between us. There is something unnerving about the intensity of his pale eyes. "As you know, I need to wait longer before collecting the more valuable items, to make sure we can stabilise their condition once they are brought up on land. In the meantime, however, I propose concentrating my efforts on the captain's journal."

"I thought the Danes said that any paper would be all rotted away by now," Lord Purdie says.

"Well it has survived better than expected, there was very low oxygenation at the original site. I wouldn't ordinarily recommend disturbing something so fragile, but this could provide a fascinating insight into the family history," I say. In truth, it will probably only contain wind speeds and compass directions. All the journals in these kinds of ventures are property of the voyage and make for dull reading.

"Do you like liquorice?" Lord Purdie says, reaching into the pocket of his dressing gown.

"No!" I am almost shouting. I have a horrible presentiment that he is about to withdraw his penis and force me to inspect it. To make some off-colour joke from another century, where men like him spent their boyhoods imprisoned in draughty boarding schools, developing fetishes for pleading for women called "matron" to smack them on the buttocks with chamber pots.

"That's a shame," he says, mildly, taking out a rope of liquorice and chewing on it.

I steady myself against the armchair. "Yes, the journal," I continue. "At the very least, it may have some answers on the route of the final voyage."

"Gosh, how exciting."

"But it would require my being here for longer. Since the journal will likely deteriorate quickly after I bring it up, I'd need to work on it for a concentrated period of time. I'll need to take detailed photographs, create a transcript, perhaps work on whatever restoration is possible. I'd also need to consult a colleague at the museum, a textual expert." My mouth fills with an acid taste as I think of Sophie.

He leans forward and peers at me earnestly. "Thank you for the recommendation, Mary," he says, before retreating to an armchair close to the fire.

"Will you talk to Lady Purdie?" I stammer. "About me staying for longer?"

"Yes, why not. I love an excuse to talk to my wife." I'm not sure if this is a joke, so I offer a half laugh.

"It's quite a timely matter," I say.

"Yes, of course. Everything is, these days."

"Thank you, sir. After all, this is a once-in-a-lifetime historical find." I will promise him anything. I'll get my chamber pot ready. I give him a respectful nod as I leave.

"Did I ever tell you about the rock up at Trier?" he says, as I'm halfway out the door.

I'm not sure if he realises we've exchanged only a few words. I come back in.

"There's a local story that says that it's where Auld James dove into the water to rescue a local woman from drowning. The first act that inspired him to take up a seafaring life. There's a sort of depression in the rock, you know. People say that it's Auld James's footprint." He looks at me. "What do you make of that?"

I feel as if I'm being tested. "I've heard many stories about the captain, sir."

"Yes. People say a lot of things about him," Lord Purdie says, crossing his legs. "But people see what suits them. That's why we launched this venture." He leans back in the armchair. "I don't want to see what anyone can see. I want to know the man for who he really was, what he really achieved. I want to get the true measure of my kin."

§

THAT EVENING I WAIT for Elsie at the bench in the cocktail bar. She asked me to be ready for ten p.m., and the rest of the hotel is silent. The only light is the glow from Mr. Tibalt's desk lamp. After dinner, Mrs. Eleanor and Francis both retired to their bedrooms; I suppose everyone is exhausted after yesterday's party.

"Shall we have a wee dram before we set off?" Elsie says, from behind me. She's wearing her cat-eye makeup, and a duckling-yellow sweater with corduroys.

"Yes, please." I cross to the counter and take a seat on one of the stools. "My brain feels like rice pudding." I spent the afternoon writing up what I hope is a convincing proposal for further research into the ship's condition. It's hard to know how much of an expert Lester is, exactly, so I've alluded to some technical-sounding details about salinity levels and temperature fluctuation and oxygenation. And as much as it pains me, I've had to defer to Alex as the big man back in the office. Lord and Lady Purdie have hired me to perform a service for them. They haven't hired me to think. For that, they will want a man in charge.

Elsie dips under the bar and pours us both glasses of Auld James's whisky. We clink glasses.

"Do the Purdies stay here often?"

She comes under the counter and sits on the stool next to me. "Not really. Sometimes, if they have some business to do in town. Lord Purdie stays more than she does."

"Imagine having a whole hotel at your disposal. As if a castle isn't enough."

"It's not as if we don't have the space," Elsie says, with a shrug.

"Yes, I suppose that's true. How does this place make a profit?"

Elsie's shoulders sag. "It doesn't." She runs the dram of Auld James's whisky around the glass, watching as it clings before sliding back into an amber puddle. "We've been expecting to be put out every year since the war."

"I'm sorry, I shouldn't have started talking about it," I say, feeling the anxiety squirm in my own gut.

"Thank you." She sets her glass on the counter. "Now, let me see your shoes."

I point my tennis shoes towards her.

"That'll never do," she scoffs. "You'll need proper walking boots."

With a flick of the wrist, I drain the rest of my glass. "That's one of my least favourite sentences."

She laughs. "And a proper coat, too."

"I only have this one." I pat my tartan coat, which is resting on the stool behind me.

"You can borrow one from the coat check. Get your shoes and we'll pick one out for you."

I dash back up to my room to collect my boots. They're still scuffed with mud, so I hold them in my hands and come back down in my socks so I don't make a mess for Flora to have to sweep up later. When I reenter the lobby, the door next to the telephone booths is open. I poke my head around. The coat check smells of cedarwood and camphor and runs along the length of the wall behind the telephone booths. Elsie is looking absently through a drawer built into the wall, smoking a cigarette. Along the right-hand side is a brass pole holding maybe twenty coats in garment bags. "How long have these been here?" I say, running my hand along the bags of coats. Through the cloth I can feel the distinctly lush texture of thick, soft fur.

"The oldest ones are prewar," Elsie says.

"But how could anyone forget a fur coat?" I say. "They must be worth a fortune!"

"You'd be surprised what people leave in hotels," Elsie says, her cigarette smoke trailing in loops under the glow of the single bulb overhead. "And sometimes it's not that they get forgotten." She stops and looks at me.

"Go on."

"Well, we used to be a popular winter spot for hunting. There was a whole cohort of older ladies like Mrs. Eleanor who lived here. And died here too."

"In the hotel?"

She nods, tipping her ash into a teacup. "Happens much more often than you'd expect."

"And their families never come to claim their belongings?"

Elsie shrugs. "If you spend your final days in a hotel, your family probably isn't that invested in your well-being to begin with."

I let the comment hang. After a moment, Elsie lifts herself up to sit on the vacant ledge next to the coats, her legs dangling. "Mine moved to Australia. Melbourne."

I only nod, not wanting to seem prurient. Given that neither she nor Alice has brought up her parents before now, I'd assumed that they had died.

She takes a drag on her cigarette. "They both wanted better than was here, more opportunities. I stayed behind with Gran while they got established, found jobs, a house. And then they had another baby. And they forgot I was ever here."

I cross and stand in front of her knees. She has the defensive tone of someone who isn't courting sympathy, but I want her to know that she has my attention.

She shrugs, self-consciously. "They came back to visit once, when I was ten. Brought the baby. They even had Australian accents, complained about the cold, the food. Originally the plan was that me and Gran would go back with them. But the longer they were here, the less we talked about it." She draws on her cigarette and stubs it out in the teacup. "They didn't even have a room for us in the house. By the end of the visit, they stopped even mentioning about us coming with them. I think everyone was a little relieved when they left and we could all stop pretending. We still call on my birthday and Christmas."

I put my hands on her thighs, and her legs wrap around my body. "They must be the stupidest people in the whole world."

Elsie's laugh is a valve releasing steam. "Gran always said Mum was a ninny."

"And you're happy here, on the island?"

She thinks about it. "Sometimes. The other day with the—" She gestures, and I know she means the shelter. "I keep thinking about it at night."

I put my hand on her cheek and she leans down, rests her forehead on mine. "I feel responsible," she says.

It's my turn to laugh. "Don't. I'm apostate, remember?"

She looks puzzled, but I don't want to dwell. "So, which one of these coats should I borrow?"

She jumps down from the ledge. "This one should do the trick, I've used it a few times." It's a green surcoat with a tie waist, at least ten years old. I put it on, and she hustles me gently out of the coat check by patting me on my behind.

As we leave the hotel, my eyesight is fuzzy, unaccustomed to the dark. It's a cloudless night, a pencil scratch of moon. I almost trip on the front steps, and she rights me. We walk down to the coastal path and along the water towards the strip of white sand beach.

"This isn't a midnight swim caper, is it?" I say, as she climbs down the ledge and onto the beach. The water is calm, spreading skirts of trimmed lace onto the sand. Regardless, I'm overcome by a sudden, uncharacteristic squeamishness about the darkness, about Lewis, here, watching me with Elsie, waiting.

"Oh gosh no, I hate cold water. You're the diver, not me." She bends down to inspect the ripples of seaweed strewn across the tide line. "Choose a rock."

I select one that is smooth under my fingers, with a coffee-coloured streak through the middle.

"Back up." She points towards the path, and I pull myself over the wall before helping her up.

"Now where?"

"The top, near the castle." She gestures away from the water, up into the black hills. She links elbows with me as we follow the path along Roiner's Point. The stars overhead are pinpricks through velvet. "You have to promise not to make fun of me," she says.

"I promise."

"I'm a very rational person," she says, looking sideways at me as we pass the phone booth. I hope she doesn't notice that her bike is lying there, unlocked. "This is my one and only concession to whimsy."

There's an uneasy burbling in my stomach. I wonder if she's about to tell me that she's felt him too. "What is it? You haven't seen anything at night, in the hotel?"

"No, don't be daft. This is just a silly tradition of mine." She lets go of my elbow and climbs down from the muddy ledge by the fields and walks in the road.

"Careful!" I say, looking behind us.

She laughs, pointing up into the gloom. "Marta, I could take a wee nap on this road if I wanted. There's no cars coming by."

"Oh, right."

Every now and again, Elsie passes me a flask from her pocket filled with rum and apple juice, and we take swigs as we walk. As we approach a gate near the turning for the castle, she stops. She takes a torch out of her pocket and shines it on the latch for the gate; then I follow her through.

It's harder walking after this. The field is hillocky and thick with mud. The torch beams on the crescent pupils of a goat, and I have to stop myself from calling out. As we climb the hill, I hear the faint sound of what I'm almost certain is Mr. Scruff barking in the castle. The ground finally begins to level out and Elsie walks west, away from the castle and towards the loop of copse.

"Here," she says. In front of us is a four-foot-tall pyramid of grey stones: a cairn. She takes the pebble from her pocket and puts it at the top of the pile.

"I didn't even know this was here," I say, taking the stone from my own pocket and adding it to the cairn.

"Why else do you think it's called Cairnroch?" she says, amused.

"Of course." It seems so obvious that I'm embarrassed.

"This one is one of the old ones," she says, lightly placing her hand on the stones. "But there are some really ancient ones up north."

My stomach twinges. "Near the museum?"

She nods.

Thinking of the Neolithic museum now has made me agitated. I'll have to go back to the castle and ask for a special audience with Lady Purdie, give her my report and beg her for more time here. I put my hands in my pockets. "Is this the silliness you were speaking of? Or should I do a wee jig, get the silliness going?"

She looks at her watch. "Well, it's a few minutes to midnight, so I suppose the silliness is starting soon enough."

"What happens at midnight?"

Elsie lets out a breath. "Oh, nothing." I feel somehow that I've deflated her, spoiled her fun. She takes a swig from the flask and hands it to me. Now that we're standing still, the cold creeps up into my bones. An owl hoots from somewhere in the castle forest. "It's a Hallowmas tradition my mum used to do with me when I was wee. After they left, Gran felt sorry for me, I suppose, and she'd bring me up here. Then, last year, she insisted she could make it up the hill, but she really couldn't. Her face went completely white."

I move closer to her and put my arm around her shoulder. "Thank you for bringing me," I say, although I'm not sure what I'm thanking her for. My boots are sinking into the frigid mud, and my fingers are numb.

She checks her watch with the torch. "Here we go, midnight."

"What do we do?" I pull her closer. "Do we kiss?"

She kisses me back, hard, and my body starts to ache, a deep throb, but she pulls away. I remember that this was a family ritual, and probably not one that she wants to violate with some illicit frolicking.

"Now we make the cast," she says, shining the torchlight around us. A grey mothlike creature approaches the mouth of the torch, and I think of Francis and his worms.

"What's a cast?"

Her voice grows a little squeaky with self-consciousness. "Like a spell. A fortune-telling superstition. You go up to a cairn on Hallowmas at midnight, somewhere that no animals can reach, and then the first animal you see on the way back down tells you of the year ahead. I know, it's ridiculous." She laughs at herself.

I clap my hands together. "Well. I saw a goat on the way up, what does that mean?"

"Lust."

"That sounds accurate," I say.

She pushes me, laughing. "It doesn't count on the way up, just the way down."

I put my gloved hand out for hers. "Shall we?"

We start to descend the hill; it's harder going down than it was going up, and the torchlight lends only unhelpful glimpses of mud and nocturnal flies, searching for something mulchy to rest on. "What are some of the meanings?" I say, trying to inject some jollity into the atmosphere. I can tell that coming up here has made her feel glum. I don't want to be the source of her disappointment.

"An owl is wisdom, a starling is a new home, a mouse is grief, a sheep means wealth."

"Wouldn't you do this on New Year, if it's fortune-telling for the year ahead?"

"But it's Hallowmas," she says, astonished.

When I don't reply, she continues. "It's one of the days when the ties are loosened. Good for fortune-telling. Not that I believe it," she says.

"I understand."

"It's just that I used to love coming here with my mum. She'd wake me up and it would still be nighttime, and we'd have sweet tea, and—" She almost slips on the clods of wet grass, and I steady her by the elbow. "Wait, can you hear something?"

I listen. "Not really." The night is so still I can smell the fires from the castle.

"No, I can hear something. In the forest." She points into the ribbon of trees that runs parallel to the castle. Something about the spotlight of white against the feathery strips of silver birch and the cracked pine trunks makes my insides squirm. I picture the dripping handprint against the glass of my window.

"There," she whispers. "You really can't hear it?"

But I do hear it now. A kind of snuffle, like a snoring breath, an unwell, sleeping child.

"Elsie, can we just go home the normal route?" I say. "I don't want to get lost."

She's already walking down to investigate. "Come along. I bet it's a sheep. I could really use some wealth this year."

My legs are stiff as I follow her down towards the tree line. Her torch flickers from bough to bough; shreds of hanging skin from the birch, scratches in the wood, from antlers, maybe, or birds. Pulsing in the undergrowth the quickening throats of toads, the pearl of their eyes glowing in the beam. Elsie's boots crunch through the leaves, a thick, vegetal smell; rotting peat, mushrooms. "Slow down, I don't want to lose you," I say. My voice sounds stretched and plaintive.

"Shhh." She points farther into the copse. "Just over there, I think."

My skin feels taut over my body, my skin prickling. The sound from here is more like a croak, a rough, crackling rasp.

And then, ahead of us, something moves.

A man.

I jump forward, grabbing Elsie's arm and pointing the torch at the figure. There are only trees. Lightning is running up and down my arms, my pulse jabbering in my skull. I pull her closer to me, squeezing her elbow.

She is laughing. "Gosh, I thought I saw it too."

I spin her to face me. I want to ask her what she saw, but my whole body has seized with fear.

"What do you think it means if the first creature you see is a ghost?" she says.

When she sees my expression, she stops laughing.

LATITUDE 78°, 53' N, LONGITUDE 69°, 01' W

Commanded men to remain on ship during mooring to much discontent... Gilchrist foolish and as useless as a maid... I set down alone to recruit Huskies from crude winter settlement.

14

SATURDAY, NOVEMBER 3, 1962

ANOTHER DREICH MORNING AND I'M HEADING DOWN TO THE harbour before sunrise. Another futile shouting match across the water while—but no, this time, there he is! Colin. I have to stand on the top of the hill and squint against the rain to be sure. After running down to the harbour, I stand around shifting my weight on the dock while he supervises another man hauling fish from his boat onto the boards, where they are dumped into a silver mound, glossy eyes rolling.

Colin and the other man are talking to each other, but so softly that I can't tell if it's in Gaelic or English. It takes a few minutes for Colin to notice me lingering, and when he does, his expression becomes puzzled, annoyed, even. I nod towards a wind-blasted bench and sit there, in the drizzle, until whatever exchange over the fish has been completed. Colin is wiping his hands with a rag, and finally, when the other fisherman is in his own boat, he gestures for me to approach.

"I need to talk to you," I say. The rain is pattering on the hood of Elsie's raincoat, and since I have to tip my head back to look at him, drops of water tap down on my eyelids.

"What are you doing now, then?" he says.

"Is there somewhere private we could go?"

He looks horrified. He should be so lucky. "It's about Purdie's ship," I say, pressing my fingernails into my palms. If I were a man I might punch him in the face, right here. No one would blame me.

"What about it?"

Blinking into the raindrops isn't helping me to feel authoritative, and I rub the water away from my face with the heel of my palm. "How much did she pay you?"

He looks me up and down.

"Violet. She's already told me," I lie. "I don't have much, but I may be able to get something together, as long as you still have some of the things."

"Violet McCloud?"

My patience is fragile. "Are there many Violets on the island? Yes, Violet McCloud. Do you still have them?" I look over his shoulder into his boat, as if I might be able to see a bag with Purdie's gold ring shining out of the top of it.

"I haven't talked to Violet McCloud since my old dad's funeral," Colin says.

I take a breath. "So she had a broker, or an intermediary. It doesn't matter. Do you still have them? Let's start there."

Colin makes a noise that might be a laugh. "I don't know what you're talking about."

I take a step forward. "Auld James's things. Did you go down yourself?"

"Down there?" He points into the water.

"Of course down there."

He lifts the brim of his cap off his head just enough to run his hand underneath it. "For a start, I can't swim. And as far as I'm concerned, what's sunk can stay sunk." He turns away from me.

Without thinking about what I'm doing, I seize him by the arm, and he spins to face me as if I've branded him with an iron. "Colin." I keep hold of his elbow. "I can pay. I just need them back."

He shakes me off his arm, his expression sickened. I realise I've made a terrible error coming here to talk to him without Elsie. She would have known how to talk to him.

"I've never seen anything from that ship," he almost spits.

"Did you take someone out there?" I say. "Only you know where the site is."

"Anybody can see the buoy," he says. "Anyone could get out there."

A terrible desperation falls over me. "Please," I say. "I can't lose my living. It's all I have. I need this. Someone's been down there. I just need to find out who."

He stares at me. His expression doesn't change, but there's an attentiveness in his posture.

"Have you heard anything?" I can see in his face that he has.

His apron squeaks as he undoes one of the buttons.

"Please. I won't tell anyone you said anything."

He looks out at his boat, dips his head, and turns his face to the side, so that I have to follow the shape of his lips. "Eddie Grimball's skiff was out near there," he says, at last. "Usually he's . . ." He points to the west. His shoulders slump, as if he already regrets telling me. "That's all I know."

I pull myself upright. "Thank you." I take a step towards him. "Thank you, really." I put my hand out for his, but he only looks down at it, then back out at his boat, as if I'm not even standing there.

15

FRIDAY, NOVEMBER 9, 1962

I HAVE TO WAIT ALMOST A WEEK BEFORE ELSIE HAS ANOTHER day off work. It's a long cycle up to Edward Grimball's house, and after learning my lesson in front of Colin, I know I need Elsie to accompany me. I'm on Elsie's bicycle, and she's borrowed Cook's, without telling him what we need it for. I'd imagined, stupidly, that it might be a chance for us to spend some time together, but as we cycle the path through hills and under the late autumn trees, the path is steep and I'm not much able to catch my breath to say anything. The leaves are dropping now, butterscotch and flame, and pinecones skitter under our wheels, sending us veering into patches of heather. Around eleven we come to a bothy under the shelter of a stone wall and climb off the bicycles. I peer in through the doorway. The bothy is the size of a stable and smells dankly of old puddle. In the corner, sunk deep into the floor, is a crude wooden statue of the Virgin Mary, her hands clasped in prayer. At least I think it's the Virgin Mary. It's hard to tell, because a filthy sackcloth rag has been tied around her face. Dribbles of water over the years have stippled the cloth in black mould. I point mutely at it.

"Italians built the bothy during the war," Elsie says.

"But—"

"Not a fan of statues, are we, on this island? But no one's going to actually chop down the Virgin Mary, so . . ." She trails off with a shrug.

The bothy has evidently been the arena for some kind of avian battle, as scattered over the hearth are blood-matted feathers still attached to grisly chunks of flesh. The whole place emanates foreboding. I refuse to step foot inside. Instead we crouch in the doorway, huddled away from the drizzle, while Elsie unpacks lunch. She opens a margarine tub to two hard-boiled eggs and a twist of salt in wax paper. Two corned beef sandwiches, a thermos of tea, a blackberry tart that sticks to the roof of my mouth. We eat wordlessly, but even through the door I can feel behind me the stunted eyes of the blinded Virgin.

When we've finished, Elsie stretches her back and throws the eggshells into the herbal-smelling moss behind the path. As she turns, she smiles at me, and I'm overcome by how strange it is that a month ago, I didn't even know her. Since the night in the cellar, things have been chaste between us—some light flirting, but nothing more. I don't know where we stand with each other, and I don't want to interrogate it too much.

After an undignified pee concealed behind the outside wall, I get back on the bicycle. Elsie leads the way along an old shepherd's path tracked between the trees. They are all young pine and slender birch, planted for cover during the war, and still learning how to grow against the winds. Their limbs travel sideways rather than up, as if they're trying to listen in on a juicy piece of gossip. Eventually, the hills give way to the coastline again. We're about fifty kilometres north of Port Mary, now. As we get closer to the water, there are no trees as far as I can see, only withering chickweed splattered among nubbly fields. The water to our left looks calm but it is thunderously dark, almost ink coloured. Sheep and goats mingle in the fields, birds that look like storm petrels swoop overhead, and I wonder if there is bad weather farther out to sea.

As we slide down along the coast, I catch enough breath for a conversation. "Tell me about Edward Grimball, then," I say.

Elsie sighs. "He's a bit of an odd one. Mainly misunderstood, I think."

"Is that your way of nicely saying he is a mean old pain in the arse?"

She laughs, and her bicycle sways across the road. Instinctively, I look behind us for cars, before remembering that the last time I saw a car on the road was ten days ago.

"So he's a fisherman?"

"Of sorts," she says.

"What does that mean?"

"Mainly crabbing, oysters, used to sell them to the hotel, but we don't buy enough to make a living. He's sort of a boat for hire, I suppose."

"And Colin doesn't like him," I say.

"What makes you say that?"

"There's no way he would confess to having seen him unless his dislike for him was stronger than his dislike for me."

"I don't know that anyone really likes Eddie Grimball," Elsie says. "Other than his brother Duncan, and he's a queer fish as well. Their family has a bit of a long history with the Purdies."

"In what sense?"

"Well, one of their ancestors was on the *Deliverance*."

I almost crash my bicycle into the rickle of a derelict byre. "Why didn't you tell me?"

"Honestly, I forgot you wouldn't know. We're a small island, there are a fair few families who had a relative on that ship. The story is that Grimball talked himself on board as the chef. Problem is, he was a redhead, so . . ." She shrugs.

"So?"

"Oh, come on, you must have heard the superstition: Redheads are bad luck on boats."

"But that can't be enough to ostracize generations of a family?"

"No, no, they're odd enough to do that on their own. Still, it hasn't helped." She stands up on the pedals of her bicycle and points down at a curve of black rocks that arc out into the water. "That's what we call Girl's Neck. It's not far now."

THE SALVAGE | 125

Slate rocks spiderwebbed with lichen and algae lie jagged in the fields, cracked blades piercing the weeds. "It doesn't look like it would make for great farming land around here," I say.

Elsie shakes her head. "It used to be all kelp. See?" She points to deep puddles along the coast that reflect back the puncture of rain and sky on water. Remains of the kelp pits. "Used to be a good trade in this part of the island. Gran talks about how the smell sometimes used to float down as far as the hotel when the wind was south. Everyone used to complain on a bad day." We cycle past low stacked walls that look out over the water. "That's where it was put to dry. No market for it now."

As we cycle farther along the water, a slumped and tumbled stone building up on a hillock appears in the distance. "Is that it?" I say.

Elsie nods.

As we get closer, the house appears more tumbled and slumped, the stones at crooked angles to one another, speckled in furry algae. Despite the rain, a middle-aged woman is sitting outside under the awning of the house, scrubbing clothes in a bucket. She looks up at us, putting a hand to her forehead and frowning when she sees me. I give silent thanks that Elsie has come with me.

Elsie slows and dismounts from her bicycle, and I do the same. She calls ahead a greeting that I don't catch, and the woman replies.

"Mary, this is Marta," Elsie says, resting her bike in a patch of heather by the cottage wall. "She's staying at the hotel."

"You're the new one, are you?" Mary says. Up close, she's a little younger than I thought; maybe in her thirties. She has sleek black hair that is parted down the middle and heavily lidded brown eyes that rest on me as Elsie fumbles in the basket of her bicycle.

"Gran sent you this," Elsie says, handing Mary a loaf wrapped in a hotel tea towel. "We made too many, and you know how she gets about bread going stale."

It's clear that we all know this is a lie, but Mary tucks the loaf under her arm. "Well. I suppose you want to come in?"

"If it's no trouble," Elsie says.

"No trouble, no trouble," Mary says, unconvincingly.

The house is neat inside, low ceilinged with a large, old-fashioned open hearth above which dried mackerel have been strung on a length of fishing wire. In the corner is a coal-fired stove from the 1940s, and Mary takes the kettle outside to fill, before returning and placing it on the fire.

"How's your granny?" Mary says.

"She's well, she's well."

"Did you hear about Cuddy Irene, down the road?"

"No."

"She's dead," Mary says, putting three enamel mugs on the table in front of us.

"Oh dear, what a shame."

"Her sister's gone to a home for the bewildered. And you know Teethie Jock up in Carherd?"

"Aye."

"He's dead too."

"Oh, I didn't hear."

"Aye, it just happened."

As they trade more tragedies, I look around the room. Other than a knitted wool blanket on the back of a chair by the fire, there is little ornamentation. The windows are book-sized, and the low, drab light picks up threads in the chocolatey smoke from the coal fire. Of course Eddie and his wife would take a chance to make some extra money by dredging up trinkets. The Purdies' largesse doesn't seem to stretch to this part of the island, and if there's tension between the families anyway, I suppose they'd feel there was nothing to lose. Would more tourists really be a positive thing for them? I shift in my chair. Here I am acting as the Purdie bodyguard, but who am I to hold the Grimballs to account? This cottage is cleaner than the tenement I grew up in.

"And how's your Eddie?" Elsie says, at last.

"You know," Mary says, pouring tea into our cups. "His knees give him trouble, but you can't complain, can you?"

"Is he home at the moment?" I say.

Mary turns to glare at me. She has a freckle, right on the end of her nose, that looks like a speck of dust. "And what would you be wanting with Eddie?" Her tone is sharp.

"His boat was out by the Purdie wreck," I say. "I have some questions for him."

Elsie flashes me a warning look, but I don't think this woman would appreciate me any more if I approached the subject sideways.

"Is that so?" Mary's face has taken on a furtive expression, and finally, I know that we're on the right track. He was down there. "Eddie's round the back," she says. "You can ask him yourself."

She puts her head to the door and shouts, "Eddie?"

A couple of minutes later, a short, powerfully built man appears at the door of the cottage. "What is it this time?" He pauses at the door and takes off his cap. "Elisabeth Drever, if you're not even bonnier since I last saw you," he says, with a laugh. He has heavy features and greying curly hair that has been left to grow a little too long. His eyes are lined, and he has a swarthy handsomeness about him, like an old-fashioned pirate in a child's picture book.

"Oh, stop, Eddie," Elsie says.

He waves his cap at me. "And who's this?"

"Someone here about your boat," Mary says.

"I'm the diver for the *Deliverance*," I say, standing up.

"Is that so?" His tone matches his wife's. I watch the synchronicity with which they move around the room, how their movements match each other. He takes a seat opposite me, rubbing his kneecaps reflexively.

"I'm here because I need your help," I say, looking directly at him. "The Purdies don't know anything is missing yet, and no one needs to find out."

He looks from me to Elsie. "What is she talking about, Elisabeth?"

Elsie puts a hand on my wrist, tugging me down to my chair. "Give us a moment, we were just talking about the boat, that's all."

He shakes his head with a cluck of his tongue. "You girls have the wrong idea."

"No one is saying anything," Elsie says, softly. "Between us girls right now, we just got onto the subject of Auld James's boat, that's all."

He places another enamel cup on the table and gestures to the kettle. His wife has the tight, pained expression of someone who has sat on a pin and doesn't want to let on. I grip my hands together under the table. Not only has he been down to the wreck, but there's something still here, in the house.

"If anything was broken during the retrieval, I might even be able to mend it," I say, hazarding a guess. "I wouldn't say anything to anyone."

"I told you I don't know what you're talking about," Eddie says, standing up. "And I'd thank you not to go accusing me in my own home."

"No one is accusing anyone," Elsie says.

"I am," I say.

Elsie takes a sharp inhale of breath. Eddie looks as if I've slapped him.

I try to walk back my temper. "I just mean, I know that you were down there. I don't even care. But whatever you still have, I might be able to buy back from you. It's worth more to the Purdies than to anyone else."

"Elisabeth, I think you and your friend should go," Eddie says, looking at Elsie instead of me. He walks to the door and opens it.

"Please, Eddie," Elsie says. "If you hear anything."

"Don't make me ask again," he says, gesturing to the door. The sparkle in his eyes has been replaced by a steely glint. Elsie nudges me.

"Come on," she whispers.

As Eddie shuts the door on us, he shakes his head. "I thought your gran would have taught you better."

§

"THERE'S SOMETHING STILL THERE, I know it," I say, pointing at the cottage.

Elsie sits on the wall, unsettling one of the stones and jolting sideways. "Marta, honestly. What's wrong with you? You can't go around accusing people! I told you the ship is a touchy subject for them!"

"I don't have any time to waste." My breath is quickening.

"But aren't you here for longer now?"

I shake my head. "Lord Purdie didn't agree to anything. Colin was a dead end. I know there's something in there." I hug my arms around my waist. "No one says no to a Purdie, isn't that what everyone says? I have to be the Purdie, now."

Elsie grimaces. "You have to cool it—people don't actually like the Purdies, remember? I know you're under pressure, but you're trying your best. Your boss will understand."

"No, you don't understand. Alex hates me. He *hates* me." A rising sense of panic is climbing my insides.

Elsie looks almost frightened. "Why?"

I stare down at the crumbling wall instead of answering.

She watches me a moment before turning away. "I can't believe that you still won't trust me."

"It's not that," I say, loosening my scarf. It feels as if I'm being strangled. "You'd never want to talk to me again."

Her expression softens. "That's not true." The rain starts drumming down more heavily, flicking up in dramatic plumes off her raincoat. "Come on, let's not sit here getting soaked. If you'd let me tell Granny, maybe she can do something. We could try bringing her up here, if you can sweet-talk Murdo at the castle into giving us a lift. They'd have a harder time saying no to her."

Elsie hoists my bike, and I take the handles from her. My backside is sore from the ride here, and it will be hours before we get back home. My neck is stiff, my chest tight, as if I had a belt cinched around it. I take one more look at the cottage and we start pedalling along the road.

Then I hear a voice over the sound of the rain. I look around us, then behind. It's Mary, halfway down the road from the cottage. She's wearing a fisherman's oilskin jacket that clearly belongs to her husband as it's several sizes too big for her.

"Els," I shout.

She looks over her shoulder. "Don't say a thing," she mutters, as she pedals around and passes me.

As we approach, Mary wipes her face. "Oh good. I thought you might have gone. Your granny's tea cloth," she says, holding the bundle out to Elsie with a tremoring hand.

My spirits drop. I'd hoped that they'd had a change of heart. But as she passes the cloth to Elsie, Elsie looks meaningfully at me. She hands me the bundle. There is something sharp and heavy wrapped inside, and I open the cloth to see the captain's knife and fork.

"Oh my God," I say, my breath catching. "It's them." I show Elsie a glint of silver.

"Thank you so much," Elsie says, at the same time as I say, "Is that all there is?"

Mary shakes her head. "That's all we were meant to keep. The rest has gone on."

I take a step towards her. "Up north?"

Mary looks between me and Elsie. "No, I don't know where. He must have took it already."

"Took it where, Mary?" Elsie says.

"I don't know where he goes to," she says, crossing her arms in front of her chest.

"Eddie really didn't say anything about where he was going, or anyone he might be meeting?" I say.

Mary frowns at me. "Not Eddie. Him at the museum."

I still don't understand. "Lord Purdie?"

Mary tuts. "The other one."

I almost drop the bundle. "Lester? Lester from the museum?"

"Aye," Mary says, looking quickly over her shoulder. "It was him that asked Eddie to get down there. Collect anything that could go to market. But Eddie said it was like a grave, he won't go down again."

My mind is reeling. "Are you sure it was Lester? It doesn't make sense—"

"Of course I'm sure," Mary snaps. "He's helped Eddie with some bother . . ." She trails off, wiping a raindrop away from her forehead, and I fill in her meaning. Lester has something on him, so he couldn't refuse.

"Mary, thank you so much," Elsie is saying. "We won't tell a soul."

I feel sick. Lester. That bastard, with his half-moon spectacles and his avuncular little chuckle. He looked me right in the face and stole from me. And him being the agent for the receiver of the wreck—any report would have to go through him in the first place. But why? The objects were destined for his own museum.

"What else was taken?" I say, interrupting them.

Mary looks over her shoulder again at the cottage. "I don't know. Not much, it fit in a potato sack. It'd call too much attention if Eddie had too many pieces, so he were only supposed to sell one thing and send part of the profits back to himself. I wouldn't know if there are others out there doing his dirty work with the rest of it." She wraps the coat more tightly around her. "I should get in. Give your granny my regards."

"Wait, but you won't make anything back on the cutlery, now," I say, as she begins to walk towards the house. "I might be able to pay, I'll just need to work some things out."

Mary shakes her head. "Oh no, I don't want any money off that ship. Eddie should know better by now. Purdie gold only brings you more grief."

"Grief in what way?" I say.

"Them and their ways. Hovering over the island like vultures and slipping in at the last minute. They're eating us up, piece by piece. And it's all with cursed gold." She nods down at the cutlery. "Those things as well."

"What do you mean?"

"At night I could hear them moving around in the drawer," she says. "All by themselves."

16

FRIDAY, NOVEMBER 9, 1962

"ARE YOU SURE SHE'S TELLING THE TRUTH ABOUT LESTER?" I call to Elsie as we cycle back under darkening clouds. Rain is dripping off my cap, and ahead of us the woods are thick with a dusky mist.

"Mary Grimball's no liar," Elsie says.

"But what about the jinxed cutlery?" Underneath my sweater, the silver feels icy against my chest.

"Oh, that. This part of the island always were a bit odd," Elsie calls to me, over the rain. "It's the kelp. Leaves arsenic in the soil. The families up this way are strange in their ways, for sure. But you don't go around accusing people for a laugh."

I say nothing. We pedal up the hill, against the rain. It drives inside my borrowed anorak, trickling down the back of my neck. I hear Lord Purdie's voice from the other day: *People see what suits them.* I can't believe how foolish I've been, trusting Lester so willingly. I wanted to see an ally, and that's what I found. Since I arrived on Cairnroch I've been allowing my expectations to lead me, instead of using my brain. Letting an older man trick me with a kindly chuckle. Jumping at shadows of my own invention.

ELSIE TAKES US a different route back to the hotel, following a path that twists along the hilly coastline, swerving back and forth between white sand scumbled with mist, rocks fuzzy with lichen, abandoned slate cottages, sheep, sheep. We trace a curve around a steep hill by the ocean and she slows, motioning for me to get off the bike.

"Come on, there's something I want to show you. We have time before sunset."

She begins to climb the hill, and reluctantly, I follow her, digging my fingernails into the stubbly grass, cowering under wind that whisks my breath out of my lungs. We reach a crude stone bield half dug into a channel in the ground and we crouch in there, flexing the blood back into our fingers.

"It's a sea cave," Elsie says, as if she's giving me a present.

"Up here?"

"There's a way in from the top," she says. "You're supposed to say your name into the cave and you hear the name of the person you're going to marry in the echoes. The story is that Auld James came here on Christmas Eve, but instead of a name, he heard an angel's trumpet, so he knew his life was supposed to be dedicated to God."

"Have you ever tried it?"

Elsie smiles, embarrassed. "Oh, we all did it while we were at school. I only heard the wind, but Irene McLennon swears to this day she heard Graeme's name." She cricks her neck. "Come on, before it starts raining again."

Near the shelter are three wooden stubs in the earth, the remains of a guideline for tourists that have been blown away or chewed by goats in the years since the war. It's hard to see the aperture until you're almost right on top of it; the rocks drop away in a circle onto the gloom of the cave under our feet. The darkness inside is so thick, it's like peering into a nest of black wool. Even over the wind, the roaring boom of the water inside the chalice of the cave thunders below us. Elsie nods to an almost imperceptible foothold along the right-hand side of the rocks, where she bends, sliding backwards, and my heart leaps: For a moment she is almost suspended over the drop into the foaming water, and then she's under the ledge. "Watch yourself," I hear her calling, and the answer of birds, bats, fluttering in the murk of the cave. I wait until my adrenaline has settled and follow her, sliding under and guiding my feet onto a path that slithers down along the rim of the chasm. It's slick with bird droppings and slimy moss, and Elsie hobbles farther along, edging towards a wide ledge that overlooks the camera beneath us. The cave smells vegetal and dank, rotting and sacred, a flooded chapel. Down below, the water rolls in cannon shots, and above, trickles of rain or condensation pour in a silvery veil through the hole. I begin to feel squashed somehow, not claustrophobic but as if I'm being held between two giant magnets. It's a horrible feeling. I take a deep breath, trying to pull more air into my lungs. Auld James's cutlery clinks together under my sweater. Below us, the water creams and whirls. It looks cushiony, like you could jump from here and plunge straight into a mound of lace instead of guaranteed death.

"Go on," Elsie says, nudging me.

I think she has heard it then, my own urge to leap. I shake my head, my mouth dry. "I'll do it for you then," she says. And I realise that she means to say my name into the cave. I reach out and pinch her on the arm; she looks at me sharply, confused. All I can think is that I already know the name of the person I will marry; I'm married to him. If she calls out into this cave, I have the sense it will tell her the truth. Suddenly I want to get out. The magnetised feeling looms inside me as if I'm too big and too small all at once. A slant of grey light through the hole flickers back and forth on the torcs of foam circling the hidden rocks below, and then I see it. Him. Lewis. Sitting on a ridge above the black water, his feet dangling over the edge. My throat is choked. He has come here. For me. This is the place you fall from. This is the place you drown. The light fades. He is still here, locked inside this chancel with us. My heart is racing. I know, immediately, that he is coming up here, that he will appear here on the ledge, next to Elsie.

Desperately, I turn and crawl for the opening, not thinking about anything except getting out of the cave. I claw in the bird droppings, levering myself around the ledge, and pull myself through the opening, crawling into the grass. I crouch there, shaking.

Elsie appears a few minutes later. "Are you all right?"

I am sweating under my anorak. My mouth is so dry I can barely speak. "Gave me a strange feeling," I croak.

"It does, doesn't it? Like being inside a big heartbeat."

I nod weakly, waiting for my arms to stop trembling. Gusts of wind roar through Elsie's hair. A tide of hopelessness tugs me under. There is something horrible on this island, I can feel it. What good did I think I would do here? How did I ever think this would make amends? And distracting myself with Elsie when I'm still married to a man who hates me. Everything I have worked for is falling apart in my hands. I should have thrown myself into the water.

One of the island's swerves from sterile to summer flashes over the hill, an instant reprieve in the wind, a slather of sunshine, the call of a sheep in a distant field, and as quickly as it came on, my despair is flushed away. Now all the misery seems like idiocy. Lewis wasn't in that cave. Lewis is dead. The poor bastard has better things to do than spend the afterlife torturing me. There are real things I need to concentrate on: my work, Lester, the woman standing next to me.

"I thought you'd like it, you like old places," Elsie says, examining me as we scrabble back down the hill, sliding on our backsides across juddering crags in the grass.

"I like *warm* old places," I say. My voice sounds steadier now, but my limbs are still weak.

She laughs. "That water can't be warm."

Eventually we are back down on level ground and begin to wheel our bikes to the road. "The water is different," I say. "Old places underwater—with what I do, I can go anywhere in the world. I get to see things no one else has, it's like opening a wrapped present. Old places in general, they're just so . . ." I don't know how to explain it to her. It's not that I have a passion for dead things and flinders of bone, for rust-coloured clay mud, dank cloisters. It's that underwater, even temporarily, I get to feel untethered from everything terrible. "Mossy," I finish.

"Going anywhere in the world," Elsie repeats, thoughtfully. "It sounds nice."

"Do you even like living on Cairnroch?"

"I don't know. I'm used to it, I suppose. And Granny's here. I wouldn't want to leave her alone."

I think of a morning two weeks ago when I spotted Alice climbing a ladder near the ballroom to oust a noisy oystercatcher from the guttering with the handle of a broom. It was early enough that her hair rollers were peeking out from underneath her plastic rain bonnet. I don't see the frail old woman that Elsie seems to see. But then perhaps that isn't what she means by not wanting to leave her alone.

"I can't imagine living my whole life here," I say, only realising as it comes out of my mouth how patronising it sounds.

Elsie doesn't seem to take it personally. "Oh, it's not so bad. Everyone knows your business, that's the main thing."

"And what about our business?" I say, glancing sideways at her. It's the closest I can bear to gauging how she feels about me.

She laughs. "People around here don't have enough imagination to think of us as more than pals. They likely think I'm odd for spending time with an outsider."

The word "outsider" hangs for a moment. And it occurs to me that maybe it isn't the condemnation that the islanders thought it was when I was standing at the doors of the bunker. That maybe all it means is I need to rely on myself—just like I've always done.

§

IT TAKES US another two hours to get back to the hotel. By the time we return, it's half past seven and we've missed dinner. My calves are throbbing, my hands tight around the handlebars, like claws. Elsie takes the bikes to leave them under shelter behind the ballroom, and I shuffle through the side door of the hotel, thinking of a hot bath, and soft towels, and warm soup and a cigarette and a whisky.

Mr. Tibalt calls to me as I pass through the corridor. "Marta?"

I pretend not to hear him.

"Marta . . . glad," Mr. Tibalt says, stopping me before I can go up the stairs. I am dripping onto the floorboards. "Message for you."

"A message?" I hold my shrivelled white hand out for the pink slip.

"... hour ago. Mr. Dimiroulis."

My hands shake on the slip of paper. The side door swings open to Elsie, and she pulls off her hood with a sigh of relief. "Watch that water, Elisabeth," Mr. Tibalt calls, pointing down the corridor at her. I crumple the slip into my bra next to the cutlery, where it's relatively dry.

"Message?" Elsie says, as she limps down the corridor towards me. Her cheeks are coral coloured from the wind and the rain.

I only nod.

Mr. Tibalt takes measure of the strange silence between us and turns discreetly back to the lobby. Elsie's face falls. She runs her hand over the stub of her ponytail, wringing a rope of water from the ends of her hair. "Your boss?"

"Yes."

"You don't want support?"

"Better not." I try to produce a smile. "I'll find you later."

Elsie disappears up the servants' staircase. I should have followed her, thanked her for today. But I can't think straight. My throat hurts. I pull out the slip of paper; the pink is now red from my wet fingerprints.

I don't know how you did it but well done. Ps won over for another month. Speak next week.

I stare at the note in disbelief.

Well done? Well done! To me! From Alex!

More funding from the Purdies! Another month!

At the telephones in the lobby I put a call through to the museum, but nobody answers. Of course not, it's after seven on a Friday; they will all be in the pub. I call Alex's answering machine too, knowing as I dial that it's a bad idea. But I want to hear him say "well done." He doesn't pick up, of course, but I leave a message. "Thank you for ringing. Call me back as soon as you can," I say.

I run up the back stairs two at a time, leaving marshy footprints. I knock on the door of Elsie's bedroom, and she opens it, confused, in her dressing gown. Her face is still raw from the rain and the bike ride. I kiss her on the mouth, her lips, tongue, cold against mine. She pulls me into the room, laughing. "What is it?"

"Another month," I say, my hands either side of her shoulders. "The Purdies have agreed to pay for more time. Alex—my boss—that's what he called to say. I'll have to catch the Boxing Day ferry after all!"

Elsie's face lights up.

"And now I have the cutlery, there might be more. He'll never know. My career is safe. I'm safe." I start laughing.

She looks at me, her eyebrows pinched.

"And we'll have until Boxing Day together," I say.

"Finally."

I step towards her, purposefully, put my hand against her cheek. She gives me the hint of a smile. I gather her to me, kiss her again, tug the hair tie out and run my fingers through her damp hair. As I kiss her neck, she makes a soft sound, and a pulse of warmth throbs inside me. She shrugs off her dressing gown and it falls to the ground; she pulls the knitted sweater off my head. We laugh as my belt sticks, my sodden socks peel off.

"You're freezing," she says, as my bare skin touches hers.

"So are you."

She jumps into her bed, and I do as well. And when I kiss her throat, her breasts, the dark blonde hair between her legs, she tastes like the rain.

17

**FRIDAY, NOVEMBER 9, TO
MONDAY, NOVEMBER 12, 1962**

"SO THIS IS WHERE YOU LIVE?" I ASK LATER THAT EVENING. We are both spent and cramped and flushed and hot and cold. Our wet hair is mingled on the pillow and there are damp patches on the linen. I am lying against her chest, covered in blankets.

"Nice of you to visit," she says, with a laugh.

I sit up, holding the blankets around me. The electric fire in the room is on, and it is pinging in metallic chimes. It's a dry, synthetic heat that comes off these kinds of fires and strikes you in bands across the face like you're a piece of bread in a toaster. Elsie's room was likely always meant for hotel staff. It has a little sitting room area with two armchairs with stuffing tumbling out of the seats. I help myself to a cigarette from her bedside table and pass her the pack. She sits up in bed, watching me, amused, as I pace around the room. I examine the books on her shelves, her vinyl collection—mostly Dixieland, the sort of music my parents might have listened to if they ever switched out the Oum Kalsoum.

"They're my parents'," she says, as if she's reading my mind. "They left them behind when they moved. They used to make me sad in a sad way, but now they make me sad in a happy way. Does that make sense?"

"Absolutely. But don't you listen to any modern music?" I say, hating how much I sound like Alex as I do so.

She stretches over her bed, tipping her cigarette ash into a seashell on her windowsill. "I'd need to make a trip to the mainland to buy others, and the last couple of times Granny wanted to come with me to Inverness. I'm not exactly going to drag her to a record shop."

"I suppose you can't get Radio Lux out here?"

Elsie shrugs.

"Yikes," I say, inspecting a 1950s pressing of the Ardgay-Bonar Pipe Band. "I'll take you to Billy's Records on Sauchiehall Street, you'll lose your mind."

She laughs, tipping her head back. In the rumpled bedsheets, her cigarette in hand, she looks like a French film vixen. Another pulse of desire thrums over me. I want to eat her with a spoon, like a hot pudding. Jumping back onto the end of the bed, I rub the instep of her foot, and she kicks me away lightly. "Ticklish," she says.

A spasm of hollow neediness comes through me, as if I've been cored. "Do you have a lot of girlfriends?"

She rests her cigarette in the seashell and combs her hair away from her face with her fingers. "Why?"

"It's a fair question."

"Is it?" She laughs, retrieving the cigarette.

I pull the top blanket from the sheets and back up over me. "Yes, I think so. Didn't we just spend the last—" I look at my watch. "Jesus. Three hours making love?"

"Marta, you're here until Boxing Day, didn't you just say that?" She sits up against the pillows.

"I did. So?"

"So, I don't think that automatically gives you the right to feel nervous about my love life."

I know she's correct, but I can't keep the sunken plughole feeling in my stomach from dragging me into despair. I get a petty urge to provoke her into confirming that she doesn't want me.

"You do this kind of thing often, that's what you're saying, is it?" I say, with a casual sort of smile, trying to goad her into thinking that I wouldn't mind hearing it.

"Mrs. Eleanor isn't exactly my type."

I laugh, I can't help it.

She kicks me lightly again on the shoulder. "I'm not going to play some silly game of who gets to feel more threatened. We can argue another time when I'm not so hungry," she says, leaning over the sheets and kissing me on the lips. It's a perfunctory kiss, but an affectionate one. I recognise I'm being deflected, but I don't feel wounded by it. Rather, her casual disregard for my neediness is reassuring; it proves somehow that she isn't going to tire of me straight away. Even as this crosses my mind, I rebuke myself for how hypocritical my anxiety is. After all, I technically have a husband.

"Shall we find some food?" she says, climbing out of bed and mincing across the cold floor to her dressing gown.

"I have some oatcakes and gin in my room," I offer.

"I'm not having oatcakes and gin for supper," she says.

Dressing in Elsie's knitted sweaters and thermal leggings, we tiptoe down the back stairs of the hotel, the mirror on the wall above the landing reflecting back my pale ankles and Elsie's even paler ankles. The hotel is dark downstairs apart from the light on Mr. Tibalt's desk, an amber dome shining across the hallway landing.

"He always keeps it on," Elsie says. "Granny and him grumble about the rates, but he doesn't want anyone who would need the hotel to come in and find themselves in darkness."

"Are the doors open?" I say.

She looks bemused. "Of course."

There is something unnerving about the front doors of the hotel, unguarded out to sea. I feel a stab of unease, but Elsie grabs my hand and we swing through the door into the kitchen.

She clicks the gas stove and lights a candle, melting the end until it sticks in a saucer. "If we put the light on, it'll wake Cook," she whispers, pointing diagonally.

"How often do you do this?"

"Often enough to know not to wake up Cook."

She pulls open the larder and takes out a loaf of black bread that we spread with margarine and salt. In the fridge are cold scalloped potatoes, thick with cream. There is a leftover blackberry crumble that we eat with vanilla custard from a tin. We sit at the counter, the candlelight shining off the polished surfaces. Elsie rubs her foot against mine every now and again. I feel impossibly happy.

Behind us, one of the windows above the sink creaks open and shuts again with a slam. I drop my spoon into the custard, little yellow globes splattering over the silver.

Elsie nudges me with her shoulder. "Just the wind."

I try to smile.

"The Cailleach got you?" Elsie says.

"Don't," I say. I think of the Purdie cutlery, picturing it waltzing away upstairs in my pile of abandoned clothes on Elsie's bedroom floor.

"What's wrong?" Elsie says, alarmed now.

"Nothing."

"You know that Mary was just imagining things, don't you?" Her expression is puzzled.

"I know." Her eyes are the colour of hazelnut toffees in the dim kitchen. I wonder what I can tell her. "You don't believe in ghosts?"

She laughs. "No. Of course not." She licks custard off her spoon.

"Wait. You do?"

I look down at the bowl, tracing a shape in the berries. "I think it would be arrogant of me to think I know everything about how the world works."

Elsie's eyes are wide. "Marta, come along, you can't possibly be serious. Ghosts don't exist."

I stare at her, longing to find the words to make her understand. "I've seen some things," I say, weakly.

"What kind of things?"

"Shadows. A shadow." I wish that I hadn't said it now. The flicker of candlelight against the chrome feels slick instead of homely. A light breeze from the floorboards swoops over my ankles. "Never mind," I say, quickly.

Elsie is looking at me, sympathetically.

I take a deep breath. "Did you know someone called Lewis Ince? He grew up here." Saying his name aloud sounds like an invocation.

She squints. "I don't think so. The name rings a bell."

Thank God. If she had known him personally, I don't know how I could have borne it.

"His family were from up on the north coast," I say. "They used to come down to Port Mary for holidays. His dad was a miner."

Elsie is watching me.

"That doesn't sound familiar?"

"Not really. There are a lot of Inces here. We can ask Granny if you like."

I shake my head. "No, it's all right. It's just, I knew him, Lewis. Before he died."

She puts her hand on mine. "I'm sorry."

I pull it away. "No, it's not like that." I don't want her sympathy. I don't deserve her sympathy. "I keep feeling . . ."

"You keep feeling him everywhere?"

"And now with the cutlery—never mind." I look down at my knees.

"But that makes sense, Marta, of course you would. You can't have met that many people from Cairnroch. But what does Auld James's cutlery jumping around have to do with your friend?"

The watery grave, the sense he would be here, waiting for me, that I would deserve it. What I owe to him. Tears drop along my nose. "I don't know."

"It's not easy, missing someone."

I wish it were that simple. It's awful, but I don't think I really miss Lewis. I didn't even know him very well. I was intoxicated by his desire for me and entertained by his quirks; how unlike Alex he was, with his jiggling and whistling. Now, though, I feel like I'm dragging him around with me, a horrible tumorous weight. I'm more attached to him in death than we ever were when he was alive. "Since I got here, I've had this sense that he's—" I can't finish my sentence.

"Marta, I'm sorry about your friend. But"—she jiggles my arm—"look at me."

I meet her eyes.

"The only ghosts are the ones we make for ourselves. Whatever you're sensing, it's coming from you."

I put my head in my hands, tears rolling through my fingers and onto the chrome tabletop. "Do you really think so?"

She puts her arm around me. "Of course. Don't you think that if we can split an atom, send a man into space, we would have proof by now if there were such a thing as ghosts?"

Something inside me aches to hear it.

"What you're feeling isn't your friend, it's your grief."

I'm crying in earnest now. A slimy feeling pulls through me, a sinewy kind of loss. All this time, I was so sure it was him. That he was here, waiting for me, that he was here to punish me. Like I deserve to be punished. Elsie's hand rests on my back, and a pressure releases from around my organs. Lewis isn't here, but I am. Elsie is almost right—what I've been feeling isn't my grief, it's my guilt. Eventually, I wipe my eyes.

"Feeling better?"

"Yes. I'm sorry, I must look a mess."

She pats me on the shoulder.

"Part of why I wanted to come here was to do something for him, because he loved this place so much. I owe him that, at least."

Elsie gives me a half smile. "That sounds like a really nice thing to do."

The way she is looking at me with appreciation, empathy, respect. I feel a twinkling sort of happiness spreading over me, and without another word, I pull her back upstairs.

§

ON MONDAY I wake up in Elsie's room, my nose in the back of her hair, and she turns over to face me. She smells of sweat and sex and I roll her nipple under my fingers, touch her, taste her, until we are both exhausted, her hair knotted in snarls.

"Oh my goodness," she says. "I smell shocking. I need to wash." She shrugs on her dressing gown. There are light bruises on her neck from my teeth, a flush still mottling her collarbones, her thighs still slippery. "Don't go anywhere."

As she leaves, I lie in bed taking in the detritus around the room—our jumble of wet clothes from Friday, the seashell ashtray, the half-drunk cup of tea from downstairs—and it all seems merry instead of sordid. We spent most of the weekend in her room tangled in the sheets, heading downstairs for Sunday lunch where we both ate thirds of roast beef, our ankles hooked together under the table. I can't remember the last time I felt this happy. The faint plummy light of an overcast day peers through the curtains. Since Elsie's room is on the other side of the building from mine, the sea is in full view, a washing line strung up hopefully in someone's back garden farther along the street. The door opens again and I yelp. It's Elsie, naked. "Forgot my washcloth," she says, grabbing it from a hook behind the door, and she's gone again. I watch in amazement as the door closes on her nude stroll along the hotel corridor back to the bathroom. I realise I may have underestimated her.

The hotel sounds busier than usual, people scurrying around the back staircase. My arm is numb, and as I rub it back into life I part the curtains, spotting a trail of people gathered along the harbour, looking expectantly towards the dock. The mainland ferry. I check the date on my watch—it's a week early.

Taking advantage of the general commotion in the hotel, I dress and run along the corridor to my bedroom. Purdie's silver cutlery is still locked in my desk drawer where I left it, and even as I close the drawer and turn the key in the lock, I laugh at myself for having been so nervy when we collected it on Friday. I look out some clean clothes to change into. With the ferry there will be fresh newspapers today, at least. I'd like to have a chance to read up on what's happening with Cuba. As I fasten the last button on my blouse, there is a knock on my door, and I open it, expecting Elsie.

"Marta, there you are." Flora is frowning.

With a drop in my stomach I realise she must have been looking for me. Does she know I was in Elsie's room? What we've been doing? Despite Elsie's nonchalance, a stab of terror juts into me on her behalf. We should have been much more careful. "Here I am," I say, as cheerfully as possible.

"There's a visitor for you downstairs," she says, retreating. "Mr. Tibalt says if he'd known she was coming, he would have been able to have a room aired for her," she adds, with a hint of reproach in her tone.

"A visitor? I'm not expecting anyone." I step forward and look over the banister. There, on the ground floor, standing at Mr. Tibalt's desk, is Sophie.

LATITUDE 78°, 53' N, LONGITUDE 69°, 01' W

Ugly quarrel at village when terms of recruitment were rejected again by the Huskimen. Left my pistol in the haste and cleaned my hands of their blood with snow . . . goggles will be of use as lighter than . . .

18

MONDAY, NOVEMBER 12, 1962

IT'S REALLY HER. SHE IS TWISTING HER RINGS, RUNNING HER fingertips anxiously over the strap of her bag. I find myself frozen to the spot, unable to formulate a thought. She must feel me looking at her because she glances up and catches my eye. Her expression hardens. Finally, my limbs cooperate and I pull back. Sophie. I run down the stairs so quickly I trip and have to catch myself on the banister.

We stare at each other. Up close, her curls have been flattened by drizzle, her clamdiggers reveal a startling expanse of goose-pimpled brown skin, and she is wearing sodden ballet slipper–type shoes. I view her with eyes that are now accustomed to the Cairnroch way of dressing, and she looks like she is in costume for something—is this how I must have seemed before I started living in Alice's knitted sweaters?

"What are you doing here?" I croak.

"Marta." Her expression is regretfully wary, as if she has discovered a snake sleeping in her shoe that she must now kill. I know now that Alex told her about Lewis. A prickle of panic snares through my chest and I look behind her, back at the front doors of the hotel.

She must read my expression because her lips tighten. "He's not here, it's just me."

I lean on the wallpaper to steady myself.

"I thought this was your idea?" she says, adjusting the strap of her bag.

I want to slap her. I don't want to touch her. "What?"

She sighs, shaking her head, bitterly. "He didn't tell you. Of course he didn't."

"Alex sent you?"

"Lady Purdie wants a textual expert." She shrugs. "So here I am. He said it was your idea. I thought . . ." She trails off. "Well, anyway." She shifts her bag again. "I'm here now."

My voice has dried in my throat.

"Listen, Marta." She straightens her posture. "I know you and Alex—"

I put my hand up. "Don't talk to me," I say. "Don't."

Her eyes blaze but she says nothing.

Flora appears and stands to attention between us. "When you're ready, miss," she says, still giving me a disapproving look, as if I'm responsible for Sophie's surprise visit.

"Allow me," George says, picking up the suitcase at her feet.

"Thanks, I'd prefer to carry it," Sophie says.

He frowns at her.

"This one has equipment in it, I'd rather—"

I leave them to scuffle, walking straight to the phone bank and dialling the museum.

Emily at the front desk answers. "Curatorial?"

"Alex Dimiroulis, please. It's Marta and it's urgent."

I tap my feet, squeeze the phone cord around my finger.

"Hello?" It's Alex.

"You sent Sophie? You sent Sophie?" I say. My brain is swirling with static; I can barely see in front of me.

"Yes, I sent Sophie. The Purdies offered to pay, and I said yes. You know we don't exactly turn down funding."

"But this is my project!" I am almost shouting.

Alex sighs, as if I'm a child threatening a tantrum. "All they cared about until now was the objects, but *you* got them onto the journal.

That's all they wanted to talk about, the diary, logging an exploratory sea route they think they could petition to be named after the captain."

"I—" I stop. I did do that. I used the journal to convince Lord Purdie, and he went straight to Alex.

"Lady Purdie said you haven't retrieved anything. She seemed confused about why. Is there an issue?"

My heart flares. "No issue, it's just the conditions aren't great so it's taking longer than expected to do a thorough site survey. We won't get another chance if they are bringing day-trippers out there next summer."

"OK. So do it properly. I can't say I haven't enjoyed having some peace around here. And don't take it out on Sophie, she's just doing her job."

I wince. Here he is defending Sophie, prioritising her feelings. "This isn't easy for me," I say, my voice breaking. I hate myself for being so pathetic.

"Marta," Alex says. "I don't much care what's easy for you. Just don't make things difficult." And he hangs up. I stand, looking at the receiver before sitting in one of the armchairs, resting my head in my hands.

I feel a familiar grip on my shoulder. The smell of her cardigan I now recognise. "Marta? Is everything OK?" Elsie says.

My vision is bleary as I look up at her. How can I begin to explain it? Then a creeping realisation draws over me. Elsie and Sophie. Together in the hotel. It's only a matter of time before Elsie talks to her. Finds out about Alex. Finds out the whole truth about Lewis.

19

MONDAY, NOVEMBER 12, 1962

HUDDLES OF ONLOOKERS ARE GATHERED ALONG THE CAIRN-roch waterfront to watch the lightship being guided into anchor near the remains of Auld James's lighthouse. I squeeze among the crowd, conscious only of Sophie's eyes on me from the hotel window and barely paying attention to what is evidently an important moment in the island's history. The lightship is bright crimson with a squat mast; she carries the lurid institutional authority that signifies both cataclysm and contingency. At the top of the mast are the light and warning bell that will have to take the place of the lighthouse until the slackening of winter storms will allow for construction.

"Followed the ferry," one middle-aged Irene is saying to another Irene, who is carrying a freckled baby. "No doubt the crew will be all day at the Black Hare before it goes out again."

"Before the ferry goes out again?" I ask, interrupting.

She looks at me for a moment before deciding if she wants to reply. "Aye, it'll be out tomorrow. Not keeping lightship lads here over the winter, are they?"

"And the next ferry after that?"

The second Irene shifts the baby on her hip. "Saint Stephen's Day."

I frown, and they look at each other. "Sweetie Scone Day?" she tries again.

"Oh." Still December 26 then. If Sophie's not on the ferry out tomorrow, we'll both be here for Christmas. I allow myself a brief moment of perverse satisfaction that Sophie will be forced to spend Christmas Day on the island, instead of snuggled up at home with Alex. Not that he would be much fun in any case; Greek Orthodox Christmas Eve is a sombre affair, all candles and dark hats and self-abnegation. But no, instead, Sophie will be here.

I push past the two Irenes and jostle through the crowd farther along the street towards the kirk. Sophie will be in the hotel for weeks, following my comings and goings. She's not stupid; she'll work out what's happened. She'll see all the mistakes. She could go straight to the Purdies. She will *definitely* go straight to Alex. And then there's Elsie. There's no time to lose—I need to find a way to get Sophie out of the hotel.

Picking up my pace, I slip down one of the side lanes and follow the high street to Roiner's Point. Elsie's bicycle is not in its usual place by the phone booth, and for one horrible minute I think it's been stolen, before I remember that she left the bicycles behind the ballroom after we returned from Eddie Grimball's house. I dash back towards the hotel, collect Elsie's bike, and push it back up the road to the castle. My legs sting, the rain whistles in my ears—I didn't even think to put on a coat—but I don't rest for breath until I've reached the doors of the castle. By the time I let the bicycle clang to the gravel, my knees are shaking and my stomach is jabbing against my ribs. Janet fusses me into one of Lady Purdie's coats before letting me back out of the kitchen, down to the field on the far side of the castle where she last saw Lady Purdie. I hobble through the rutted grass, my heartbeat bouncing in haphazard leaps inside my chest. She is down at the end of the field with a groundsman. Between them they are wrestling with a wild goose that has become caught in a stretch of fencing. The groundsman is holding the wire aloft, and Lady Purdie is on her knees in the mud, one elbow against the goose's neck, the other arm easing its leg back through the knot. I stand at a respectful distance while the goose shrieks and Lady Purdie talks to it with an air of brisk efficiency. "One more step," she's saying. "Yes, that's the idea."

With a ruffle of feathers the goose shakes free of the fence and limps across the field. Lady Purdie stands and takes off her glove to wipe a smear of mud from her chin. She gives some directions to the groundsman about the wire, then pauses to watch the retreating goose.

"Lady Purdie," I say, clambering down the slope towards her.

She doesn't turn but removes the binoculars from around her neck and hands them to me. "Magnificent, aren't they?" she says, tipping her head towards the flock of geese at the end of the field. "They should be away already, I don't know what they're waiting for."

"Yes." I pretend to look at the geese. "Quite."

"Lord Purdie would've wanted to add that old girl to the pot, but it doesn't seem sporting when the poor fool has already entrapped herself, does it?"

"Sophie Ndiaye is here," I blurt out.

She squints at me, mildly.

"The textual expert. For the books."

"Oh, good." Lady Purdie nods. "That was quick. I was worried they'd miss the ferry, it's running early on account of a storm predicted this week. Mr. Dimiroulis said it would be close."

Hearing Alex's name in her mouth is disorientating.

"Yes, lucky that she was able to make it," I say, tersely. "Anyhow, I wanted to check with you as to when I should take the microscope down."

Lady Purdie cocks her head in my direction.

"If Murdo will give me a lift, I could take the microscope down to the hotel today."

"You want to take the microscope?" Lady Purdie says, striding back in the direction of the castle. God, she's fast for an old woman. I try to match her pace, even though my knees are shaking. There's nothing that the countryside gentry respect less than a physically frail youngster.

"Well, she'll need to use it, of course. I'm sure she'll try her best to be careful with it," I say, trying not to let on that I'm short of breath.

"Yes, for heaven's sake, don't break the contraption, it cost an arm and a leg. I've been told it's a good one?"

"It's top of the line. Even better than the model we have in the museum in Edinburgh."

"Is that so?" Lady Purdie nods. "Lester chose it."

My stomach churns at the mention of his name. Another mess I'll need to clean up. "He chose well. And I'll ask him about the materials, of course. The fluids."

"What fluids?"

"The fixatives," I say, trying to think of convincing-sounding technicalities. "And preservation fluids and chemicals. We can mix up the solutions in the stillroom and then transport them, I suppose."

Lady Purdie frowns at me. "Whyever would we do that?"

I bite my lip as if perplexed. "The next mainland ferry back is Boxing Day, so she has six weeks here, and there's an awful lot of material to get through. I apologise, I assumed you'd want her to work as much as possible"—I search for a suitably aristocratic, puritanical idiom—"really muck in. And it'll be tricky if she's coming back and forth, that's all. I thought it would make sense to bring everything down to her rooms at the hotel."

Lady Purdie pauses. "We can't be moving heaven and earth for her."

"No, of course not."

"Not a princessy type, is she?" Lady Purdie says.

How delicious it is to hear someone say it. "I'm not sure about that," I demur, politely.

"Don't touch the materials," Lady Purdie says, at last, as we approach the castle doors. "Let me think about Princess Sophie."

I give her a bow before I realise what I'm doing. "Absolutely," I say.

§

I SPEED DOWN the hill on Elsie's bike even though the road is slippery with drizzle, and I take the turn near Lees Farm at far too wide an angle and teeter into the brambles. Lady Purdie's coat fills with air like a parachute, and I feel irrationally that it is slowing me down; hampering me from returning in time to prevent Sophie from producing diagrams of my failures. Murdo's car overtakes me as I round the corner near Roiner's Point, and I cross my fingers on the handlebars that he's not delivering the microscope. I ride through the high street, bouncing down the uneven cobbled lane, and cast off the bicycle behind the ballroom.

As I stagger in through the side door, George is wheeling a chrome trolley through the lobby to the front of the hotel. Sophie is standing there, still in her damp trousers. Murdo's car is parked outside, and Mr. Tibalt is holding a jinking umbrella overhead as Murdo opens the trunk. The front doors slam open in the wind, and Mr. Tibalt supervises as George loads Sophie's luggage into the back of the car. Sophie draws her coat around her as Mr. Tibalt holds the door open, and she climbs up into Murdo's car. Mr. Scruff is already in the car, his paws printing muddy clovers on the seats, and Sophie flinches as he gambols around her. She catches my eye then. It takes all my power not to wave as Murdo drives her back up to the castle.

Charts wrong

20

MONDAY, NOVEMBER 12, TO
SUNDAY, NOVEMBER 25, 1962

AS LADY PURDIE PROPHESIED, THE RAIN BUILDS INTO A storm that I watch from my bedroom window as it crosses the horizon farther out to sea. Lightning flickers in whips of a blanket. Alice has lent me a polishing cloth, and I rub the captain's knife until a slice of my own face wavers in the silky gloss of the silver. My throat is sore, and I can see in my reflection the effort at each swallow, as if there are shards of jagged roast potatoes stuck in my gullet. I need to get down to the ship and collect the journal before more winter storms roll in. Keep Sophie busy. I put the cutlery down on the desk and massage my temples. Here I'd thought that being on the island for another month might give me room to breathe. But the idea of Elsie finding out—looking at me the way the rest of the island did when they shut the doors of that bunker. I couldn't bear it.

Elsie knocks on the door before putting her head around. "You weren't at dinner."

"I thought I'd get an early night," I say.

"The Purdies asked for Sophie to go up to the castle?" She crosses to the desk and reaches idly for Auld James's fork. I yank it away from her, instinctively, as if it might scald her to touch it.

"There's lots to be getting on with," I say. I wonder if Sophie is the first Black guest they've ever had stay here. I try not to picture their stilted inability to cover their surprise when they are introduced to her. Elsie rests her hand on the back of my neck. "You're hot."

"I'm fine." The captain's cutlery glints in another flash of lightning. A lance of cold air jabs through a chink in the window frame, filling the room with the tonic smell of seaweed and wrack tossing in the waves along the coast. I pull the curtains across the window.

"You don't want to watch the storm?"

"Who likes storms?"

Elsie crosses to the edge of my bed. "I love storms. The feeling of being tucked up safe inside. In my granny's old house growing up, I never felt so cozy as when the wind came wailing down the chimney."

"People who like storms don't have to work in the water," I say, knowing that I'm being a bitch.

Elsie gives me a sour look as she slips off her shoes, and I feel immediately contrite.

"OK, Marta. It's been a long day, let's go to bed."

That night I dream that I'm in the playground outside my old school, plucking the stones out of the pebbledash and eating them one by one. The stones are made of metal; they chime in my stomach as I gulp them down. I wake with a start, the sheets sticking to me.

"What's that sound?" I say.

Elsie props herself up on one arm. "Hmm?"

"The cutlery, it's moving in the drawer, I heard it."

"What?"

A thin, brattling noise comes from the far corner of the room under the dresser. It seems to be moving in circles, dancing. My pulse is screaming in my temples. A flash of white judders across the floor.

Elsie yelps. Then she clicks on the light, lying back on the pillows with a laugh. "It's just a mouse. Oh, my heart."

"A mouse?"

She stands up, tutting. "Dragging a bit of paper or a hankie. Must have gone out here." She leans down and peers at the skirting boards. "Have to put a trap down tomorrow."

"But I heard it moving," I say. "Auld James's cutlery."

Elsie comes back over to the bed. She stands there for a moment, listening. "Marta, that sound is you wheezing."

"We should sleep in your room," I say. "Or lock it somewhere. The safe."

"Marta, hush, listen."

Falling quiet, I hear it too, a crackling noise in my chest, like tissue paper rustling.

In the morning, Elsie brings broth on a tray with some headache pills, but the rustling paper turns to buckling cardboard by the afternoon, and I have to build a slope from pillows to catch my breath. At some point after night falls, Alice is in the room. I find myself too weak to protest as she undoes the buttons of my nightshirt and rubs menthol paste onto my chest. A man I haven't met before with red hair appears by the bed; the island doctor, I gather from his black bag. He slides a cold instrument across my back and gives me some tepid, reassuring pats on the shoulder. It's around dawn when I'm alert enough to realise that the hissing sound I had dreamt was Auld James's snake is a kettle on the coal fire in my bedroom, piping steam into the air.

Dr. Brode returns the next day and, finding that I'm now spitting up a horrible sludge, declares me on the mend. But I can hardly limp to the bathroom without skewering pains through my ribs, and I'm yawning compulsively, even as Elsie tries to talk to me. Over the next week I'm restricted to bed, graduated from the kettle to bowls of hot water over which I must sit and breathe with a towel over my head. I continue to cough up more and more slime, perplexed and morbidly fascinated at how much horror there could possibly be lurking inside my lungs. Every hour that I'm stuck in bed gives Sophie more time to poke around at the castle. And Lester, God knows what kind of poison he could drip into her ear.

Elsie sits with me as I eat bland invalid's food, toast, mashed potato, broth, jelly, sweet tea. Whenever I ask her about Lady Purdie, Sophie, the castle, Elsie reassures me they have been preoccupied with preparing for the castle museum, but I can tell from the deliberateness of her cheer that she's lying. When Flora comes up to collect my tray on Saturday, she's less politic and appears almost gleeful to report that yes, Lady Purdie has called several times to ask when I'll be ready to get back to work. And Sophie has rung from the castle every day. I pull back the curtain and tug open the window. The detritus of the storm still litters the coast: corks from lobster pots, birds feasting on the kelp shredded by the black rocks near the ruined lighthouse. The water itself is jabbling towards the horizon, waves like frayed ropes. There's a flinty chill in the air, and there's no denying that autumn has turned, the swift cloak of winter has fallen over the island.

I need to go back down to the ship.

§

WHEN SUNDAY the twenty-fifth approaches, I'm awake and dressed before dawn to take my equipment down to the lobby on the lift so that Elsie won't notice that my strength is diminished enough that I can't carry it down the stairs. I'm along the front path, testing my still-raggedy lungs in the brisk morning, when the hotel doors slam open and Elsie comes tumbling down the stairs.

"Not creeping away," she says, catching up with me. I deduce from her hat and padded coat that she's intending to come on the boat.

"You really needn't join," I begin, but my heart's not in it. She puts up a mittened hand to stop me, and I don't bother to finish my sentence.

"What can I carry?" she says, eyeing my equipment, and I hand her my camera bag.

It's a gruesome morning, with an icy breeze that carries mushy, gristly shards of sleet, and when we arrive down at the docks, there are circles of ice floating on the surface of the water between the boats. They are large as dinner plates, light as lily pads. I kick one and it rustles sloppily against its neighbours. Elsie's expression is as alarmed as mine, and a sense of foreboding broods inside my stomach as we approach Colin's boat.

"What is this?" I call, pointing down to the ice.

He barks a laugh, which I gather means that I have said something stupid.

Elsie shifts the camera bag on her shoulder. "Won't this interfere with your . . . visibility?" she asks.

Colin reaches out with an oar to prod the strange orbs. "It's only pancake ice."

"I've never seen it before," I say.

Elsie shakes her head. "I don't like this at all, Marta."

"From the river," Colin says, pointing along the white sand beach where the mouth of the river pours into the North Sea.

"Surely it's not wise to go out if it's cold enough for ice?" Elsie says.

Colin shrugs. "Up to her."

Elsie hooks a finger around my elbow. "Marta, it's freezing. You're still not back to full health. Don't do this."

I look down at the milky disks. "I've done ice dives before. The water can't really get that cold. Anyhow, I have to."

Elsie looks horrified. "You *don't* have to. You can say no."

I aim for a smile. "No one says no to a Purdie." I pull away from her and climb onto Colin's boat. "Let's go, whenever you're ready," I say.

As Colin guides us out of the harbour through the disintegrating plates of ice, I can feel that Elsie is furious. Her posture is rigid, and I decide against going to sit next to her in case it makes her tip over into total frustration.

Out of the harbour, choppy waves smack the boat in lurches, and I find it difficult to keep myself upright. I lock my legs around the seat, not wanting Elsie to notice I'm struggling to maintain my balance. The wind is bitter, swirling clouds shedding splinters of sleet overhead. Colin slows as we approach the buoy, but I ask him to steer farther north so that we're as close to the wreck as possible, to give me less time in the water.

As the motor turns off, the boat lobs from side to side. I shuffle closer to Elsie and pull out a jar of Vaseline from my bag. "Would you put some on my face?" I ask. "I can't touch the journal otherwise."

Her expression is grim, but she dutifully pulls off her mittens. I take off my coat, and when Elsie sees I'm wearing the knitted red sweater that Alice made for me, her lip twitches. I strip down to my wetsuit, and Elsie's cold fingertips stroke the Vaseline over my cheeks and forehead, her touch gentler than I have any right to. "Marta," she begins, as she screws the lid onto the jar, but I shake my head.

I sit on the gunwale and start my breathing exercises, ignoring the catch at the bottom of my lungs on the exhale. Then I tip a bucket down into the water and pour it over myself, careful not to splash Elsie. Feet, thighs, arms, heart, then head. It's like a rug of nails, a form of penance. I can feel Elsie's eyes on me, but I don't look at her. I don't want any excuse to stop.

The wind screams over my body, and I'm so cold that my fingers are already starting to go numb. I give Elsie a pitiful wave, then lean myself back and drop into the water.

A glacial grip tightens over my chest and I cling to the anchor rope, floating near the surface as the shock pierces my limbs. I can't help but gasp into the mouthpiece. As soon as my breath steadies, I plunge down. The water feels sludgier, soup-like, though it may just be my lethargic movements. The guideline twirls through my fingers, and my lungs crunch all the way through to my spine.

I struggle through the hatch, my fingers too numb to grip the edge properly. The ship is much darker than it was on my previous trips. I drop the torch, and it floats down to the bottom of the passageway, rolling in the slippery algae; again and again it spins from my clumsy grip, and the deep blue of the ship presses against me. I feel drunk with cold, slathered with it. When I finally catch the torch, I force myself forward, into the galley. The flash of my camera lights up the rows of plates, the drifting silt. The saloon next. At the cupboard in the corner, I try to make out the scratches in the wood. Could a fish really have made them? I take a couple of photographs, and in the enclosed space, the white flash sears my eyes. The water shines around me, broken with pale streaks that I realise are in my own vision. I find myself floating against the ceiling, a warmth slinking over my body. The camera smacks against the porthole and I snap back to attention, pushing now along the corridor. I point the camera indiscriminately through the doors of the crew rooms, then at the bottom of the corridor, at Captain Purdie's room. The bunk looks almost lonely without his body. Even though I know that Eddie has been down here, that he has taken the coin, the goggles, there is a childish part of me that nursed an absurd hope that somehow they would all be back down where they were. Of course, there is still a gaping hole in the algae where the coin should be. I lever open the top drawer of the desk and take further pictures of the two leatherbound books before carefully wrapping them in the oilcloth.

I turn to swim back down the passage, clicking off the torch temporarily since my hands are full. The space is utterly black. It's then I have the distinct sense I'm being watched. All the hairs on my body twist in their pores.

The weight of someone's fingers grips hold of the other end of the books and tugs on them.

Without thinking, I pull the books back with a muffled yell into the regulator. I'm turning, then I'm spinning, it's too dark to know which way I am facing, I can't hold the books and the torch, I am groping through the slime I hope forward, and then at last, a shimmer on the ladder leading up to the hatch.

I'm out of the ship.

Now, now, it's cozy in the water. The softness of it cocoons me, lulls me. What's the rush to go anywhere? It will be colder on the surface. Nicer to linger down here, the seaweed suckling tenderly at my legs. And then the guideline is being shaken, the jiggle travelling through my shoulder. I suppose they are waiting for me, back in the upstairs world. I picture Elsie's face, anxious under her hat, and reluctantly, I pull myself along the guideline, up towards her.

Elsie is heaving me into the boat, and Colin too. I'm almost giggly as I slide on board. The bundle of books is taken away and towels and blankets are thrown on top of me. Elsie removes her hat and pulls it over my ears. The waterline of the boat has collected more of the pancake ice, the orbs floating, clicking together with a crunchy tap, like little bones.

"Go on, another bowl," Alice says, from her chair at the end of the dining room table.

"I'm half liquid." I shift my weight, producing a distinct sloshing sound from all the soup in my stomach.

She narrows her eyes. "I'm under strict instructions. Go on, it'll do you good."

I bring another spoonful to my lips and pretend to sup from it. Mrs. Eleanor politely follows the movement of the spoon, willing me on with a birdlike insistence. On the other side of me, Francis is drumming his fingernails pointedly on his bowl. We typically wait for everyone to be finished before pudding is served, and Francis has the petulant frustration of a child who has been promised his custard.

"I really can't," I say, putting the spoon down. "We both did our best."

Alice tightens her lips before conceding. "All right, I suppose that'll be enough for her."

I wonder how much she's guessed about me and Elsie. Alice is canny enough; she knows, even if she doesn't know she knows. I push the bowl away from me. There is a light brume of sweat on my forehead from the exertion of guzzling soup.

"Right." Alice whisks away the bowls and returns with slices of jam tart. I nibble around the edges, Francis eyeing my serving, and when Alice turns to poke the fire, I slide it onto his plate, leaving a jammy sluice across my bowl.

The wind shrieks through the hotel, and the coals rumble in the grate as Alice goads the fire into more flame. I picture Sophie up at the castle, the marble floors, that bathroom with the cracked soap, sitting alone in her room, looking out over the empty fields.

As we leave the dining room, Francis pops his knuckles. "Anyone up for a game of whist?"

Mrs. Eleanor tuts. She considers all card games to be a form of gambling. Francis will have to make do with Mr. Tibalt again, who takes pity on him after dinner each evening, even though I suspect he has officially finished his hotel duties by then.

Elsie has set up her ironing board in the deep pantry next to the bar, and she looks up from the napkins as I approach. "How many bowls of soup did you have?"

"Twenty," I say.

She rolls her eyes at me, her lips twisting into a little keyhole of annoyance as she bears down on the fold in a napkin. "It's straight back to bed after dinner, you know. You need to rest up."

I help myself to a glass of Auld James's whisky and sit on a stool on the other side of the counter. She continues to press and fold and flip without acknowledging me.

"Is something wrong?" I say, finally.

Elsie shakes her head. "That was stupid, what you did today." The way she shakes her head, the tension in her lips, she looks a lot like her grandmother.

"My job is dangerous, sometimes."

"There's a difference between stupid and dangerous. Today was stupid."

I light a cigarette and look down into my glass. "I didn't ask you to come." I can hear the sulkiness in my voice. Even if that is technically true, it's petty to express. I certainly wanted her there.

Elsie lets out a bitter scoff.

I sneak a look at her. "Leave that a second, will you?"

She drops the iron on the board with unnecessary violence. "I don't understand. You don't seem to have a problem standing up for yourself."

"What makes you say that?"

She waves her hand around. I feel a sting of shame that she's noticed I have difficulty controlling my temper. "Because I'm such a bitch," I finish for her.

"I like that you're not false," Elsie says. "But still, you'll take unnecessary risks for the Purdies. For your boss."

I shift the cigarette between my fingers. "That's what they pay me for."

"Couldn't Sophie have gone down there?"

"She's not trained," I say, stabbing out the butt in the ashtray. "No one is trained, Elsie. Me, I'm trained. Do you know how expensive my time is?"

She looks almost disgusted with me.

"I'm good at this, I last longer than the men on the same tank of air because I'm smaller, more careful. It means I can log more hours than any of them. This is maybe the only thing I've ever been good at, and it's all been for nothing." I know how petulant I sound, but the small victory of finding the cutlery and gaining the extra weeks here feels inconsequential with Sophie looming over me, a witness to my failures.

Elsie is watching me, confused. Her shoulders fall as she lets out a sigh. She ducks under the counter and comes to stand next to my stool. Taking a sip from my glass, she reaches over and gives me a resigned, one-armed hug. Even as she hugs me, a sense of terror drops heavily over me. She's this exhausted with me, already. When she finds out the kind of person I truly am, she'll never talk to me again.

§

LEWIS'S WATCH washed up two days after I left the hotel. I'd gone straight to my parents' flat in Glasgow after that weekend at Crag's Head and sat there numbly in the piles of rubbish, not knowing if it was day or night. I couldn't bear to face Alex, to face myself. When Alex returned from his "camping trip," I suppose he realised where I must have gone. He called there to break the news that Lewis was missing, presumed dead. My lips made the movements, but nothing came out. And there was something else, worse. It wasn't true relief but something in the shade of colours related to relief. The affair had ended, and Alex wouldn't find out. I'd lit a fuse for a bomb that never went off. I spent hours walking the length of Ruchill Park, convincing myself that it hadn't truly been my fault. Lewis had been gone for hours by the time I realised. He was reckless, going out in weather like that. And now I was abandoning Alex while he was grieving for his friend. How was I supposed to support him? Wouldn't it look more suspicious if I wasn't there?

Alex was sitting at the kitchen table, waiting for me, by the time I had gathered enough nerve to return to Edinburgh a week later. I found him hunched over a full ashtray, a blue fug of mentholated smoke looping around the kitchen. There, on the table, was a book from the in-house museum library.

"The police found this in Lewis's hotel room in Crag's Head," he said, sliding it over the table without looking at me. "His mum returned it to me."

He opened the cover of the book, and I saw my own name listed on the borrowers' slip.

I felt nothing. I only stared at my name written there and waited for the horror to start.

Alex looked up at me, his face white. "Why?"

I felt the tears rolling down my cheeks, but I didn't go to wipe them away. I didn't deserve to cry, to be sad. Being sorry wasn't enough. "I don't know," I said, in the end.

Alex looked back down at the table. "What a waste," he said. "What a total waste."

21

FRIDAY, NOVEMBER 30, 1962

ON FRIDAY, ELSIE GOES WITH COOK TO COLLECT CRABS, AND I have my opportunity to escape my sickbed and go up to the castle. The wind is blowing from the north, and I'm pitiful on Elsie's bicycle; no matter how hard I press against the pedals, the bike hardly moves. It takes me ten minutes of coughing before I give up, pushing it up the hill.

Over an hour and a half later I finally throw the bicycle into the ornamental hedges and slump against the kitchen doors. Janet lets me in, and I grope towards a chair at the kitchen table while Mr. Scruff lollops all over me, turning in delighted circles.

"Bitter out," Janet says, leaning her broom behind the kitchen table. She comes over and rests her hands on my shoulders. "And are you feeling well?"

I reach up for her hands, her knuckles knotted against my cold fingers. "I'm fine, thank you."

"We were all worried. Your chest, was it?"

"It's really fine," I say, trying not to release the incipient cough knocking at my throat.

"Well, Miss Sophie will be glad. Oh, you should have seen her face when Auld James's books arrived."

Suddenly, I wonder if Sophie may have said something to Janet about me.

"How is it, with herself?" I say, tipping my head into the building.

"Oh, she's a nice lass," Janet says. "Very educated," she says, pointedly.

"Right," I say. She's correct, of course. Sophie is more educated than me. A degree from the Sorbonne, no less. But I suspect what she means is that Sophie is wealthier in affect than Janet had anticipated from a Black girl.

"She were up all last night. I saw the light on as I came downstairs," Janet says.

I feel irrationally territorial. I didn't appreciate the antlers in the hallway and the cedar smell of the Ceylonese Room and the marks on the soft wood of the kitchen table and the love of Mr. Scruff. Maybe I made a terrible mistake, suggesting Sophie come up to the castle. I don't have much, and she's still helping herself to all of it. A bleat of rage flares into my chest and I put my hand to my heart.

"They're almost like sisters," Janet is saying, as she picks up her broom again.

"Sorry, who?" She *can't* be talking about me and Sophie.

Janet tuts. "This castle and the boat." She sees the confusion on my face and continues. "That's how I like to think of it, anyhow. Both spruced up at the same time with the same money, made nice again and set off into the world."

I hadn't remembered the link between the two, and I think now of Mary standing outside of her cottage in the rain, talking about "cursed gold." The same thread of money flowing from Jamaica through the castle, through Auld James, injected back into the island. Auld James's whaling industry boosted local livelihoods in the same way the Purdies are attempting now. No wonder he's the island hero.

The carpeted corridors thicken my steps as I walk through the building towards the museum. Lady Purdie isn't at her desk, and through the windows of the reading room a light, sharp sleet is falling, like little silver quills.

In the museum, Lester is leaning in a circle of lamplight next to Sophie, inspecting the provisioner's ledger on the table. He turns, confused, as the door opens, as if he'd forgotten I ever existed. Again, a froggy lump of anger bounds inside me.

Sophie's face grows tight as I come closer to her.

"Hello," I say.

Sophie sits back, takes off her glasses. She's been working for some time; there are doe-foot indents either side of her nose. "You're better?" she says.

"All better," I say, giving her an insincere smile.

"I'm so glad." Lester squeezes me on the shoulder. "We've all been worried about you."

I have no patience for his pretence. "Do you mind, Lester, sorry, I need to talk business with young Sophie here." God, the way that sounds out of my mouth. Young Sophie. I've never said that in my life.

He looks affronted. "Of course. You ladies don't need an old fusspot like me in your way," he says, giving us a bow and shuffling out the door. "Nearly teatime anyhow."

As he closes the door, Sophie straightens the pencil next to her notepad. I resist the urge to smack it off the table. "No need to be cruel to him," she says, tightly.

I lean on the table. "Lester is a snake." I stop myself, just. After all, I don't want her to know anything is missing.

"Marta." She puts her hand to her head, groaning. "Must we begin with the paranoia already?"

I shrug. "You'll see."

She sits back and evaluates me. "Some place that you've stuck me."

"A castle not good enough for you?" I say, raising my eyebrows.

"The room I'm in." She looks upstairs, a dart, towards the door, before lowering her voice. "I would have stayed out of your way at the hotel."

"You need as much time as possible with this, surely." I gesture towards the journal.

She gives me a long, clear look, then shakes her head in exhaustion. "Did you not retrieve anything else? Just the books?"

I stare down at the table, running my knuckles over the wood grain. "Just the books. I need to do a proper site analysis survey before

I excavate anything. Once they have boatloads of tourists coming through, there won't be another chance."

Sophie chews on the earpiece of her glasses, unconvinced. "But it's almost December, you're really going down there again? Do you even have enough air for another dive? Why not just collect what they need for their museum? Heaven knows they're talking about it enough."

"Look, I have my methods," I snap. "Or do you want to do the underwater survey?"

Sophie runs her tongue around her teeth.

"Let's just do what we need to do, then we can both get out of here."

"Yes. After a lovely Christmas by myself," she says, bitterly.

"Instead of with my husband, you mean."

She gives me a perplexed look. "What are you talking about? Is there something you want to say to me, Marta?"

I walk out of the room instead of responding.

§

IN THE STILLROOM I pull the curtains and mix up my chemicals. I hadn't noticed before that of course it doesn't have a fireplace, and now the weather has turned, the room is frigidly cold. With numb fingers, I unwind the camera roll into the reel, pour in the developing fluid, rinse, then add the fixer. The negatives already look promising; I've practically memorised the contents of the cabins by now, and it doesn't look like anything else is missing. This means that since I have his cutlery, I still need to find his horn cup, the mirror, the snow goggles, the coin, and finally, the gold ring. But it could have been worse—I had been half expecting the photos to show that the rooms had been ransacked beyond repair. The relief that trickles over me is so intense that I feel light-headed enough to lie down on the floor. The stones are unforgiving, even through Alice's knitted sweater. I drag myself to sitting and go in search of Lester.

I find him in a small room off the kitchen that must once have been an office for a butler. A low, round table at his elbow holds a teapot and a plate of brittle shortbread biscuits. Above him a cuckoo clock is ticking, something more expensive and whimsical than I'd expect to see in the servants' quarters—it must have been relocated from upstairs. Mr. Scruff is sitting in the corner of the room, gnawing heavily on something with a slobbery enthusiasm.

"My dear, please." Lester motions to an ottoman on the other side of the table. "Janet will bring us another cup."

I hate him then, for volunteering Janet's labour so casually. "I'll just use this one." I draw a delftware teacup sitting on the mantelpiece towards me, but it contains some loose change and Lester's key chain. "Never mind." I take a seat on the ottoman, which slumps beneath me with a puff of dust.

I look at him for a long moment. "I know," I say.

He blinks at me, mildly.

"I went to Eddie Grimball's house and spoke to him."

There is the faintest twitch at the corner of his eyes, but he doesn't say anything. He feels confident that Eddie would never have said anything to me about Lester's role in stealing from Auld James's grave.

"I also spoke to his wife," I say. And at that, he licks his lip, a tiny tip of tongue. "She gave back the cutlery. I have it somewhere safe now."

"My dear, I don't know what you're implying," Lester says, raising his teacup.

I lean forward. "They are Auld James's things. They belong with the Purdies."

He looks at me pityingly. "Any objects found floating from the ship are, in fact, the responsibility of the agent of the receiver of the wreck. Which, if you remember, is me."

"Floating?" My voice squeaks. "Exactly how is solid silver cutlery floating around in the sea?"

He gives me an extravagant shrug. "Perhaps it was attached to a piece of cork, or inside a wooden basket of some kind."

"Attached to cor—" I force myself to take a deep breath. "Aren't you risking both of our careers? It doesn't make sense why you'd do this, the objects are worth more to you here in the museum than—"

Lester gives me a light roll of the eyes. "My position here is safe."

I stare at him. "So that's it? You have the guarantee of a job dusting Ceylonese moths, so you're fine to make a quick profit from the wreck—you don't care about anything else?"

He leans forward. "And why are you taking it so personally, my dear? What does it matter to you?"

"I'm taking the fall for your theft," I say. "That's why it matters to me."

"So you care because it will keep your job safe. Pure self-interest. Same as me."

My face is burning.

"They cast you out," he says. "We all heard what happened at the shelter, they threw you away like a piece of litter. Wash your hands of them. Put the absences down to looting and take your cheque and go back to Dundee."

"I'll report you," I say.

"If you report it now, then Little Miss Muffet next door will find out you've been covering it up for weeks," he says sweetly. "And won't that look even worse?"

Damn. I clear my throat. "Sophie already knows."

"Oh?" He sits up. "Shall I call her in now?" He reaches for the speaking tube in the corner of the room.

"Fine." I swallow. "Fine." A dark feeling bubbles in my stomach.

"Marta, with respect." He crosses his legs. "You have what, three weeks before the next ferry? Why don't you spend the time kissing your girlfriend goodbye?"

A flare of heat ignites my face. Resisting the urge to kick the ottoman, I stand and leave the room. Janet isn't in the kitchen, and through the windows on the other side of the hearth, I watch the slivers of hail thicken into snow.

22

SATURDAY, DECEMBER 1, TO
FRIDAY, DECEMBER 14, 1962

OVER THE FIRST TWO WEEKS OF DECEMBER, IT SNOWS IN frightened little flurries, laying a layer of slush on the island that churns up into brittle peaks on the paths before freezing again. Along the coast, the sea spray etches loops and weirs into the powder. Elsie is delighted. It never snows on Cairnroch, apparently. I had expected that Christmas would not mean much to the dour island elect; and I peer through the front rooms from the high street and note, with grim satisfaction, the absence of garlands or mistletoe or candles. But I was wrong. Cairnroch Islanders don't do their Christmas festivities at home, they do them in the pub. The hotel cocktail lounge starts to acquire visitors that I've never seen before. Irenes drinking shandies, Jocks with whisky. Then at ten, Auld James's whisky comes out and people begin rounds of toasts to Auld James, to the fishermen, the miners, the Cailleach herself. Sometimes, Alice and Cook even perform recitals at the piano, mainly wartime songs. It's not meant to include me, so I don't try to be included. I move between my room and Elsie's room and smoke cigarettes down to the filter. The date of my final dive is set: Saturday, December 22. I had to choose the last possible day before the ferry goes out so that I can leave swiftly after my disgrace. I will have to make a good show of looking surprised and shocked when I surface. Perhaps I should invite one of the Purdies to come out on Colin's boat, to avoid having to break the news later. I thought this year was my lowest point, but what will 1963 look like for me? I haven't wanted to truly imagine it until now. Back to the soot-crusted windows of the bedsit, eking out the shillings into the metre, waiting for my final paycheque, for the scandal of my situation to spread among my colleagues. What do divorced brown women do to survive? I can't type, I can't sew or cook. I dream of crawling through a maze of mouldering rubbish in my parents' flat, my knees sinking through slimy floors oozing with rot. Outside, a nuclear flash that bleaches the windows white.

§

ON FRIDAY THE FOURTEENTH, after Elsie's shift, the door to her room opens and she tiptoes in, creeping over to the sink to wash her face. I sit up in bed.

"Sorry, I was trying not to wake you."

"I wasn't really sleeping."

"Oh, Marta, you're still not well, you need your rest," Elsie says.

"Lester knows about us." I'd not intended to mention it to her at all, but I've been tossing in the sheets for hours, building up more and more frustration at every single person on Cairnroch Island. Including myself.

She stops lathering for a moment. "What did he say?"

"It was a couple of weeks ago, but I didn't want to worry you. He mentioned something about you being my girlfriend."

She shrugs. "At least he doesn't think we're being casual," and she raises her eyebrows at me, mischievously.

I'm annoyed instead of reassured by her dismissal. "Shouldn't you be worried?"

She runs the tap and splashes water on her face. "It rather sounds as if you'd *prefer* me to be worried."

"He's evil," I say. "Who knows what he could do."

Elsie dabs her face on the towel. "Trust me, not a single person here has enough imagination to think you and me are having sex. According to the minister, marriage is a contract between God and the elect. No frilly stuff."

I scuff my feet backwards and forward between the bedsheets. I'm not sure what kind of reaction I was aiming for, but this isn't it. Part of me was hoping that Elsie would be scared, that I would shock her into solving my generalised growing panic. "I'll be gone on the twenty-sixth," I say. "Doesn't that make you sad?"

"But you're coming back," Elsie says, smiling as she jumps into bed with me. "Next summer, you'll be coming back to do more work on the ship." She lays her cold hands on my stomach, and I squeeze them between mine to warm them up.

I had almost forgotten about that lie. I say nothing.

Her eyes search my face, and then she turns over in the sheet. "I knew it."

"What did you know?" I raise myself on one elbow.

"It wasn't true. I knew it."

"It's not . . ." I start, then I trail off. "Why *would* they have me back? I'm going down there next week to pretend to collect things that have already gone. No one will hire me again after this. And after the Purdies have paid for my time, and for Sophie's. There will be nothing to show for it."

"Oh, don't get me started on Sophie," she says. "Since you're so keen on keeping me and her apart, let's not even bother with her." The electric fire pings.

I put a hand on her arm. "It's not—"

"Marta, I've had a long day. I think you should go sleep in your own bed." Elsie rolls away from my touch, pulling the blanket up around her shoulders.

I think about apologising, but instead I get up and dress hastily in the dark, feeling a glum kind of victory that I provoked her into rejecting me before we have to qualify our goodbyes.

LATITUDE 81°, 01' N, LONGITUDE 65°, 33' W

Ice set fast around ship. Fired the engines day and night for four days but no movement. Ordered rudder and . . . raised. Enough provisions for a year with tinned stores and hard biscuit pemmican. Interrupted insubordinate discushions in the saloon, men whisper we should have turned back at 72° and not proceeded through the straits in search of further recruits. I ordered any with treason on his lips would have no melted snow to drink. Strange sounds from the ice as if screams from Huski village, but that is empty now.

23

SATURDAY, DECEMBER 15, TO MONDAY, DECEMBER 24, 1962

THE SNOW SUGARS, THEN SETTLES. THE SLENDER TREES THAT struggle up the hill towards the castle are shrouded in icicles; confused sheep call from snow-clogged fields. The small lane that leads to the high street becomes impassable; as soon as the bellboys dig channels away from the hotel doors, they collapse in on themselves in slurries of wet powder.

By the Friday before my final dive, the waves nudging against the sandy beach are syrupy with glitter, and the lightship bell tolls faintly through the falling snow. Visibility is so poor that even men who have fished here for their whole lives are unable to leave the harbour. I join the fishermen who are pacing the waterfront, chewing on the ends of pipes sizzling from snowflakes. The air is woollen, heavy with the catmint smell of deep winter.

It's obvious there will be no way for me to get back down to the ship before I leave.

When it truly hits me, I'm overcome with relief. Conditions are too terrible; the Purdies can't argue with the weather. I'll get on the

Boxing Day ferry and leave it all behind me. Yes, I'll get a smack on the knuckles for not retrieving their museum objects earlier, but no one will find out anything is missing, at least not until next spring. And by then, it won't be my fault. The snow has released me. In a flash of exultation I scrape a handful from the bank beside the beach and bring it to my lips. It tastes like coal fire, like gasoline. I put the whole bitter scoop into my mouth.

The sun sets at three thirty these days, but the snow retains the last echoes of light until five, cradling it around the hotel. It's a small mercy because the wiring is increasingly erratic, and the longer I can wait before switching on the lights, the better. Stubbornly avoiding Elsie, I stick to my room, smoking in bed, overlooked by the watchful eye of HMS *Deliverance* in her icy noose. Balanced on my lap is the third draft of my explanation letter to the Purdies. The phone lines are down, so I can't call them. And while I probably *could* climb the hill up to the castle in the snow, a letter left behind for someone else to deal with is far easier. The coward's retreat. A drop of cigarette ash falls on the paper and I rub it with my thumb. I've decided not to apologise, since that might make it seem as if I had something to apologise for. Instead, I'm aiming for a clinical, slightly officious tone: *Regrettably the inclement weather has made another dive impossible at this time, so final retrieval will have to be revisited by our team at a future date.* Around me, the hotel creaks from the shifts in temperature, the chimneys shifting against the cold. The creak eases off, returns, eases, and I realise that the creaks are regular. Footsteps. I put the lid on my pen. The footsteps are coming from overhead. The room above mine.

As quietly as possible, I close my door, creep along the squeaky corridor, and climb the stairs up to the third floor. From the top of the corridor, I spot the whirl of a cherry-pink pinafore at the far end. It's Alice. She's withdrawing from the room above mine, locking the door with a key on her chain. When she turns, her face is pale.

"Alice?"

She spins towards the stairs and shrieks, a hand to her chest.

"Sorry, I didn't mean to scare you."

"Oh, it's not you, hen," Alice says, with a fraction of a glance at the room behind her. She straightens her pinafore. "Anything I can get you?"

I rub one stockinged foot against the other. The carpets are so cold they feel wet underfoot. "What do you mean, it's not me?"

"Oh, don't give me any mind," Alice says. Her eyes slide over the key in her hand, down to the floor, to a scuff on the banister. "Nothing to worry yourself about."

Immediately I feel there is something to worry myself about. "Mice?" I offer.

Alice laughs. "Bless you, no, not mice. Well, if there are any mice, you didn't hear it from me."

I look along the length of the third-floor corridor. It's dank smelling, the carpets less worn here than they are in the lobby, the teal colour bright and nautical. I don't know why I never thought of it before: that evening I spent locked in the linen cupboard, the footsteps that I heard. What if it wasn't from my room but the room above? Truthfully, I had almost forgotten the third floor of the hotel even existed. "Are these all abandoned rooms?"

Alice approaches the staircase and, with a groan, takes a seat on the top stair. I sit next to her as she rubs her left knee absent-mindedly. "It makes more sense to put guests downstairs. We don't get many these days, and it means less climbing."

Overhead, the chandelier flickers.

There can't be much housekeeping up here if all the rooms are abandoned. Alice is still rubbing her knee, her lips pinched. Even though she seems hale and hearty, she must be at least seventy. How much longer can she really keep working such a physically demanding job? We spent only one summer in Latakia when I was around five, before Mum's accident meant she hardly left the house, never mind travelled on an airplane. I remember very little of my grandmother—I have impressions of the satiny softness of the crepey skin on her arms, a pair of heavy silver earrings I liked to weigh in my hands. I picture my own mother scrubbing strangers' toilets well into her seventies and try to ignore the flutter of guilt at the thought that I am about to abandon Alice and the hotel without fulfilling my end of the promise.

"Alice, have you ever heard footsteps in the hotel when no one is here?"

Her expression tightens. "Don't you go listening to Flora's stories."

Prickles run over my scalp. "What kind of stories does Flora have?"

"Just blether," Alice says, with an unconvincing scoff. "Bless her daft wee head."

"Are there stories about the hotel? I never heard any."

Alice sighs. "This used to be where Auld James's schoolhouse stood, before they built the hotel. Well, everyone's schoolhouse, I suppose."

"Oh. Wouldn't he have had a tutor at the castle?"

"Aye, you'd think so. But Auld James was the youngest of the Purdie sons. The least favoured. They used to have a saying about sons: One for the land, one for the infantry, and one for the Lord."

"And Auld James was for the Lord? I thought he was for whaling."

"There's nothing written down to say you can't be both," she says defensively. "Well, even as a wee boy, he was all about the common man. Insisted on being among the people. So the Purdies sent him down here to the village for his schooling. One day there was a squabble in the schoolhouse, him and a boy from the village had a confrontation. In the scuffle Auld James lost one of his wisdom teeth. They say he buried it down under the schoolyard rather than tell on the boy."

"Children don't have wisdom teeth," I say, before I can stop myself.

Alice waves her hand. "Well Auld James was born with his. You haven't heard the song?"

I shake my head, picturing the wisdom tooth of Captain James Purdie nestled snugly underneath the floorboards of the hotel. I don't recall any obviously missing teeth when I collected his remains, but it wasn't my main worry at the time.

"Anyhow, when they built the hotel it was tough work to dig deep in this soil, and they didn't find any teeth. But still, that's the story."

"What does a tooth have to do with footsteps?"

Alice laughs, and for a moment she reminds me of Elsie, stinging my heart. "Even a saint might come back to collect all their wisdom before Judgement Day."

I sit with this. "So people around here believe in Auld James's ghost? It seems like it wouldn't fit with what the minister has to say about salvation."

"The Lord gives the gift of faith to his saints," she says, cryptically.

I think of how the stone kirk up on the hill separates the world into pure and evil, saved and damned. That maybe it's squeezed any experience that falls in between into places so crooked that they have no choice but to fester. "But surely if you think he was elect, then it doesn't make sense that he'd be lingering—"

Alice draws her breath in through her teeth, interrupting me. It's a frustrated sound, like she is instructing a poorly trained dog. "There's lots of things that don't make sense in this world."

This feels like a grannyish way of telling me to stop being so literal. I picture Mary's face as she passed over Auld James's dancing cutlery. Could I have misunderstood what has been happening on Cairnroch? That I *did* hear something here, feel something, see something, down in the ship. But the answer isn't Lewis; it's much more obvious. The captain himself. I feel as if an icy pebble of hail is sliding down the back of my neck. "It would be a good omen though, wouldn't it? Being visited by Auld James?" As soon as I say the words aloud, I regret them. I've been trying to put all idea of spectres out of my mind. But that last dive down to the ship, the grip on the books in the darkness. It felt like the pull of something unhappy, unsettled. If Auld James truly were slinking around among the living, of course he would choose me to watch, judge, patrol. I cut a path into his grave. The word "defile" comes to my mind. My stomach churns acid into the base of my throat.

Alice cracks her knuckles. "Auld James is part of us, and we're part of him. Sightings of him are supposed to be a herald, a warning sign, like that lightship out there. What you make of the sign is up to you."

"I never heard anyone say anything," I say weakly.

"Oh, there's plenty around here who have happened on the know of a person on a dark road. Or seen an event happening before it does. These hills are old, they have their old ways. There's just things that you don't go around talking about."

"What kind of things?"

"The sort of things you turn the key on," Alice says, "and you don't look back."

LATITUDE 81°, 01' N, LONGITUDE 65°, 33' W

Bitterly cold . . . crew plagued by agueish headaches and tempers raised . . . to stand on one leg for an hour and afterwards he did regret his actions. Gilchrist talks an awful muttering about visitation from the devil and it can be heard throughout the ship. Ordered him to camp on the ice overnight but the crew did protest they heard his footsteps walking around the vessel scraping at portholes. Later he was discovered asleep in the coal store and the men were much confused by the scraping.

24

TUESDAY, DECEMBER 25, 1962

ON CHRISTMAS MORNING I WAKE UP TO A PLUSH CARPET OF snow so white that it makes my eyes ache. At first, it doesn't look too deep. But when I come down for breakfast, Cook is out in the little terrace behind the old ballroom, gawping at how it reaches his knees. I've never seen so much snow in one place in my life. The temperature drops over the morning. It sinks even lower, until it's ten below freezing. Cook and Mr. Tibalt, heading home for the holidays, are given a ceremonial farewell at the front steps of the hotel, and although Cook refuses to shake my hand goodbye, he makes eye contact with me, at least. Mr. Tibalt makes me promise to keep in touch, and I agree, even though I fully intend to try my best to forget that Cairnroch exists the moment I leave this island.

By midmorning, Francis, Mrs. Eleanor, and I are in the reading room, trying to find a card game that won't scandalise Mrs. Eleanor. I'm bored with them both and they're bored of each other. The fire is roaring and we are all heaped with blankets, but it's impossible to keep warm without jiggling.

The lights flicker overhead, and Mrs. Eleanor looks up, surprised.

"They were doing that yesterday," I say.

Then the lights fall, a dim, ominous buzzing resonates through the building, before flickering back up to full power. God, I hate Christmas. It has always felt like an in-between time, neither celebration or punishment. Just a stretch with nothing to fill it except creeping thoughts of how much better things should be. When we were children, Jenine and I would be forced to spend at least a week in the flat, scratching our chilblains and eking out treacly welfare orange juice and stale biscuits, too cold to loiter anywhere outside, our friends snug in their own intimacies. My mother's guttering candles, my father's rosary clicking. Alex and I had that in common, a collective nursery of solemn yuletide rituals.

The last Christmas Alex and I spent together, he'd forgone his usual visit to his parents, and I was relieved that we'd both be spared the long church service and the customary fast. It was going to be just the two of us—a chance for us to start making our own traditions. Around noon on Christmas Eve he claimed that he was going out for messages in town, but I suspected he'd forgotten to buy me a present, so I didn't press him. I lit the oven and set a chicken to roast and deliberately didn't wear stockings under my skirt. But then four came and went and six came and went. I ate the overcooked meat by myself, standing over the stove, falling asleep eventually on the sofa.

When Alex came in close to eleven, I startled up from the cushions.

"What are you doing on the sofa?" he said, fumbling over his shoelaces.

I felt my eyes blazing. "Waiting for you! Where have you been?"

He chuckled, then looked affronted. "You don't really care?"

"I cooked," I say, my indignation faltering under his disdain. "It's Christmas Eve."

"But we're not those people," he said, sitting beside me on the sofa. "We're not suburban."

I stared at him. "What kind of people are we then?"

He laughed. "We're fun." He pulled me towards him. I could smell lager and menthol cigarettes on his breath.

"This isn't fun." I pushed him off. "I'm not having fun." It was as if I had been running against a strong wind and all my energy was expended. I'd been worrying so much about him having fun in our marriage that I'd forgotten to check if I was.

He turned his head aside, disappointed. "Bloody hell, Marta, don't turn this into a fight."

This made me prickle with suspicion. "What were you doing all this time, anyway?"

He shrugged. "I bumped into Sam and that crowd."

"Which crowd?"

"You don't know them. Friends from school."

"Friends from school that I don't know? Like who?" I sat up now, alert. "Women?"

He sighed. "Don't be like this, Marta."

"You're not answering me."

"It's insulting, that's why."

"It's insulting to answer questions from your own wife about where you've been on Christmas Eve?" I threw my book in his direction, only intending to emphasise my point, but it clipped my wineglass on the table. The glass shattered onto the floor, dripping red wine through the floorboards. I saw immediately that I'd gone too far, been too dramatic, too intense, but I was scared that if I relented, I would lose the righteousness I'd acquired a moment ago, when he was the evasive husband and I was the wife waiting at home for him with a chicken roasting in the oven.

He looked at the smashed glass. "You tidy it away this time," he said, standing up. "I'm tired of cleaning up your mess."

It frightened me more, then, that he wouldn't argue with me. I screamed something after him, I don't know what. The front door slammed behind him, and the woman in the flat next door knocked on the wall like she always did when the door slammed. He had not come back by Christmas morning, and I spent it alone in the flat, smoking in the chair, crouched, like a gnome. I couldn't believe he would leave me alone on Christmas Day. I decided if he didn't come back by noon, I'd leave him, go somewhere, so that when he returned there would be nobody in the flat and he'd be frightened. But I didn't leave, and by three he still hadn't arrived. I felt frantic, convincing myself that I wasn't afraid he'd left me, no, I was a normal person waiting for my normal husband with a normal amount of concern.

It was just after four when I heard his footsteps in the corridor. "Trick or treat," he said, into the keyhole. When I opened the door, he was smiling, pleased with himself, wearing a cheap paper hat. I lost my nerve to hate him. He kissed me, hard. "Look what I have," he said, sliding a box of tangerines onto the table. As he peeled them I ate one after another.

§

FOR CHRISTMAS LUNCH in the hotel, Mrs. Eleanor, Francis, and I sit with Alice, Elsie, and Flora in the dining room and eat the chicken and potatoes that Cook left for us. We pull Christmas crackers and afterwards nibble on cold fruitcake doused in brandy with a slice of cheese on the side. I keep trying to make eye contact with Elsie, but she is deliberately not looking at me. I suppose it makes things easier, with me leaving. She never even asked about my final dive.

After lunch, Alice tries to lead us in some Christmas carols, but the mood is glum. Flora seems ill at ease in our company, Francis is too embarrassed, and Mrs. Eleanor is too agitated on account of there being such a poorly attended service at the church. It's difficult to strike up merriment. The lights flicker on and off. The wind is cloyed with snow and it freezes mangled shapes on the edge of the roof that cast fantastical shadows in the low light. As we pass around a tin of brazil nuts left over from Halloween, the gears of the lift begin creaking down through the building. I don't think anything of it until Alice raises her head, and I see her catching Flora's eye. Then I realise. Who is in the lift? There are only the six of us left in the hotel. The lift grinds slowly towards the ground floor and there is a sickening lump in my chest as we all pause, waiting for the doors to cough open, none of us wanting to admit that it's really happening. There is the ping of the bell and the doors open. Nobody moves. Nobody breathes. I can't help it. I put my head around into the empty corridor. Francis starts laughing, a little nervously. I stand up to get a better look. The lift doors close again, and up it goes into the building, the dial on the top of the mechanism resting on the second floor. My room. I think of that sharp, proprietorial grip in the watery darkness. The footsteps overhead in the shuttered-up room.

"Whisky?" I say.

Elsie doesn't respond to me, but she does nip down to the bar and bring back another bottle of Auld James's whisky, and we all pour generous slugs into our glasses.

By seven my nerves are on edge, despite the whisky. I can't bear listening to the lift moving endlessly up and down through the building. I'm going to go to bed, pull the blankets over me, and wait for the morning.

"My last night here," I say, standing up. "It's been a pleasure." I don't even attempt to make it sound convincing.

Francis frowns. "What do you mean, your last night?"

"Mainland ferry tomorrow," I say.

Everyone in the room looks at one another. It's the same look we've all been exchanging since the lift started plunging of its own accord. Like nobody wants to say the bad part out loud.

"Marta, hen," Alice says. "I doubt the ferry will be running tomorrow."

"Or this week," Francis adds, with a scoff. "Or this year."

"There's only six days left in the year," Mrs. Eleanor scolds. "No need to be dramatic."

"But," I object, "the winds aren't that high."

"It's not just the winds, Marta," Alice says, kindly. "They can't see anything for all this snow. You must have realised. If Colin can't take you out, they won't be able to come in."

I let the reading room door swing behind me, and I'm not even up the first few steps before I'm crying in earnest. Of course, I knew already. The soupy slush of the harbour, the hushed tones of the lightship bell. No way in, no way out. Not a reprieve but incarceration. In my room I cry for being stuck here longer. I cry for Lewis who's dead and Alex who doesn't love me and Elsie who isn't talking to me and for myself. Eventually I'm spent from crying, and I climb into the blankets, my face raw, and watch the falling needles of ice.

25

WEDNESDAY, DECEMBER 26, TO MONDAY, DECEMBER 31, 1962

OVER THE NEXT FIVE DAYS, THE TEMPERATURE LINGERS around twelve below zero. It becomes too cold even for snow. I sit in my room, watching the surf along the coast congealing into a slurry. The phone lines are still down, but I have to assume that Sophie has also understood she's not going anywhere, and that we will both be trapped here indefinitely.

The night before Hogmanay I shiver under my blankets, watching the coal fire smudge thumbprints of meagre light across the walls. It takes a few moments for me to realise that there is a movement near the desk, the curtains stirring from the breeze. But no, the stirring is tracking across the wall, rippling through the pattern of the wallpaper. I raise myself on my elbows. Some kind of air bubble maybe, caused by the warmth of the fire meeting the cold air. It loiters, that's the only word for it, in the corner of the room by the door, directly opposite my bed. Somehow I know that whatever it is, it is watching me. I can't move, can barely breathe. The ripple collects, warps, settles into the shape of a figure. A man. There, in the corner of the room, crouching. A jolt of the bed wakes me and only then do I realise I must have been asleep. Gasping, I scramble for the light switch. There's no bubble in the wallpaper, no rippling in the pattern. Only a nightmare. A tiny blade of icy air from the window next to my bed is parting my hair and the nape of my neck; maybe that's what prompted the bad dream. Bunching all the sheets around my knees, I wait for my heart to stop knocking at my chest. My eyes fall on the painting of HMS *Deliverance* above my bed. Trapped, like me, by the ice. Except Auld James was a hero, beloved by his community, a leader to his crew. To him, I would seem unworthy of even touching his remains. Tainted. I stare at the painting for so long that the flag on the mizzenmast looks as if it's rippling. Even though I know, rationally, that it's a painting, that nobody is actually inside the ship, I reach up and unhook the painting from the wall and slide it underneath my bed.

As soon as day breaks, I tiptoe along the corridor to Elsie's room. She grumbles at my knock, and I open the door a crack.

"Oh." Elsie stirs from the pillows. "Is everything all right?"

"It's snowing," I say. "I thought you might like to see it." I invite myself into her room and pull open her curtains. The air is swollen with snow, a cascading thicket that falls so quickly it's impossible to rest your eyes on it.

"Oh my God." She sits up in her bed and rubs her face. "Am I dreaming?"

I shake my head. But I understand how she feels; the days have been so icy and so similar, and this sudden onslaught of snow feels unreal.

"It's not normal, this weather," she says, softly.

"I know."

She turns to look at me. "What do you think it means?"

"I don't think it means anything."

Elsie chews her lip. "It's not going to be like this forever, is it?"

I laugh, the sound surprising me. "Of course not."

"What if—" She stops herself.

"Go on."

She hugs her knees to her chest. "What if there *was* a missile and we didn't know because the radio's been down? And now everyone out there in the rest of the world is dead, and this climate is the result of a bomb in the atmosphere, and we will all just have to wait and die?"

"Jesus, Els."

"Have you read the novel *On the Beach*?"

I shake my head. "Not much of a fiction reader, sorry."

She crosses her legs. "There was a picture too? Anyway, it came out a few years ago, it's set in Australia in 1963, and it's about these families after the nuclear war. The war's already happened and everyone else in the world is dead. But this town in Australia has no choice but to get on with things, knowing there's nothing they can do, that they just have to wait to all get poisoned and die. And with my parents being there—" She breaks off, gripping my wrist. "Don't read it."

I take her hand in mine and squeeze it. "Thanks for the warning." I sit on the edge of the bed and work the squeeze up her arm, her shoulder, testing, until she relaxes into my embrace. "I'm sorry," I say. "I should have tried to make things right between us sooner."

"You don't want to get involved in anything serious, is that it?"

"Oh, it's not that." I realise the words are true as I say them. It feels as if the string attaching me to Alex has been letting out and letting out, and with enough concentration, I could allow it to slide away. But am I crawling to Elsie's bedside now because I need her, or because I need someone, anyone? I'm not certain that even I know. "I panicked. Sophie . . ." I begin.

I can feel her waiting for me to finish the sentence.

"Sophie is Alex's girlfriend. My boss. She doesn't like me much. I don't know why I didn't tell you before. I suppose I was embarrassed. I wanted you to think well of me."

"And it worked, did it?"

I laugh, bitterly. "I'd say it worked splendidly."

She watches me with an evaluative expression. The skin around her eyes is chapped; I wonder if she has been crying, or if she's just cold-burned.

"The snow is just snow, Els. Neither of us are used to this much time indoors, that's all. Don't read any more books about atomic bombs."

She takes a deep breath. "Let's go join the others and start drinking. It's Hogmanay, after all."

§

DOWNSTAIRS, ALICE IS DETERMINED to complete the ritual Hogmanay cleaning, and she arms us all with brushes and pans and cloths, and we spend the afternoon keeping ourselves warm with furious rubbing and polishing and scrubbing. Dinner is soup coaxed from melted snow and some wilted carrots that Flora boils on the kitchen coal fire. We open a box of shortbread afterwards, though, and distribute plenty of Auld James's whisky. It's a poor mimic of Hogmanay festivity, and I can't help but think wistfully of the mounds of black bun laid out at the Purdies' Samhain party. No doubt Sophie is feasting from the Purdies' stores up there right now.

Right before midnight there is some argument about whether to open the windows, the traditional way to let the old year out and welcome the new one in. In the end, Alice just begins barking orders, and we all follow her role as commander of Hogmanay. We're told, three seconds of air, no more, no less. I am assigned to the window above the bar, Elsie to the front door, Francis to the side door, and Alice herself takes the reading room windows. We run to our stations as Flora and Mrs. Eleanor count in the new year. Then we cheer and brace ourselves for the onslaught of ice. None of the windows have been open since the cold snap, and I hear the echo of frustrated laughter as we all struggle to wrench them up against the frost. Finally, I wriggle the bar window up just enough that a wedge of freezing air pierces the room, stirring the coals in the entranceway fireplace. The snow looks beautiful in the dim candlelight across the front garden; all glisten and glitter. As my eyes adjust to the lumps of smothered heather, I notice something: There are dents in the snow along the path.

Elsie pulls open one of the front doors with a groan. "One, two," she counts, but I run to stop her from closing the door, swinging it open farther.

"Good grief, it's baltic," Francis shouts, from the corridor.

Elsie wrestles with me. "Marta, don't let the snow in.".

But I don't care about the snow piling now through the open doorway. Ahead of us there are clear footsteps leading up to the front doors, and none that lead away.

LATITUDE 81°, 01' N, LONGITUDE 65°, 33' W

... abominable lustful acts ... passions inflamed ... close quarters without reprieve. . . . This talk of the visitor is a product of judgement clouded by feeble mindedness. Men report hearing humming music from crows nest but repeatedly it has proven to be empty.

26

SATURDAY, JANUARY 5, TO
SUNDAY, JANUARY 6, 1963

THE SNOW KEEPS SNOWING, SEETHING, FOAMY THICKETS OF snow. By the fifth of January it's six feet high, and both the front and the side doors are sealed with the pressure. We try to unblock the side door by pouring melted hot snow from the window above it, but it only collapses an arc of snow into a perilous, glossy cement. The hotel begins to produce clicking sounds, peculiar breathy noises as snow sloughs from the roof, tumbles suddenly onto gutters. Alice and Elsie take a detailed inventory of the hotel store cupboards, and we plan in earnest. The coal store is more than generous but has already been diminished, and we decide to prioritise the reading room fire and the kitchen fire, and to block off the other fireplaces around the hotel, closing the dining room completely. Unused coals from the rooms of the usual hotel staff will have to be collected and redistributed. The larder is well stocked: Island living demands preparedness, even at the best of times. Over Alice's shoulder I spot shelves of tinned salmon and ox tongue, cans of kidney soup, sacks of sultanas and haricot beans, tins of custard and evaporated milk, sour apples wrapped in newspaper, jars of pickled eggs. Flora shoos me away so "the real women" can make a meal plan. I try not to overthink what she means by that. Alice and Flora decide to be conservative to save what we can, in case the winter stretches for even longer, but it's hard to stay warm without proper meals. We are all famished each evening, despite not having done much more than sit together and shiver. We divide into pairs—Mrs. Eleanor and Francis, Alice and Flora, and me and Elsie—and undertake cold-proofing the building. We gather old newspapers and sackcloth and bedding and towels and rags, and unlock the empty rooms to collect any wood, coal, newspapers. Of course I'd known that it was only us six left in the hotel, but it is different to unlock empty room after empty room and fully realise how many dark, unused spaces are quietly resting in the building. We check for leaks, pad the windows, plug any cracks where the cold could creep in. The work keeps us warm at least, although it doesn't help to assuage our hunger pangs, and even I begin to feel sorry for Francis, who takes on something of a pained look each night, despite an extra bowl of snow-melted soup. As with any marooned community, our conversations turn to comfort, to warmth, and to food.

On Sunday morning Elsie and I are sitting on the landing on the third floor of the hotel, rolling towels to be stuffed under the door of room 16. She is telling me about her favourite sweeties growing up: cinder toffee and Alice's homemade tablet.

"We weren't allowed sweeties," I say, eventually. "There was a dried apricot leather that my grandmother would send over from Syria. You're supposed to turn it into juice—but we chewed it dry. It was very sugary, though it gave us both runny tummies." I laugh, telling her the story of Jenine's devastation when the traitorous sweeties turned on her. "That was before," I say, then catch myself.

"Before?" Elsie says, companionably.

"Nothing," I say, squeezing the towel into a sausage and stuffing it under the door of room 16. The silence between us is pointed; I know that she is waiting for me to continue. We shift along to the end of the corridor, to room 15. As Elsie unlocks the door, I realise that it is the room directly above mine. The same room that I saw Alice turning the key on just before Christmas. The room is papered with pink wallpaper decorated with little red roses, the furniture shrouded in dust sheets. No one has been assigned this room for over a year, according to Elsie, and the air feels stale. The windows have already been stuffed with old newspaper, and I step across the boards experimentally, wondering if I really would be able to hear the creaks from two floors down.

Elsie peers hopefully into the empty grate, and I cross to the sink, where an unwrapped tablet of hotel soap is sitting next to a glass resting on a paper doily. I add the soap to our collection, since the hotel's supply is still running low from the mysterious disappearances around the missile crisis. There's a crocheted blanket over the back of the chairs that neither of us recognises, but Elsie hangs it over the crook of her arm.

"Are there really stories about the hotel?" I say, to the roses in the wallpaper.

Elsie motions for me to come to the other side of the door and turns the lock. "What do you mean?"

"I saw your granny up here a couple of weeks ago. I thought I heard footsteps. I think she heard them too."

Elsie laughs. "Not that old tale about the wisdom tooth. Half the island has a story like that. It's a wonder he had any teeth left."

We sit cross-legged on the carpet and roll another towel to stuff under the door.

"My mum had a sort of accident," I say, after a moment. "I must have been about six, Jenine eight. Mum was frightened to leave the house after that." It sounds so simple, as I say it. I sit back, stunned at how much sense it makes, when I explain it in that way. It doesn't capture all the funereal uncertainty of the following months. The sense that something irrevocable had happened and none of us would be safe again.

"A car accident?"

I shake my head. "A deliberate injury. From a total stranger. We never even found out who he was." The shuffle of my mother's rosary, her entreaties for forgiveness on his behalf. The energy she expended on absolution for this man; a nobody, a shadow. As if she could cleanse us all and undo the damage, all by herself.

Elsie nods, concentrating on the towel. She seems to know that if she urges me on, I won't be able to continue.

"Mum was unsettled. Soon after that she started keeping hold of things. Storing things."

Elsie makes an understanding noise.

"But not useful things, not . . ." I cast around for items that people usually consider useful. "Maps." My face stings; that's not right at all. "No, that's a silly example. What's something useful?"

"Candles?" Elsie offers. "Matches? Batteries. Toilet paper. Firewood."

"Right, nothing useful," I say. "Well, I suppose they were once useful. Burned candles, for example." I picture them now, their gruesome sooty pistils, the way the waxy tops of the candles would become sticky with dust and oil that had settled from the stove. "Or empty Izal toilet paper boxes. Or used-up batteries."

I feel so grateful that Elsie's expression is neutral. That she's not laughing or looking disgusted. "And you couldn't just throw the useless things away?"

I shake my head. "We did in the beginning. My dad became frustrated now and then, and we'd cull it all. But it made her so upset. Distraught. And in the end, I suppose we got used to the collecting. It seemed . . ." I stop. It never felt normal. I can recall even now the terror of an unexpected ring at the doorbell, the fear that somebody might have taken it upon themselves to call in. That the gas and electric men would come by. That the postman might see. The milkman. The worry at school that we smelled, that the tin baths in front of the fire weren't enough to wash away the scent of mildewing rubbish. The shame of having to keep going to school for hot dinners all through the holidays, because the kitchen stove was unreachable. "We didn't talk about it," I say, eventually.

"I'm sorry," Elsie says. "That sounds like a difficult way to grow up."

"Thanks," I say. Alex never liked me talking about my upbringing; I think it depressed him, and his reaction was always to hurry me on so that he didn't have to dwell on it too much. I trace my fingertips through the carpet, making nonsense shapes in the weft. "I send money, but I've only been back to visit them once since I left home."

That was after that weekend with Lewis. It feels like a dark spell, those ten days. "My sister doesn't go back there either. That flat, it makes me feel . . ." An involuntary shudder runs through me as I think of it. "It makes me pity them and hate them at the same time."

Elsie nods. A low wind whistles quietly along the hallway.

"I think about it often, the flat. As a child, I thought it was my fault. That there was something wrong that I did." I pause.

The distinct sound of a single glass shattering echoes from inside room 15.

Elsie and I look at each other; a tingle runs along my scalp. She moves to stand up and I put a hand out to restrain her. "No, don't," I say.

She shakes me off. "Something broke."

I tug her arm back. "Please."

She's laughing. "Marta, come along, I can't leave broken glass in there for someone else to clean up." She unlocks the door. I climb to my feet, my every nerve twitching.

The pink room is gloomy with no natural light, the rosiness of the walls lending a sickly, uterine sheen to Elsie's reflection in the mirror. A good half a foot from the sink, the glass that was sitting on the ledge is now smashed on the floor.

"I'll need to get a brush," Elsie says, wrinkling her nose as she bends down for the largest shards.

"Don't touch it!" I yelp.

Elsie turns her head. "I do this a hundred times a week." She stops, holding a large shard in her palm, then puts it down. "Whatever is wrong?"

"How could that have fallen? There's no breeze—the windows are stuffed up."

Elsie shrugs. "It must have toppled over."

"No, I just saw it, steady and sound. See, the paper doily is still just where it was, in the middle."

"Perhaps you brushed against it when you picked up the soap?"

I'm shaking my head. All I can think is that it looks as if it has been thrown. Deliberately. I take a step back, out of the doorway.

Elsie's smile falters. "Do you know how they make glass?"

"Of course I know," I snap, before catching myself. "Sorry, yes, I know."

"Well then, there was probably a fault in the glass and the cold set it off and it smashed."

I grip my elbows. I picture the footsteps in the snow leading up to the doorstep, think of the first-footing tradition that the first person over your threshold on Hogmanay should be a dark-haired man, bearing gifts. What gift would Auld James bring me? Judgement. Condemnation.

"You know those weren't footprints, don't you?" Elsie says, as if she's reading my mind. She kneels and collects the largest shard of glass in her palm. "A mouse or an animal, jumping through the snow. It'll be madness out there for the poor things," she says. "Nothing to eat or drink."

I nod, but I'm not really listening. All I can think is that there is somebody else here, listening to everything that we say.

§

WE GATHER ROUND the table in the reading room later for something approaching a Sunday dinner. The candles probe jabs of light across the ceiling, and I'm alert to every scrape of every spoon. After eating, we move closer to the fire. Flora takes the bowls to the kitchen to wash them out with snow, and when she returns, we roll towels under the door to seal in as much heat as possible. We take turns reading from a book of Walter Scott's collected works, but I can't stop thinking of the glass, imploding inside a locked room.

"Wait," I interrupt Francis during *The Lord of the Isles*. "Do you hear that?"

The room falls silent, except for the glugging sound of the fire.

Francis shrugs and continues. But I hear the noise again, a knocking sound. "There it is again," I say.

He shoots me a withering look.

There is silence once more as everyone humours me. A piece of coal shifts in the grate. "There you go, it's the fire," Elsie says. "Carry on, Francis."

He takes a breath, but I know what I heard. "No, it's not, listen, it's like a knocking."

They exchange a slightly annoyed, slightly concerned look.

"It's probably the wind," Elsie whispers, patting me on the arm.

"I know what the wind sounds like in this miserable place by now. It's knocking. Somebody knocking."

Just then, a loud tap comes on the outside of the reading room window. Everyone screams, including me. I can't move, I feel rooted with horror as Elsie pulls back the curtain and rustles a gap in the newspaper.

"Who's there?"

"I don't know," Elsie says.

The room starts to spin; I have to hold on to the back of Mrs. Eleanor's armchair to steady myself.

"I think it's a woman," she says. "Come, let's open the door. She'll be frozen to death."

But of course, the door won't open. It's frozen shut, the ice too impacted. "Hold on," Elsie shouts, through the door. "We can't open it, come round, we'll have to try the window."

Between Elsie, Flora, and Francis, they shake the window next to the bar back and forth in the frame until it gives way with a pop and they can push it farther up. The bundle of clothes slowly shimmies in and drops, with a slop of wet snow, onto the leather booth.

"Thank you!" she says.

I take a step forward. "Sophie?"

She pulls off her hat and hood. "Oh my gosh, it's so warm in here," she says. She looks thinner than she did when I last saw her.

"Well, I never," Alice says.

In the corner of my vision, I can feel Elsie looking at me. "This is Sophie Ndiaye," I say, my voice tight.

"How did you even get here?" Elsie says. "Is Murdo's van going?"

"What in heaven's name are you doing out on a night like this?" Mrs. Eleanor croons.

Francis dashes to the bar. "Let me pour you a dram of whisky."

I stand uselessly in the centre of the room, watching Sophie being ministered to, trying not to begrudge the attention she is garnering. I wait until all the fussing has simmered down, until she's pulled off her wet layers and been given a blanket and a glass of whisky. Her hair is staticky, her cheeks flushed, her nose dripping.

"What are you doing here?" I say, eventually. "Have they all killed each other at the castle?"

As I say this, Mrs. Eleanor and Alice gasp, clutching their chests. "Oh, they haven't?" "Whatever has happened?" they chirrup. Francis is paused, his hands outstretched, ready to do what, I don't know, at the mention of danger. Elsie gives me a reproachful look.

"No, no, everyone's fine," Sophie says, breathlessly. "Sorry to make you all worry. I didn't mean to be so dramatic an entrance," and she smiles. Everyone softens.

Alice touches her arm. "Oh, no, hen, don't mind us, we're just being fretful old ladies. With this weather, you can't help but be worrying someone will have a wee fall."

"I thought I'd get here well before it got dark," Sophie says. "I got turned around in the snow."

"You could have come to real mischief," Mrs. Eleanor says. "What if you'd fallen in the snow and killed yourself dead?"

Sophie nods, sombrely. "I know, I was getting a little cooped up, and the telephone lines aren't working. It was a silly idea, really."

"Well, you've just missed our Sunday supper," Alice says. "Let me fix you something. We still have some soup. If Flora puts the pot over the fire, it'll warm right up."

Even Flora doesn't seem to mind being volunteered. "Oh, aye, it'll warm right up."

"Don't go to any effort," Sophie says, and I roll my eyes. Typical. Even when she is starving and frozen half to death, she's still being polite.

"Oh no, it's no trouble, it's no trouble at all," Flora says. Alice and Mrs. Eleanor follow her out of the room to gibber nervously about what they can offer to their Sunday night miracle.

Elsie nods next door. "Let's go into the reading room. There's a fierce draught here." She helps Sophie up, unnecessarily, obviously, and Francis takes Sophie by the other hand; again, clearly, not required.

Sophie hobbles next door and is offered the seat nearest the fire. As Elsie pulls a footstool out under her feet, Sophie smiles at her and a stab of fear plunges into my gut. Elsie and I are only recently back on good terms; the last thing I want is to give Sophie an opportunity to turn her against me. Alice and Mrs. Eleanor reappear with a bowl of soup and oatcakes and a pack of Garibaldi biscuits that they must have uncovered somewhere. Sophie shifts to get out of the chair, but they tut, urging her back. "Oh no, no, don't you go anywhere. Much warmer in here, anyhow."

"I couldn't possibly eat all of this," Sophie says. "I don't want to take more than is fair."

"Don't worry about us, hen," Alice says. "Aren't you a dear."

I scrunch my blanket into my fist.

Sophie drinks deliberately from her soup, while we all watch her.

"And you say you know each other," Alice says. "You and Marta, here."

Sophie nods. "That's right. We work in the same department, back in the museum."

"Do you do the—" Alice makes a swooping motion with her hand.

Sophie laughs, catching a drop of soup at the corner of her mouth. "Oh no. I'm not a daredevil like Marta. She's the risk-taker."

Mrs. Eleanor and Alice chuckle, good-naturedly.

"No, I'm more of a researcher," Sophie continues.

I want to say that I'm a researcher, too, but I force my mouth shut.

"I do the dusty parts," Sophie says. "Mainly restoring old books, documents."

"Clever girl," Alice says, beaming.

"We thought it would just be Marta here, for the ship," Mrs. Eleanor says.

"Yes, we thought so too," Sophie says, mildly. "But Lady Purdie was interested in some more thorough investigation."

"Is that so?" Alice tuts. "Well, I suppose it's their pockets, though what you want to keep digging around down there for is beyond me."

"Disturbing Auld James's grave," Mrs. Eleanor says.

They both cross themselves in a gesture that makes them look briefly like synchronised dancers.

Francis rolls his eyes, and for once I'm glad of his presence. "Marta's been mapping the site," he says. "Why on earth would they need someone else?"

If I could bear to get close to him, I might hug him.

"Anyway," Sophie says, ignoring him, "I'm certain no one wants to hear me natter on about work."

"We're glad for the diversion," Elsie says. "We're all running out of things to talk about, here."

I look at her. Is that true? I should have been trying harder to be nice, friendly, entertaining.

Sophie grimaces. "I feel terrible, not being able to even sing for my supper."

"Can you sing?" Flora says, hopefully.

"No, unfortunately not." Thank God for that. "But is that a piano I saw?" She points outside into the corridor.

I'm certain nobody will be interested in leaving the warm reading room, but Flora claps her hands together in excitement. She bounds from the room and lifts up the lid of the piano.

"It's a little out of tune," Alice says.

Sophie stands up, gathering her blankets like a cloak around her, and takes a seat on the stool. "Do you play?" she asks Alice.

Alice holds her hands up. "Oh, we've exhausted all the tunes I know."

Sophie plays some experimental chords. "It's not too bad, given the weather," she says. "We'll have to avoid"—she presses a key—"D-flat. But I think we can manage." She blows on her fingers. "Any requests?"

"Do you know any hymns?" Mrs. Eleanor says.

"Some," Sophie says.

"How about 'Stand by Me'?" Francis says, quietly. He has crept to the side of the piano and is looking down at it, hawkishly.

"Oh, I can do that one," Sophie says, starting, then stopping. "I'll have to change the key." She thinks for a moment, then goes into a slightly altered rendition.

Francis's eyes grow hungry. I watch the line of his breath delving a parting in Sophie's hair, how close he is standing to her. His hand rests on the back of her chair, his grubby fingers brushing against her shoulder.

I pull him away. "Leave her be," I say. "Nobody wants you breathing so closely on them."

He frowns at me, offended, but Sophie catches my eye, and something like a fraction of thanks passes over her face.

The old ladies have the time of their life now Sophie has arrived with some new tunes. A bottle of whisky is passed around, toasts are toasted, drinks are drunk. I sit in the reading room with the door closed against the jollity, trying not to nurse the sense of being shut out. Elsie puts her head around the door, makes some *come along* gestures, but eventually gives up and leaves me to glower by the fire.

When the clock in the reading room chimes ten, I stand deliberately in the doorway. I want to go to bed, but I'm not about to leave Sophie and Elsie alone together without my supervision. Sophie widens her eyes. "Oh, my, how late it's got."

"You won't be thinking of going anywhere," Mrs. Eleanor says, putting a bony claw on Sophie's shoulder.

"If it's not too much trouble," Sophie says, gathering a garland of blanket around her. "It would be so terribly nice if I could stay here."

"Of course you'll stay here, I wouldn't hear of it. Let me go make you up a room now," Alice says. She leans over to Elsie. "What would be the warmest? The Purdies' room?"

"Oh yes," Elsie says. "That'll be nice and cozy for you. It'll be warm enough on account of the stove in the kitchen."

"Normally we keep it ready for themselves," Alice says, "but there's fat chance of them coming down at the moment, is there?" And she starts giggling. I realise she is a little tipsy.

"If it's a warm room, then you should be taking it," Sophie says, her expression horrified.

Alice waves her away. "Oh no, hen, I like my own room. Give us a hand, will you, Els?" She groans as she stands up.

Flora transfers a few hot coals from the reading room into a zinc bucket, and the three women go up to the first floor. From the corridor I hear their footsteps overhead. Mrs. Eleanor and Francis excuse themselves, and as Francis climbs the stairs, he gives Sophie a longing stare. "Thank you for a beautiful evening," he says. "It's been a long time since I had the pleasure of such lovely company."

Mrs. Eleanor beams at her. "I haven't been up so late since I was a lass."

"We were up this late on Hogmanay," I say.

"Oh, well, you know what I mean." Mrs. Eleanor flaps her hand. "Thank you." She gives Sophie a kiss on the cheek.

As their respective doors close upstairs, I lean against the piano. "What are you doing here?"

Sophie's expression of agreeable accommodation drops from her face. "I need to talk to you."

I shuffle. The slide from pleasantries into business has unnerved me. I lift my chin, determined to show I'm not intimidated by her. "About Alex?" I congratulate myself for my voice not breaking.

Sophie frowns at me, disbelieving. "No, not about Alex, good grief. About the site, Marta."

"Oh." I flinch. "What about the site?"

"The diary," she whispers, sitting forward. "Have you read it?"

I shake my head. "How would I have read it?"

"You were down there," Sophie says, in an exasperated tone. "You didn't look at any of it? You must have pictures?"

"I was busy trying not to die," I say.

Sophie sighs. "OK, Marta, fine."

"Anyway, what's the urgency in talking about the diary now?"

She pulls her blanket over her shoulders. "I had to get out of that castle. The Purdies have elaborate formal dinners each evening. I have to sit there and discuss the journal in the most excruciating detail. They are obsessed with it."

I shrug.

"I can't hold them off much longer. I've been fabricating all sorts of excuses about how I need longer to do the transcriptions, but I don't know what I'm supposed to say to them. And it's a problem for both of us."

"Why is that?"

Sophie holds my eyes. "Auld James was a monster," she says.

I scoff.

"I'm serious."

"So he wasn't perfect," I begin, but she interrupts me.

"No, Marta, it's very clear from the journal, there's no getting around it. He's worse than you can imagine. Cruel and stupid, clearly not even good at whaling. Everybody hated him—the crew, the islanders. Selfish, prejudiced, a poor leader. The men who disobeyed him, he would take away their water rations and gloat about it! He was a monster."

Smoking makes my cough worse, but since Elsie isn't around to give me a row, I light one of her cigarettes from the pack on the side table. The smoke probes the tight corners of my lungs. Auld James. Precious, saintly Auld James. Protector of the island, paragon of virtue, representative of the Cairnroch elect, all chosen personally by God to be saved from damnation. Man of the people, friend to the friendless, plougher of sacred fields, emissary to heathens. A fraud! I start to laugh until I'm choking. I have to lean over the corner of the table until the wheezing subsides.

When I finally look up, Sophie is watching me with a mixture of annoyance and confusion. I wipe my eyes. "Sorry," I say. "Enjoying the irony."

"There's something else. When you went down there, Purdie's room, was it all shut up?"

I stub out my cigarette. "I suppose. The door was stuck quite firmly, it had sunk down into a lip in the corridor and become gummed up with seaweed. Why? Was there some kind of contamination of the paper?" I'm getting ready to defend myself in case she is about to accuse me of damaging the books.

She has a strange expression on her face that I can't decipher. "No. The door didn't drop down."

"What do you mean—it had sunk into the lip of the floor, I had to cut the seaweed away. The hinges probably rusted or rotted."

She's shaking her head. "It didn't drop down. The crew nailed him in there. They locked him in his room and left him there to die."

27

MONDAY, JANUARY 7, 1963

IT'S JUST PAST THREE IN THE MORNING WHEN THE SLUGGISH gears of my brain click together. I wake up with my cheek pressed against Elsie's shoulder. Violet's face in the bathroom mirror at the castle on Halloween. I thrash around in the blankets until Elsie mutters, clamping her arm around my waist. "Stop wriggling," she says.

"Violet knew that Auld James wasn't the saint everyone seems to think he was," I say.

"Mmm," Elsie says, pulling me closer.

"And Lester must have set her up. He sold off those Pictish objects and then had her blamed for it. She lost her career! She must know something about what he's up to."

"In the morning," Elsie says, patting my head, clumsily.

I try not to wriggle, but my mind is gathering speed. I slip out from under the blankets and feel my way into the hallway. I stand in the dark holding on to the banister at the turn of the staircase, listening. I don't know what I'm listening for. The sound of unquiet footsteps, roaming for wisdom. When I start to shiver, I tiptoe back into Elsie's bed and concentrate instead on the thick sounds of her sleeping. She starts to stir around six, and I slip my hand around her stomach, bundling her soft warm weight farther towards me. I burrow down next to her, breathe in the smell of her unwashed hair.

"Don't." She pats her head, self-consciously. "I must smell like a barnyard. Why don't we melt some snow and wash our hair today? We can do it over the sink."

"Must we?" I have a powerful hatred of sponge baths left over from my childhood.

"Just think how much better we'll feel. And smell." She rolls away and uses two fingers to part a cleft in the newspaper against her window. "And it's stopped snowing!"

I put my eye to the hole. It is dazzling. A scrap of sun is veiled behind a satiny cloud, and the island is crisp and unblemished as wedding stationery. The harbour has frozen over, collecting a perfect sleek lacquer that stretches out to the horizon. "Let's have tea, then get the fur coats from the cloakroom and see how far we can walk. We'll never see anything like this again."

"Deal," Elsie says.

We open the kitchen doors quietly so as not to wake Sophie, but she is already sitting by the stove, drinking a cup of tea. "I hope it's OK," she says. "I melted some snow from the front garden."

"Of course," Elsie says. "Just maybe avoid the terrace. There's a drain at the back where we've been emptying the pots." She gives her a meaningful eyebrow.

"Ah, I see." Sophie looks into her tea, embarrassed. Ridiculous. What were they doing for toilets up at the castle?

Elsie hovers by the table as I pour us both a cup of weak tea and add one spoon of milk powder. I can feel Sophie's eyes tracing us, her gaze flicking from Elsie to me and back again.

"I'll take this up to Granny," Elsie says. This is clearly a ruse. Elsie treats her first cup of tea of the day like a sacrament; she wouldn't donate it, not even to her granny.

There's a moment of silence between me and Sophie.

"I suppose we should talk, then," I say.

"Yes." Sophie's voice is hollow.

We look at each other.

Sophie puts her teacup down on the table. "I know about the missing artefacts," she says.

I wince. Somehow, I could feel it was coming, and yet it still stings. "How?"

She raises her eyebrows. "The photographs, Marta."

"But . . ." I brought all of them back to the hotel, I'm sure of it.

"The last set of negatives are still in the reel."

I close my eyes. "Damn."

She rotates the teacup in her hands. "What happened?"

I sit down at the bench with a sigh. "Someone went down there and took them between my first and second dives."

"Well, yes," Sophie says, with a wry smile. "I'd deduced that much."

I swallow. "Alex—"

Sophie tenses as if she's bracing herself.

"I needed more time to try to retrieve everything." I look down at the metal surface of the table, where my fingerprints have left smudges in the chrome. "I thought I might be able to make it right."

Sophie pinches the bridge of her nose. "If I don't tell him now, it's going to make things so much worse. I can't cover for you."

"I'm not asking you to."

"But don't you see? You've been careless, and now I'm implicated."

I balk at this. "I haven't been careless. It's not as if I advertised the dive site in the island newspaper. There were only a handful of people that knew, and one of them was Lester. He's the one who commissioned someone to go down there and ransack the site, by the way."

"Lester?" Her forehead wrinkles.

"Yes, Lester."

Sophie runs a dismissive tongue around the inside of her cheek. It's obvious she doesn't believe me. "Well, the looting itself may not have mattered as much as you expect. It does happen. You shouldn't have concealed it."

"It will matter because it's me," I say.

She fixes me with a pitying expression. "What I don't understand is, why do you even want to continue working for Alex? It can't possibly be pleasant." Pleasant for her, she means.

"I don't work for him, I work for the museum," I snap. "But one bad word from him and my career is over. Not even a word. An insinuation. A suggestion. You *know* what a boys' club it is. And after how hard it's been to get this far . . ." I trail off.

"Alex told me about—"

"I'm sure he did," I interrupt. I can't bear to hear her say Lewis's name out loud.

She looks down at her knees. "I don't pity you."

"I'm not expecting your pity," I say.

There's another moment of silence.

At last, Sophie says, "What should I tell Lord and Lady Purdie about the diary?"

I rub my shoulders, relieved for the change in subject. "If they ask, the material is too degraded, and we have to take it back to a laboratory in Edinburgh. Then we send them the transcript when it's published and let Alex deal with any complications."

Sophie lets out a breath. "I don't feel comfortable lying to them."

"So don't lie," I say. I find myself standing up. "Just don't disclose the truth. What about the provisioner's ledger? There must be something in there you can talk to them about."

"Come on, Marta. There's only so much conversation I can make about how many tinned vegetables the crew ate."

"Well, I'm sure you'll work something out. I'm going up north for a while."

"What?"

I was just as surprised to hear myself say it. "The curator in the Neolithic museum, she has a reason to hate Lester. I think she might be able to help me find out what he's done with the items."

"It's—" Sophie points outside. "Have you lost your mind?"

"I'll find a way. Someone will drive me." Again, it's like hearing a stranger's voice come out of my mouth. I feel like Sophie's arrival has slapped me back into action. "She also has more insight about Auld James. It might help you contextualise the journal."

Sophie licks her lips.

"So, what do you think, shall we make an agreement? You don't mention anything about the missing objects, and I'll try to collect whatever information I can about Auld James."

She stares at me. "The telephone lines have been down for weeks. Who exactly am I going to talk to?"

LATITUDE 81°, 01' N, LONGITUDE 65°, 33' W

... though I have forbidden it, they are given to discuss among themselves of the visitor and its visitations. Ince caused panic walking while quite asleep and seizing Grimball upon the shoulder. For my part I have not seen anything but the cracking from the ice does not allow for sleep, sounds like bones snapping.

28

TUESDAY, JANUARY 8, TO WEDNESDAY, JANUARY 16, 1963

NOW THAT THE SNOW HAS STOPPED FALLING, THE ISLAND begins to break out of its lacteal cocoon. The snow has smothered every road, buried sheep in the fields. From the harbour comes the occasional deafening boom, as desperate fishermen turn to dynamite to crack the ice; but it is frozen solid for half a mile. The only colour on the horizon is the red ribbon of the lightship hull, stuck so still that even her bell has ceased tolling. The fishermen turn to digging out doorways and front paths, to chopping down even the smallest sapling for firewood. They walk the coast, cracking holes in the ice at Roiner's Point for any seals that managed to survive this long. Tragedies are uncovered: Mungo Ince, a seemingly fit forty-year-old man, is discovered frozen in his bed. The perfectly preserved body of Jock Gilles turns up in his sheep field, where he must have got disoriented in the snowfall. Morag Brode is found at the bottom of her staircase, her door slightly open, a sheath of snow covering her body. The ground in the kirkyard is too frozen to bury anyone, and the unfortunates are laid to rest in Morag's now disused potato shed. Improbably, a hero emerges: Meadow, the fluffy black cat belonging to Irene Gilchrist, is found both alive and hale, sheltering inside a cellar where he spent the worst days of the chill apparently gorging himself on the mice driven inside.

There is no table salt to be found in any meal. Instead it is spread on doorways and footpaths. Icicles are snapped off eaves for cups of weak tea. Cows are brought inside back rooms. School has apparently been cancelled and children ride tea trays down the hill near the castle, their whoops carrying far over the village. Old women take old side tables into their gardens and chop them down for the fire. Puffins lie stiff where they have dropped from the rocks near the other lighthouse, too iced over even to pluck. The jet at the air base is frozen, the runway unusable, since there's not enough grit to melt the snow. A helicopter passes overhead and parcels of sugar and milk powder are lowered by a rope onto the high street, schoolboys holding knitted hats over their ears in transfixed and unadulterated exultation. Dr. Brode moves from house to house, pulling teeth, lancing boils, meeting at least one new baby. The hotel is overrun by a constant stream of visitors ostensibly dropping in for conversation, yet all the talk is of the Lord's hands on the island, God's will enacted through ice and snow, as if the Cairnroch elect are relishing their puritanical cleansing by ice, its sterile, unyielding embrace. Typical of the island perspective to see all this snow as abluent instead of aberrant.

The hotel feels like a war-scarred encampment, people wandering from room to room crouched over against the cold, dressed in huddles of bizarre clothing. They come with complaints tempered in stoical refusals to complain; they leave with whisky. None of the visitors have useful suggestions about how I could get up north; the island cars are no longer working, the fuel frozen solid in their pipes. Jock Lees tells Irene Gilchrist, of Meadow fame, who tells Alice, who tells me, that Murdo up at the castle even tried lighting a fire under his car to get the engine going before Lady Purdie intervened.

§

THE SMELL of the wallpaper in the hotel is sickening me. Dampness and cold and dust and coal fires and condensation. Around the fireplaces it is buckling in blisters, slithering into curls, revealing pink cloudy speckles, spectres of prewar velvet. Murky dribbles of mildew skid into the carpet. I can smell it on me, on our clothes, on Elsie's breath. She insists I'm exaggerating, but she didn't grow up in a damp home. The scum of it stays with you.

I walk in the trails carved by the men between the houses, watching the faint glower of embers through cracks in newspapered front windows. The game Jenine and I used to play feels distinctly unsatisfying now, those meagre fireplaces crawling smoke into rooms fusty with dirty, cold islanders consulting their Bibles in blades of daylight. I have no interest in going up to the castle and enduring the Purdies. Instead, on Monday, I watch hopeful gulls blown in from distant ocean rocks shuffle across the frozen harbour. The fishermen have been continually walking back and forth between the boats, so I know the ice will hold my weight. I let myself down from the pier and wander among the hulls secured in place by puckered lips of ice. Here and there are blasts where people have tried to shoot or chip away at the rime, but the blessing of Cairnroch's shallow harbour has been its downfall here; under my feet the ice is steady as concrete.

Keeping close to the boats, I trudge through the snow farther out until the coastal street stretches behind me. Beyond, a strange, pearly flatness, the odd shine from distant open water glinting on the clouds. It can't be that different from the sight Auld James and his crew spent all those months looking at. Stuck without any hope of rescue. I understand why the crew set off in search of something, anything. Better to perish out on the floes than to be trapped like animals, waiting to starve slowly to death. On my right, the blackened chunks of the Purdie Lighthouse have been gifted a white mantle. The rocks around the lighthouse are treacherous underneath the snow, and I steer clear of the hillocked halo around the islet. If I slipped here, I doubt anyone would notice me bleeding red against the hull of the lightship.

As I get closer to the lightship, her crimson stripe of paint seems almost outlandish to my colour-starved eyes. If I were a little taller, I could just about reach the ladder at the far end. I picture myself returning to the hotel with a sack of pilfered coal; a fire big enough to roast away the dampness in a scour of heat. The bottom rungs of the ladder are too slippery to hold on to, but I pace back and forth, carrying over armfuls of snow and compacting them, until, after a few minutes, I have just enough leverage to pull myself up and grab the railings. Two scrabbly steps more and I'm over. The bridge must have accumulated a foot of snow; I should have realised it would weigh down the hatch. Kicking through the powder, I trace the edge of the hinge with my boots. I've come this far, surely it's worth a try? It's thirsty work trying to scrape away the ice from the hatch, and I have to resort to eating snow, scratching the inside of my mouth. At least this far away from the Cairnroch fires it tastes clean and faintly metallic, like water from an old garden hose.

And then, with a heave, the hatch yields. I open the hatch flush against the deck and lower myself down into the belly of the ship. There's nothing much to these unmanned lightships; the main space below deck is an engine room fortified by ballast tanks. There'll be a crew room on the aft deck, but this is where the fuel is kept, usually a combination engine and—yes, there it is—a coal store! Down here, the belly of the ship feels almost warm, insulated by all that ice and snow. I don't have a bag with me, but I can take off my sweater, tie knots in the arms, and fill it up. I'll keep warm on the way back if I walk quickly enough. But after fifteen minutes wrestling with the wheel on the coal stores, it still hasn't budged. The mechanism must have seized with the cold. I'll have to come back with oil, maybe find a way to heat the springs.

Just as I am rubbing the dents of the wheel out of my numb hands, the lightship bell above me tolls. I fall back with a yelp. My heart is racing from the surprise. When I have enough breath, I raise my face towards the hatch. "Hello?"

No answer.

"Hello? Is someone there?"

Silence. Perhaps it was me, moving around down here just enough to shake the bell. I take a step back towards the ladder when the hatch above me closes with a sharp, short slam. Without the window of wintry light, the engine room is completely dark; I can't see my own boots. It's so black that I can see dots and zigzags from my own eyeballs. *Everything is fine*, I tell myself, groping for the rungs of the ladder. I clamber up, pushing at the hatch. These are designed to open from the inside. My fingertips are slippery against the cold metal; there is no handle. My heartbeat pounds in my ears. I take a deep breath, another. *You can do this. Imagine you are diving.* I hold the breath deep inside me, filling my belly.

Then I hear, clearly, someone sigh.

It's close enough to feel it on my face, a light, sweet, cold breath.

It's coming from the corner of the room.

Biting off my left mitten, I scramble to the very top rung of the ladder until I'm squashed against the hatch. Pressing my back against the opening, I push up from the knees with all my strength. The hatch squeaks an inch, and I thrust the mitten into the gap before it can crash shut again. With one more shove, the hatch swings back open, and I pull myself out, crawling on my hands and knees into the wet snow. It is impossibly bright, my vision scored with lightning. Without daring to look down into the dark mouth below, I kick the hatch door shut.

Around me, footprints in a circle, but I can't tell if they are only mine. Above me, the bell rings again. From my place lying in the slush, I can see there is no one else here. In every direction around the ship, only an expanse of white.

"Lewis?"

My voice steams the air. I know, somehow, that it isn't Lewis. I can feel it. Instead, Alice's words sting in my mind—that Auld James's spirit is just like this lightship: a herald of destruction. I brace myself against the gunwale and rise on unsteady legs. Now that I know from Sophie that Auld James was a horrible person, the idea of his presence feels even worse. Maybe that's why he's following me. Because I'm just like him. A secret monster, heading for a miserable end. A breeze scatters crumbs of snow into my eyes, and I climb slowly down from the lightship and begin my walk back across the frozen harbour. And as I walk, I can't help but keep looking behind me, checking for shadows lurking on the ice.

§

WHEN I COME BACK to the hotel, all I can think of is a stiff drink. I make eye contact with Elsie, who is mid-conversation with a Jock who is sitting at the bar with his own tumbler.

"Hi," I say, taking the seat next to them. My hands are still shaking, and under my trousers, I can feel the frozen track of a trickle of blood.

"Go on, tell Marta what you told me," Elsie says.

The Jock looks at the floor in distaste. He takes a long minute, releasing a clucking sound before raising his eyes to somewhere on my shoulder. "Soviets have done it."

I blink at Elsie. "A missile?"

"Not a missile," the Jock says. "Some other kind of bomb. A snow bomb. The Soviets have done all of this." He waves his hand at the window. "Frozen us. Part of their plan. They're going to make us like them. Siberian."

"Oh?"

"It's a ploy to turn us pink. Then they'll come across the ice and communise us."

Elsie lowers her eyes, and I know she's thinking of her own spell of paranoia about the weather. "Not about the Soviets," she says, kindly. "About the train that goes up to the mines."

"A train?" I say. "But I thought all the fuel was frozen?"

"Steam," he says.

Elsie claps her hands. "Steam!"

After ten days of continuous digging along the line, the tracks between Port Mary and the colliery have been cleared. It seems that every available man and woman and child from coast to coast has been toiling to get the train to and from the mine running again. Elsie tells me that while they make use of it on the island, Cairnroch coal is not the quality usually sold for homes. Although she does tell

THE SALVAGE | 223

me never to mention that if I value my life. Instead, the mine produces a small contribution to industry that is usually exported. But since mining is one profession not especially affected by the extreme temperatures, the miners have been able to keep working. At least while it's still too cold for a thaw that would risk flooding.

What this means is that I can get the hell out of Port Mary.

29

FRIDAY, JANUARY 18, TO
SUNDAY, JANUARY 20, 1963

"THAT'S TRUE," ELSIE'S VOICE SAYS, THROUGH THE READING room door. It's low, urgent, engaged. I feel a cough crawling into my throat and have to step back into the hallway, treading on the floorboards as I do so, giving myself away.

There is a knowing, gathered silence from the other side of the door.

"Hello?" Sophie calls from inside the room.

I curse myself, coughing into my hand.

"Marta, is that you?"

I open the door slowly. Sophie and Elsie are in the armchairs by the fire. They are sharing one large blanket, trimmed in Purdie hunting tartan. I look at the lumps in the blanket, trying to discern if their knees are touching underneath. "Am I interrupting?" I say, churlishly.

"Come in and close that door," Elsie says. On the other side of her, Sophie is sucking her teeth, clearly irritated by my intrusion.

"We were just talking about pesticides," Elsie says.

I glare at them, almost insulted that Elsie thinks this lie would satisfy me, when it is so obvious that the only thing they have in common is me. "Is that so?"

"Yes, Rachel Carson's book? Have you read it?" Sophie says, resting her head back on the armchair as if she is a university lecturer.

"Sophie lent it to me." Elsie is flushed, animated. I notice the book on her lap. She's been carrying that book around for the past few days, and stitches of jealousy prickle over me that on all the occasions I saw her with it, the source of her absorption was Sophie.

"No," I say. "I haven't."

"It's about the environment, and DDT. There's a chapter about this town where everything has been just—silenced—and we were talking about all *this*." Elsie waves her hand around.

I fold my arms, leaning against the wallpaper. The dank chill of it wavers through my clothes. "How could pesticides cause snow?"

Elsie looks simultaneously annoyed and disappointed in me.

Sophie clears her throat. "Well, I don't know that there's a direct correlation, per se, but the silencing of nature, the lack of birdsong, the ground where nothing grows, this is exactly the type of destruction Carson is describing."

God, I hate her.

"Or do you have an alternative explanation?" Sophie says, waving her hand as if she's gesturing to a freshly laid table.

I lick my lips. A vindictive spell cast by the man I left to die? A curse from a Victorian tyrant? "Low pressure front," I say, shrugging. "I suppose I should leave you to your book society."

I leave the room and feel behind me, with a petty vindication, that Elsie is following.

"What's wrong?" she whispers.

"You know that she hates me," I hiss back. "Why are you even speaking to her?"

"Marta, do you want me to go crackers? She's the first new human being I've had to talk to in months."

I take a long breath, rubbing my face. "I'm sorry. I feel as if I'm losing my mind too, cooped up like this." I take her hand. "Come with me up north. Please."

Elsie looks down at the ground. "Granny," she begins. We've been through variations of this conversation on and off since I found out about the train.

"I need you. And don't you want a chance to look at something that's not this wallpaper? Bring your book, I promise that you can tell me all about pesticides."

Elsie softens with a sigh, and I know that I have succeeded.

§

THE NEXT DAY we begin the long walk down towards the train, heavy in borrowed furs from the cloakroom. The stationmaster's cabin is only one room and smells of bacon, a scent that I have never enjoyed, although I notice Elsie gripping her knees in hopeful anticipation as she turns her head in search of the source of the aroma. There are two other men in the cabin, teenage boys in overalls who I gather have volunteered to run the line to help distribute the coal. The train itself has not been much used since the war, as it's apparently cheaper to transport the coke on the puffer. On account of the condition of the rails, it is running at a horse's pace, and it's not until close to midnight that Elsie and I are finally shown to the train by the bemused stationmaster. There are only two carriages, and he shows us to a booth on the right-hand side of the train and, before closing the door, advises us to lock it as soon as he leaves, "to prevent any bother from the lads."

We heed his advice and pull the curtains across the door for good measure. A leather bench bolted to the left-hand wall slides out into a makeshift bunk, and we huddle on the seat under the blankets we brought from the hotel. We have a hot-water bottle between us and a thermos of smoked cod stew, courtesy of fish donated by one of the hotel visitors. Just the taste of salt in the broth makes me ready to renounce my total depravity and turn my back on my heathenish ways.

The train whistle blows, and slowly, with shrieks against the rails, it pulls out. We ignore the raps against the door, which, since they are followed by laughter, we decide to interpret as cheeky rather than menacing. From the other booths we hear the stamp of men's boots, coughing, some low voices, eventually snoring. The train moves steadily through the night, and against the gentle thrum of the engine, I slide my hand between Elsie's thighs where she is warmest and touch her until she has to bite into the blanket.

The train crawls along the tracks, frequently stopping and starting, and each time it pauses, I jolt awake, feeling the engine rumble beneath my back and worrying that we are going to be trapped here under another burst of snow. But around five a.m. we reach the end of the line near the colliery. We wait until we hear the boots receding from the carriages, and jump down from the train to find a dingier replica of the stationmaster's cabin we left the night before. The two teenage boys in overalls are frying eggs on hot pans over a stove, and wordlessly, one of them shoots us a plate. After we've eaten, Elsie wipes out her thermos with snow until there is no lingering scent of stew and fills it with sugary tea.

As Elsie begins to walk west along the road that leads towards the Neolithic site, I take a look back behind us at the colliery, a squatting, rusty cage of iron and piping steam on the horizon. Lewis grew up in the collier village—there must still be families there who knew his dad, people who remember him as a boy. Someone would know where they used to live. I imagine myself standing at the front gate of his childhood house. His silhouette appearing at the window, watching me. I turn my back on the village. Elsie is navigating the channels dug into the snow and I follow the back of her white fur coat. At first, it feels disorientingly like we never left Port Mary; every tree, hedge, field looks so uniform in the snow. Gradually, small differences between the north and south of the island become apparent. There are far more trees up here; the snow itself has a sleek, glassy sheen. About an hour into our walk, I begin to hear an echoing rumble behind us that initially I take for thunder, even though the sky is clear. Pulling myself to the top of a slate wall, I balance against Elsie's shoulder and spot a giant horse and carriage approaching us from the east. When the man driving the horse is close enough to shout, he calls, "You all right there? Someone taken ill?"

Elsie starts. "Colin Gilles, is that you?"

The man peers down. "Elisabeth Drever! You're the last person I expected to see today. What does your granny have to say about you being out on the road like this?" His voice is younger than his face; he must be closer to our age than I'd realised.

"She gave me a right earful," Elsie laughs.

"Where are you going?" he says.

"Visiting Violet at Drisher's End."

Colin gestures into the cart. "Climb on in then." I pull myself into the carriage and help Elsie up after me. The back of the cart contains three crates of slightly green potatoes and a sack of dried cobnuts. Elsie spreads the blanket over us, and we huddle close to the tea thermos.

As the horse trots up along the lane, Colin and Elsie trade what they can over the wind. The collier village has fared better than Port Mary through the cold snap, although they are all low on paraffin.

"And how is Mr. Ben?" Elsie says.

"Poor old chap, I thought he'd done his last winter, but I don't have a choice." An anxious expression crosses his face. "He'll have some nice warm mash when we get done."

It takes me a moment to realise they are talking about the horse. Elsie sees me inspecting him and leans closer. "Coldblood," she says, as if that explains anything. But I give her an understanding nod.

Half an hour later, he slows Mr. Ben, and Elsie and I climb down quickly so neither of them cools off too much in the wait. Colin passes down a sack of potatoes for us to give to Violet and waves us a quick goodbye. As they pull down the path, I look around us. The lane is as frozen and lifeless as any stretch of the road we've travelled. Shrubby hedges are coated with white. Here and there in the snow are the tracks of enterprising birds that have managed to keep themselves alive this long.

I can't help myself. "Are you certain we're in the right place?"

Elsie gestures towards a crooked rowan tree. "There's a path down there to the museum."

It's only after we climb around the rowan tree that I realise a cottage is built into an odd hollow in the ground, so it's almost concealed from the road by the hedges. It's a haphazard one-storey slate building with a barely perceptible stream of smoke from a chimney attached to what must be the kitchen. Outside the front door, I trip on the boot scraper hidden in the snow and Elsie catches me. I go to knock on the door, but she stays my hand. "We don't knock around here."

I stare at her. "What do you mean, you don't knock?"

She laughs, a little curl of steam from her breath. "You just sort of call out a hello and wait. Then you call some more and only knock when the other person has responded, right before you open the door. Knocking first is something a policeman would do."

And she calls out for Violet. We wait, but there's no answer. She puts her face to the window and calls again.

"You don't think she could have gone out, do you?" I say. The cold from the carriage ride is catching up with me now.

Elsie shakes her head. She presses her nose closer to the window. "I think I can see her. There's a grey shape on an armchair, but it's not moving."

"Oh my God." I wipe the glass with my arm and try to discern what it is that we're looking at. Elsie and I exchange a grimace. "Well, we can't stand around on her doorstep." I push on the front door, and it gives with a squeak. As it opens, I call, "Hello, Violet?"

The cottage must once have belonged to a farmer; the front door opens straight into one large room, with a huge open hearth on the left wall where a square of peat is burning. The ceiling is filled with a thick blue smoke from the peat fire, and my chest immediately seizes into a cough.

"Oh, hello, ladies," Violet says, stretching.

Her movement is so sudden that both Elsie and I jump, clinging on to each other.

"Potatoes, how lovely." Violet stands up, casting off her grey rug. She's dressed in an odd full-coverage pink-and-white knitted suit, rather like a baby might wear. Her hair is plaited in an elaborate braid, with a halo of frizzy curls that have flattened against the back of the chair. "Tea?"

"Uh, yes, thank you," Elsie says.

"Please, have a seat." Violet points to a surprisingly modern-looking sofa underneath the window. Elsie and I sit next to each other, our knees touching.

"Did you tell her we were coming?" Elsie whispers.

I shake my head.

"Sorry to drop in on you uninvited," Elsie says, taking off the white fur coat and her tartan scarf. Her nose is pink as a berry.

"Oh no, it's nice to have visitors." Without warning, Violet bangs aggressively on the window next to the hearth. "You, get away, get away from there."

Elsie shoots me a concerned look.

"Bothersome squirrel keeps on stealing the seeds I leave out for the birds. Poor things don't have anything to eat with all this ice." She knocks on the window again. "Don't make me come out there!"

Violet puts a kettle on the peat fire, and then seems to forget what she is doing and begins pulling lengths of string from a basket hanging from a hook near the sink. My eyes are watering from the smoke, and I cough uselessly into my handkerchief as Elsie pats my back.

"You need an onion on that chest," Violet says, from her basket of twine.

"I'm fine, thank you," I say. Although the cottage is an improvement on the potato carriage, the longer we sit still, the less comfortable the room seems. Waterlogged books speckled with mildew are crammed against the windowpanes. The house is designed around the peat fire, but it doesn't give off much more than a suggestion of warmth.

"How has your health been?" Elsie asks, but Violet bats away the attempt at camaraderie.

"Good," she says, peering into an assortment of ceramic cups that sit in a plastic bucket by her window ledge. I dread to think what she is inspecting. The kettle burbles, and she has deciphered whatever she needed amongst the cups, putting three on the table and digging into a brown paper bag with her hands, distributing a loamy substance into the cups that looks suspiciously unlike tea. "Raspberry leaf is all I have," Violet says. "Good for your wombs."

Elsie gives me a sideways look that I take to mean, *I told you this was a bad idea.*

Violet delivers the cups, and I look into the murky potion. "I wanted to talk to you about Lester," I say, deciding that there is little point in preamble.

"Who's Lester?" Violet says.

Elsie splutters on her cup of tea.

"Lester at the castle museum," I say.

Violet pulls the grey rug back over herself and strokes it as if it's a cat. "Oh, him. What about him?"

"I know what he did to you," I say. "How unfair it was that you got blamed for items going missing."

"Unfair?" Violet looks between us both. I notice now that, improbably, she seems to be wearing lipstick. Had she put that on before we arrived, or else somehow applied it without my noticing?

"Lester, he's trying to do to me what he did to you," I say, hoping to appeal to a sense of solidarity. "This time it's Auld James's items, and I'm going to end up taking the blame."

Violet says nothing. I look uncertainly at Elsie.

"Do you know what his sources are, Violet?" Elsie says, softly. "Who he sells on to?"

Violet slurps her tea. "Poor Eddie. Never been the same since that lightning storm."

My heart picks up. "You knew that Lester sent Eddie down into the ship?"

"Oh yes," she says, absently. "I've got Auld James's goggles right here."

My mouth falls open.

She turns to a shelf next to her chair and, from an egg carton, withdraws the whalebone ice goggles. My hands are shaking as I take hold of them. Even though I'd worked out their dimensions, they are still smaller than I'd expected, lighter too. There are holes scored into each end, which must have been used to tie them to the wearer's head.

"It cost me an arm and a leg, but they'd be safer here with me. I knew he would come for them."

"Lester's been here?" Elsie says.

"Oh, not *him*, no. Auld James."

I stare at her.

"He's been hanging around outside the window, trying to get in at all hours of the night," Violet continues.

Elsie is rubbing her forehead.

"Horrible man he was. Is." Violet takes a breath. "Mean tempered as hell."

"What did you see?" I say. My voice is croaky. Elsie shoots a horrified look at me.

"Wait, wait." Elsie raises a hand. "Lester. How did you know that he sent Eddie down to the ship?"

"I bought some oysters from Eddie's brother, Duncan. They had this beautiful antique mirror for sale. I knew straight away it must have come from the ship. Oh, I told Duncan it was bad luck, that Auld James was an evil man, that keeping something like that would only get his spirit coming after them. You'd think they'd be more wary of him, what with the family history. But he wouldn't listen."

"Mary could have spared us a lot of bother if she'd said Eddie's brother was involved," Elsie says.

Violet shakes her head. "Oh, Mary's hardly going to get her own kin in trouble, is she?"

"And so Duncan gave you the goggles?" I say, trying to urge the conversation on.

"Ha!" Violet breathes a dimple into her teacup. "Duncan wouldn't give his own dog a slap. No, no, I had to buy them from him, of course. But I know how to handle malevolent energies. I told Eddie and Mary as well, I told them they don't know what they're dabbling with, but they wouldn't listen." She shakes her finger at us. "No one listens to old ladies, you'll see. Overnight, people stop listening to you."

"I listen to my grandmother," Elsie says, a tinge of defiance in her voice.

"They never listen when you speak," Violet says. "Oh, no, everyone else knows better."

Elsie grits her teeth. It's the first time I've ever seen her obviously irritated with someone other than me. I look down at the goggles in my hand.

"You can have them if you're so keen," Violet says. "I didn't buy them for my own health. You'll need to keep a watch out for Auld James, though. Get yourself some pearlwort, lay down some salt."

"So you took the goggles," Elsie says, "and Eddie's brother Duncan has the mirror. What about everything else?"

"Duncan had already passed on everything else before I got there," Violet says. "Callum will sell the rest, down at the Black Hare. No one will say a word against Callum."

Elsie and I look at each other. Back in Port Mary. "And where does Duncan live?" I say.

"He's on the coast near Gluckathy," Violet says. "The best oysters on the island."

I slump on the sofa, suddenly spent. I feel as if I've fallen to the bottom of a well and don't have the strength to climb back to the top. Yes, Violet is eccentric, and right now doesn't present the picture of the most reliable witness. But still, the thought skulks around in my head: If she has seen the figure too, then it means I haven't been imagining things. And it means that since I first went down to that ship, I've been followed.

Elsie's voice breaks me out of my reverie. "Marta, are you feeling all right? You look pale." Then to Violet she says, "Do you have anything to eat? She had a bad chest cold a while back."

My heart swells with gratitude as I watch Elsie conferring with Violet, bickering over a pot on the stove, raking yellow ashes from the peat fire. What have I ever done to deserve her? It can't be long before the bad luck that has been trailing me starts to infect her too. A bowl of barley soup appears in my hands, and Elsie peers at me closely. "You're not about to faint, are you?"

"Not the type," I say, although I do feel light-headed. The soup tastes of nothing; rainwater and grit. Elsie and Violet return to the hearth and chat with the squabbling cadence of two women who have known each other a long time and have got used to talking at cross-purposes. After the soup is finished, I look down at my own face in the puddle of broth at the bottom.

"Auld James," I say. Elsie and Violet turn to me. They are on the other side of the room inspecting some onions that Violet has smoked over the grate, I hope not with the intention of rubbing one on me.

"Horrible man," Violet says.

"What makes you think he's been here?" I say.

Elsie's mouth twists into an exasperated grimace. "Marta, really."

"Sophie needs to know more about him," I say, looking up at her. "More context for the journal."

Elsie blows air from her cheeks. "Fine." She sits cross-legged on a high stool near the fireplace. "Go ahead."

"James Purdie would have hated women like me. Wise women. Healers. A zealot is what he was," Violet says. "Dragging islanders out of their beds to go up north, for what? Religious maniac, trying to convert those poor Eskimos."

"Inuit," I say.

"An emotional man. Unpredictable. They say the crew didn't want to join that doomed voyage, but it's not as if they had much of a choice. Stay behind and they'd have trouble making their way on this island without looking like reprobates. No one says no to a Purdie, after all. Oh, he had a vision right enough. Nations of Christendom for the glory of bonnie Scotland. No respect for traditional wisdom, just the Bible or damnation. You must have noticed all the misfortune we've had since you went down and got him?" Violet shakes a knuckle at me. "The lighthouse, this snow!"

"But what makes you think it's him?" I say. "Here?" I need to know if he's marking me out specially. If he knows that I'm corrupted. Like him.

"Oh, I can hear him breathing, over the wind," Violet says. "Only reason he can't get in the house is because of that rowan tree out there."

"Right." Elsie claps her hands. "We will have to go if we're going to make it back to the train on time."

"Really?" Violet's face falls, and I feel a little sorry for her. She can't have too many visitors out here.

"We were lucky enough to get a lift from Colin and Mr. Ben," Elsie says. "We don't want to wait until it gets dark. The train heads back at midnight."

"I'll raise the flag, then," Violet says, with a sigh. "But it might take him an hour or so." She rummages in her kitchen drawer, withdraws a pair of voluminous red nylon underwear, and climbs up onto the counter.

"Don't!" squeaks Elsie, darting forward.

Violet gives her a perplexed look. "I'm not about to jump, silly girl. I'm just hoisting my flag for Colin to see." She creaks open the window, attaches the underpants to a loop on a wire running parallel to the frame, and pulls the other end so that it raises high in the air. "I've not completely lost my mind," she mutters, as she pulls the string. She climbs down from the counter and dusts her hands. "It may be a wee while yet before he sees my flag. Shall we take a tour of the site?"

"Is it far?" The idea of more walking in the snow is only slightly worse than sitting here in the smoke.

Violet laughs. "Goodness me, no, it's right out the back."

She lets us out the back door of the cottage and through a vegetable allotment that has tin cans placed at even intervals, "to keep away that squirrel," Violet says. We pass through a gate at the end of the garden, climb a small hill, and Violet points ahead of us to an old corrugated steel Anderson shelter that has been repurposed as an information booth. "That's the museum," she says. "I'd open it for you, only it's frozen shut."

I nod, trying not to show how shocked I am. From the castle, to this? How could she possibly not want to ruin Lester's life?

"And here we go, Cairnroch's only Neolithic site," Violet says, as we follow a track around the back of the hut and through her snow-covered allotment. The site is a compact arrangement of stones built into another depression in the earth, much like the one that Violet's cottage occupies, and I wonder if her house was built on top of another Neolithic site, although I don't volunteer the thought. As we walk down into the depression, the stones reach our knees, and ahead of us is one shallow opening, about the size of a chicken coop.

"I tried to clear the snow away from the top out of respect. But then I realised the snow keeps a really nice insulating layer when you get into the space. It made me think about it in a whole new light. Neolithic winters would have kept this warm," Violet says, with evident fondness for the site. "Do you want to go in?" she says, nudging Elsie forward. "Go on, there's just enough room in there if you bend over."

Elsie shuffles inside the cavity. In her white fur, she looks uncanny there, hunched over.

Violet is making a strange sound, her hand to her throat. I turn to her.

"Oh, it's odd when I see her like that, all in white. She looks exactly like him for a second."

"Like who?" I say, but I already know what's going to come out of her mouth.

"Like him. Auld James's spectre," Violet says, with a shudder. "When I see him, he's always in the corner, just like that, crouching."

LATITUDE 81°, 01' N, LONGITUDE 65°, 33' W

... all talk is of the visitor ... bound Gilchrist's mouth with rope.

30

SUNDAY, JANUARY 20, TO
MONDAY, JANUARY 21, 1963

THE TRAIN BACK TO PORT MARY DOESN'T RUN ON A SUNDAY, and it doesn't end up leaving until ten the next morning. The stationmaster takes pity on us, cooking us sausages and mashed potato from a packet before letting us into the bunk at the back of the cabin to sleep for the night. It is mercifully warm from the stove on the other side of the wall, but the sheets are rich with the onion-and-musk smell of unwashed man, and it's a relief in the morning to get back onto the train and into the same carriage we occupied on the way up. People along the route must have been warned about the late departure, because on the way down to Port Mary, there are scraggly-looking figures waiting by the tracks every few miles, wrapped in an odd assortment of winter clothes. The train slows to a jog at these apparently prearranged intervals, and a window at the front slides open with a slam. One of the teenage boys leans out and tips a bucket of coal into a makeshift receptacle held out by the waiting audience.

"You can't listen to Violet's superstitions," Elsie says, out of nowhere. We haven't spoken about what Violet said, more concerned with the mechanics of how to pee behind the stationmaster's shed without being seen by any of the men working the trainyard. My cough wouldn't let either of us get much rest last night, and Elsie's face is drawn.

I choose my words carefully. "I agree she's a little eccentric, but it's not just her—"

Elsie laughs. "Eccentric, aye, that's a polite way to put it. She's daft as a brush, Marta." She takes a breath. "Let's say that Eddie Grimball went down to the ship, and it was a bit unsettling. Would you say it's unsettling?"

"Yes," I say, reluctantly.

"So Eddie went down there. Him and his brother have been diving in those waters their whole lives, but they've never seen anything like this. The boat, it's hard to swim in, and dark, and dangerous. And Eddie doesn't have your equipment; he has to keep going back, each time getting more scared. He probably thought he was just picking something up discarded from the seabed."

"Flotsam," I say. "Or jetsam."

"Exactly," Elsie says. "The sea belongs to everybody."

I twitch. The sea absolutely does not belong to everybody. There have been wars waged over who seas belong to. Elsie notices the twitch. "Our sea, around our island, belongs to our fishermen," she says, with deliberation.

I nod, willing to give her that, at least.

"But instead, it's all set up like someone's living room. He feels he's doing something immoral, and it weighs heavily on him." She leans in closer. "I don't know if you've noticed, but the Cairnroch Islanders have a particular perspective on good actions reflecting a good heart."

The image of the woman with the flowered headscarf at the door of the shelter flashes in front of my face.

"Don't forget, the Grimball family have been carrying around guilt and superstition about that ship for a hundred years. And then, imagine, Violet turns up. She's got her odd ways and her potions and her big red underpants on a wee string like a kite." Elsie mimes flying a kite overhead.

I can't keep myself from laughing.

"Violet says he's looted a grave, ooh, and it's all cursed treasure, and Auld James, the saint of the island, who *your* ancestor infected with his bad luck, is going to be rattling his bones on your hearth and asking for his gold back?" Elsie shifts her weight against the banquette. "Well, is it any wonder if your conscience is going to catch up with you and make you think you see things and hear things?"

My chest feels lighter from laughing, as if I've taken a swig of sweet cherry cordial. "No, I suppose not."

"There you go." Elsie dusts her hands in victory.

With a shrieking on the rails, the train slows down again. Coal is emptied from the train window into a basket held out by an old lady wearing a tea towel wrapped over her head. She pushes a bottle of milk into the hand of the boy in the train driver's carriage. The milk has frozen solid, a plume of iced milk jutting through the neck of the bottle.

"This weather doesn't help, either," Elsie says, as the train picks up again. "The snow, the cold. The wind. It's no wonder people are seeing things."

"But Mary heard the cutlery moving before the freeze," I say. "Remember, it was back in October?"

Elsie looks at me. "Why are you so determined to believe in ghosts?" Her tone is earnest, imploring.

I hold her gaze. A churning rumbles through my insides. It feels as if all the secrets I've been carrying around are stacked against a door straining at its hinges. She has a right to know. My heart quickens, and I know that I'm about to tell her.

"Someone died because of me," I say.

Elsie is watching me carefully. "What do you mean?"

"You remember my friend Lewis, who grew up here?"

Elsie nods.

"It's my fault he died. We were on holiday together, he went swimming and he never came back." I can feel the tears in my throat, but I don't let them out. "I didn't tell anyone, I just left." I feel a terrible release as I say it, like jumping from a great height. Now I've told her, it can't be undone.

"You had a shock," Elsie says, quickly. Too quickly. "You panicked."

I shake my head. "If I'd called someone, lifeboat, fisherman, I don't know, anyone, they could have found him in time."

"Anyone might have done the same," she says. "You don't want to make a fuss, then it's too late. It doesn't make you responsible."

But I don't want her to absolve me. "I am responsible. He never would have been at that beach that day if it weren't for me."

Elsie takes a breath, but I interrupt her. "I didn't want anyone to know we were there together. I didn't want to be discovered."

She shakes her head, confused.

"We were having an affair," I say. "Lewis and me. He was Alex's friend."

Elsie stares ahead, her whole body tensed. "Alex, your boss? Were you two . . ."

I know I should give her time to absorb what I've said, but I feel like a child's toy that has been wound up by a key, and now I just have to spin until I'm untangled. "I thought Alex was leaving me—I don't know, I suppose I wanted to punish him first, before he could hurt me. And then when Lewis went missing, it was as if I suddenly realised what I was doing. I panicked and I left him and he died and it's my fault." My body feels lighter but dirtier, as if the process of telling Elsie has stirred up the mess.

She is still staring ahead, her posture fixed. I go to touch her arm, and she holds up her hand. "Not yet, Marta."

"At first, that's who I thought I was seeing. Lewis. That he was here, waiting for me. But now—well it doesn't make sense that Lewis would be at Violet's. I just keep thinking about Auld James and how—"

Elsie puts her hands to her hair. "Enough, Marta! Why are you telling me all this now?"

Because right now she can't walk away from me. Because no one has ever been so kind to me as she has. Because Sophie will tell her if I don't. Instead I say, "I don't know."

She begins to pace around the bunk, stumbling whenever the train tilts. "So you and Alex, you were together?"

I nod.

"Not calling anyone because you didn't want to get caught!"

"I know."

"And the ghost? What am I supposed to say to all this?"

"Also, Alex and I are married," I say.

Elsie's face flushes with what could be disgust or anger. She looks at me for a long moment before bursting out in a bark of hysterical laughter. "Jesus Christ!"

"But that's everything, I promise."

Elsie leans against the wall of the compartment. "Don't talk to me for an hour. In fact—turn the other way, would you?"

"We're only married on paper," I whisper. "Sophie really is his girlfriend. He hates me, not that I blame him. We just haven't divorced yet."

She points at the door. "Look that way. I get the window." She pulls her coat over her shoulders and sits at the farthest end of the banquette.

Obediently, I turn my head towards the door, tracking the hand on my watch as twenty minutes pass. I feel less heavy, but now the terror starts. This is when Elsie truly understands the kind of person that I am. This is when she makes a choice. My stomach is making volcanic growling sounds.

"Is that the train or you?" Elsie says, eventually.

"It's me."

She is still staring out of the window. "You should have told me you were married."

"Only on paper."

She shakes her head. "It's not fair to me. I have the right to know if I'm getting involved with a married woman, don't I?"

"You do. I'm sorry." And I am.

"How long were you, have you been married?"

"Three years," I say. "But it started going sour quickly." She opens her mouth, but I interrupt both her and myself. "I know it doesn't excuse me. I don't want to make excuses for myself."

Elsie tugs her coat closer around her. "There's a drunken kiss in a pub on Hogmanay, and there's sneaking around for months."

"I know."

"When Lewis went missing, were you worried about him?"

"I was, but I was also worried about me."

Elsie bites her lip. "Marta."

I should be trying to defend myself, but I also know that there is no defence.

"I just—" Her voice is flat. "I just feel like I've been falling for someone who has been wearing a mask."

My heart bleats, a little lambing jump. A jittery dance of sugary terror. "Elsie, I love you," I say, my eyes watering. Her head twitches but she doesn't reply. "I'll never keep anything from you again, I promise." I kneel on the dirty, juddering floor of the train. I would promise her anything right now. "And as for what happened, no one could feel worse about it than me. I came here thinking I could make up for it somehow, and . . ." I trail off.

Elsie turns to me, her lips white. "Christ, Marta. What a mess you've made of everything. It's just such a waste."

MONDAY, JANUARY 21, TO TUESDAY, JANUARY 22, 1963

THE TRAIN RUMBLES SOUTH AND ELSIE STILL ISN'T TALKING to me. It's only when we plunge through a copse of young birch trees that I realise if we get off the train an hour or two before it approaches Port Mary, we will be closer to Duncan Grimball, and one step closer to collecting everything. I fidget on the banquette until Elsie asks me what's wrong.

"I just want to go home," she says, after I tell her, resting her head in her hands.

"But if we get off soon, we can cut across at the narrowest part of the island. It seems mad to go down to Port Mary and then come back up again in the cold."

"It'll thaw," Elsie says, and even she sounds unconvinced.

"What if it starts snowing again, and there's no way back up to Duncan's for weeks?"

Elsie frowns. "What if it starts snowing again and we're *trapped* near Duncan's for weeks?"

I take out my notebook. "Violet said Duncan was trying to sell the mirror; I just don't want to risk waiting any longer. If you draw the route for me, I'll find my way on my own." I give her a smile that tries to communicate that I understand why she wouldn't want to help me, but also that I desperately need her help, regardless of what I say.

Elsie is quiet for a long moment. She lets out a resigned sigh that I'm both terrified and relieved to hear. It means that she might be about to relent, but it also means that her patience with me has worn down to a spindle.

§

THE OLD MAN waiting for coal by the tracks near Collack recognises Elsie, and although he refuses help carrying his newly replenished bag of coal, we walk alongside him to his farmhouse. He stops at the door and invites us in, but through the window I see a makeshift bed occupied by a yawning sheepdog next to the fireplace, and it's clear he's been living in that one room. Elsie thanks him and reassures him we can make it along the road to Duncan's house before nightfall.

For three hours we walk on numb feet over snowy fields. Elsie and I don't talk, except once, when I see a robin, and the sheer relief of a flush of colour against all the unbroken white makes me call out without realising.

The day is even more bitter than the previous one, the sky the downy grey of a pigeon feather, and an icy wind is slicing towards us from the east. Walking uphill like this in the snow means that each step requires thought and effort. My breath freezes in my eyelashes. I find myself trailing behind Elsie, her white fur moving through the snow, only reassuring myself she hasn't melted away into the frost by the crunch of her footsteps and the occasional swear word as she loses her balance.

It's another hour before we reach the top of the ridge. From here, we can see down to the coast, the water a sloppy, sludgy frozen churn that looks as if it's grinding rather than splashing against the shore. Duncan's house is not much more than a stone hut on a ridge overlooking a wide, flat tidal reach. There is a large yard behind the house enclosed by a series of outhouses, and as we get closer, Elsie points me to a shed that must usually be a pigsty while she walks ahead to the house. Despite the shelter, I have to jig in place to keep warm—the easterly wind is even more fierce without the protection of the hill, although the ground has less snow cover, presumably from carrying sea spray. The yard behind the house is littered with farm debris: sharp scraps of metal, wooden barrels, dangerous-looking rusty gears and equipment I can only guess the purpose of. It's been so long since I've even seen mud that I'm mesmerised by the rich brown colour.

Elsie reappears to wave me forward after about fifteen minutes, and to my disappointment we bypass the house entirely and go round to the other side where a man is breaking ice along the front path with a spade.

He straightens as we approach. Without introducing himself or acknowledging me, he nods to the far side of the building. "This way," he says.

"Duncan, this is Marta."

He doesn't look at me but picks up his pace, striding towards a long, narrow outhouse. I am aching from the walk here, and both Elsie and I have to hobble to keep up with him.

"There," he says, pointing through the doorway of the outhouse. It must usually be a chicken coop as there are perches covered with sackcloth flecked with droppings. On the far side of the shed is a bundle of white linens. For one horrible moment, I think it's a baby, wrapped in cloth.

"The mirror," Duncan says.

"From the ship?" My voice is ropy; I cough until it clears. "The mirror from the ship?"

"Yours if you want it. I'd throw it back in the water, but it's been frozen to soup."

I cross and unwrap the bundle. Here it is! It feels strangely familiar handling it here in this chicken coop, like finding an object from a dream in real life.

"I put it out here meaning to get them speckles off before selling it," he says, adjusting his cap. "But the chickens didn't like it one bit."

"Chickens don't like to be reminded that they're not peacocks," Elsie says, smiling at her own joke, but her expression falls when she sees that neither of us is in a smiling mood.

"And then, this." He lifts up one edge of the sackcloth to a row of fractured eggs. "Soon as I put the mirror in here, they were all like this. Sucked dry."

"Sucked dry?" I repeat.

He looks at me now. I can see the resemblance between him and Eddie, the hooded eyes.

Elsie steps in front of me, as if by blocking my view of the eggs she can somehow intercept my nervousness. "By a mouse or a fox, surely? All the frozen ground, they're probably thirsty."

"I've never seen a fox suck an egg dry, have you?" he says, to Elsie.

Elsie puts her hands on her hips. "I've never seen it snow this much, have you?"

He snorts a little laugh. "Agnes thought I was off my head too, until that." He points up to the wooden roof of the coop. I follow his gesture. Above us is a series of dark marks tracked across the ceiling that look exactly like a set of bare-toed footprints. They start just inside the entrance and span across the boards until they reach where the mirror was lying. All the hairs on the back of my neck stand up. It's like something, someone, was crawling upside down until they found what they were looking for.

"It's frost marks," Elsie repeats, as we follow Duncan back to the house. "It's just frost."

I don't reply.

Duncan opens the door to a small, cold kitchen, and gestures for us to enter before walking away. I look around the kitchen for a jug of melted snow or a kettle, anything that I could drink. From another room comes the sound of a woman retching. "Should we go and check on her, do you think?" Elsie says.

I shake my head, unable to think about anything other than footprints across the ceiling. I reach into the sink where there is a pail of snow, still frozen, and scoop some into my mouth. My fingers are so numb I can hardly feel them, but the ice burns against my tongue.

The retching fades to coughing and sighs, and a door at the far end of the room opens to a small, hunched-looking woman in a black oilskin raincoat.

"Oh," the woman says. She is carrying a pink plastic bucket in her hands. She lets herself out of the house and tosses the contents into the yard, then swirls around the inside of the bucket with a handful of snow from a trough.

"Do you need a doctor, Agnes?" Elsie says, as she comes back into the room. "We could try and reach Dr. Brode when we get back to Port Mary?"

Agnes shakes her head. "No, it's nothing like that."

Both of us understand at the same time. I say, "Congratulations."

Agnes nods in my direction without making eye contact. "Sit," she says, pointing at the table. Elsie and I follow her orders. There are only three chairs, so I hope that Duncan isn't about to come back in and stand behind me. Agnes must be at least forty-five. Her hair is grey, and she is very thin, with deep hollows under her cheekbones. I'm impressed that she could even get pregnant.

"Agnes, this is Marta," Elsie says. "We were on the other side of the hill and thought—"

"You came for the mirror, I suppose?" she says, interrupting Elsie.

I nod. "Thank you. We left it in the coop for now."

Agnes leans forward. "The mark of Cain on our house, that's what this has brought upon us."

"Cain?" I repeat.

She slaps the table with both hands. "And the Lord asked Cain, 'What have you done? The voice of your brother's blood cries out to me from the ground. So now you are cursed from the earth, which has opened its mouth to receive your brother's blood from your hand. When you plough the ground, it will no longer yield to you. A fugitive and a vagabond you shall be on the earth.'"

Elsie and I sit in startled silence.

"I keep telling Duncan, but does he really hear?" She drills into her temple with her finger.

She begins rocking back and forth in her chair, and I want to make a signal to Elsie, but I'm afraid Agnes will see me.

"Strange beasts, strange beasts, slinking across land and sea. Well, there's naught stranger than the depravity of a man's heart," she says, with a laugh. "Isn't that so?"

Both Elsie and I nod, enthusiastically.

"'And if you do not do well, sin lies at the door. And its desire is for you, but you should rule over it.' Oh no, but the sinners are bound to evil." She puts her hands and wrists together in a twisted configuration. "'You have driven me out this day from the face of the ground; I shall be hidden from your face; I shall be a fugitive and a vagabond on the earth.' A fugitive, laying his cold mark where he has tread."

As she talks, a kind of frantic desperation grips me. I'm too cold and thirsty to tolerate a sermon. I am seized by a giddy sense that I may be about to do something insane—jump over the chair and lick her face. Set something on fire.

Elsie coughs, and it seems to break Agnes from her recitation. She turns to Elsie. "And I suppose you'll be wanting some food," she says, in an accusatory tone.

"Oh, we're fine. Don't be bothering with us at all," Elsie says.

"No, no, I won't have any guests of mine going hungry." Agnes stands and pulls a tin of pears from a shelf, slamming it onto the table. "There, will that do you?"

"We wouldn't want—"

Without waiting for me to finish, Agnes throws a tin opener against the tin. "Anything except bread makes me sick to my stomach," she says. "Don't make this a waste."

"Thank you," Elsie says, struggling to open the tin with cold hands. She makes a jagged mess of the lid, and I have to use two fingers to scoop the pears, at risk of cutting myself. They are grainy and slippery and so cold I can hardly taste them. The syrup is thick and makes my teeth hurt. I am aching for something more to drink, but I don't dare ask Agnes.

"And you'll have to bed down with the chickens," Agnes says. "We had to move them into the house in the cold."

Elsie looks at me. "Oh, we'll probably be on our way, won't we, Marta?"

"Yes, that's right," I say, slapping my knees. "In fact, oh, look at the time, we best be getting off."

"And where will you be getting off to?" Agnes says, leaning forward in her chair.

As I'm stuttering, Agnes cuts in. "Can you not hear that wind? It's getting up something fierce."

I stand and inch towards the door. "We'll be all right. We can walk quickly."

Agnes raises her hands. "Well, don't mind me. Elisabeth, when your granny comes asking for your frozen corpse along with that mirror, I'll tell her you were in a hurry to get away."

Elsie hesitates, and my heart sinks.

"Right, that's what I thought," Agnes says. "Sacks are by the door. We go to bed early in this household."

§

NOT LONG AFTER SUNSET, Elsie and I are shown to the back room of the house, where the occupants of the chicken coop have been relocated. We're given a candle in a jam jar that gutters in a draught from an unseen source. The vinegar-and-lye smell of chicken droppings is suffocating, and I'm almost glad of the paltry light from the candle that prevents us from seeing the full horror of the room. It looks as if there is the shape of something resembling a bed frame in the corner where the chickens are huddled high off the floor for the night. We move the soiled straw from by the door until we clear an area from the worst of the chicken droppings. I lay down the sacking and pull one of the wooden boards across to buffer against any curious birds that might wander down. I volunteer to take the side nearest the chickens, and Elsie lies in front of me closest to the door. Despite how tense things have been between us, there is no comfort to be found except from squeezing up next to each other. Sleep is impossible. The stench is sour in my mouth, the floor hard underneath my hips. The birds move restlessly, clicking, snuffling, scratching. The wind knifing off the ocean bores holes around the room. I picture the frosty, deliberate footsteps across the ceiling.

"I don't understand what she meant about Cain," I say, quietly.

"You know about Cain and Abel, surely."

"Yes."

"Well, people here believe Cain was cursed to be a fugitive on the earth. He's an example of someone non-elect, I suppose. Doomed."

After a moment, I say, "Like me."

Elsie is silent for so long that I think she may have fallen asleep. I'm envious of her. The chill is seeping into my bones from the floor. The pick and scratch of chickens at the back of the room mingles with the shriek of the wind. I'm reminded of the feeling from the sea cave, the sense of pressure and desolation; of abandonment. The frozen sea and the frozen ground. I'm the one who dragged us here. Elsie will never forgive me for lying to her. I'm seized with the deepest sense of dread. I should just stand up and walk straight into the waves.

Out of nowhere, Elsie rolls aside. "What *is* that?"

I sit up, scanning the shadows above our heads for something crawling across the ceiling, watching us. "What's what?" My heart hammers into my throat.

"Oh, here we go." Elsie retrieves a feather from underneath her ribs. "Just a sharp one." She settles back onto her side. "God, I'm so fucking hungry," she mumbles.

My pulse retreating, I lie down again, reaching my arm back tentatively around her, ready to withdraw if she resists. But she shifts her elbow to make room for me, and my desolation floods away. Now I'm just sleeping in a pile of chicken droppings on the hard floor of a shack, trying to keep the only person I care about close. "Me too," I say, into the warm skin at the nape of her neck.

LATITUDE 81°, 01' N, LONGITUDE 65°, 33' W

Men mutter of a contamination from my quarters, of items moving although there is no wind, of footsteps on deck while we are all below. They claim to hear a bird trapped within the vessel that clicks its beak through the unrelenting hours of darkness.

32

TUESDAY, JANUARY 22, TO WEDNESDAY, JANUARY 23, 1963

THROUGHOUT THE NIGHT I FEEL ELSIE SHIFTING POSITION on the hard floor every few minutes. Around three a.m. a rooster in another room of the hut starts crowing. And crowing, and crowing.

"Let's go next door," I whisper into her hair. "Surely anything has to be an improvement on this."

But when we push open the door into the kitchen, Duncan and Agnes are huddled on the kitchen floor in front of the fire, the blankets on top of them moving, back and forth. Agnes moans loudly and I hustle us back into the chicken room, shaking my head. "Abort the mission."

Elsie lies back on the ground, covering her head with her arm. "Tell me a story," she says, as I settle on the floor beside her.

I'm so exhausted I can barely muster a scoff. "I'm no good at stories."

"Tell me anything," Elsie says. "Do anything except crow."

I think for a few seconds, then say, "Fish and chips."

She is so quiet I think she may have fallen asleep. Then she says, "Peeling sunburn."

"Soft towels, right on the pebbles, and you can feel the hot stones underneath the towel."

We talk like that until a faint pinkish light steals into the room. Productive, waking-up noises can be heard from the kitchen, a chair scraping, a pot banging, hinges squeaking. I sit up; my neck is stiff, and I can't turn it all the way to the left.

"That was the worst night of my life," Elsie says, rubbing her hip.

I can't help it, I start laughing. She tries to shush me, but I can't stop. Soon we are doubled over, gasping with laughter.

§

AGNES SERVES US PORRIDGE with water boiled from the snow. I'm so hungry that even though it tastes like glue, I would be happy for seconds, thirds. Agnes sits at the table without eating. Instead, she rocks back and forth, the wooden chair legs screeching against the floor. When Duncan stands, both Elsie and I follow his cue.

"Right," Elsie says. "Thanks so much for everything. We'll be off."

Agnes looks directly at me. "And Cain said to the Lord, 'My punishment is greater than I can bear.'"

I stand caught in her gaze until she turns away.

Elsie waits with Duncan while I collect the mirror from the chicken coop. Even bending over to pick up the bundle, I can feel the footsteps over my head. They do not look like frost marks. They are dark, as if the wood has been water stained, and smallish, smaller than my feet. Would I be able to reference the size against Auld James's skeleton? I shiver, gathering the mirror, and hurry back along the path to where Elsie and Duncan are standing, seemingly in silence.

"Thank you," I say, to Duncan, motioning the bundle towards him. He takes a step back, as if I'm holding a knife.

"It would help Marta if you remember exactly what left the ship," Elsie says, softly, to Duncan. "Just to be sure."

He takes so long to respond that I begin to think he won't answer her, but eventually, he says, "Mirror, the ring, a coin. Goggles. Silver knife and fork, cup." After another pause, he looks at me. "I didn't want to."

"I never thought that," I reply.

He wipes his face with the back of his hand in a swift, savage gesture. "I wish I never went down there. Will he leave us be now?" He is looking straight at me.

My voice is trapped in my throat. Soothingly, Elsie says, "There's nothing to worry about."

Duncan's eyes don't leave my face. "It's not me I'm worried about. I don't want him to mark the bairn."

"Who?" I say, holding my breath.

"Him. The wanderer."

The way he looks down at the ground, it becomes clear to me. I know something about shame. It's not just that Duncan and Agnes are worried they are being haunted. It's that they are frightened they are being condemned. That they aren't saved. That something on this island knows they are bad people, rotten on the inside, and is stalking them, marking them. A flash of hatred passes through me. The Purdies and their empire. Lester and whatever blackmail nonsense. The preacher in his poky little church. This island doesn't deserve to be rescued.

"Duncan, do you want to come back with us?" Elsie says. "Plenty of rooms for you at the hotel until the weather lifts, help keep Agnes and the baby strong."

Duncan's mouth tightens as he shakes his head. It's not just about pride; he doesn't want to be drawn into any more debt to the Purdies, even by extension.

"Please don't go back down to the ship," I say. "Not for Lester. It's not safe without special equipment, anything could have happened to you."

Duncan releases a bitter laugh. "I'm not going back there for all the tea in China."

Elsie is tugging gently on my arm. "Come on," she says. "Thank you, Duncan. We best be off."

He gives us a brief nod, relieved, I think, that the mirror is finally leaving his possession. Elsie and I follow the path along the ridge that looks out over the water. The sea down on the pebbles is congealed, lumpy, not unlike the watery porridge Agnes served us for breakfast.

Duncan calls from behind us. "River's that way."

"We're not taking the river," Elsie says, gingerly, as if he's lost his mind.

He shrugs. "Don't say I didn't warn you. God preserve you."

We follow the ridge, snapping through wispy reeds that are starched with ice. "I thought they were going to murder us and feed us to the chickens," I whisper.

"Good thing Agnes only has a stomach for bread right now."

I want to laugh, but I feel too stiff and cold. "Was she always so odd?"

"She's always been intense. But nothing like that."

"She was unhinged!" I say. "She is unhinged, isn't she?"

Elsie shushes me. "With the snow, you can hear everything for miles, remember?"

"And the river? What are we going to do, swim home?"

"Imagine suggesting that in this weather."

I stop. "Wait."

She pulls ahead. "If I stop, I'll never get going again. Please don't slow down."

"No." I tug on her arm. "No, wait, we're the stupid ones. The river!"

"Not you too. I should warn you, I get antsy during sermons."

"The river will be frozen solid. We can follow it straight to Port Mary."

She gapes at me. "Wow. We are stupid."

§

WHEN WE GET to the river, it is a light blue ribbon that cuts through the hillsides. Under the surface, tobacco-coloured fringes of sedge lie suspended like a mat. If the harbour is frozen all the way through, then the river is likely to take our weight, but still, I test it first, holding on to frozen roots shackled into the ice and stepping back and forth until I'm sure. A fresh dusting of snow stops it from being too slippery, but after a few minutes I slide forward and my weight yields with a smack that goes right through my buttocks and into my jaw. Elsie reaches for me and tumbles too.

"Are you all right?" I say.

Elsie gasps, and I think for a moment that she's hurt herself, but she's pointing at a hedgerow overgrowing the river. "Rose hips!" She gets to her feet and brushes off the dusting of snow to reveal the lozenges still frozen to the trees. They are such a bright scarlet, they look as if they're glowing.

"We're like those sailors," Elsie says, as she uses my penknife to cut them from the branches, filling her pockets. "Antiscorbutics."

As we start walking again along the river, I put one of the rose hips in my mouth, even though it's frozen solid. Anything to trick my brain into thinking I'm not hungry.

"You need to stop torturing yourself," Elsie says.

For a second I think she is talking about the rose hip. I turn to her in confusion.

"You're not being haunted."

"Oh."

"That's what you think, isn't it?"

The only sound is the crunch of our boots across the ice. A dead branch has lodged between the banks, charcoal fingers against the white sky. "You can't deny the odd things that have happened," I say, cautiously. "And Sophie has proof of how unforgiving Auld James really was."

Elsie rubs her face. "Marta, please tell me you're pulling my leg?"

I don't reply. This isn't the moment to try to convince her, not when I'm at risk of losing her. We come to a sparse clump of young pine trees. Their branches have sheltered strips of river ice from the heaviest snow, revealing glinting stipples of silver and olive water.

"It makes me feel tricked that you weren't honest with me about everything from the beginning," she says.

I stop and take her gloved hands in mine. Her eyes are wet, and a pang of guilt twinges inside my stomach. I've been so selfish, thinking only about what I stood to lose, not about how it would make her feel. "I'm sorry. I was frightened that you wouldn't be able to forgive me."

"Don't make it my job to forgive you, it's not fair."

"You're right."

"You need to find a way to live with what happened. And if we have any chance—"

My heart leaps. I squeeze her hands more tightly.

"I don't want to worry that you're keeping things from me because you think you know how I'm going to react."

Elsie is looking at the ground, and I know that she's afraid I would be unfaithful to her.

"Alex and I were terrible for each other. It's nothing like you and me, how we are with each other. How I feel about you, I've never felt that way about anyone."

"Do you promise?" Elsie says, her voice ragged.

"I promise." I pick her up and we both stagger in the snow. I kiss her on the mouth, and our lips are so cold I can hardly tell when mine are pressed against hers.

"I love you," I say.

I can feel her smiling. "I love you."

"I'm sorry about everything," I say. "I wish I could undo all of my mistakes. I want to try."

"I know."

§

AS WE STUMBLE back through the village, I'm surprised at how relieved I am to see all the familiar depressing buildings, the frost sparkling off the pebbledash. The troughs dug to navigate the streets have accumulated a filthy crust from coal smoke and dirty boots, and an unattended sheepdog trots purposefully through the trenches, sniffing eagerly for something unseen. The smell of thin gruel boiling trickles from chimneys, and a racketing cough echoes from inside one of the houses. Behind us, a window is shuffled open with a creak, and an old woman puts her head to the inch-wide gap. "Elisabeth, is that you?"

Elsie turns around, giving a full-armed wave. "Hello, Mrs. Gilchrist, how are you getting on?"

"How's your grandmother?" the old woman says.

Elsie stops on the street. I stop as well.

"She's fine," Elsie says, although there is a note of uncertainty in her voice.

"The doctor's already left, then?"

Elsie looks briefly at me before turning to run towards the hotel.

Sophie is in the lobby, apparently waiting for me, when I enter through the hotel's side door.

"Hello," she says. "Elsie just went up."

I pull off my hat. "Alice?"

"She's OK," Sophie says. "The doctor is in there with her now."

My pulse bounds up and down. I put my bag containing the mirror and the goggles on the table and lean on it while my heartbeat steadies. I had pictured the worst—Alice, lying out on an icy bier, a spray of pearlwort over her heart.

"What happened?"

Sophie grimaces, looking around us into the clearly empty entranceway. She drops her voice. "She had a bit of a turn."

"What do you mean, a turn? Dizzy spell?"

She shakes her head. Her hesitation is both irritating and nerve-racking.

"Sophie, for Christ's sake, just tell me."

"It's just, well, it's that someone found her yesterday afternoon, walking around the village. Naked."

33

WEDNESDAY, JANUARY 23, 1963

"PARADOXICAL UNDRESSING," THE DOCTOR SAYS AGAIN, AS Elsie writes it down onto the reading room telephone message pad. She sits back and stares at the words on the page.

"Is it likely to happen again?" I say.

Dr. Brode shakes his head. "I would hope not. People who get cold enough to undress usually don't last long after that. A very cold person thinks they are warm again right before they decide to go to sleep. It's a good thing Mrs. Brode was watching her from the window and came down to fetch her right away."

Elsie folds her hands over her stomach and leans over as if she might be sick. I touch her shoulder.

"And you're sure it's the cold, and not—" I hesitate. "Not her mind?"

He sighs. "Older people often behave strangely when they haven't been drinking enough water. Could be that. Could be a sign of a confused mind. We won't know, really, until she's all rested up."

Elsie is still leaned over on the chair, and I rub a circle on her back.

"But," Dr. Brode says, shrugging on his coat, "she was very, very cold indeed when I got here, and that was a couple of hours later. You've got to keep our Alice nice and warm."

Elsie looks up, her eyes bloodshot. "I don't understand how she could have been freezing to death, right in front of us, and no one realised."

Sophie clears her throat from the reading room doorway, and I flinch. "Do you need something?" I say.

"It's just," she says, twirling the ring on her index finger, "we brought her to the reading room, it's the warmest. But when I went up to Alice's room later to fetch her a change of clothes, the grate was clean." She looks at Elsie. "I don't think she'd been using the fire."

"Why the hell would she do that?" I say.

"To save coal?" Sophie says, almost apologetically.

"Oh my God," Elsie groans. "I should never have left her here."

The doctor acquires a look on his face I recognise from Alex; it's the expression of a man who has suddenly found the overwhelming presence of women and their accompanying domestic concerns to be distasteful, or beneath him, or both. "Well," he says, getting up and lifting a bottle of Auld James's whisky to Elsie. "Thanks for this. Keep taking her temperature, lots of soup, send someone round to get me if you're worried."

"Thank you," Elsie says, without getting out of the chair.

As the doctor passes by her, I give Sophie a glare. "We could use some privacy."

She looks at me, then at Elsie, then nods. "Flora and I are supposed to be helping Curly Irene with her grandson. I'll come back in an hour or so."

I'm relieved when she closes the door but still bristle with irritation. She should have been taking better care of Alice, not trying to make friends with the villagers. I snap to attention on Elsie, who is wiping tears away from her eyes. I kneel down in front of her chair and embrace her. "Your granny is tough. She'll feel much better soon, now she's had some food and she's all warmed up."

She pulls back from me. "I shouldn't have left her. I should have been here to look after her."

There it is—the dropping feeling. Elsie's always been convinced of her grandmother's frailty, and now her fears have been confirmed.

I'm the one who took her away. She regrets spending time with me, being with me. Someone else is more important to her. Of course her family is more important to her, more important than me, that's natural. The ugly thoughts wrestle each other. Elsie needs me right now; I have to be supportive. I mustn't give any hint of pouting or disappointment. "There's nothing you could have done," I say, even though I know that's not true.

"I would have noticed if she was freezing, or acting strangely, or not eating and drinking, or being confused, or getting naked!" She shakes her head. "This will kill her. No one will ever talk of anything else. They'll be whispering about it until Judgement Day."

I say things like, "It's been a strange couple of months," and "These things brush over," and "Everyone has been swigging Auld James's whisky for breakfast, I doubt they'll remember," and Elsie nods absently each time, even as she rises from the chair, turns the door handle, and climbs the stairs back up to her grandmother's room. I follow, and then, at the doorway, Elsie turns.

"Do you mind?"

I realise she means she wants me to leave.

"Oh." I want to cry. "No, no, of course not."

"I just wouldn't want her to get confused, having someone she doesn't know in the room."

I want to say that Alice does know me. That Sophie has been sitting in the room, so why shouldn't I? But I don't. Instead I wave Elsie goodbye and give her a chaste, chapped kiss on the cheek.

My own bedroom is like a freezer. Icicles have formed in a crust over the window, and a glass of water I left by my bedside has a frosty scab across the surface. Sophie should have known better than to leave it to get this cold. Cold enough for icicles! I pull some clothes out of my drawer and dress in a fresh sweater and two pairs of woollen tights underneath corduroys. I nap in front of the fire in the reading room, approaching warm for the first time in days.

I wake with a start to find Sophie sitting in the other armchair by the reading room fire. It was a tapping sound that roused me, like fingernails on a window. But when I startle from the chair, I see that Sophie has a bundle of blue wool on her lap and she's knitting. Jesus.

"Did I wake you?" Sophie says.

I don't like the idea that she has witnessed me asleep and vulnerable, perhaps snoring or dribbling, so I shake my head. I shift in the armchair and stand up, crossing to the fire and pretending to warm my hands in front of the flames. Being back in the warmth after the last few days has made the skin on my hands itch and peel, and holding them now near the fire is punitive.

"How is Alice?" Sophie says.

I turn around. "Better, I think. Elsie is with her."

"Poor woman," Sophie says. "She must be so glad to have Elsie back."

I set my teeth. "Elsie was only gone for a couple of days. This is her worst nightmare, and you could have prevented it. You should have kept a more careful eye on Alice, taken even basic care of her. She's an old woman."

Sophie gives a rueful laugh as she clicks her knitting needles.

"Is something funny?"

Sophie tongues the inside of her cheek. "You always see the worst in people."

My head snaps back, brushing lightly against the mantelpiece. "You don't even know me."

Sophie shrugs. "OK, Marta."

I pinch my fingernails into my palms, trying to restrain the rage boiling inside me. That this woman, who is sleeping with my husband, has the nerve to sit there and criticise me. "Why don't you stay out of my business?" I say.

Sophie's clicking pauses as she counts her stitches. "I have no interest in your business, believe me." She gestures upstairs with the tip of her needle. "But Elsie is a nice woman. Don't sabotage it by being, well, being yourself."

My rage is replaced with a flash of terror. Sophie has worked out that there is something between me and Elsie. But no, Elsie knows now about what happened with Lewis. She knows about Alex. Sophie has no power over our relationship. I straighten my posture. "I'd thank you not to talk about Elsie either."

Sophie lifts her hands in the air.

I want to leave the room, but I have nowhere to go. I turn around and poke the coal in the grate more fiercely than it needs to be poked.

"Elsie mentioned that you found the mirror."

I nod, into the fire.

"So, what's left?"

"What does it matter to you?"

The sound of her knitting ceases. "I'm going to have to answer for you at work, remember?"

I grip hold of the poker. "Go to hell, Sophie."

After a moment of silence, she says, "And did you find anything out about Captain Purdie?"

"Must we talk about this now? We've had a miserable couple of days. I haven't eaten properly since I don't know when."

She doesn't reply.

I return to my chair. Five awkward minutes pass before I say, "Violet thinks Auld James was some kind of religious maniac. That he wanted to build an empire of believers in the name of Scottish glory. She said the crew couldn't refuse his mission without losing face as a member of the elect."

Sophie tilts her head. "So she sees him as a faith-driven coloniser? I suppose that wouldn't be far off the other Purdie family enterprises. It might soften the blow for the Purdies if I can reframe his behaviour as motivated by devotion, appropriate for the era. Did she say anything else?"

The image of Violet's face as she pointed into the Neolithic shelter flashes in front of me. "Not really." I adjust my weight in my seat. I am itching to talk about Violet's sense of being followed by Auld James, about the footsteps across the barn, but there is no way to begin without sounding like a lunatic. The last thing I need is Sophie feeling even more superior over me. "Find out anything useful about him while we were gone?" I bring my knees up to my chest. "Was he vengeful?"

Sophie gives a soft bark of a laugh. "Oh, absolutely."

"I was thinking more about God while we were up north."

Sophie raises her eyebrows, and I ignore her. "I mean about this island. The entire concept of the elect—the saved and the doomed. The minister will know more." I picture the bland, myopic face of the minister at the doors of the shelter, watching impassively as his brethren cast me out into Armageddon.

"Hmm, the minister. I'll consider it," she says. I feel the sense of the words "thank you" floating around her, but that she can't bring herself to say them.

"I'm going to check on Alice," I say, more to get away from her than anything else.

Upstairs, nobody answers at my knock and I open Alice's door a few inches. Elsie and Alice are bundled up under the covers together, Elsie's blonde hair tangled on Alice's neck. I creep in and put a hand on Alice's forehead. Her skin is dry but warm; she's breathing regularly. They both look so sweet like that that I feel an unexpected pang of loneliness. I collect a tray of empty bowls and teacups from the top of the dresser and tiptoe out of the room.

I have to put the tray down on the floor of the corridor to close the door, and as I pull it softly shut, a howl of wind rides through the building. The crockery rattles in my hands on the stairs, and as I approach the landing on the first floor, I pause. Was that just the wind? It sounded distinctly like a scream. I put the tray down again, listening harder against the synchronised chorus of the wind through the hotel. There it is again—a faint yelp. It's not the wind. It's a woman. I bound back up the stairs and reopen Alice's bedroom door. They are still sleeping as softly as kittens. I think of where I was standing on the stairwell—the sound must have come from the other side of the hallway, not directly above me. Mrs. Eleanor's room. Now that I think of it, I haven't seen her all afternoon. I'd expect her to be hovering anxiously around the edge of a tragedy like Alice's illness, conspicuously fretting. I cross quickly along the corridor and knock on the door. A muffled knocking sound is clattering from within, and I steel myself. She must have fallen over. Slipped, or a stroke, even. I should have thought to check on her earlier. I turn the handle and open the door onto a full-length mirror on the opposite wall, which reflects back the image of Francis vigorously fucking Mrs. Eleanor, her head rapturously slamming against the headboard.

LATITUDE 81°, 01' N, LONGITUDE 65°, 25' W

... to set out with our equipment across the floes ... the stars unusually bright and behind us did cast shadows against the mist and far beyond I saw an extra man following us at some distance, although all were accounted for. This I affected not to give credence to but the men did see it for themselves and grew much agitated that the visitor had joined us.

34

**WEDNESDAY, JANUARY 23, TO
THURSDAY, JANUARY 24, 1963**

THAT EVENING AS I HELP ELSIE WASH HER HAIR IN THE kitchen, I tell her what I saw in Mrs. Eleanor's bedroom.

She blinks water out of her eyes, sputtering in surprise. "No."

"Oh, I would not want to invent that. I promise, it wasn't my imagination." I shiver. "And I'll never stop seeing it."

"The cold really does do odd things to people," she says, dunking her head back into the bucket. I massage soap through her hair; it's the colour of wet clay under my fingers.

"Do you think that's all it is?"

She opens one eye. "Hmm?"

"That it's only the cold, having a strange effect on people? Mrs. Eleanor and Francis, your granny?"

Elsie laughs. Upside down, her laugh has a strangled quality. "Of course it's the cold. Too much whisky, too much time."

I continue to rub her scalp. "Sophie is going to talk to the minister about Auld James, find out more about him."

"Oh?"

"For context. It might help to ease things over with the Purdies. Keep his reputation intact, if he really was as awful as Sophie says."

"That's good. That you two are getting along, I mean," she says. I decide not to correct her. Now that I think of it, Sophie has been so taciturn about the journal, it's entirely possible she won't share anything the minister has to say about him.

I nudge Elsie forward and wrap a towel around her hair, catching the cold drips. She shudders. "After the last few days, I feel like I'll never be warm again. It seems as if it's getting even colder."

"You'll feel better tomorrow morning," I say. "But we can wait until the afternoon to try the Black Hare?"

Elsie readjusts the towel. Her expression is a mixture of disappointment and sadness. "Oh, Marta."

A horrible flash of premonition stings inside me. She's finished with me. I flinch back as if I've been struck.

Elsie motions for another towel and uses it to mop around the back of her neck. "I can't leave Granny right now."

I look down at my lap. My eyes are burning. I feel childish, for pouting. "Not even for an hour? I really need your help. You know nobody around here will talk to me."

She smiles, sadly. "You'll find a way around it."

"I really need you," I say.

Elsie shakes her head. "My grandmother needs me, Marta. You just want me."

I open my mouth and shut it again.

"You'll have to do your treasure hunting on your own, I'm sorry. I should never have left her alone in this cold. I can't be out—" She gestures to the window. "I understand why this is important to you. But it can't be my priority right now."

There is a lump in my throat, and I have that precarious, vertiginous sense from before. If I don't behave perfectly at this moment, I will lose her forever. I take a deep breath. "I understand," I say.

"Thank you," she says, leaning in for a kiss before pulling the towel closer around her neck. "It's definitely getting colder."

I embrace her. "I'll warm you up tonight. We can have seventeen blankets, and I'll just sleep directly on top of you."

I expect her to laugh but she goes a little still. "I thought I'd go in with Granny tonight. I mean probably for a few days at least."

"Oh." Again, the plunging feeling in my chest. "Oh, of course. Yes."

§

THAT NIGHT IS a torment in my old bedroom. The room is ferociously cold—I think Elsie was right, and the temperature is dropping even further. I have blankets and fur coats on the bed, and I'm wearing a hat and two pairs of socks, and there is a fire in the grate, and yet I feel like I'm being pricked with nails. I roll in the sheets, trying to generate enough static to warm myself up. There is hardly any wind, but the icicles on the window are creaking like a rowboat. At three a.m. I can see my own breath in the room, and I can't take it anymore. I gather blankets and the fur coats and take them down to the reading room. Sophie is already sleeping next to the fire, and I don't think twice before settling down next to her. She gives a little groan and drifts back off to sleep.

After dawn, I pick myself up from the floor, stiff, thirsty, my chest crackling. I use the pail to scoop snow from the front garden and set it to boil on the stove for tea. Sophie pads into the kitchen as the kettle boils, yawning as she unwraps her hair from her scarf.

I don't know what I'm going to say until I hear it coming out of my mouth. "I need your help."

35

FRIDAY, JANUARY 25, 1963

MINISTERS, WE DECIDE, PROBABLY WAKE UP EARLIER THAN publicans, so Sophie and I agree to visit the minister first. The thermometer reads fifteen below zero, and the road is as glossy and slick as glass. Even with the nails attached to my boots, it's safer to trudge in the thick snow than to risk the black stone, and I lead the way to the church through the hedgerows along the coast. The boats are frozen in place in the harbour, but farther out across the ice, men are congregated around a break in the water where there is a smear of blood from a beaten seal.

At the manse, the door is opened by a short woman in her fifties wearing an apron and a harried expression. "A death?" she says.

Sophie and I look at each other. "Not a death."

She puts her hand to her chest. "Oh, thank goodness for that. I heard about Alice, up at the hotel. I thought, Oh, this'll be the news that she's gone."

"She's fine," I say. "Are you—"

"I'm Mrs. Ince, the housekeeper," she says, with a hint of irritation.

"Lovely to meet you," Sophie says. "We'd be ever so grateful for a few minutes of the minister's time, if he's available. We can come back, if now isn't convenient."

I scuff my feet on the doorstep. Is this how she asks for favours? Is she sitting in my flat, at my table, asking Alex for a cup of tea if it would be convenient for him?

Mrs. Ince furrows her brow. "I can check, if you like."

"Yes, please, thank you." Sophie beams at her. She should know better. Nobody smiles in this part of Scotland unless they are a simpleton.

"I suppose you'll be wanting to come in, then?"

Before we have to go through another recitation of gratitude, I push past Sophie and into the hallway.

"I can't promise you anything. We've had an awful lot of people recently, and I don't like to trouble him when there's people in spiritual need," Mrs. Ince says.

"We're in spiritual need," I say, interrupting Sophie before she can insist that we're not a priority.

Mrs. Ince gives us an evaluative look. "Yes, I can imagine."

I am fighting with the urge to roll my eyes.

After a hushed knock on a door at the back of the house, and a hushed conversation, Mrs. Ince creeps forward. "He'll see you now, in the study."

I wait for her to offer us some tea, but nothing is forthcoming.

The minister's study is a poky, small room, which should mean that it is heated generously by the coal fire on the left wall, but only a few meagre cherries smoulder in the grate. He is writing something in a notepad and doesn't look up as we enter. I wonder if Mrs. Ince told him who was calling, if he feels any kind of shame and regret about what happened at the shelter during the crisis.

Sophie clears her throat. "Excuse me?"

"Yes, yes, sit," he says, without lifting his eyes from the paper, gesturing to the seats in front of his desk. They are two hardback wooden chairs. Probably good for inciting confessions rather than indulging in consolation.

I take the seat closest to the sad little fireplace. The minister continues to write, scratching on his pad. A station clock is ticking by the window. The time is wrong, but the second hand continues to flick against itself.

Finally, he looks up at us, putting his pencil down on the desk. "Yes. How can I help you?"

Sophie shifts in her seat. "First of all, I just wanted to say, thank you so much for your time, I really appreciate that you're able to see us. It's a beautiful church."

He is watching her but doesn't respond. She coughs nervously. "Um, and, well, I could really use some advice on something that I hear you're a local expert on."

"Yes?" he says.

"As you may know, I've been working on a journal, well, transcribing a journal, that was recovered—"

"We're here about Auld James," I say, unable to restrain myself.

"Yes, and what about him?"

Sophie glances at me. "Well, I suppose, do you know anything about his religious beliefs?"

"Do I know anything about his religious beliefs?" he repeats.

"Yes."

"Do I, as a man of the church, know anything about the beliefs of our child of the island? The man whose bones are resting out there in that kirkyard?" He points to the window.

"Yes," I say, making deliberate eye contact with him. "We would like to know more about him."

He gives no sign of recognising me. It must be a professional kind of detachment that they also teach soldiers and surgeons. How to excise without mercy.

The minister folds his hands on his desk. "I should say that if I, as a man of the church, who oversees the bones of Captain James Purdie in this kirkyard, don't know about his religion, I would be doing a very bad job."

I get the slightest sense that perhaps this is the minister's idea of a joke. Sophie offers a tentative laugh, and he nods at her, accepting her gesture.

The minister sits back in his chair. "Captain James Purdie was born in 1809. He grew up here on the island at Purdie Castle and, after an early interest in the church, followed a calling from the Lord into the whaling trade. When his elder brothers died, he recommitted his life to missions and forged north."

Sophie scrambles in her bag for a pencil and a pad. She takes down notes in practised shorthand.

"The captain had met many heathen Eskimo during his time in the north, and he made it his personal mission to take the gospel out to them."

"Inuit," Sophie says, reflexively. "And could you explain more about how they were known to be heathens?"

The minister laughs. "How could they be elect when they have no faith in God? When they do not labour in righteousness?"

"What would be righteous labour—" I begin, but Sophie cuts me off.

"So Auld James was a deeply religious man who acted out of his conviction," Sophie enunciates slowly. "And his whaling trade was an extension of his interest in mission work?"

"Absolutely."

"But," I say, unable to help myself, "was he trying to save them? The Inuit?"

The minister turns his bland eyes on me. "Yes, naturally."

"But God decides the elect, doesn't he? God has already determined who has been redeemed?"

The minister nods.

"So why would Auld James bother trying to convert people? Why be a missionary at all, if God has already decided who is saved? They can't *not* be saved, if God has decided that they're saved. What's the point?" There is a faintly hysterical tone in my voice.

The minister runs his tongue around his teeth. "We are commanded to spread the gospel, Matthew 28, verses 19 and 20. A member of the elect follows the commandments of God."

"But," I persist. Sophie kicks me lightly on the ankle. I ignore her. "But how can people have free will to choose to be redeemed, if God has also determined in advance?"

The minister leans back in his chair. "These are parallel truths."

"What does that mean?" I say. "Two things that are both true at the same time, even if they contradict each other?"

"If you like to put it in such a crass manner," he says.

I'm feeling desperate. I need to know why Auld James has been visiting me the past few months, what he wants from me. "So would Auld James have wanted to punish people if they wouldn't convert?"

The minister fixes me with a fishy stare. "Why would the captain take into his own hands the destitution of hell?"

The sound of two female voices arguing breaks in from the hallway. Grunting, followed by a scream. The minister stands and opens the door to two Irenes wrestling with each other. The taller woman has her hands in the other's grey hair, and the smaller of the two is digging her fingernails into her opponent's hip. Mrs. Ince is trying in vain to keep them apart, her face flushed.

Sophie and I look at each other. I've never seen elderly women in a fistfight before.

"Ladies!" the minister shouts, with the full, trumpeting voice of the preacher. They immediately drop their hands to their sides, their eyes wild, chests heaving.

"You two." He gestures to us with his head. "Goodbye."

And just like that, we are dismissed.

"In!" He points to his study, and one after the other, the women shuffle past along the corridor, their eyes downcast. As he closes the door forcefully behind them, Mrs. Ince tidies her hair.

"What was that about?" I say.

Mrs. Ince sighs. "It's a bad business, this weather. I tell you, the minister has been called out day and night recently for trouble just like that." She gestures into the study. "Satan prowling out in this snow."

"Prowling?" I repeat.

"Yes, prowling. And creeping, and tempting. All this snow is here to lighten our sins, to cleanse us. So Satan is here, all right, and he's trying." She cackles. "The elect might wobble on the path, but we always return. The Lord loves his bride too much to let go of her hand."

AS WE MAKE our way back down to the village, I can feel Sophie looking at me.

"You never struck me as a theologian," she says.

"When they lock you out to die and call themselves holy, then you start to pay greater attention."

Sophie is quiet. "What do you mean?"

I check to make sure that she isn't being wilfully cruel. But no, her expression is puzzled.

"You didn't hear?"

She shakes her head.

"It doesn't matter," I say, turning away.

She quickens her step after me. "No, don't do that, the Marta door slam. What are you talking about?"

I pat the pockets of my coat, but no cigarettes. A half-frozen rose hip is still lolling in the bottom of one of my pockets, and I dig my fingernail into the flesh. "I'm surprised nobody told you. We lost radio signal the day we thought the missiles were coming. The whole village went up to the shelter and closed the door on me."

She looks as if I have slapped her. "What?"

"The island is special because everyone is elect, apparently. Not me, though. Outsider. So I suppose not you either. If there's an atomic bomb, we'll both be grilled toast."

Sophie's fingers lightly graze my elbow, before she withdraws her hand. "They just left you outside to be bombed?"

"Not Elsie," I say.

Sophie looks as if she's doing some complicated algebraic equations in her head. "But then why do you want to help the Purdies at all? Surely you can't feel much loyalty towards the island after all that?"

"Lewis was from here, he loved this place. The least I can do in his memory is not let it self-destruct, even if they don't like me. I don't blame them."

After a long moment, Sophie gives me a nod.

§

THE WINDOWS of the Black Hare are streaming with condensation when we approach. The curtains are drawn, but the beads of water on the glass must mean that there is a fire indoors, and a strong one. Remembering what Elsie said, I tap on the windows and call out before trying the front door. A door at the side of the building opens, with a squeak and a puff of hot air that floats around to the front.

It's a young boy's voice that answers. "Yes?"

Sophie and I follow the voice around the side of the building to see a child, maybe seven years old. He's dressed in a woman's coat that is far too big for him but has been pinned at the arms.

"Hello," Sophie says, in a cheery voice. A far too cheery voice. "Is your mummy or daddy in?"

The boy frowns. "Hurry up, don't let the cold in."

We follow him into the pub, a fug of coal smoke and spilt beer and stagnant water. I'm surprised to see there is already a group of four youngish men in the corner near the fire, slumped over a table. With the drawn curtains and the poorly ventilated fire, the room is dingy enough for it to be nighttime instead of noon.

The boy lets himself behind the counter and steps up on a stool, putting his hands on the wood. "What can I get you? Auld James's whisky?" He taps a sign that has been made out of the back of a cornflakes packet that says *Swaps only* in thick, childish handwriting. "Don't need any more potatoes," he says. "Coal, powdered milk, that'll do nicely."

Sophie and I exchange a glance.

"Either of your parents around?" I say, in the least sugary voice I can summon.

The boy's expression hardens. "Why?"

"I need to check with them about something." I pause, not wanting to offend him. "Something adult." Then I add, "Sorry."

"Well, Mum and Dad are upstairs. You can go get them if you like. I'm not going."

I feel an overwhelming pang of terror for this child, performing an adult's work in an adults' house. "Are they ill?"

He releases a froggy laugh. "Ill! No. They're busy, though. If you want to see what I've been seeing, go on ahead." He points to the stairs.

I think of Mrs. Eleanor and Francis. "Oh."

He smacks the table of the counter with small, dirty hands. "So. I've got Auld James's whisky or there's rum. Lager's frozen. If you want a can opener and a spoon, you have to promise not to cut yourself."

"Let's come back," Sophie whispers.

"We've got clean towels back at the hotel, and pickled eggs," I say. "Would that do for two whiskies?"

He thinks on it. "Done." He pulls out a soft grey school notebook and writes the details of the barter carefully on the page. "Name?"

"I can write it," I say, and his face relaxes. He tips up his little cap as he watches me write the letters upside down.

"You're the diver."

"Yes."

His face gets a line of concentration down the centre of his forehead and his ears go a bit pink. He knows about the objects.

As he pours Auld James's whisky into two jam jars, I look over at the men slumped by the fire, who have propped themselves up on their elbows now and are talking softly to one another. Sophie and I take a seat at the bar and look into our jam jars. "I've drunk more whisky in the last month than I have in my whole life," Sophie says, wincing as she takes a sip from the jar. She raises her jar in my direction. "Happy Burns Night."

"Is it today? I feel as if I've been stuck in the same day since Christmas," I say. Across the counter, the boy is pretending to write in his notepad. I lean forward. "What's your name?"

"Joe." He sounds almost shy.

"Do you celebrate Burns Night on Cairnroch, Joe?"

He frowns as if he's trying to remember who that even is. "The heathen singer?" he says at last.

"I suppose that's our answer," I say, to Sophie. "Joe, this is Sophie. She works at the museum in Edinburgh with me."

He examines her from under fair eyebrows. "Are you a diver too?"

She shakes her head. "I'm more of an indoor person. How about you, do you like the outdoors or the indoors?"

He sniffs. "Outdoors, definitely."

"Do you have any siblings?" I try not to let him see that I'm inspecting him. He's grubby but seems well-fed enough. He's wearing boots that have been carefully patched with red rubber disks.

He nods. "Billy's out collecting dulse. You can eat it, you know."

"Is Billy older or younger than you?"

"Older. He's ten."

I gesture behind me to the men in the corner. "And are they here often?"

Joe nods. "Yeah. Every day. But miners bring us extra coal, so I don't mind."

"It's clever, the swaps. Was that your idea?"

He nods, then another pink tinge crosses his ears. "Well, me and Billy."

"And your parents, they haven't been down here much, I take it?"

He shakes his head, clearly embarrassed.

"Cold does strange things to people," I say.

Joe frowns. "Yeah," he says, with a sense of conviction. "All of them have been acting up since the big snows. My pal Greg runs the shop now."

Sophie sips from her whisky. I can feel her bristling with the urge to say something, and I'm glad that she is winning restraint.

"Greg, is he your age?" I say.

Joe nods, then thinks about it. "Well, he's born in June, so he's younger than me." He puffs up his chest.

"And there's no school at the moment?" Sophie says, sweetly.

He chuckles. "No."

In the corner, a man is murmuring something. The others laugh, with a cackle. It's the first real sign of animation they have given since we came in. Joe's face becomes alert.

"And they don't cause any trouble?" I say, quietly.

"No," Joe says. "I've known them since I was a child."

I try to smother my smile. I remember so well that sense of wanting to distance myself from childhood, even while it was moving away from me. "So. Dulse, is it? But you're getting enough to eat?"

His expression grows proud. "Oh yeah. We're eating lots. Dulse, barley soup, salt cod. We had a rabbit brought in here once, though all we knew what to do was boil it. But that's all right, isn't it?" He looks troubled.

"Yes, absolutely," I say, and he nods, reassured. "You're doing great." He shrugs, trying not to look embarrassed.

"Me and Sophie, we're up at the hotel, with Elsie. You know Elsie, don't you?"

Joe nods, a little too eagerly. It occurs to me that Elsie is probably beloved by schoolboys all over the island. I feel a flicker of pride that she belongs to me.

"I'll come back with the towels and the eggs later. But if you think of anything you need for the barters, you come on by? Or send Billy?"

He acquires a businessman's appreciation for commerce. "All right."

"Your dad, Callum, does—" I start, but the cackling starts up again, and I look over my shoulder, recognising the man on the right as the miner who brought the hoist for the second dive. I flash back to the trace of his elbow across my arm, the night of the fire. Losing my train of thought momentarily, I turn back around to the bar.

Sophie must notice, because she looks behind us, curiously.

"Whisky?" Joe says, over my shoulder.

"Aye," a voice says. The miner is standing unsteadily at the corner of the counter, looking down at us both.

"There she is," he says, peering at me as if we're long-lost companions. "Haven't seen you in a wee while."

"Hello," I reply. I don't remember his name; I'm not sure he ever introduced himself.

He leans over Sophie and runs a heavy, proprietorial hand along the length of my back. "Certainly a sight for sore eyes. The mermaid herself. Wouldn't mind myself a little swim with you."

I stiffen, jostling my shoulder until I've shaken him off. "OK," I say, swallowing the last of the whisky in my glass and standing up, carefully out of reach of any further clumsy embrace. "Maybe you can let your mum and dad know that Sophie and I were here, that we were talking about Auld James's ship," I say.

Joe nods.

Sophie follows me outside. "Wow, I'm so stupid," she says, under her breath, as the pub door closes behind us. I turn to her just in time to catch an expression of exhausted amusement across her face.

"What is it?"

"Nothing." She stares down into the snow, shaking her head with a smug kind of irritation. "I don't know what I expected."

"Expected about what?"

"I just thought, for a moment, that you had changed," she says. "Elsie—the way you are with her. I've been telling myself, give Marta a chance, everyone deserves a second chance. Even after what you did."

I am stunned by her sudden change in tone. "What do you mean?"

She scoffs, gesturing to the door of the pub. "That man? You just can't help yourself, can you?"

"Oh, come along, Sophie, he's just some handsy chap in a pub. You're not going to blame *me* for that?"

She huffs a bitter laugh. "Oh no, it's never your fault. Who else is there, Marta?" she goes on. "Francis? What about Mr. Tibalt? Murdo? The minister? Jesus, Marta. What's wrong with you?" I turn away from her and hunch into my coat. "Leave me alone. You don't know the first thing about me."

"Really," Sophie calls after me. "Really, I'm genuinely asking. What on earth is wrong with you?"

I walk even faster now. If I slow down, she'll see that she's got to me, and she doesn't deserve to see me upset. Sophie picks up her pace to match mine, her voice insistent.

"I thought that maybe you were learning a lesson," she says. "But no, you're just bored and cold. I should have known that you're clinging on to Elsie the same way you throw yourself at anyone else in your path."

"Don't you dare talk about Elsie," I say, swivelling around. "I love her." It feels vindicating to say it out loud, like I'm forging it into iron.

"Do you?" Sophie says, raising her arms. "Are you even capable of love? Of taking responsibility for yourself?"

I take a step towards her. "Oh, and how responsible is it to be sleeping with my husband, exactly? Whatever you're accusing me of, maybe you want to take a look at yourself."

Sophie splutters. "You are so paranoid you can't even hear what you sound like."

"Come along, no need to be coy with me, the whole office knows!"

Her face drops. "I'm not sleeping with Alex. He gave me a raise, that's all. Are people saying that I'm sleeping with him?"

"What?" I snap.

Her lower lip is wobbling. "I'm not having sex with—"

From behind us comes a small, pointed cough.

We turn to see Joe, standing knee-deep in the snow. From the way he is rubbing his arms, I'd guess he's been standing there for some time.

"Joe, sweetie," Sophie says, all sugar. "I'm sorry about us shouting. When grown-ups—"

"I don't want my mum and dad to hear," Joe says. His expression is so tense and urgent I know that there isn't much time before he changes his mind.

I walk past Sophie and approach Joe. "You don't want them to hear us talk about the objects?"

He nods.

"Have they been sold already?"

He shifts his weight. "The ring went to Miss Gilles, in the village."

He looks so frightened that I want to reassure him. "That's OK," I say. "What else?"

"That's all that's gone. Miss Gilles gave me ten pounds for it. I've already spent it. I didn't have a choice, there was things we needed." He is shaking.

I stand next to him. "Don't worry, I understand."

He sucks in his cheeks. "Do you want the rest of it?"

Behind me I hear the crunch of Sophie's footsteps. "Very much, yes," I say.

"OK," he says, swallowing. He gestures towards the pub. "It's in the back room."

§

THE DOOR TO the back room of the pub has frozen from the cold, and I have to put my shoulder to it before it bursts open into what must once have been a formal dining room. The wallpaper is stippled with mould, and on the floor there is a wooden crate containing three frozen red apples. Joe pulls open the top drawer of a chest of drawers and hands me a potato sack. I can't wait. I tug out the knot. Inside are the horn cup and the coin. My heart flares as I withdraw the coin. It's British, a copper halfpenny token from 1794 with Neptune embossed on one side. I won't be able to check a catalogue until I'm back in the museum, but I doubt it's especially valuable, and Purdie must have kept it for sentimental, rather than pecuniary, reasons. The reverse is slippery smooth, and when I turn it over, there is only the faintest image of men in a boat, what looks like a whaler raising a harpoon to strike a jet of water foaming from an unseen beast below. The engraving of the boat crew has been worn down to a gloss, as if someone had taken to rubbing it absent-mindedly, or even for luck. I squeeze it briefly in my palm before dropping it back into the bag.

I turn to Joe. "Joe, thank you. I'll collect some money together, and I'll write a note for your dad, I'll explain everything and take the blame. I don't want you to get into trouble."

He puts his hands into the pockets of his coat. "It's no bother," he says, but I can tell from the way his lip is twitching that this is a considerable act of bravery.

I tie up the bag. Only the ring left. I feel almost light-headed.

Sophie steps forward and crouches to his eye level. "Before we go, I want to ask if you've seen anything odd in the pub since you got these items from the ship?"

"Odd like what?"

"Oh, I don't know. Strange sounds, maybe?" She clears her throat. "Seeing a person hanging about. Or the shape of a person?"

Slowly, I turn around. Joe is glancing between us both. I have the irrational thought that Sophie is mocking me, that Elsie must have told her about my fears.

Joe hesitates. "Do you mean the Bodach?"

"What is the Bodach?" Sophie says.

"Crone's husband," Joe says.

Sophie leans in. "Someone in the village?"

"He's like a spectre," I say, my voice hoarse. "A winter goblin."

Joe edges away from the chest of drawers. "Comes down the chimney to get naughty children. Not that I believe it," he adds, with a quick, unconvincing cough. "But Billy, he didn't like it. That especially." He points to the fireplace in the corner of the room. It clearly hasn't been used in some time, and there are sooty streaks stretching out from the chimney across the wallpaper.

"What about it?" Sophie says, in a gentle but urgent tone. "What did you see there?"

"The scorch marks."

"Yes," Sophie says, sounding almost disappointed. "Though we'd expect to see those around a chimney, wouldn't we?"

He frowns at her as if she's stupid. "Them marks aren't from fire at the bottom. No, that's from something that burned as it went up the chimney."

Sophie stands up and walks towards the fireplace. He's right. The wallpaper around the fireplace is charred with black licks that spread downwards and spray across the floor. Whatever was burning here was hot enough to sear bubbling blisters into the wallpaper and melt tracks into the floorboards. And it travelled upwards, into the chimney. When Sophie turns around, her expression of horror matches my own. There's no disguising that she's afraid.

Elsie hasn't said anything to her. She believes it too.

"What do you know?" I say.

LATITUDE 81°, 01' N, LONGITUDE 65°, 33' W

Fearful of the visitor, the crew insisted on returning to ship, and when in the morning I woke they had all broken camp and begun a return across the floes. I had no choice but to walk after them, having left my pistol in the Huski village after quarrelling.

36

FRIDAY, JANUARY 25, 1963

I FOLLOW SOPHIE UP TO HER BEDROOM ON THE FIRST FLOOR. I knew that this was the room usually reserved for the Purdies' use, but the scale of it still surprises me—it must run the length of the kitchen below, and a couch and two armchairs are settled into the recess of a bay window on the far side. A four-poster bed in the centre of the room faces a fireplace containing a few glowing coals. Sophie has already laid out her nightdress on top of the bedspread, along with a silk scarf for wrapping her hair. I resist the childish urge to jump on the covers and disturb her peaceful arrangement.

"This way," she says, picking up a towel that was rolled under a door next to the bed. This leads to what must usually be a dressing room, with a large wardrobe and a mirrored vanity. Sophie has pulled two card tables together to make a desk, with matching oil lamps at either side. It is spectacularly tidy, one pre-sharpened pencil lying obediently on a lined notebook next to a cardboard box. In the centre of the desk is a sheaf of papers that I at first mistake for typewritten, but no, her handwriting is just that neat.

I take a seat and point to the cardboard box. "Are the books in there?"

Sophie winces. "I'd rather you didn't touch either the journal or the ledger. The paper is extraordinarily fragile—I risked deteriorating their condition even further by bringing them here. You'll just have to trust I've transcribed accurately." She gathers up the manuscript and holds it protectively to her chest before putting it back on the table. "So. The men start seeing a figure in the ship not long after it gets trapped in the ice."

"Lack of sun? Vitamin deficiencies?"

A dimple forms in her cheek. "Yes, possibly, I thought that too. But it's not just the captain. It's the whole crew. They see it, slinking around. They hear it too, footsteps."

"It?"

"It, them, she, he." She shakes her head. "I don't know. The crew can feel something. And it's not long after that that everybody starts disintegrating." She turns the pages of the transcript. "Fighting, jealousy, arguments, 'lustful acts'—I think they were all sleeping together, although he doesn't exactly spell it out. Auld James blames the crew for lax morals. And the crew blames Auld James for bringing it upon them."

My scalp prickles. I almost don't want to ask her. "Like a ghost?"

Sophie raises her hands.

"I don't even read my horoscopes. I'm not a superstitious person. I'm sorry. I've just been doing nothing but reading the diary all the time. All the cold, the lack of electricity, the candlelight, the castle—my God, the castle, the wind. I can't help it. I've just got away with myself." She laughs halfheartedly.

But I don't believe her. There is no way that Sophie, meticulous, careful Sophie, comes to the conclusion that the island is being haunted, unless she has reason to. "Tell me what you saw," I say.

She turns aside. "Nothing."

"Sophie."

"I'm sure it was nothing." She tugs on a loose thread in her fingerless gloves. "My room in the castle. One of the windows looked out over the field, onto darkness. After the sun sets, all you can see is shapes from the fire reflected in the glass, these little dancing triangles. The evening before I came here"—she waves around the hotel—"I woke up in the night and the triangles were, they were settling. Gathering into the shape of something solid. I thought I was dreaming at first. I told myself not to be foolish. I dared myself to get out of bed and poke the fire up enough to see if there really was anything in the room. And when I did, the glow from the fire showed it up, in the corner. It was just there, watching me."

"What?"

"A shadow. The sense of a shadow." She meets my eyes. "The crewmates think it's a creature, or a man. But I don't think it was ever alive."

I pull my knees up onto the chair. "What do you mean?"

"I don't know. It didn't feel human. It felt more like, more like how a seagull watches you when you're eating. It was as if I was in the way, somehow. Like it found me there and it was—disappointed."

She's seen it too.

I put my head in my hands. The overwhelming relief I feel is mingled with frustration that Sophie, of all people, is the person who believes me. "I've seen it."

"Where?"

"There was something in the ship on my first dive. Watching. And then in my room upstairs. The lightship. I—I thought it was Lewis, at first," I say, my voice barely louder than a whisper. "I thought that he was here waiting for me, after—"

"It's not Lewis, Marta. The whole crew of HMS *Deliverance* sees it. It's not Lewis in 1849."

"I know that," I say, unable to keep the bite out of my voice. "But then it seemed like, well, Violet thought she was seeing Auld James. It made sense. I went down there, took things from his grave . . ."

Sophie shakes her head. "The crew of the ship were sailing away from an Inuit settlement when their boat got trapped in the ice. I can't be sure what happened in the village, but Purdie was a violent man at the best of times, and he didn't like to be told 'no.' He was still alive when the visitations began—that's what they call them, 'visitations.' I know what the minister said, but it seems as if the plan was never to actually convert anyone. This was some kind of recruitment drive for seal hunters, not a missionary trip. And when Purdie insisted on stopping at more settlements, they lost valuable time before winter. When they got stuck in the ice, they became so terrified by the visitations they decided to abandon the ship. At that point they saw another man among them, an extra figure on the ice, following behind them." She runs her fingers along the top of the page. "When they go back to the ship, the crew leave everything inside it, including Captain Purdie. They blame him for the haunting, lock him inside his cabin, and he hears them knocking a hole in the engine room."

"So that's why the ship is so well outfitted? They left everything inside it deliberately?"

"It seems like it."

"I kept thinking about Auld James's horn cup. It makes no sense to leave an item like that behind, if you're making an escape across the floes."

"Yes, or his snow goggles." Sophie opens the bottom drawer of the vanity behind her and withdraws a half-empty bottle of Auld James's whisky and a Bakelite tooth mug. She pours herself a slug into the cup and hands the bottle straight to me.

Something slides into a groove in my understanding. "The crew thought Auld James specifically was cursed by something that came in from the ice."

Sophie nods. "But what is it?"

"I'm not sure. A manifestation of some kind. I don't understand it, I just know what I saw."

I picture the footsteps in the snow, leading up to the doorway, on Hogmanay. "The weather allowed it out from the ship," I say. "The snow. If it came from the Arctic—but what's it doing here? What does it want?"

"Well, it went to Violet, Duncan, the Black Hare. It's following anything connected to Auld James. It's following what was taken from the site."

I grip the bottle of whisky tighter. "But that means if we wanted to stop what's been happening, I'd need to put everything belonging to Auld James back down there, back down in the ship."

Sophie wriggles her fingers, as if revealing a magic trick.

The room is lilting around me, whether from exhaustion or whisky on an empty stomach, I'm not sure. Before I realise what's happening, I'm crying. Sophie glances around her helplessly, before dashing next door and returning with a handkerchief. A terrible, ridiculous sense of loss is rolling over me. This haunting hasn't been about me at all. "But I deserve to be punished," I say. "Lewis—and then I thought Auld James—"

Sophie takes a breath. Next door in her room a coal in the fireplace tumbles into the grate. "For what it's worth, Marta, I think you're punishing yourself plenty."

I try to regain enough control to say something, but every time I try to speak, a croaky sob breaks through me and I gibber into the handkerchief. After a moment, I feel a hesitant, cold hand on my shoulder, and I cry even more.

"What happened with Lewis, it wasn't your fault," she says, eventually.

I shake my head. "Don't be nice to me."

Sophie laughs, bitterly. "I'm not, believe me. Even Alex said he used to swim in all kinds of weather. It wasn't the first time he went out when he shouldn't have. Accidents happen."

"I should have noticed earlier, said something earlier."

"Yes," Sophie says. "And it still may not have made any difference."

I hold the handkerchief over my face. It smells faintly fusty and old-fashioned, like lavender and mothballs.

"You're going to need to make peace with it," Sophie says. "Or you'll end up causing more damage."

We sit in silence, and Sophie motions for the whisky. I pour another measure into her mug.

"Are you really not sleeping with Alex?"

She grimaces. "No. He asked me out for dinner and drinks. I felt..."

She looks down at her lap. "I couldn't exactly say no to my boss, could I? You know what it's like for girls like us."

I try to cover my surprise that she would put us in the same category. "He said you threw a joint party at our flat."

"That? Good grief, no. That was an ambush, not a party. He asked me to get there for seven; no one else turned up until nine. He was already drunk when I arrived, talking about you and Lewis. I think he wanted me to feel sorry for him."

I laugh, wiping my eyes. "He always was a gentleman."

She gives me a sidelong look. "If he's told you we are an item, then it's to hurt you. Make you paranoid. Even more paranoid. I'm surprised he didn't think you and I would put two and two together, being here."

"Oh, he knows me well enough to guess I'd alienate you from the start."

Sophie gives me a tired smile.

"But what are we supposed to do about this?" I gesture to the diary. "Do we call a priest?"

"A priest? You'll get in trouble for papism like that around here! No, you heard the minister. He thinks Auld James is proof of how godly the island is."

"And we're heathen outsiders," I finish. "No one on Cairnroch will want to think Auld James is being punished."

"Maybe he deserves to be punished," Sophie says. I feel the echo of what I said earlier dancing around the room. She looks abashed. "It's not the same, Marta," she says, softly. "He was a tyrant. The Purdies are corrupted. The things they did to collect their wealth—the plantations, the tea, the sugar? The castle, the hotel, it's all sitting on poisoned gold. They've *earned* a family curse."

I look down at the floor. "But it's not just the Purdies, is it? It followed me, it came to you. The lighthouse fire. Those scorch marks at the Black Hare, it was there too. Other people on Cairnroch might get hurt."

Sophie raises her eyebrows. "Didn't they lock you out to get blasted to dust? Maybe they all deserve to be punished."

"They're not evil. They're just . . ." I trail off. I don't know how to finish the sentence.

"If it wants Auld James so badly," Sophie says, "then maybe it should have him back."

37

SATURDAY, JANUARY 26, 1963

"I don't understand the joke?" Elsie says, the next day, after breakfast. She is wearing a willing, bemused expression. In the light of day, with the bowl of porridge mixed with snow water sitting on the table beside her, some of my conviction from last night has faltered.

Sophie shifts her weight and glances at me.

"It isn't a joke," I say.

Elsie looks between us. "You think some kind of apparition has hitchhiked here from the Arctic and is haunting the island?"

Sophie and I look at each other again.

"Um, yes?"

Slowly, Elsie puts her spoon down into the porridge and pinches the bridge of her nose. "I haven't had enough tea for this."

"I know how it sounds. But perhaps if you wanted to look at the diary for yourself, it might make more sense," Sophie offers.

Elsie stares at her. Then she blinks, pointing up above the kitchen. "Oh yes, please, anything that would help this to make more sense."

Sophie beckons with her head, and we follow her upstairs to her room. In Sophie's makeshift study, I watch as Elsie turns the pages of the transcript. "Here," Sophie murmurs. "And here, see."

After about twenty minutes of pointing and reading, Elsie leans back in the chair, bouncing against the springs. She turns to us with the expression of a sportsman, eyeing up his cricket team. "You've both gone crackers."

Sophie's shoulders drop. "But the whole crew sees it—the extra man."

"They were starving to death, trapped in the ice in the darkness," Elsie says, articulating each word. "What's the word for when people stir each other up?"

"Hysteria," I say.

Elsie points at me. "Yes, hysteria. One person thinks they see old Billy out by the well, and then everyone else does too."

"But we *have* seen old Billy," I say.

Elsie bursts out laughing.

I feel the heat in my face. "I mean—we've seen things too. Surely even you have to admit that it's been getting odd around here?"

Elsie shrugs. "No TV."

"The arguments, the—" I shift my eyes quickly to Sophie. "The sex, the tempers."

Elsie is shaking her head as if she's delivering a terminal prognosis. "You're supposed to be scientists, aren't you? Both of you?"

Both Sophie and I dip our chins.

"Should I send Flora to fetch Dr. Brode?" she says.

"No."

Elsie rubs her temples, springing a flush into her skin. "I don't know what you expect me to say."

Sophie slips her palms between her knees. "I suppose we want your help," she says, in a meek, winsome voice.

Elsie's expression softens. I make a mental reminder that maybe I need to try being more meek.

"Maybe we got a little," Sophie chuckles, "a little carried away. You know what it's like—long nights, ghost stories. But the Auld James from this diary poses a problem. It won't help anyone on the island lure tourists here if he was a hateful idiot."

"The Purdies will select the parts that don't sound too awful and keep the rest in a drawer," Elsie says, with a shrug. "And no one on

Cairnroch is going to mind that he's a religious maniac. It might make him even more liked, if that's possible."

"And what about when the Purdies find out the crew murdered Auld James?" I say.

Elsie looks at me sharply.

"The way the Grimball family have had that superstition around them? When people on Cairnroch find out that their ancestors ganged together and nailed Auld James into his cabin, how will that fit with their godly self-image? The Purdies aren't going to swallow that well, either."

Sophie gives me a slight congratulatory nod as Elsie stares into the paraffin lamp, absorbing this.

After a long few moments of silence, Sophie clears her throat. "Do you know who Miss Gilles is?"

"Miss—oh, you must mean Morag," Elsie says. "What do you want with Morag?"

"She has the ring."

"You found it!" Elsie grins. "Old Morag, is it? Well, if Morag has it, you might need to haggle. She's canny, sells island blankets and sweaters to shops on the mainland. She won't give up something valuable without making a good profit."

"Maybe we'll need Lester after all," Sophie says, more to herself than to anyone else.

Elsie scoots forward in her chair. She makes a gesture as if she wants to take my hands in hers and then thinks better of it. I forgot to tell her that Sophie knows about us. "Isn't this everything you wanted?" she says, in a low voice. "You've done it. You've found everything you needed."

I nod, unable to meet her eyes.

"Why aren't you more excited? I thought you'd be happy."

Discreetly, Sophie lets herself out of the room. I offer her a glance of thanks as she passes. When she has closed the door to her bedroom, Elsie takes my hands and jiggles them, lightly.

"Be happy," she says.

"I am happy." My voice is glum.

"But you have all the items now. And if Morag has the ring—your job is safe! The Purdies have their collection. You did it!"

I chew the inside of my cheek. "I'm not sure."

"Marta—"

"I know something is happening. I know there's something wrong here. I've felt it since I arrived. I still feel it. I *know* it."

She searches my face. "Marta—"

"There's no way for you to understand," I say, turning aside.

"I do understand," she says, gently. "I understand why you think that you're being followed."

"This isn't about Lewis. It's not all in my head."

"I didn't say it's all in your head."

"How can't you see what is happening?" I feel close to tears again. She is looking at me with the sort of pained resignation of someone on a train that is pulling out of the station. "I don't understand how we can be so close, but you can't see what I see."

Elsie lets out an exhausted breath.

"We are still close, aren't we?"

A brief flash of frustration passes over her face. "Of course we are."

"Then come back with me on the next ferry."

"We've been over this, Marta. It's not that simple," she says. "I have Granny."

"Doesn't she want the best for you?"

"She does, but the idea of her being here, alone . . ." She trails off.

There's a lump in my throat. She doesn't want her granny to be alone, but that means she'll be alone too. We both will. I shuffle my chair closer to Elsie's and kiss her. She kisses me back, but reluctantly.

"I'll think about it," she croaks. "About leaving." Her eyes trace over my face. "I do love you."

I stroke a strand of hair away from her cheek. "And it's not just the effect of the figure?" I say. "Racy dreams, inflamed passions?"

Her lip twitches. "You're joking, aren't you?"

"Yes, of course," I say. "Yes, of course I'm joking."

38

SATURDAY, JANUARY 26, 1963

SOPHIE AND I SET OFF FOR THE CASTLE AFTER LUNCH. IT IS six below zero and a gritty wind plunges down the hillside, stinging my eyeballs. We don't have the breath or the strength to talk to each other as we climb the hill, and I'm glad for the excuse not to discuss how I failed to convince Elsie. The road is too slippery to risk, so we trudge heavily through the fields, each footstep an effort. Near the stile, Sophie shrieks, and when I return to her side she is standing with her hands at her cheeks. Under her foot is a dead blackbird, frozen solid into the field. She shudders. "It made a crack."

When we arrive at the castle, we let ourselves in through the kitchen door to find Janet sitting at the table, wearing a dazed and exhausted expression. Her hair is sticking out from her bun, and from the corridor comes the sound of shouting, the soft scuffle of objects being thrown.

"Janet?" I approach her carefully, as if she's an animal I want to capture. "Janet, what's happening?"

She doesn't register any surprise at seeing me after what must be weeks. "Oh, they're fighting again."

"Who's fighting? Lord and Lady Purdie?"

"All three of them," Janet says, shaking her head.

Sophie gives me a worried glance, unwraps her scarf, and puts the kettle on the fire for Janet. I creep along the velvet-lined corridor and down to the curtain that opens onto the formal entranceway. Lord Purdie is in only his nightgown and slippers, red-faced and shaking his finger up at the first-floor stairwell. I peer cautiously round the corner to see Lester wearing a Purdie tartan dressing gown and threadbare woollen socks, standing at the banister on the upstairs landing.

"Don't you talk to me like that!" Lord Purdie is shouting up at Lester.

"I'll talk to you any way I please," Lester shouts back. "You don't talk to *her* like that."

"She's my damn wife."

"In law only!" On the floor next to Lester's feet is a wooden box, and he bends down, reaches within, retrieves a handful of flimsy papers—perhaps receipts or letters—and tosses the bundle into the air, releasing fluttering scraps over the banister and down onto the marble floor of the gallery. One envelope catches near the grate and begins to singe. Mr. Scruff, oblivious to the tone, scampers in delight amongst the falling papers, trying to snatch them in his jaws.

I tiptoe back along the corridor to the kitchen. "Are Lester and Lady Purdie involved with each other?" I whisper.

Janet takes a sip of her tea. "The lady, the lord, and Lester. All three of them," she says, distractedly.

I raise my eyebrows at Sophie. "Did you know?" I mouth, over Janet's head.

"Of course not! When I was here, it was all, 'Pass the butter, if you might.'"

"Should we come back later?" I say.

Sophie's eyes sparkle. "No, this is the perfect time. He'll be so unsettled."

Heavy footsteps approach along the corridor, and Sophie and I freeze as Lester passes in profile on the way to his study. Sophie motions with her chin, and I follow him along the hallway, turn the handle to his study, and slip inside, Sophie behind me.

Lester is looking out the window, his hands worrying at each other. When he turns, there is a livid blush across his cheeks. "What on earth? What do you two want?"

"Nice to see you too." I sit on the sagging ottoman. My sudden dip in posture diminishes my authority somewhat, so I fold my arms in front of my chest.

"We're here because of the items from the ship," Sophie says. "We need something from you, and in return, we give you our word not to file our report on your activities." She gives him a polite, polished smile.

Lester huffs with scornful laughter. "Honestly, girls. I've already been through this with . . ." He gestures at me. "I don't have anything."

"Oh, but we do," Sophie says. "A signed and witnessed statement by Edward Grimball, testifying to your involvement in the black market."

I snap my head to look at her. Bringing up Eddie Grimball was not what we agreed. In fact, Sophie expressly promised me she wouldn't mention him. We were supposed to bluff Lester with vague references to the authorities. I try to compose a neutral expression on my face.

"I don't believe you," he says, but his eyelids are heavy, the speckled flush on his cheeks spreading towards his ears.

"That's fine," Sophie says, "I thought you might not. We'll just hand the allegations straight over to Mr. Dimiroulis at the museum. Let's leave the investigations up to him and the museum administration. That won't cause any embarrassment or alarm for Lord and Lady Purdie, I'm sure."

He looks from me to Sophie. "You wouldn't—"

"We will," I say. My voice is hoarse. Sophie's unexpected invocation of Alex has spiked my pulse. "You haven't left us any choice. The repercussions for us will be minimal in comparison."

"But—"

"Oh, something you may not know is that Marta here is Mr. Dimiroulis's wife. I suppose that hasn't come up?" Sophie adds, sweetly.

Lester holds my eyes, and whatever assessment he makes in that moment, it's clear that I have passed. His face slackens. "What is it that you want?"

"We need an item from the Purdie collection," Sophie says. "Something that won't be missed."

"And it needs to be valuable," I add.

He shakes his head. "Impossible."

"OK," Sophie says, gripping her knees. "We'll leave it in Mr. Dimiroulis's hands. He's been in communication with Lady Purdie before, so she can expect to hear from him soon."

"Wait," he says, as I stand. "I can give you a moth. A valuable moth."

"What's the best moth?" I say.

He stutters, "Not the sultan's moth. It's priceless, its absence would be noticed instantly."

"Fine," I say. It wouldn't benefit us to draw attention to the complicated algebra of lies in the castle. "What's the next-best one?"

His eyes trace over the carpet. "I suppose the jade moth. There are three in the collections."

"We'll take that, then," Sophie says. She pulls the delftware teacup from Lester's mantelpiece towards her and shakes the change and keys resting inside. Then she reaches behind it and pockets a bronze letter opener. "And we'll take this too." When Lester looks confused, Sophie shrugs. "Interest."

LATITUDE 81°, 01' N, LONGITUDE 65°, 33' W

Although I beat my hands against the door the nails hold fast... I grow hoarse from calling, and I fancy I hear sometimes an echo.

MONDAY, JANUARY 28, 1963

THE LITTLE BELL ABOVE MORAG'S DOOR TINKLES AS WE PUSH on the button. A hollow, hacking cough echoes along a narrow space before the door opens, and I can feel my surprise register on my face. I'd expected someone stout and Celtically inspired, like Violet; but this woman has the fragile, piteous demeanour of an underfed zoo animal from a desert climate forced to eke out its existence in Aberdeen.

"Yes?" she says.

"Good morning, Miss Gilles," Sophie says, in her treacly Edinburgh accent. "It's ever so lovely to meet you. We've been referred to you by a mutual friend, Lester."

"Lester sent you?" Morag says, gathering her coat in front of her chest.

"Yes, he has a special consignment for you," I say. I think of opening my bag to show her the moth, but something about the idea of flashing her this hairy creature seems so obscene that I just lean forward onto the doorstep. "I think you may be interested."

"Well, if Lester sent you," she says doubtfully, retreating into the corridor so that we can follow. Worn crescents at the heels of her socks flash as she climbs the staircase up to the flat. Upstairs, her front room is surprisingly warm, although the air is grainy with dust. Textiles are piled on every surface: knitted shawls, woven rugs, tapestries, woollen sweaters in bright, Christmassy colours.

I clear a space on a stool fashioned from an old fishing barrel. "I have a trade for you."

Sophie gives me a sharp look, with a ferrety little frown.

Morag blinks at me in confusion. "Oh, really?"

"It's in exchange for the ring," I say.

Morag's gaze slides around the room, slipping off rabbit fur blankets and crochet doilies. "Ring?"

"Auld James's ring," I say, more clearly.

Morag scratches the side of her nose. "I don't know that I've seen anything like that in here."

"May I see Purdie's ring before we show you what Lester sent?"

Morag moves around the space, touching a scarf, a ball of liquorice-coloured yarn, another scarf. Her fingers are quick and thin. "Now I think of it, I do have some Victorian mourning rings, but where have I left them?"

Sophie sighs, looking at her watch. "Listen, Miss Gilles. I didn't want to have to be so blunt, but Lester needs the captain's ring back. It's not a request."

I cough, pointedly, trying to encourage Sophie to soften her tone, but she ignores me. "Lester has some information about you that you really wouldn't want shared."

"He," Morag stutters. "Oh, but—" She rubs one of her stockinged feet against the other. "Oh, but he promised—"

"I'm sorry," Sophie says. "But we don't have a choice. Would you really want people around here to whisper about your being condemned?"

I shoot her a frown, but she is focused on Morag.

Morag says something so softly that at first I don't catch it. I have to lean down to her rabbity mouth. "I like it," she says. "The ring."

"Yes, I'm sure it's very pretty," Sophie says, in a bored, condescending tone. She goes around the room, picking up rugs and letting them drop as if she's sifting through manure.

"I like the dreams," Morag says.

Sophie pauses, her hand grazing a lambswool cape.

"What dreams?" I say.

Morag's face has acquired a hectic flush. "The dreams."

Sophie is looking at me, uncomfortably.

"Are they"—I clear my throat—"intimate dreams?"

Morag shuffles to the edge of a low table and puts her fingers around a cup of tea that is clearly already cold, a frilly scab of old milk on the surface.

"I don't see what that's got to do with the ring," Sophie brays, a little too loud.

"It's got everything to do with the ring," Morag says, breathlessly. Her eyes are febrile, liquid. The passion in her expression is alarming, like seeing an equatorial flower blooming in a greenhouse—all unguarded poison and sticky liquid. Morag peers at me, earnestly. "It's better than romance novels."

Something about the scum on her tea turns my stomach. The flat seems unbearably hot, the sweet scent of rubbish mouldering somewhere under the piles of rugs. It smells like my parents' flat. I tug at the top button of my coat.

"I'd never give up the dreams," Morag says, closing her eyes. Her papery, pink lids flicker with an insectile motion. "Not for anything."

"May I see it?" I say.

Her eyes dart protectively to a margarine tub on a lacquer tray by the window. "Oh, no."

Over Morag's shoulder I give Sophie a desperate expression. "I've heard all about its properties," I whisper. "I'd love just to see what it looks like."

Morag's eyes widen. "I'm not going to sell it. I want to keep it, just for me."

"I understand," I say. "But we have a good trade for you. You won't be out of pocket."

Sophie walks over to the other side of me and, with a theatrical stumble, sends the cup of cold tea smashing onto the ground, and a pile of rugs sliding after it into the puddle. "Oh dear!" she says, tossing blanket after scarf. "Oh no, oops, dearie me."

As Morag's head tilts over the mess on the floor, Sophie dives towards the margarine tub. I seize a stiff tea towel and help Morag dab at the liquid. Her fingers are twitchy on the rugs. Over Morag's shoulder, Sophie nods at me.

"Has anything else unusual happened, while you've had the ring?" I say, quietly. "Have you seen anything strange?"

Morag runs the tip of a grey tongue over her lips. "Only him."

"Who?"

"The captain," she whispers. "He visits sometimes at night. I don't get that many visitors."

"What is it that you see?" I say.

Her expression acquires a kind of moony hunger. "He comes after dark. He's looking for a bride."

"Well, thanks for your time, but we have to go," Sophie says. "Come along." She tugs me up from the floor. I drop the moth onto a pile of sheepskin rugs and follow her into the hallway.

Sophie goes first down the stairs, and I prod her on as she struggles with the bolt at the front door. "Round the back," she hisses as we leave the building, and instead of running down the high street we hustle into the gap between the wool shop and the pharmacy. The snow has impacted in the narrow space, and there is barely enough room for us to both squeeze between the buildings. Sophie puts her finger to my mouth; I can feel her heartbeat pounding through her coat.

It takes only a few moments before a cacophony of crashing and banging comes from upstairs. Sophie grimaces. Footsteps thud on the stairwell, and the bell jingles as the door opens. I hear Morag say, "Oh," in a plaintive, small voice. I almost feel sorry for her. She shuts the door, and a soft wail, mingled with a cough, reverberates through the walls. Sophie and I wait between the buildings until my knees cramp. Sophie guides my hand into her pocket where I can feel the hard mouth of the ring.

"What if she tells people?" I whisper. "The police or something?"

Sophie frowns at me. "It's a stolen ring to begin with. She can't say anything."

"Oh, you're right."

"We left her the moth, it's not like she can't get some money back. Nutty old freak," Sophie says, with a steely glint in her eye.

"Who are you and what have you done with Sophie?" I whisper.

"She never would have given it to us willingly," she says. "Sometimes you have to take matters into your own hands."

I nod, both unnerved and impressed by her bravado. Perhaps I underestimated her. Then I think maybe the figure is having an effect on her too.

40

TUESDAY, JANUARY 29, 1963

AULD JAMES'S COLLECTION IS SPREAD OUT ON A TRAY IN THE lobby of the hotel, and it's not long before the word spreads. By eleven, people are thronged into the space to run inquisitive fingers over the rim of his personal cup, the smooth face of his lucky coin. Looking at the coin now, I have to wonder if he had the sense that something was following him, if the buffed image of the leviathan was his own superstitious method of warding off disaster.

Familiar faces join the crowd: Joe from the Black Hare brings his brother, and they both examine the items with their hands tucked respectfully behind their backs. Mrs. Ince, the minister's housekeeper, sniffs at the captain's ring, no doubt scandalised that such a worldly item would even be associated with such a revered member of the elect. When Colin's face appears at the doors, I leave Sophie to relay the explanations and join him in the passageway.

"Come to see the fruit of your labours?" I say.

Colin shoots me a suspicious expression. He removes his cap and runs a quick hand over the pate of his head. He opens his mouth but doesn't speak.

"Wasn't it lucky that we were able to get back out there?" I say, giving him an insincere grin. "The Purdies are delighted."

He blinks at me, putting his hands into his pockets and walking straight to the bar. If he's curious about how I managed an impossible dive, I feel confident he won't ask any awkward questions.

Just before lunch, one of the Irenes peering over the tray meets my eyes, and with a jolt I recognise the woman with the flowered headscarf from the shelter. She recognises me at the same time, her lower lip twitching. I raise my head and hold her eyes for as long as I can, until she looks away. Moral superiority; it's a new sensation for me. I can see why Sophie likes it so much.

After a quick meal of thin barley soup, I collect the paraffin lamp, pack the items into a shoebox, and announce to anyone still loitering in the lobby that Auld James's belongings are returning home. Glasses are raised, toasts are summoned, and just as we'd hoped, Sophie and I are followed out of the side doors of the hotel by a coterie of cheerful chaperones. Mr. Tibalt joins us, along with Flora, George the bellboy, and at least five Jocks, who strike up a chorus of "Nearer by the Long Road" as we climb up the icy path to the castle. Perhaps they are bored, or perhaps they are hoping to ingratiate themselves with the Purdies, but as we navigate the troughs carved into the snow, more people trickle out from the farms to join our procession. In the still, icy silence, our voices echo in the hills.

We arrive at the castle just before three, greeted by Mr. Scruff barking himself into a frenzy. Janet is standing with her face pressed against the kitchen door, her expression wary and confused, Lady Purdie behind her, clearly interrupted during afternoon tea. Lady Purdie's eyes are flashing, a sandwich crumb still teetering on the lapel of her collar.

"Marta?" she barks as if this is an act of schoolgirl japery. She's not completely wrong.

"We've brought Auld James's belongings home," I say, holding the cardboard box aloft.

It is the first time I have seen Lady Purdie wrong-footed, but after a quick conferral, the grand oak doors are winched halfway open, as far as they will swing given the months of packed snow in the hinges. Our motley party is admitted through the doors, and we pour into the formal hallway. A scullery maid hastens to set and light the fire,

Mr. Scruff gallops between muddy boots, and Janet bustles trays of glasses and whisky back and forth.

Lady Purdie sidles close to me. "Thank you so much for such a lovely surprise visit, Marta."

I nod, pretending not to notice her tone. "Is Lester here?"

"Of course he's here," she snaps, looking behind us until we both spot him loitering near the velvet drapes. She clicks her fingers impatiently in his direction, and he obeys the cue, walking rather woodenly towards us.

I hand the box to Lester. "The Captain James Purdie collection," I say, a bit too loudly.

His expression is glassy, his ears pink at the shell. He gives the box a gentle, experimental shake.

"Wait," Lady Purdie says, putting a hand to her necklace. She slips through the crowd and returns with Lord Purdie in the crook of her arm, positioning him so that they are standing in the light of the fire.

"Please, the honours," she says, gesturing to her husband. With a nod at his wife, Lord Purdie lifts the lid, and all three of them peer at the contents. A reverent hush falls over the gathered crowd.

"Good grief." Lord Purdie beams at the congregation. "After many months of toil, I can't express how delighted myself and Esme are to have you all here at this moment. The Purdie belongings delivered to their rightful home."

Lady Purdie's cheeks are bright, her eyes shining. I try not to pity her.

"Let us all raise our glasses to Auld James, safely returned from his long voyage at last," Lord Purdie says, and as he lifts the box, the objects rattle within.

§

WHEN THE LAST of the Jocks have finally drunk their fill and retreated, it's past eight, and Lord and Lady Purdie's smiles have worn a little thin. As one of the footmen fastens the bolt on the oak doors, Lady Purdie puts an exhausted hand to her head.

"You'll join us for supper," she says to me and Sophie. It's not a question, and she doesn't wait for an answer.

"I'd suggest keeping everything in a stable environment," Sophie says, with a nod towards the box. "Residue from coal fires—"

"Oh, of course." Lord Purdie hands the box to Lester. "You have just the place, don't you, old chap?"

Lester nods. He carries the box towards the museum with a gliding stroll, as if he's sleepwalking.

The formal dining room is sombre without electric light. A single guttering candle casts yellow spindles from the centre of the table. We are served rabbit so lean that it tastes like shoelaces, while Lord Purdie talks at length about the farmers breeding them indoors over the winter. The bones are the size of matchsticks.

"The ship won't be safe for people to swim through," I say, interrupting Lord Purdie's description of the symptoms of myxomatosis.

Everyone at the table turns to look at me. Lady Purdie dabs her mouth.

"The site isn't safe," I continue. "Sophie and I have looked extensively at the area, and it's important to ensure no one has access. In fact, when the weather thaws, the hatch must be boarded up to stop entry."

"Well, we never thought people would be swimming *inside* the ship," Lady Purdie says. "Wouldn't that be impossible, without your Aqua-Lung?"

I look at Lester. He is concentrating on his meal, the tines of his fork clattering over the bones on his plate.

"Even one person entering could result in a fatality, which I'm sure is the last thing that you would want."

"Oh, absolutely, absolutely," says Lord Purdie.

Lester clears his throat. When he looks up, his face is in high colour. "The collection is all that matters," he says. "People will be coming here in droves for the chance to see the captain's personal items. Purdie Castle will be the talk of Scotland."

Lord and Lady Purdie are watching him with a dewy combination of tenderness and pride. There is no doubt they will all be warming one another's beds again tonight.

"It's the achievement of a lifetime," Lester says. He raises his glass of red wine to the table. "And may I say what a sincere honour and privilege it is, to have the legacy of Captain Purdie intertwined with my own."

Sophie pushes her chair away from the table with a scrape. "Well, thank you so much, but I'm afraid we have to begin our walk back to the hotel."

"But it's pitch-black out there. Why not stay in one of the rooms upstairs? You still have belongings waiting for you," Lady Purdie says, with a sharpened edge.

"That's so kind," Sophie says, "and I'll return to collect those on another occasion. But we are due to take a shift looking over Alice. She's still not fully recovered."

"Of course," Lester says, standing up politely from the table as we rise. "Of course, you must go. Duty first." He wrings his napkin in his hands. "And thank you."

Janet fusses handfuls of bullet-cold raisins into our pockets before she will let us leave. We wave goodbye to her at the kitchen door and trudge down the road, Sophie swinging the paraffin lamp. Above us is only the tiniest sliver of moon, a baby's fingernail. We slide down the glittering path, past the hedge, then stop. Mr. Scruff is barking from inside the kitchen, and the sound of Janet tutting him carries in the air. Sophie extinguishes the lamp, and we turn back on ourselves, following the outside of the hedge, stumbling in treacherous dollops of snow suspended over ankle-turning divots. The hedge leads around the loop of the castle to the garden where the bonfire was held on Samhain. From our place on the other side of the field, I can see the blank glass doors of the Ceylonese Room, the balcony where Elsie and I stood that night of the ceilidh. A light snowfall drifts on the breeze, feathering our eyelashes and filling in our footprints.

"We're going to freeze to death," Sophie whispers.

"Let's just keep walking." I nudge her forward.

And so we skulk slowly around the grounds, creeping in the falling snow, breathing froths of breath, slithering on glips of wet ice. From inside the castle, shivers of candlelight spill in arcs over the silent gardens; slim dancing triangles of reflected firelight settle on Sophie's face. Half an hour goes by, an hour. One by one, candles are snuffed, windows grow dark. I crouch on the other side of the dining room, the drawing room, pressing my bare hand to the glass windows; they grow cooler as fires are dampened. The snow has stopped now, and the air is so still I can hear my own heartbeat in my ears.

Footsteps echo up the stairs; the glowing trickle of bedtime candlesticks retreats inside the building. The grand hallways of the house are emptied. In the kitchen, Janet yawns as she finishes sweeping, leaning her broom behind the kitchen table. She covers the hearth, impatiently hushing Mr. Scruff, who is jumping up at the windows, yipping softly at us, crouched on the other side.

I give Sophie the signal. She holds two frozen sticks in place under her arm and trudges as quietly as she can towards the morning room. I wait. A few minutes later, she begins to rattle the sticks along the building, drawing them in clicking grooves through the ancient stones. Mr. Scruff bounds towards the noise. Janet puts a hand to her heart, cocks her head towards the sound. She steadies herself on the corner of the table and follows him along the velvet-draped corridor, the stub of a candle wavering in a saucer.

I unlace my boots at the kitchen door and let myself in, tiptoeing across the kitchen and down to Lester's study. There, on the mantelpiece, his keys are nestled inside the delftware teacup. Sophie is creeping her tapping now towards the dining room, and I edge along the narrow corridor, across the formal hallway to the museum, and unlock Lester's cabinet. The objects return to their trusty potato sack, and I turn the key on the empty case. With a lollop and a snuffle, Mr. Scruff comes towards me, his nails clicking over the floor, and I nuzzle his ears, easing one of the rabbit bones from dinner out of my pocket and into his soft mouth.

Janet's irritated chirrup comes from the other side of the hallway, and he bounds back obediently towards her. The chime of her key chain echoes now up the stairs, and he settles on the first landing, guarding his meagre prize between territorial paws.

Lester's keys return to his teacup, and I collect my boots, as well as Janet's broom from behind the kitchen table. Sophie is waiting to meet me at the other side of the garden door, and she brushes over our tracks as we retreat. Goodness knows what Janet will make of it in the morning, when she sees an extra set of footprints leading up to the kitchen door, and none leading away.

LATITUDE 81°, 01' N, LONGITUDE 65°, 33' W

I continue to try against the door although my nails have peeled. Cold is unrelenting.

TUESDAY, JANUARY 29, 1963

IT'S LONG PAST MIDNIGHT WHEN SOPHIE AND I SPREAD ALL the objects out on her bedspread: Auld James's cutlery, his horn cup, his goggles, his mirror, his coin, and, finally, his ring. We stare at the collection in silence, not knowing what to say to each other.

Elsie gives Sophie's door a cursory knock before letting herself in. She's carrying a bottle of Auld James's whisky and three enamel mugs. She stands for a moment looking at the artefacts, shaking her head. "I can't believe this bag of junk has caused so much trouble."

"Shh, don't call them junk," I say.

Elsie laughs, handing me a mug. "I don't think they know they're worth money, Marta," she says, but that's not the first thing I'd thought of. Instead, I was picturing the figure hunched outside, listening to everything we say.

"Let's keep everything in the ballroom overnight?" I say to Sophie, and she nods. Now that we have all the items, the idea of their being in the hotel while we sleep feels like a provocation. I can't bear another night of lying awake, my pulse racing at every creak in the hallway.

Elsie pours all three of us a slug of whisky, and we clink our mugs together. I reach the bottom of my mug as Sophie takes a sip of hers.

Elsie refills my cup. "Will you report Lester, once the lines are up again?"

Sophie and I exchange a look. "No," I say. "The Purdies should be able to manage Lester themselves. I don't think they'll want to draw much attention to their prize collection going missing, which suits us."

Elsie shakes her head. "After all this trouble, just to make everything disappear again."

Sophie and I shift in our chairs.

"I don't want to risk it hurting more people," I say, softly. "Look at what happened with your granny."

"Don't be ridiculous," Elsie says, a hiss of her spit landing on a hot coal in the grate, blazing a flicker of orange.

"Really, we're just returning everything to where it was," I say. "Back in the water."

Elsie turns to glare at Sophie. "I can't believe you're going along with this."

Sophie looks crestfallen. It's oddly reassuring that Elsie's scorn stings other people as much as it stings me.

"Archaeologists occasionally have to make uncomfortable choices for the sake of preservation," Sophie says. "Climb scaffolding to take a photograph we're not supposed to take, slip someone a bribe to take some measurements. No one is going to open that tomb again and find out—"

Elsie raises her hands, then covers her ears. "No, don't tell me anything about it. I don't want to know. I don't want to hear it."

Sophie grimaces at me.

"Come, it's late, let's go to bed." I pull Elsie up from the chair, and she doesn't even look at Sophie as we leave the room. I mouth, "Sorry," at Sophie, and she offers me a double blink, which I take to mean *Good luck*. I hope that she will remember to hide everything down in the ballroom tonight, and not sleep with that invitation anywhere near her perfectly made bed.

"Please don't do this." Elsie turns to me on the staircase, one hand on the banister. "I'm beginning to get really worried about you."

"There's no need to be worried, I promise."

She is shaking her head. "I think there is."

"Don't you trust me?"

Elsie hesitates. Before I have time to generate offence, she begins, "You're impulsive. You take chances at things, I like that about you, but this—" She points back in the direction of Sophie's room. "Marta, this is just so stupid. Stupid and weird. You're not using your brain."

I quicken my pace on the stairs so that she has to follow behind me. In my room, I poke up the fireplace and crawl under the blankets. "Aren't rational people allowed a few weird ideas? Remember your Hallowmas cast?"

"Marta—"

"But we fixed it. Everything. People can still visit the ship, just not go inside. And the Purdies will have their transcription, the drawings and photographs of the items—they can make re-creations if they want to. I don't understand why you're so worried."

"What about—" Elsie cocks her head towards the door.

"She won't say anything. I'm safe from Alex finding out. And everything going well out here means more work for me. Turkey, Greece."

Elsie opens her mouth and closes it again.

"You won't believe it out there," I say, stroking her hair behind her ears. I lie on my side, drowsiness stealing over me. "The food, the coffee. The sunshine."

She makes a noncommittal noise. I know that I haven't convinced her yet, but I will. Right now, I feel impermeable, like someone has poured molten silver through my insides.

I lean in and kiss her. "I love you."

"I love you too."

"You'll see. I'm going to be so professional and rational, you'll get bored to tears of listening to me talk about decompression calculations and stratigraphy."

"You're going to have to do a lot of rational things to make up for this," Elsie says, and I think perhaps she will, in her own way, permit this act of madness.

"I promise. I'll mend lots of bicycles. And write letters about improper grammar to the *Scotsman*."

She gives a reluctant laugh, and I feel encouraged enough to continue. "And I'll go around picking up other people's rubbish and throwing it away, while tutting at them. And I'll read the map before we take any trips and plot out the journey in advance and pencil it in so you can rub it out later."

I've gone on for too long; it's given her a chance to reflect. She's biting the inside of her cheek. I give her a gentle shake of the shoulders. "Please just bear with me a little longer. After Sophie and I have taken care of this, I can focus on taking care of you."

Elsie frowns. "I can take care of myself."

"Of course you can," I say. "But I want to put this all behind me, behind both of us. There is so much we can look forward to. I just want to fix things here first."

She concentrates on me. "Is this helping you come to terms with what happened with Lewis?"

"What do you mean?"

I have the sense she is choosing her words carefully. "Do you feel as if you're doing the right thing?"

"I do." I can hear the certainty in my own voice. "I just know this is the right thing to do."

She closes her eyes for a long moment before opening them. "None of this has anything to do with me. I never want to know the details."

I wriggle closer to her, touching her cold nose to mine. "Thank you."

"But whatever you do, you'll have to find somewhere other than the hotel to keep all that—" She gestures vaguely. "And anything else you *collect*. God knows what would happen if the Purdies found out it was here. Put it all back down in the ship, I don't care how. Boil some water, or drill, or borrow some of that dynamite they were trying to explode the harbour with."

"I'll find a solution. I'm rational now, remember?"

Elsie gives me a rueful chuckle. "I'll hold you to that."

I kiss her, tracing the teardrop freckle under her left eyelid. "And you have to promise you'll still love me once everything is returned."

She pulls back. "What?"

"If we were to leave here together, nothing would change between us, would it? After everything's back, after all this is over. You promise, don't you, nothing will be different between us?"

She looks at me strangely, but she says, "I promise."

42

WEDNESDAY, JANUARY 30, TO
FRIDAY, FEBRUARY 1, 1963

THE TEMPERATURE RISES SLOWLY OVER THE NEXT FEW DAYS, settling somewhere around zero. The sudden tug from frozen into cold prompts a slough of heavier ice; snow tumbles from the hotel roof, eliciting queer squeaks from the tiles. The blades of icicles turn pulpy and slide farther downwards. The ice in the harbour is old enough by now that it has acquired the yellowish colour of cake batter, and in the morning light, the tide is lapping more insistently against the edges. Down on the beach, the water is milky soft against the shingle, shouldering plates of ice with gentle sighs. The weather is turning. After a hushed debate in the ballroom where Elsie can't overhear, Sophie convinces me that the time has come to collect Auld James. I would rather wait for a full thaw and get down to the ship immediately afterwards, but Sophie points out that the moon is waxing, and the longer we wait, the more chance we have of being spotted.

§

FRIDAY EVENING'S DINNER of boiled duck is sitting hard in my stomach as Sophie uncovers the hurricane lamp behind the slate wall overlooking the church.

"Not yet," I hiss.

"No one will see it," she says, batting me away.

"Yes, they will. We're up on the hill; any light up here and people will see it for miles." I nudge her until she covers the lamp again. It turns out to be a stroke of luck that Auld James wasn't buried belowground in the kirkyard. Given the cold, if Auld James had been lowered into a grave instead of placed inside the family mausoleum, we wouldn't have been able to retrieve his skeleton, even from the sandy loam of the kirkyard.

I take one last look around us. It's almost ten in the evening, and the windows of the manse are dark. Some muffled voices carry on the wind from a field farther up towards Lees Farm, but we've been waiting by the wall for an hour, and the voices haven't come any closer.

"Follow me," I whisper. The bolt cutters from the hotel are heavy, and I stagger around the yew tree to approach the mausoleum. But when we get to the door, there is no bolt.

Sophie laughs. "They don't even lock their front doors here, why would they lock their graves?"

Her laughter has a bright, irritating quality, and I elbow her forward. "OK, now increase the light, just a little."

She turns the valve on the lamp, and I use the blade of the bolt cutters to score the ice between the door and the hinge. After a few minutes it is still sticking, so we light a candle from the lamp and hold it against the gap until pricks of water appear in the wedge of ice. Then I lever the cutters back and forth again, against the hinge. Finally, the door begins to wiggle, and I give Sophie a nod. She pulls her sweater over her nose; I do the same and heave open the door. But of course, it's been below freezing for months. The air is stale and oddly dry, but there is no smell beyond a lingering dankness. Sophie holds up the lamp, and it shines a quiver on two rows of plain stone tombs with slate lids balanced across the tops. Auld James's final resting place is identified with an engraving in the stone that simply reads: *James Purdie, 1809–1850*. Good old Calvinism.

As Sophie goes to enter the crypt, I hold her back. "Wait." I wrestle the cutters into the gap at the bottom of the door so there is no chance it can slam shut and trap us.

"What if someone sees," Sophie begins, but I shake my head at her. "Trust me."

Between us, Sophie and I push the slate away from the cover of the tomb, and Sophie shines the lamp on Auld James's wooden casket. I lean in and use the nose of my penknife to lever a hair's gap in the lid.

There are the bones of Auld James, iced to the bier with a frosty white sparkle.

"On three," Sophie whispers. I stand at the feet of the skeleton, Sophie at the head, and we ease the casket out from the stone tomb. As we jiggle it back and forth, I hear a clinking sound from inside the box. One of Auld James's teeth has rolled loose and is chiming around against his bones.

We lower the casket down to the mausoleum floor and heave the slate back in place. I dust my hands, and we both stare down at the box. A light sweat shines on Sophie's forehead through the gloom, and she pulls the Purdie tartan blanket from around her shoulders and throws it over the casket. Turning down the hurricane lamp, she rests it on top of the lid, and slowly, we shuffle out of the door of the mausoleum and back into the kirkyard. I feel acutely conscious of each crunch of our footsteps, out in the night. There is a damp breathing sound from the far side of the church, and my pulse thrusts into my head before I realise it is only the noise of waves trying to simmer through the ice and break against the black rocks below the church. We heave the casket behind the yew tree; then I return for the bolt cutters, brushing the snow over the door of the mausoleum, smoothing and scattering it with my bare hands, walking backwards to cover my steps.

I crouch down under the cover of the yew tree and thrust the bolt cutters under the snow to retrieve later. "It's so obvious," I say, a nauseous lurch in my stomach. "God, it's so obvious. Anyone would be able to tell straight away. Elsie will get blamed, I just know it. Oh, God, this is crazy. This is crazy!"

Sophie pinches me on the arm, hard. "Snap out of it, Marta. Look at me."

Through the gloom I focus on the whites of her eyes.

"Don't lose your head now. Nobody will be poking around in this kirkyard for fun. And even if they do, they're not going to suspect for a moment that someone would take Auld James's body."

I bite down on my tongue. "I think we made a mistake, this is a bad idea. We should put him back."

Sophie kneels closer to me, her breath bitter. "Do you want to be followed by a shadow for the rest of your life?"

I picture the endless nights that in my imagination are filled with endless snow, an unshakeable icy draught, a figure crouched in the corner of my room. I shake my head.

"Good, so stop panicking. Let's finish this."

"But wait." I rub the back of my hand over my dry lips. I wish we had thought to bring water. Or whisky. "Wait, don't you think the Purdies deserve to be punished?"

"Yes," Sophie says, leaning closer. "But this thing is out for revenge, and what it wants is Auld James. So I'm going to help it. Now, let's go."

She helps me up and we ease slowly through the graves in the kirkyard and then over the gravel road and into the field beyond. Sophie's breath is white in the air, and we have to keep pausing as she readjusts. I should offer to switch places, since she is walking first and carrying most of the weight as we head down the hill, but it's more slippery at my end, and I decide that I'm more athletic than she is and will be able to keep my balance better. As we pass the turning near Lees Farm, we have to cross the road again, and just as my heels touch the starched grass, I hear a slathering pant, and suddenly, something hot and furred is on me. I scream, almost dropping my end of the casket. But it's Mr. Scruff. I gape at him as he scampers between me and Sophie. "What are you doing here?" I whisper to him.

A woman's voice calls from behind us. "Hello?"

Sophie draws in a sharp breath.

"Oh, girls. I wondered why he shot off like that." It's Lady Purdie. She is dressed in walking clothes, Wellington boots and a waxed jacket, and despite the late hour, is carrying no torch.

"Lady Purdie." My hands shake on the box, and the loose tooth rattles around inside.

"Going up to Lees Farm, are you?" she says.

Sophie and I glance at each other. "Yes," I say.

Lady Purdie nods. She looks at the box. "What is that?"

"Driftwood," Sophie says, immediately. "From the beach. My hands got splintered so I put a blanket on top. Marta teased me but I can't help it if my hands are soft." She begins to giggle, and I nudge the box into her thighs.

Lady Purdie is nodding, absently. "Well, pick up the pace, girls. It's quicker this way," and she strides left, across the dark field. "Come along."

With a desperate look back at me, Sophie begins to follow her, while Mr. Scruff gallops between our legs happily, sniffing at the box, leaping his muddy paws on our coats. I use my elbow to gently nudge him away.

Lady Purdie pauses, her hands on her hips, and waits for us to catch up with her.

"Actually, I'm rather glad we ran into each other," I say, wheezing as we manoeuvre the hillocks in the slippery grass. "Sophie and I were planning to come up tomorrow and take some final measurements of the collection. Would after lunch be convenient?"

Lady Purdie's mouth tightens. "What? No, that won't work at all."

"Perhaps Monday?"

"Girls, I think it's best that you relinquish the collection to our care. Leave the expert to make his own determinations."

"Lester?" Sophie says.

"Yes, of course Lester," Lady Purdie snaps. "The Purdie collections are with their rightful owners. We will make the decisions regarding any future display."

I can't help myself. "You don't want us to take the final measurements?"

"Focus your efforts on finishing that transcription," Lady Purdie says, to Sophie. She turns away, resuming her long stride up through the pitted fields. "Then I'd say we can conclude our business together, wouldn't you?"

Even through the gloom I can sense the smile on Sophie's face. "No one says no to a Purdie," she whispers.

"Ah, here we are," Lady Purdie says. From the top of the knoll, I can now see lamps shining in a loose circle around a storm drain, a group of five men gathered at the grate. It must have been their voices we heard earlier. "Surprised they called for you two," Lady Purdie says, turning and looking us both up and down. "But I suppose extra hands are extra hands, no matter how soft."

"Put the box down," I mutter to Sophie. She pauses abruptly and I stagger against the coffin. We edge sideways, dropping the casket in the shelter of a slate wall. I yank heavy stones from the top of the wall to weigh down the lid; the last thing we need is for Mr. Scruff to come bounding over with a chunk of Auld James's arm in his mouth. Wiping our hands on our trousers, we walk towards the congregation.

"Oh my God, oh my God," Sophie says, through gritted teeth.

"Is it my turn to tell you to snap out of it?" I say.

A man I recognise from Lees Farm is closest to the drain, hunched over and peering down through the bars. The others are holding lamps aloft to illuminate the drain, a slurry of icy mud and wet snow seeping into their clothes. Mr. Scruff runs around the grate in wild circles, barking.

The men touch their caps respectfully as Lady Purdie approaches.

"How long has the ewe been down there?" Lady Purdie says.

"Since sundown," the man from Lees Farm replies.

"And you can't reach her from this angle?" Lady Purdie is saying. She's on her knees now, next to the drain. Again I'm reminded of the rural competence of these posh women. She could probably lift the grate with her bare teeth.

"Oh, poor sheep," Sophie says, and the men turn to look at her, sharply. I elbow her in the side.

"Clogged with snow," one of the men says.

"Could we melt it?" Lady Purdie looks up.

No one answers.

"Have you tried melting the snow?" Lady Purdie repeats.

There is a moment of silence. "Isn't melting," someone says.

Lady Purdie taps at the drain. There's only a borehole between two of the bars where the ice has been chiselled and then the water has refrozen it to a glossy marble. Mr. Scruff sniffs around the hole, then scampers quickly away, back around Lady Purdie's legs, his ears flat.

From deep within the drain comes the most horrifying sound I have ever heard. It is more than animal, less than human, a low, quiet, rasping chord of scream.

One by one, the men cross themselves.

Lady Purdie flinches back from the grate. "We should put her out of her misery," she says, eventually.

The men exchange glances. "That's no sheep," one of them says.

The sound comes again, a keening wail. Mr. Scruff's fur stands on end, his lips pull over his teeth, and he crouches low, snarling at the drain. He leaps now towards the drain, unleashing a volley of barking which echoes around us in the white hills.

Lady Purdie shouts at Mr. Scruff, grabbing him back by his collar. "Down," she says, "down! What's possessed you?"

Reluctantly, Mr. Scruff is dragged backwards from the mouth of the drain, his lips still twitching. Lady Purdie is breathless, holding him by his collar so that his front legs dangle off the ground.

In the pause between his barking, the howl slithers from within the drain again. But it's even quieter now, almost a purr, as if it's drawing farther away from us.

"Going through the tunnels," one of the men says, under his breath.

In the darkness, Sophie reaches out to grip my hand, and I squeeze back. We are all silent as the wail in the tunnel fades, replaced by the sound of our collective breath, the murmurs of complaint from Mr. Scruff as Lady Purdie finally releases his collar.

The farmer from Lees Farm turns to the others, and they share a look that I can't decipher. It seems to indicate that whatever brought them to the field has now concluded, as the other men readjust their caps, blow into their hands, nod at one another in the way of people about to part.

Lady Purdie calls Mr. Scruff to her side and rubs him soothingly on his snout. He is still looking at the grate, and although the fierceness has left his face, he still has the alert, inquisitive tension of a dog who has investigations to resolve.

"Thank you for coming, ma'am," the man from Lees Farm says, lifting his cap to Lady Purdie. "I'll walk you back up to the castle?"

She gives a short laugh. "You'll do nothing of the sort, Jock. You'll go back to Irene and tell her I had no part in your being out this late."

He gives her a nod and begins trudging through the field back in the direction of the farmhouse. Lady Purdie releases a long sigh, watching as Mr. Scruff sniffs intently around the grate. "Sad business," she says.

"Yes," I say. I can still feel the sound skittering over my skin.

Lady Purdie calls Mr. Scruff to her with a click of her tongue. Reluctantly, he obeys. "This weather is making fools of us all," she says. "I don't think I've ever seen a farmer frightened before."

43

FRIDAY, FEBRUARY 1, 1963

THE SITE OF THE FORMER RATHDUNON CASTLE ENDS UP AS the temporary resting place of Captain James Purdie. Even at the best of times no islanders go there except to collect mushrooms or hawthorn berries growing in the rubble. In the recent weather, however, the snow has filled in the deepest part of the crater, allowing us to conceal the casket under six inches of snow. By the time the box has been buried, my back and neck are stiff, my arms shaking from the effort.

"What can we do for protection?" Sophie says, wiping her face as she reviews our handiwork.

I have a moment of doubt. "I thought we agreed that nobody would come here?" A whistle loops through the stones, and I turn my head to the source of the noise. Just the wind.

"That's not what I meant," Sophie says. "Is there anything we should do to protect us? From it."

I shiver. The sweat inside my clothes is growing colder the longer we stand still. "I don't know."

Sophie clears her throat. "We're going to help you. We're returning everything to the boat. Please don't curse us," she announces into the night air.

I can't help but smile. "Yes, I'm sure that will be just the ticket."

We stay close to each other as we hobble back towards the hotel, walking shoulder to shoulder through the black stones of the old castle, the black road along the coast. Despite the bitter wind, the snow feels slushier, puddles cracking under the weight of our boots, and I wonder if a thaw may not be too far away. All I need is for the temperatures to lift enough that we could motor out of the harbour. We should start trying to convince Colin soon; no one else is going to take me back to the site. From the rocks near the darkened lighthouse, a slippery rustle announces shifting snow, answered by a gruesome crack in the ice below. Sophie tenses, and we blink behind us, out into the shadows.

By the time we arrive back at the hotel, we are both in a state of delirious exhaustion and heightened vigilance. As we approach the front doors, it takes a moment for me to register that people inside are singing along to the piano. Sophie turns to me. "You hear that too, don't you?"

I nod her forward, and we enter the lobby to see familiar faces crowded around the piano, which is illuminated by a startling number of candles. Mrs. Eleanor and Francis, their arms linked—yuck—Flora, George the bellboy, and Mr. Tibalt are singing along to "Pack Up Your Troubles" as Cook plays. Alice turns and spots us. "Join us," she says, taking hold of my elbow.

"You're up late." The clock in the entranceway has long since stopped working because of the cold, but my watch reads quarter to midnight.

"And why not?" Alice rubs my shoulder, affectionately. "It's the festival of Brìghde today. Not that we can do much in the usual way of celebrating."

Sophie and I look at one another, confused.

"Time to say goodbye to the Cailleach," Alice says. "Brìghde takes over today, the spring maiden. We've been scrubbing the place all afternoon."

I look down. Sophie and I are dripping melted snow onto the floor, and I still have the dirt from Auld James's grave on my boots. "Oh, sorry."

Alice laughs. "All that matters is the weather is due for a turn. I'm ready to say goodbye to the old crone this year." She leans in closer to me, smelling impossibly clean, like Palmolive shampoo powder and lilacs. "And I hear you and Els will be saying goodbye to this crone once the ferry gets going."

I stutter.

"I won't have her putting her life on the shelf for me," she says, before I can form intelligent words.

I'm flooded with gratitude. I want to get on the floor and kiss Alice's slippers. "She doesn't want to leave you alone," I say.

"Alone?" Alice pulls back with a scoff. "Who says I'm alone?" With her other arm, she reaches out and lightly brushes against Cook's arm. He turns to her, mid-song, and smiles.

I embrace her before I know what I'm doing. She gives me surprised pats on the back, the way you settle a fussy baby. "I'll take care of her, I promise," I say.

She lets go and gives me a shrewd look. "She can take care of herself, our Elsie." Then she points a finger at me. "Not a single call put through to Glasgow since you arrived," she says. "Call your parents."

I nod obediently.

The kitchen door opens to Elsie, and she cheers when she sees me and Sophie, before her face falls as she remembers where we have been.

"I need to wash," Sophie says, and Elsie stands aside as she edges into the kitchen. I follow her, rinsing my hands with snowmelt in the adjoining sink as Sophie scrubs at her fingernails with a scoop of grated soap.

"How was it?" Elsie begins, before correcting herself. "No, no, I don't want to know."

Sophie's breath catches, and she peers down at her palm. "Ouch, splinter. I think it's frozen in there."

"Light is better in the reading room," I say, and Sophie lets herself out. "So. Your granny and Cook?" I give Elsie a smile, trying to lighten the tone, divert her attention, but she only gives me a flicker of an acknowledging smile.

"Seems like it," she says. Her body is tight with a sort of preemptive tension, and I feel as if she is holding something back.

"Lucky Alice," I say, in a forcefully cheery tone. "To have someone who knows how to cook. I should warn you that I'm not much of a chef. I can boil an egg, but I may need to take a course or something if we're not both to go hungry." I hurry out of the kitchen and across the lobby to the reading room. There's a perverse safety in being in Sophie's company right now—Elsie's strange mood feels like a bad portent.

In the reading room, Sophie is examining her palm by the light of a candle stub in an old shoe polish tin.

"Let me." I nudge her closer to the fireplace and take out my penknife. I hold her palm steady in my hands and probe the shard with the tweezers, until I can grip on to it. Sophie winces as I withdraw the splinter and toss it into the fire.

Elsie is leaning against the doorframe, her arms crossed. The dampened sounds of "Lili Marlene" float in from the corridor.

"Maybe my hands *are* soft," Sophie says, rubbing her palm. She looks up at Elsie. "Any chance of a nightcap, Els? I really need a whisky after tonight."

Elsie nods before shaking her head. "No whisky."

Something in her tone is odd. "Did we really drink it all?" I say. "Bloody hell."

"There's rum," Elsie says, one hand on the door handle.

Sophie gives me a quizzical look. "Rum is fine, though it's late, I can just go to bed—"

But Elsie has already left the room.

Sophie takes a seat in one of the armchairs. "Is she annoyed, do you think?" she whispers. "About tonight?"

"Maybe," I reply, although the drum of my stomach feels tight. She's thought it over, and she isn't going to come back with me, even with her granny's blessing. She's going to abandon me, just as everything else falls into place.

The coal rumbles in the grate. "You're not going to leave, are you?" Sophie says.

"Sophie, you didn't see what happened when we thought the bomb was coming. The way the whole village stared at me at the doors of that bunker. I'll never be able to stop seeing it."

Sophie looks embarrassed. "I meant the museum."

"Oh." I lean forward. "No, I'm not leaving. I mean, I don't want to. There's only going to be more demand for people who are trained like I am. I can go anywhere. I can be an asset, if Alex lets me."

Sophie nods. "Don't leave it up to him. Don't let anyone push you out, if you don't want to go."

I try to mask my surprise. "Thanks," I say.

The door squeaks open and Elsie carries in a tray with three tumblers of dark liquid. She closes the door with her foot, and we all take a glass.

"Here we go. We should really raise a toast to Alice and Cook," I say.

Elsie gives me the smallest hint of a smile, and my alarm grows even more urgent. An itchy sensation rustles in my gut. "What's wrong?" I say, unable to help myself.

Elsie sits between us on the footstool. Sophie lightly taps the arm of the chair in the manner of a person who is about to leave the room, and Elsie puts her hand on Sophie's arm. "No, I need to speak to you too."

Sophie and I look at each other.

Elsie takes a deep breath. "It's about the whisky."

I laugh, a floaty bubble of relief filling my insides. All this for a caution on my drinking? She's not wrong, but it's not abandonment. "I can live without Auld James's whisky," I say. "I'm happy to start paying for—"

Elsie cuts me off. "No, this is serious."

I snap my mouth shut.

She straightens her shoulders. "Ever since you said that the"—she waves her hand—"the shadow is the most reasonable explanation, I've been thinking. And I'm certain I know what's been happening." She looks at me as if for permission, but I don't move a muscle. "The whisky—Auld James's whisky. The wheat all comes from the land up north, near the Neolithic site," Elsie continues.

"Yes, I remember," I say. "Auld James ploughed all the fields by himself, and then also killed a snake. Or sang to a snake. Something about a snake."

Elsie isn't smiling. "The land is where all the old lead mines were."

Sophie coughs on her swig of rum. She looks as if she's been slapped. But I'm not following. "Does that matter?"

Elsie's eyes widen. "Of course it matters! We've all been drinking it! The whole island, gallons of the stuff. No wonder everyone's been all over the place. We've all been poisoned. Small amounts, of course, but still."

Sophie is rubbing her lips.

"Even if that were the case, it would be fractional amounts of exposure," I say.

Elsie frowns. "Tiny amounts add up over months. It's like Sophie's book about pesticides. It builds up slowly. It would certainly be enough to make people act strangely. Poor sleep, bad tempers, nightmares. That is, on top of the snow, not eating well."

I raise my glass of rum at her. "There you go, the snow. Auld James's whisky doesn't explain why everything started going odd when the snow arrived. It's the Arctic temperatures that let it—that encouraged it out."

Elsie shakes her head, a flush rising on her cheeks. "No, but we started drinking the whisky before that. You brought up the body before then. It was the missile crisis. That's when we started drinking the whisky."

A sense of tingly horror crawls over me. "No," I say.

"We opened the casks the night Auld James came back to the island. The night of the fire. It was the same evening."

I shake my head. "No, but that doesn't matter. It's the—it's him that it wants," I say. "The figure. It wanted his body. It makes sense everything would have started that same night. Anyway, what about the fire itself?"

"What about it?" Elsie says. "There were boys out there trying to fill bottles from that first cask. Whisky everywhere, everyone drunk, smoking, engine oil all over the place. Miracle no one was killed."

Sophie is leaning forward, massaging the roots of her hair.

"I saw something, on that first dive. I have a photograph. I have evidence. Sophie sees it too," I say.

Sophie is still leaned forward, staring at the carpet.

"With everything that's happened," Elsie says, cautiously, "I feel like people see what they expect. Old Jock insists the snow is a Soviet conspiracy. Duncan and his wife think they're being followed by Cain the wanderer. It doesn't, it doesn't *prove*—"

"That doesn't matter. Because the whole point is that the crewmates and the island, we're experiencing the same phenomenon," I stutter. "Phenomena. We're all seeing and feeling the same things."

Elsie gives me a reluctant grimace, as if she's about to inform me of a death.

Sophie taps herself on the forehead. "Oh my God!"

Elsie looks at me intently. "Do you remember what you said about scurvy, about the antiscorbutics?"

"Yes?" I'm trying not to sound diffident, defensive, but I can hear the clipped edge to my voice.

"Lead tins, Marta," Elsie says.

The room reels around me.

Sophie pinches the bridge of her nose. "They had fresh rations from the villages on the way up. They only started eating from the tins when they became stuck in the ice."

"Lead poisoning," Elsie says. "And the cold, and, well . . ." She trails off. Both her and Sophie are watching me.

"Imagination," I finish.

LATITUDE 81°, 01' N, LONGITUDE 65°, 33' W

The oil lamp has not much left. By its poor light I see sometimes the visitor has entered the room. It says nothing, only stays in the corner, stooped and watching.

FRIDAY, FEBRUARY 1, 1963

THAT NIGHT, ELSIE SLEEPS IN MY ROOM. I DON'T KNOW IF it's her presence or the rum or the slight thaw of the temperature, but it's so warm I feel as if I am choking, as if the room has had the air pumped out of it. Elsie feels me rolling over in the sheets and bundles me closer to her.

"I'm sorry," she says, her sleepy voice muffled by the back of my neck.

I laugh, bitterly. "You're apologising because my ghost isn't real?"

Elsie hesitates. "No ghosts are real," she says, after a moment.

"I know that," I say, a little too quickly.

She nudges me until I turn over to face her. In the dim light of the fire, her eyes trace over mine. "I know you wanted to repair—" She pauses. "Repair something. Prove something. That's nothing to be embarrassed about. It's a nice thing that you wanted to help people."

I shake my head. "It's not the product of a guilty conscience. I saw things. I saw it."

Her expression is earnest. "I believe you. Poisoning doesn't mean you didn't see things."

"But it would mean that none of it is real," I say, surprised at the lurch of grief in my chest.

"Yes," she concedes. "But I know that it feels real."

I start to turn away from her, but she pulls me closer. "You know what else is real? Me."

Tears prickle in my eyes, and I try to smile. "I'm not imagining you?"

"No, I'm very real."

"Will you still be real if we leave the island together?" I say. I'm intending to pass it off lightly, but she must catch the tone in my voice because her forehead wrinkles.

"When I was young," I say, "there was this story in one of my dad's books, about a man who marries a ghost bride, and they live happily together in his cottage, as long as she never ever leaves. And then after years, they decide that it can't really be true, that surely so much time has passed that nothing could break their bond. And they take out in a boat and cross the river. And as they row over the water, she disappears, like mist. Because she never really belonged to him in the first place." The scene passes vividly in front of my eyes. Sitting on the top of the ferry, Elsie, holding my hand. As the sun warms us, I feel cozy for the first time. And then the sheets of vapour lift off her, carrying more of her back into the sea spray. When I look down at her hand, there is nothing there, only foam, dissolving in my fingers.

"Marta," Elsie says.

With difficulty, I meet her eyes. The nebulous horror of it is still swirling around me. "The way everyone has been behaving," I say. "Agnes's pregnancy. Mrs. Eleanor and Francis. The fighting, the arguments. I thought . . ."

"You thought I only love you because of the effect of your shadow creature?"

I break into a silly laughing jag of tears. "I don't know?"

"Marta, that's insane," she says, shaking me gently.

"But now, it's just lead poisoning instead," I say, the tears flowing in earnest. "That doesn't make it much better than a curse."

Elsie is laughing in an indulgent way. "It's not a shadow figure, it's not lead poisoning. And it's not a curse."

"But—"

"I liked you before the crisis, remember? Before we had the first sip of Auld James's whisky."

"You did?"

She mops my tears away with the edging of the blanket. "Of course I did. And you liked me too, didn't you? Or is that lead poisoning as well?"

I shake my head. "The first day I met you, I wanted to impress you."

"There you go."

She nudges my head into her chest and strokes me. Eventually her hand slows, and she mumbles something, and is still.

The last few cold months on the island, Elsie has been my anchor. She tried to save me when I was refused from the missile shelter. She came with me up north, even when she didn't agree with what I was doing. She forgave me, after everything. I rub watery tears from my cheeks. All this time, I should have been concentrating on her. On keeping her, deserving her. I'm not leaving this island without her. All the desolation I felt when I arrived here is dissolved, now that I have her with me. I never have to feel it again, if I have her love. Maybe she doesn't believe in the figure, but she believes in me. That has to be enough.

I pick my head up off her chest and watch her sleeping, the milk chocolate of her eyelashes, the slack in her cheeks. She coughs, turning over, and I lie in the bedclothes. A coal skitters in the grate. There is a slopping, gurgling sound from the window where water is trickling down the icicles and into the gutters of the building.

I roll over and my hand dangling over the edge of the bed receives a cold breath from somewhere near the window. It almost feels refreshing in the stuffiness, a little slice of frosty relief. I pull myself to the edge of the bed and drop my head over to make sure there isn't a crack in the wall that is about to admit the snowmelt. I had almost forgotten that I'd stored the painting of HMS *Deliverance* under here, and the gold frame glints in the meagre light. Hunched over it, in the shadows, is the silhouette of a crouching figure.

45

WEDNESDAY, FEBRUARY 6, 1963

THE ICE IS CRUNCHING, GRINDING, SLUSHING, CRACKLING like crispy roast potatoes knocking together in a pan. Chunky, frost-churned water is sloshing against the hulls of the boats in the harbour, and as the wood of the hulls exhales for the first time in months, they creak and mumble. It is just after sunrise, and the sun is weak lemonade behind waxy clouds. In contrast to how cold it has been until now, it feels tropical. Colin is wearing only a sweater and fingerless gloves. Elsie and Sophie are perched on the back of the boat, looking almost naked in coats and hats. The safe from the hotel linen cupboard is bobbing at the front of the boat, covered with a Purdie tartan blanket.

Elsie links her fingers through mine. "It's not too late to forget about this whole idea," she says. She's been offering variations of this for the last week, and I've been offering variations of politely insisting.

"I'll take full responsibility for any difficulty in Edinburgh," Sophie says, again. The way they exchange meaningful looks makes it clear that they've been discussing me behind my back.

"Neither of you have to be here," I mutter.

They exchange another meaningful look.

"Will she hold?" I say to Colin. I cross my fingers under my knees. He has been running the engine for half an hour now, and the wheelhouse smells of diesel and hot plastic and mildew.

He nods. "I think so."

We creak out through the harbour, nudging through the lumpy mush, crumpling accordions of ice as the boat noses into the sea. I keep my fingers crossed while we pass beyond the charred chunks of the Purdie Lighthouse, waves thrumming against the hull. The surface of the sea looks almost slimy, the sun lifting soft mists from crusts of ice and smudging the surface of the water like turpentine rubbed through a painting.

When the buoy for the ship appears, I release my fingernails from my palms. Part of me expected that the guideline wouldn't be here, that something would interrupt us before I could actually return the items.

"Neither of us will judge you if you change your mind," Elsie whispers, as I shrug off my coat.

I say nothing, only grip her wrist once, before letting go.

Sophie's and Elsie's matching, frightened expressions are the last thing I see before I go backwards down into the water. The cold judders my heart and I curl with my knees to my chest in the water, gathering my heartbeat back to myself. All these months of being frozen have finally provided their use; I am more resistant to the cold now than I ever have been. The water is close to eight degrees, even warmer than the air.

I follow the guideline down towards the ship. The icy film across even this deep water has prompted a bloom of lurid green algae; it thickens the line into a slimy rope of wavering fronds. When HMS *Deliverance* appears through the murk, I kick in place, waiting for my eyes to adjust as much as possible. My torch batteries haven't survived the freeze so I will have to do this through feel and camera flash. I give the guideline one hard tug.

The weighted lobster cage appears behind me, lowered on fishing lines operated by Sophie and Elsie. I struggle with the fixtures for longer than I expected to in the darkness, and in the end, my frustration gets the better of me and I use my penknife to slice through the lines. I glide the safe out of the cage and shake it gently to ensure water has filled all the air pockets.

The black tunnel of the hatch yawns into the belly of the vessel. My pulse picks up, and I take three long breaths before sliding myself down into the passageway. The insulating ice has thickened the algae here too; the cushiony fringes brush gently against my limbs as I ease myself down the corridor and into the galley.

I lower the safe carefully into the pillows of silt on the passageway floor. Holding the camera at chest height, I snap the button and the flash lights up the galley kitchen, the saloon beyond. White arrows flicker in my vision. I have to coast in inches towards the back of the room to avoid catching myself on any rusty nails, and still manage to knock my leg against the side of the table. At the back of the room I grope for the porthole, lay the safe down in the glutinous algae. The little cupboard door ahead of me is knocking gently closed, open, closed.

This is my last chance to check. I unclip the safe and feel about inside for the muslin bag of Purdie's remains, the squash of the journal and ledger, the potato sack containing the museum items. I steady the camera and flash upon a grotesque arrangement of Purdie's bones. Still there. Of course they are. Fumbling inside the sack, I trace over each item in turn. The snow goggles, the horn cup, the gloss of the mirror, the cutlery, the ring. Even at this depth, the coin is cold under my fingers, its worn face silky where Auld James rubbed it, hoping to ward off whatever was following him. Much use that was. A knocking creak from the belly of the ship shoots my pulse into my ears, and I grip the coin. Sound travels fast underwater. The noise could be from out on the seabed, could be from miles away. Colin might have brought the boat around, and it's simply an echo of the motor from above.

The sound thuds again. It's coming from within the vessel, the other side of the cupboard; Auld James's cabin. I control my breathing. My mind flashes back to Lewis whistling, his fingers drumming on the steering wheel that day we drove to the beach. The point where I almost asked him to turn back. Then I picture Elsie's face. The little sharp teeth at the edge of her bite that she's self-conscious of. The pinkness of her earlobes. Her warmth, in bed with me this morning, the downy hair on her upper thighs. How right now, she is sitting over the edge of Colin's boat, watching for me. Waiting for me. My Elsie.

When the safe is locked, I open the cupboard and pause, my breath hoarse in my regulator. A full minute passes. The darkness folds itself around me. I slide the safe into the cupboard and turn the latch on the door.

I pull myself back across the room and come to rest at the edge of the saloon. Behind me, a deliberate, slow creak. The cupboard door has opened. I raise my camera and hover my finger over the button for the flash. After one long moment, I lower it again.

§

I'VE BARELY SURFACED before two pairs of hands are hoisting me on board, piling me with towels, blankets, a hat, a scarf. I feel weak, caved in on myself. My breathing contains the whisper of a crackle that I hope Elsie won't notice.

"How do you feel?" Elsie says, rubbing my arms vigorously with the blanket.

"Good," I say, trying not to cough. "Good, fine."

Over Elsie's shoulder, Sophie's face is so relieved I only now see how tense she must have been. She brings out a thermos from her coat pocket. "Don't worry, it's rum."

I laugh, accepting a swig. Elsie leans down through the mound of coats and kisses me on the lips.

"Colin," I croak.

"It doesn't matter, we're out of here on the next ferry," she says, kissing me again. "Oh, your face is so salty!"

Elsie is giddy as we bounce back to Port Mary. Even Colin seems in a good mood; he accepts a sip of rum from the thermos, and if he notices our exchange of kisses, it doesn't show on his face. Under the cover of my coat I peel off my wetsuit, which is even looser now than it was when I arrived here, and pull on a pair of damp corduroys and one of Alice's knitted sweaters. The wind slices through the holes in the weave, but after the past few months, I feel invincible.

The harbour at Port Mary is busy with men as we nudge back through the slimy ice towards the island. Seagulls wheel overhead, and fishermen are uncoiling new nets, choking engines, calling to one another from the boats. In all the commotion only a few puzzled expressions follow Colin's boat back to dock.

Sophie pats me on the arm as we step down from the boat. "Good working with you," she says.

I laugh, squeezing her hand.

"I'll have to go back up to the castle and pack my things," she says, waving at me over her shoulder. "See you later. I can't wait to never drink whisky again."

"We'll come with you," I begin, but Elsie yanks on my elbow. "No, I want to celebrate! Look! It's like we're finally alive again!" She stretches her arms out—gesturing to the seagulls, the Irenes tossing buckets of meltwater over the snow in their front gardens.

"How much of that rum have you had?" I say, but I understand what she means. It's as if we've been standing still for all these cold weeks.

She runs along the coastal path and clambers down onto the white sand beach, throwing the bundle of blankets and towels onto the shore. "Everything's about to be different," she says, as I climb down after her. Then she spins to face me. "I don't want to say 'I told you so,' but it's all back in the ship now, and I still love you!"

I laugh, nudging her.

"I told you it wasn't a curse," she calls, running ahead and executing a sloppy if enthusiastic cartwheel over the sand.

"I thought you didn't want to say 'I told you so,'" I say, watching her acrobatics. She turns back to me with a shrug, and I smile. As she runs farther away across the beach, I feel down into the lining of the coat pocket and run my fingers along the silky surface of Auld James's copper coin.

Acknowledgments

MUCH OF THIS BOOK WAS WRITTEN WHILE SIMULTANEOUSLY looking after a young child and pregnant with another, in the small hours before my day job, during a genocide of the Palestinian people. It has been an exercise in emotional stamina and creative persistence to believe that art still has meaning in the face of so much overwhelming horror. While writing, I reflected on the record-breaking winter of 1962 as a moment of deep freeze before profound social transformation, and I have been so grateful to everyone who has used their voice to witness and to push for justice. A particular thank-you to the writers and book workers involved with FFB for your solidarity and optimism.

Thank you to Hattie for being my tireless champion and counsellor—I'm so lucky to have you!

Thank you to Jade for your incredible editorial vision, your perceptiveness and generosity; it's been an immense privilege to have your eye on my work.

A huge thank-you to Catherine Drayton for your ongoing support.

To Masie, thank you for your guidance, enthusiasm, and insight; it is such a pleasure and an honour to work with you. Thank you to everyone in the Tin House team: Win McCormack, Becky Kraemer,

Nanci McCloskey, Anne Horowitz, Allison Dubinsky, Alyssa Ogi, Elizabeth DeMeo, Jacqui Reiko Teruya, and Isabel Lemus Kristensen. A special thanks to Beth Steidle for the fantastic cover.

Thank you to Captain Dave Briggs, my comrade in polar exploration; your reading recommendations, encyclopedic knowledge of and love for all things icy have been a huge inspiration.

A special thank-you to Dr. Georgia Holly at the University of Edinburgh for your expertise and for answering my questions on marine archaeology—all errors and fabrications are completely my own!

My WWF friends have been a lifeline while writing this book, so much appreciation and thanks to all of you: Daisy, Elizabeth, Francine, Hannah, Imogen, Jessie, Kiran, Kirsty, Rachelle, Sophie, and Nell.

Thank you to Ruhi and to Laith, I love you both so much.

Thank you to Struan for everything during the long months of writing, editing, and parenthood. I couldn't be more grateful to have you as my companion and crewmate.

ANBARA SALAM is half-Palestinian and half-Scottish, and grew up in London. She is the author of *Hazardous Spirits*, *Belladonna*, and *Things Bright and Beautiful*. She has a PhD in Theology and lives in Oxford, England.